The Philosopher's Toothache

Rethinking the Early Modern

The Philosopher's Toothache

Embodied Stoicism in Early Modern English Drama

Donovan Sherman

NORTHWESTERN UNIVERSITY PRESS
EVANSTON, ILLINOIS

Northwestern University Press
www.nupress.northwestern.edu

Printed in the United States of America

10 9 8 7 6 5 4 3 2 1

Library of Congress Cataloging-in-Publication Data

Names: Sherman, Donovan, author.
Title: The philosopher's toothache : embodied stoicism in Early Modern English drama / Donovan Sherman.
Other titles: Rethinking the Early Modern.
Description: Evanston, Illinois : Northwestern University Press, 2022. | Series: XRethinking the Early Modern | Includes index.
Identifiers: LCCN 2021021044 | ISBN 9780810144149 (paperback) | ISBN 9780810144156 (cloth) | ISBN 9780810144163 (ebook)
Subjects: LCSH: English drama—Early modern and Elizabethan, 1500–1600—History and criticism. | Stoics in literature. | Philosophy in literature.
Classification: LCC PR658.P48 S54 2022 | DDC 822.309384—dc23
LC record available at https://lccn.loc.gov/2021021044

CONTENTS

ACKNOWLEDGMENTS

This book has benefited immensely from the advice, critique, and care of communities immediate and far flung, conceptual and material. I am grateful for the support given by my home institution, Seton Hall University: a sabbatical in the 2016–17 academic year afforded me the chance to dive, with focus and vigor, into research; the writing retreat of the Center for Faculty Development, under the leadership of Mary Balkun, allowed the first sparks of this project to grow. My colleagues in the English department have offered unerring support: my thanks to Cara Blue Adams, Martha Carpentier, Jonathan Farina, Karen Gevirtz, Russell Sbriglia, and Angela Weisl. I also received guidance from Fr. Doug Milewski and Michael Maloney, my co-instructors in the Seton Hall Honors Program, in helping me learn more about philosophy and theology in early antiquity. I also owe a special shout-out to my fabulous writing partners, Marianne Lloyd and Elizabeth Redwine, for cheering me on through thick and thin.

I have been fortunate to participate in fruitful, generative dialogues at meetings of the Shakespeare Association of America (SAA) and the American Society for Theatre Research (ASTR), where fragments of the book first saw sunlight. ASTR generously granted me a research award to help defray some costs associated with the work. Longer presentations at the Columbia University Shakespeare Seminar and the University of California, Irvine Early Cultures Conference helped me sharpen and articulate many of my main points. The "Crafting Race in Early Modern Subfields" workshop at the City College of New York, organized by Miles Grier and Patricia Akhemie, offered a robust environment to think through the implications of Stoicism's claims of bondage. And my participation in the Folger Library's seminar on "Shakespeare's Virtues," organized by Julia Reinhard Lupton, proved a crucial step in developing my project by reminding me of the larger ethical stakes at play. The book received keen commentary from members of these scholarly collectives: Pannill Camp, Christopher Crosbie, Julia Fawcett, Lisa Freeman, Leticia Garcia, Marissa Greenberg, Daniel Keegan, Unhae Langis, Naomi Liebler, Erika T. Lin, Steve Mentz, Steve Monte, Ineke Murakami, Ian Munro, Scott Newstok, Benjamin Parris, Tanya Pollard, VK Preston, Jennifer Rust, Adam Rzepka, Gina di Salvo, Stephanie Shirilan, Andrew Sofer, Stephen Spencer, John Staines, Richard Strier, Jarred Wiehe, William B. Worthen, and Adam Zucker. My editors at Northwestern

University Press, Trevor Perri and Maia Melissa Rigas, have epitomized collegial and calm communication; the careful eye of Lys Weiss helped sharpen and tighten the book's language; and the two readers who reviewed the original manuscript offered perceptive considerations that strengthened the text immensely. In their stewardship of the "Rethinking the Early Modern" series, Marcus Keller, Ellen McClure, and Feisal Mohamed have assembled an impressive roster of scholarly works that I am humbled to join.

A special note is due to those who, Seneca-like, offered a sounding board and crystalline mirror for my ideas, who exhibited patience when reviewing my work, and whose lives provide examples of truly virtuous public intellectual life. Julia Reinhard Lupton has long modeled the ideal of a scholarly collaborator, mentor, and friend. Her selflessness, perceptiveness, and capacity for community creation remain unmatched. Robert Cohen, a true legend, inspires me every day to see the connections between practice and theory, action and intellect. And it is no understatement to say that my undergraduate advisor, Ellen Mease, changed my life by showing me how theater can invigorate philosophical ideas; the genesis of this book, in fact, was a lovely Iowa hike with her and Scott Samuelson at my college reunion, where we discussed Hamlet's simple, profound declaration, "Let be."

Hamlet's economic hymn to immediacy echoes a lesson I learn every day with my family: to be in the moment, to acknowledge miracles in the ambient hum of existence. My love and awe for my wife, Kasia Piekarz, is born of our extraordinary journey together and magnifies each moment of our shared life: I am ever grateful for the emotional, psychological, and spiritual nourishment of our partnership. My children, Natalie and Wally, to whom this book is dedicated, embody a lifetime of philosophical learning in their ways of being. Their dispositions remain radically open, surprising, and inspiring—I have learned much from them.

Parts of this book, in earlier incarnations, have been published elsewhere. Small pieces of chapter 1 appeared in a brief essay, "Shakespeare's Embodied Stoicism," in *The Routledge Companion to Shakespeare and Philosophy*, edited by Craig Bourne and Emily Caddick Bourne, copyright 2019, reproduced by permission of Taylor and Francis Group, LLC, a division of Informa plc. Chapter 2 appeared in *English Literary Renaissance*, volume 48, number 3, copyright 2018 by English Literary Renaissance, Inc. An expanded version of chapter 3 was published as "Stoicism as Performance in *Much Ado about Nothing*: Acting Indifferently," in the series *Elements in Shakespeare Performance*, Cambridge University Press 2019, reproduced with permission of the Licensor through PLSclear.

THE PHILOSOPHER'S TOOTHACHE

INTRODUCTION

More Things

> Philosophy teaches us to act, not to speak.
>
> —Seneca

Seneca offers this dictum as a form of consolation to his friend and pupil Lucilius, the addressee of the philosopher's *Letters on Ethics*. This particular letter begins with exasperation. "For it will be to my credit," Seneca claims, "if I manage to extricate you from that place where you are now floundering without any hope of escape."[1] Lucilius is struggling, and Seneca's advice is to focus on action, not speeches. As he does throughout his correspondence, Seneca expresses distaste for overreliance on words, the very medium of his expression. It is in actions, he insists, that philosophy resides. And only by living, rather than simply expounding on, philosophy can one calm the paralyzing anxiety that Lucilius feels.

How does one live a philosophy? The question is central to Stoicism, the school for which Seneca is a standard-bearer. The major classical Stoic texts that have survived—preeminently those of Seneca, Epictetus, and Marcus Aurelius, alongside fragments and secondhand descriptions in collections such as Diogenes Laertius's *Lives of the Eminent Philosophers*—all evince a belief that philosophy resides in active and embodied habits and decisions rather than in spoken or written words. The actual goal of Stoicism can be stated simply: to operate by reason alone through the extirpation of all passions, thereby living in complete accordance with nature. What complicates the matter is the *how*, not the what; the telos of pure reason is so nearly impossible that one needed a radical revision of their entire disposition in order to attempt its attainment. It is in this process of revision that Stoicism thrives—in the actions, cogitations, habits, and decisions by which one focuses on the North Star of the Stoic ideal.

As Pierre Hadot memorably terms it, Stoicism is less a doctrinal system and more a "way of life."[2] Hadot's influential claim that classical philosophy resides in the particularities of one's everyday behavior, rather than in a static, intellectual, and textual expression of ideas, encompasses more schools of thought than Stoicism. But for Hadot, Stoicism most vividly realizes the goal of a philosophical life: "For the ancients, but *particularly* for the Stoics," he argues, philosophy was ultimately a way of life, rather than a purely cerebral exercise.[3] Why Stoicism? Because of all the ancient philosophies it is the most public, present-focused, and materialistic. As opposed to the Cynics, who divorce themselves from civic obligation, or the Epicureans, who attempt to create their own communities, the Stoics "strive, at the cost of the greatest difficulties, to live their everyday and even their public lives in a 'philosophical' manner."[4] Furthermore, Stoicism "will insist on the effort needed to pay attention to oneself, the joyous acceptance of the present moment imposed on us."[5] This focus on the present does not attempt to penetrate the banality of the quotidian stuff of the world in order to realize a metaphysical truth lurking beyond the realm of perception; indeed, as opposed to Platonism and Aristotelianism, Stoicism revels in the immediate materiality of one's surroundings. Rejecting a "model of hierarchy of knowledge and of levels of reality," the Stoic instead celebrates "the representation of an organic unity, in which there is complete copenetration"; as a result, "the distinction between physics, as a science of the sensible world, and a science of the transcendent world of Ideas (that is, Platonic dialectics) or of the gods (theology) is completely abolished."[6] Stoicism situates itself entirely in practice, and that practice trains the philosopher's eye to remain vigilant and attentive to every detail of the world around them—not a world in a heavenly beyond, nor one hermetically set off from society, but the precise same world in which we live, in all of its seemingly uneventful happenings.

We can deduce from Hadot's account of Stoicism that it bears striking affinities with a medium often placed in opposition to philosophy: the theater. Like the theater, Stoicism utilizes the vessel of the human body as its primary instrument. Similarly, Stoicism asks that we remain "in the moment"—responsive, reactive, attentive to every shift in the energy of a scene. And Stoicism, like theater, needs an audience, a public body scrutinizing and reacting to a performer's actions to provide immediate feedback and accountability. And yet Stoicism does not conform to a traditional view of mimesis; again, contra Platonism, the Stoic's behavior does not view action as mimetic of something abstract, but instead as the sum totality of its immediately observable phenomena. The Stoic does not possess what Martin Puchner deems "the most fundamental tenets of what is usually called Platonism: a disregard of the concrete, embodied, lived experience and a desire, instead, to ascend to some realm of abstact forms or ideas, pure and simple."[7] This is not to say that Stoicism merely accepted the world as is. Indeed, the Stoic needed to train their energy almost exclusively on the ability to discern what is real or false. But this attention was focused *inward*, at the mental representations of reality ushered into cognition by perception. Here, at this level, falsehoods can be distinguished using the almighty power of reason. As Martha Nussbaum explains, Stoicism instructs the philosopher to "suspend her habitual responses, and to turn her gaze upon herself, becoming watchful and critical of each impression that she is inclined to accept."[8] It is within the mind that theater's traditionally mimetic powers can be ascertained, on the stage of consciousness.

Viewed this way, the Stoic writing that has survived operates less like holistic explanations of thinking and more like scripts for proper behavior. Texts such as Seneca's *Letters* or Marcus's *Meditations* do not contain thorough and cogently organized principles; they operate as prompts for readers to perform in a certain way. Reading and rereading passages from these works, then absorbing them as techniques of self-monitoring so as to curate one's behavior, constitutes a regimen akin to that of an aspiring marathon runner who regularly jogs, adjusts their diet, and stretches. This is barely an analogy, in fact: the Stoics referred to the implied behavior of their audience as *askesis*, or "exercise." Marcus's reader was himself, and he examined his *Meditations* daily not to learn new information but as a way to expand his capacity to act in a proper manner. One such meditation reads: "Am I accomplishing some action? I accomplish it, relating it to the well-being of mankind. Is something happening to me? I greet it, relating what happens to me to the gods and to the source of all things, whence is formed the framework of events."[9] This frequent attentiveness to activity inspires abundant theatrical analogies in Stoic works. "Remember," Epictetus implores in his *Handbook*, "that thou art an actor in a play of such a kind as the teacher may choose; if short, of a short one, if long, of a long one."[10] To absorb this aphorism properly, one must live it, not simply understand and recite it. Life must become worthy of scrutiny and curation, capable of distillation into behavior that stems solely from reason so as to become virtuous—a term that in Stoic terminology means "to realize complete capacity, to attain potential."[11] Behind Seneca's admonition to Lucilius is this core belief of Stoicism: to live a happy life, one must not seek refuge in moribund words, but instead pay attention to the life they are already living, the actions they are taking.

After its initial flourishing in antiquity, Stoicism regained popularity in the early modern era, and particularly in England, a culture that witnessed a surge in theatrical activity. Yet the intensely theatrical nature of Stoicism disappeared in this reincarnation. When Stoicism reappeared in early modern England, in fact, it came to represent precisely the opposite position. Rather than advocating a focus on lived experience, it appeared to advocate for cerebral detachment. Rather than distrusting words as the medium of philosophy, it located itself almost entirely within discourse. The entry on Seneca in William Baldwin's popular collection *Treatise on Morall Philosophy*, first printed in 1547, approvingly notes that "hee wrote in his life time many goodly bookes, out of the which shall bee picked some of the most pithie sentences, both of Precepts and counsailes, and also of Proverbs, Wages, Parables, Semblables which in their places heereafter shall follow."[12] Seneca's thought is here reduced to nothing more than the words he produced—words that he explicitly warns against reading as expressive of philosophy. The "pithie sentences" that Baldwin celebrates refers to *sententiae*, sayings familiar to students who would have copied them by rote in their humanist education. Similarly, and despite Epictetus's endorsement of the theater as an apt analogy for virtuous living, the early modern Stoic often gains visibility as an archetypally unmoving, stuffy killjoy resistant to theatrical legibility—so much so that the Stoic emerges as a stock comic character on the actual stage. In perhaps the most self-aware example of this type, Ben Jonson's *Bartholomew Faire* features Adam Overdo, a justice of the peace, strapped into the stocks for public pain and humiliation; when asked if he suffers, he replies, "I do not feel it, I do not think of it, it is a thing without me," which leads a passerby to exclaim, "What's here? A stoic i'the stocks? The fool is turned philosopher."[13] Foolish denial of obvious fact becomes synonymous with the apparent Stoic denial of felt sensation.

This disdain is in part spiritual. Augustine exemplifies an early Christian critique of Stoicism in *The City of God* when he claims that its typical practitioner is "crippled, wracked with pain, visited by every imaginable affliction, driven at last to take his own life."[14] While the Stoics did argue for suicide as an ethically defensible decision, Augustine mocks this choice as the result of withstanding, Overdo-like, extreme pain. Calvin resurrects the figure of the tortured Stoic in his *Institutes*:

> You see that to bear the cross patiently is not to have your feelings altogether blunted, and to be absolutely insensible to pain, according to the absurd description which the Stoics of old gave of their hero as one who, divested of humanity, was affected in the same way by adversity and prosperity, grief and joy; or rather, like a stone, was not affected by anything. And what did they gain by

> that sublime wisdom? They exhibited a shadow of patience, which never did, and never can, exist among men. No, rather by aiming at a too exact and rigid patience, they banished it altogether from human life.[15]

To be a Stoic, in this description, is to be inhuman, in denial of all emotion in exchange for a "shadow of patience" that cannot last. In fact, Calvin argues, by attempting to attain wisdom, the Stoics became foolish and hubristic. Even Neo-Stoics, those early moderns who sought to synthesize ancient thought with contemporary religion, admitted to the philosophy's insufficient capacity for grace. Joseph Hall, in *Heaven upon Earth*, laments that even Seneca, the wisest (in Hall's mind) of the philosophers, lacked deliverance: "No marvell, then," Hall concludes, "if al the heathen have diligently sought after it; many, wrot of it; none attained it. Not Athens must teach this lesson, but Jerusalem."[16] We are far, in these accounts, from the Stoic portrayed quite clearly in the ancient source material: the pupil who trains their mind and body to remain attentive and purposeful in their behavior, who turns to texts for dynamic interaction, and who imagines an audience to their every action. Instead, we have graceless, senseless fools who produce a smattering of wise aphorisms but fail to offer a viable mode of perceiving the world, much less a way of life.

This book recovers Stoicism as a vibrant way of life in a time and place that attempted to hammer it into a more schematic and textually dependent system. I argue that we can find in the dramatic work of early modern England the original understanding of the philosophy. To do so, I propose we take Seneca at his word and think of early modern Stoicism just as its classical forbears did: as a performance. I diverge, then, from the impressive range of scholarship on the topic that ends up reifying its stereotype by analyzing Stoicism as a set of stable principles. Many influential accounts of early modern Stoicism have informed my study, and I engage with their work throughout the readings that follow; however, few such analyses commit to an understanding of Stoic philosophy as a mode of performance, and none explicitly links this performance to the theater. Looming large in any bibliography of the early modern Stoics is Gordon Braden's *Renaissance Tragedy and the Senecan Tradition: Anger's Privilege*, a brilliant elaboration of how Stoicism's obsessive focus on self-cultivation, in an effort to extirpate the passions, operates as an internalized imperial drive and in turn results in an external expression of all-consuming anger. Braden's work culminates in a long reading of Shakespeare's *King Lear*, but his primary archive is Senecan drama rather than Stoic philosophy, more broadly conceived. Braden falls into a long and distinguished genealogy of scholarship on the influence of Seneca on early modern drama, a repository that includes works by J. W. Cunliffe, F. L. Lucas, Otto Regenbogen, A. J. Boyle, Robert Miola, and T. S. Eliot.

There have been recent notable studies of Neo-Stoicism and early modern adaptations of Stoic philosophy, though I agree with Joseph Campana that "a relatively small body of scholarship on Renaissance neo-Stoicism and English literature exists."[17] Andrew Shifflet's *Stoicism, Politics, and Literature in the Age of Milton: War and Peace Reconciled* stands out as a more nuanced reading of Stoicism, viewing it not merely as a sagacious extreme of unattainable wisdom but as a more processual set of habits; however, as his title indicates, his study focuses on the late seventeenth century and takes up the written word, not the theater, as his site of inquiry. Gerhard Oestrichs's *Neostoicism and the Early Modern State* studies the political, not performative, implications of Neo-Stoicism. Similarly, Patrick Gray's recent study of Stoicism and Shakespearean drama recovers the political implications of the early modern critique of classical conceptions of "constancy." My primary aim here, however, is not to view Stoicism as a stable set of principles that can serve as a cohesive doctrine to be critiqued. Nor do I explore the wider ramifications of Stoic philosophy with respect to issues of sovereignty or republicanism. Instead, I examine the more immediate consequences of the theater, as a place of philosophical work, on the individuals and communities who witness it. I also avoid analyzing Seneca's drama, which clearly influences the dramaturgy of early modern revenge tragedy in readily apparent ways. I am more interested in something subtler but no less powerful: how early modern drama stages Stoic philosophy *as* theater, not how it follows Stoic models or represents Stoic ideas. Rather than ask whether a certain character is Stoic, or whether Stoic ideas appear supported by the text's formal elements, or identify Stoic sentiments in the dialogue, I will see how dramatic texts, when realized as theatrical presentations, operate as Stoic exercises, like Marcus's meditations.

While education and Christianity attempted to wring Stoicism of its vital and performed nature, another, less heralded factor is at play. Too often, early modern readers of Stoicism conflated the Stoic sage with the Stoic *tout court*. It is the sage that Seneca, in the letter to Lucilius that opens this introduction, identifies as the rare figure who can align their words with their actions. Seneca claims that in theory, "actions should be in accordance with words" and that a person "should be the same in all places, a match for himself." He then asks, as if anticipating Lucilius's incredulity, "'Is there any such person?' Not many, but there are some. It is indeed difficult."[18] William Irvine, in surveying Stoic thought, notes that its proponents "talk about sages primarily so they will have a model to guide them in their practice of Stoicism. The sage is a target for them to aim at, even though they will probably fail to hit it."[19] The sage is necessarily a nearly impossible figure to emulate—someone who has extirpated their passions and proceeds purely from reason, carefully parsing out their actions accordingly. This is the figure admittedly ripe for parody, as exemplified by Cicero's reference, in his *Tusculan Disputations*, to Anaxagoras's reaction to the news of his child's death: "I was already aware that he was mortal."[20] But even in the case of the sage, Stoics did not advocate for *not* feeling. One must still absorb sensations in order to evaluate them. Michel de Montaigne, one of the more sensitive early modern readers of Stoicism, picked up on this quality in his earlier essays, before his eventual shift to skepticism. The Stoics, Montaigne explains in "Of Constancy," do not mean to say

> that the soul of their sage can resist the first visions and fancies that come upon him; rather they consent that he give in, as to a natural subjection, to the great noise of the heavens or of a falling building, for example, to the point of turning pale and tightening up. Likewise for the other passions, provided that his judgment remains sound and entire, that the seat of his reason suffers no injury or alteration, and that he lends no consent to his fright and suffering. For the man who is not a sage it goes the same way for the first part, but entirely differently for the second.[21]

Montaigne recognizes that the difference between sage and pupil is whether feelings penetrate to the level of reason, not whether the feelings exist at all. Sages register affect; they become as pale and tense as anyone, but they are capable of realizing that these sensations do not have any effect on their capacity for judgment. Martha Nussbaum, in a close reading of what she calls the "wonderful phenomenological descriptions" of the early Stoics, clarifies this point. The various accounts of attempts to uproot the passions "show us that the Stoics are not neglecting the way passions feel. What they insist is that, in each case, the thing that feels like this is an act of assent or acknowledgment. Some recognitions feel like embracing a nail; others like rubbing yourself across a rough, grating surface; other propositions 'cut' differently, so other acceptances have a different phenomenological content."[22] To practice Stoic philosophy is to acknowledge passions as they inundate one's consciousness. Thus the Stoic must experience the physical sensations symptomatic of poor judgments before they either exorcise them from their soul or allow their judgment to be clouded.

Most aspiring Stoics follow the latter path. Stoic *askesis* can last a lifetime and most likely will end in failure, but this failure designates a feature of the practice as it brings the philosopher closer to, not further from, a greater sense of embodied humanity. The Stoics hold that, in Nussbaum's words, "life, if we attach ourselves to it, alienates us from our own humanity."[23] This paradox is worth sitting with: Stoic detachment from things we cannot control—*adiaphora*, things indifferent, independent of our reason—in fact allows for intimacy with what is essentially human, the rational soul. The only way to gain this intimacy is to act with the integrity born from rigorous self-examination so as to create a philosophical way of life.

Witness, however, the specific linkage between Stoicism and *not* feeling put forth by Leonato, in Shakespeare's *Much Ado about Nothing*, as he brushes off attempts to console him:

> I pray thee peace; I will be flesh and blood.
> For there was never yet philosopher
> That could endure the toothache patiently,
> However they have writ the style of gods
> And make a push at chance and sufferance.[24]

I will have much more to say about this play later in the book, but for now, suffice it to say that Leonato's insult depends on the Stoic's apparent hypocrisy in writing divine words but reeling at the pain of a simple toothache. And yet the dynamic put forth by the Stoics themselves was the inverse: they put little faith in words and advocated for an open, present-tense acknowledgment of the feelings that accost their bodies and souls. To have a toothache was not a hindrance to philosophy; instead, the toothache could in fact inaugurate a philosophical exercise—a dash of physical pain that prompts introspection and self-exploration.

In focusing an inquiry into Stoicism on physicality, rather than solely on the intellect, this book accordingly considers early modern drama not only as a collection of textual records but as something inextricably linked to bodily realization. As such, the discipline of performance studies greatly informs my practice of reading drama. Diana Taylor offers a lucid explanation of the field's objects and methods: "'Performance,' on one level, constitutes the object/process of analysis in performance studies, that is, the many practices and events—dance, theater, ritual, political rallies, funerals—that involve theatrical, rehearsed, or conventional/

event-appropriate behaviors"; at the same time, "performance also constitutes the methodological lens that enables scholars to analyze events *as* performances. Civic obedience, resistance, citizenship, gender, ethnicity, and sexual identity, for example, are rehearsed and performed daily in the public sphere."[25] Notably missing from this list of examples is anything traditionally theatrical—anything that takes place on a stage. Instead, performance studies grants the same dignity and capacity for meaning-making to more broadly conceived enactments that occur outside of the theater building. Furthermore, as Taylor hints at here, the performance scholar does not apprehend these enactments simply as plays that happen to take place elsewhere. Instead, drawing on anthropology, speech act theory, and phenomenology, performance studies allows for greater explanatory power than merely extending theater as a metaphor. Richard Schechner, whose collaborations with the anthropologist Victor Turner provided foundational work in the discipline, defines performance as "restored behavior," a capacious term that encompasses all actions that are "marked, framed, or heightened." To restore behavior is to offset it somehow by changing its formal components or altering the way we view it. Thus, it "can be worked on, stored and recalled, played with, made into something else, transmitted, and transformed."[26]

Thinking of Stoicism as performance, in this understanding, helps solve a potential problem with my earlier claim that Stoicism bears affinities with the theater. It is more accurate to say that Stoicism mobilizes a theatrical *vocabulary* in its exercises. The actual activity of Stoic *askesis* does not make for riveting action: Marcus sitting at his study, closing his eyes and visualizing his day, does not arrest an audience's attention. Rather, while the Stoic exercise is not itself theater, it renders life theatrical. The critical generosity of performance studies, whereby every behavior can be rendered worthy of scrutiny if framed as such, finds a classical antecedent in Stoicism's exhortation to imagine the world as irreducibly material but nonetheless—or perhaps especially—deserving of intense study and prompt for reflection. Unlike Taylor and Schechner, however, I will not be studying live performance as my primary object. Instead, I will be reading dramatic texts as repositories of the Stoic performances wrung out of the philosophy's early modern textual adaptations and translations. I contend that the Stoic way of life lived on in theater even as it appeared to die elsewhere. As such, I will read the potential enactment of drama as a rehearsal of a Stoic exercise on its hypothetical audience. Like Stoicism, the theater depends on bodies for its full realization. In this way, drama bears a keen resemblance to Stoic texts, which are insufficient and incomplete remnants of a particular way of life.

Stoic performance, then, smuggles into drama, a medium of representation, a distinctly nonmimetic set of practices. Rather than a person taking on a character, or accessing a metaphysical realm, *askesis* outlines their life as already deserving of close attention. This quality compelled Michel Foucault, in his lectures at the Collège de France, to turn to Stoicism as an early example of the "art of living" (*tekhne tou biou*), a range of ancient practices that, in Foucault's genealogy, will coalesce into modern technologies of biopolitics. One quality of Stoic *askesis* that Foucault highlights is its grammar of aestheticization, of rendering the self as a formal creation *of* the self through repeated acts of distancing and focusing. To this poetics is wedded the nontranscendental quality observed by Hadot, an irreducibility of the body that provides the goal of Stoic philosophical work. Foucault, a great admirer of Hadot, elaborates that for the Stoics, as opposed to Platonists or Christians, "the self is the agent, object, instrument, and end of salvation."[27] There is no release from the tangible elements of scrutiny. The Stoic highlights their behavior without elevating it; they call attention to their performance to accord with nature, but stop short of attempting to instrumentalize the self as a gateway to sublimity. One prescription for this nontheatrical theatricality—without artifice, in accordance to nature, yet bounded as distinct from the aleatory noise of the everyday—might look like this:

> Be not too tame neither, but let your own discretion be your tutor. Suit the action to the word, the word to the action, with this special observance, that you o'erstep not the modesty of nature. For anything so o'erdone is from the purpose of playing, whose end, both at the first and now, was and is to hold as 'twere the mirror up to nature; to show virtue her feature, scorn her own image and the very age and body of the time his form and pressure.[28]

Hamlet's advice to the players brims with Stoic terminology: the action and word must be wedded, as Seneca urges Lucilius; performance must realize the full capacity of its nature; virtue and scorn must be parsed out carefully. A caution to avoid melodrama doubles as a prescription for philosophical practice.

I want to linger on Hamlet to consider briefly his Stoicism—or, more accurately, to consider how to consider his Stoicism. The critical reception has largely found him to be, in Alan Sinfield's phrase, a "failed Stoic."[29] While the play features copious clear references to Stoic texts, alongside a more broad and structural inheritance of Senecan revenge tragedy, Hamlet himself usually warrants mention as a quasi-Stoic at best. Joshua Scodel finds that Hamlet "radically deflates" Stoic ideas and "render[s] inapplicable" one of the "key tenets of Stoicism: that we can assert rational control over our thoughts and thereby make ourselves psychologically free."[30] This is surely true if we hold Stoicism to reside in a set of static principles—in "tenets." But Hamlet's failure to adhere to the near-impossibility of absolute rational control marks him precisely *as* a Stoic, one who attempts the practice of philosophy without ever attaining sagacity. The critical conflation of sage and pupil is made clear in Geoffrey Aggeler's claim that the "attitude of Hamlet himself toward Stoicism and its embodiment in the Stoic sage is obviously ambivalent."[31] The offhand equivalence of the philosophy with its ideal covers over a considerable gap of practice, one in which Hamlet resides.

The play continually lobs Stoic maxims at Hamlet, beginning with the half-hearted fragments of *consolatio* spoken by his mother and stepfather. "Thou know'st 'tis common," announces Gertrude, "all that lives must die, / Passing through nature to eternity" (1.2.72–73). After Hamlet waves this attempt away, Claudius embarks on a longer explanation that because "your father lost a father," Hamlet's persistence in "obstinate condolement" commits "a fault to heaven, / A fault against the dead, a fault to nature, / To reason most absurd, whose common theme / Is death of fathers" (2.1.89, 93, 101–4). As many editors point out, Claudius sounds a Stoic note in his echo of Seneca: "Let a person make his exit according to his own inclination. Whether he prefers the sword or the noose or some poison that spreads through the bloodstream, let him go forward with it and break the bonds of servitude."[32] Interpreting this as a prescriptive declaration, we can easily label Hamlet a failure. But this would not accurately give a sense of the Stoic way of life, just its tidy encapsulation—the kind of overly simplistic reflection of principle that leads Hamlet to call Rosencrantz a "sponge" that "soaks up the King's countenance, his rewards, his authorities" (4.3.15). To be a sponge is to passively absorb, to copy by rote, to carry a message from its origin to its destination without reflection or admission of lived experience—precisely the kind of unreflective and dutiful rehearsal of Stoic trope by Claudius.

By contrast, Hamlet himself largely avoids the simplicity of *sententiae* and instead conducts a series of Stoic exercises: he meditates on his own death, questions the virtue of his behavior, and trains an eye on his actions as if he were an actor. These are not distinctly Stoic qualities, of course: it was Plato who famously claimed that "true philosophers make dying their profession."[33] What makes Hamlet such a compelling candidate for Stoicism in particular is his insistent avoidance of the transcendental coupled with his habitual turn inward, to question his reception of the truth, rather than outward, to question the nature of external appearances. When his passions overtake him, he habitually interrogates his motivations, attempting with increasing desperation to re-anchor his behavior in reason—and, famously, question whether reason ultimately dictates his decisions. Furthermore, he does so in active contrast to the purely textual philosophical sentiments that he encounters. This dynamic gains its clearest expression in Hamlet's relationship to Horatio, perhaps the best known Stoic in the early modern canon. On the parapets of the castle, after witnessing the return of the ghost of Hamlet, Sr., Horatio exclaims that the scene of Hamlet's giddy, compulsive urges to swear silence is "wondrous strange"; Hamlet replies that there "are more things in heaven and earth, Horatio, / Than are dreamt of in your philosophy" (1.5.173, 174–75). Hamlet's "your" orients the critique at Horatio's particular mode of thinking, one that balks at accommodating the fantastic into its scheme. Crucially, Hamlet does not evince distaste for Horatio's ideas, but believes they lack a worldly component that engages with them: Horatio hesitates to incorporate into his worldview an account of what occurs in front of him. Rather than philosophize in the ethereal realm of ideas, Hamlet, a "quintessence of dust," locks into the here and now, the immediate materiality of his surroundings (2.2.308). And yet he still recognizes and admires Horatio's idealism—he just recognizes it as such, a sagacious goal rather than a realistic practice. Thus Hamlet's encomium before the "Mousetrap" scene, where he celebrates Horatio as

> one, in suff'ring all, that suffers nothing,
> A man that Fortune's buffets and rewards
> Hast ta'en with equal thanks; and blest are thou
> Whose blood and judgment are so well commeddled
> That they are not a pipe for Fortune's finger
> To sound what stop she please. Give me that man
> That is not passion's slave, and I will wear him
> In my heart's core, ay, in my heart of heart,
> As I do thee. (3.2.66–74)

Hamlet takes the model Stoicism of Horatio and wears it in his heart as inspiration to attempt to refuse the overpowering force of his passions. I see this as an encounter akin to Lucilius reading Seneca, or Marcus reading himself: the absorption of an ideal as philosophical prod, a framework for the "more things" that inevitably inundate perception, should we choose—and, contrary to popular belief, the Stoics insist we should choose—to participate in public life, rather than exist in Horatian reserve. The acknowledgment of the "more things" that stand outside comprehension should be absorbed into one's disposition, Hamlet suggests, not as ideas to be analyzed but instead as necessarily mysterious realms.

In its admission of mystery, this principle carries theological undertones. Indeed, the replacement of the unknown universe of Stoicism with the unknown mysteries of God provides a signal gesture of the Neo-Stoics. But what makes Hamlet particularly Stoic, rather than Platonic, is his subsequent turn to relentless self-examination coupled with a lack of mimetic escape.[34] Hamlet's turn inward has long been claimed as a prophetic glimpse of modernity, an uncannily relentless self-consciousness that, so the narrative goes, devours the generic demands of the classical revenge plot. By marking and heightening his own actions, however, he also looks backward at ancient practices. Over and over, Hamlet's passions overtake his reason, but he constantly interrogates *why* this is so and attempts to investigate the source of his actions. He does not see himself as simply an actor—he fails to live up to the imitative virtuosity of the players—but neither does he allow the sensations and habits of his life to slip by unremarked upon; he frames them as they relate to the tenets delivered to him. He tests himself. The key passage in this regard is yet another polite dismissal of his schoolmate, one that again draws clear limits of control and comprehension. After Horatio advises that Hamlet call off his duel with Laertes, Hamlet claims that "[w]e defy augury. There is special providence in the fall of a sparrow. If it be now, 'tis not to come; if it be not to come, it will be now; if it be not now, yet it will come. The readiness is all. Since no man, of aught he leaves, knows aught, what is't to leave betimes? Let be" (5.2.215–20). Hamlet proffers a Stoic exegesis of a biblical passage: because divinity accounts for all events, no matter how humble, we can only "let be." This final two-word exhortation could either serve as an efficient summation of his attitude or, as Harold Jenkins points out, operate more prosaically as a call for Horatio to stop their conversation as Gertrude, Claudius, and Laertes enter the scene. But even this deflating interpretation amounts to the same basic idea: stop talking, words are not needed. Here we find an echo of Seneca's distrust of a philosophy grounded in language alone, one that attempts to claim the future through augury, through mastery. Hamlet seizes instead on "readiness," the ways by which the Stoic pupil trains themselves, through carefully attending to themselves, to engage with the incomprehensible world.

Hamlet fleshes out Lucilius's side of things. If we take Seneca and his Stoic peers as holistic philosophical articulations, we miss out on the lived experiences of the philosophy, which is where it actually resides. As G. M. Ross points out, Seneca, in his own time, had "no influence" on the development of "philosophy as a technical discipline" due to his "ambition not to produce new developments in philosophy . . . but to propound and defend the Stoic view of life in a way that would appeal to the layman."[35] It was in the everyday lives of his readers that Seneca wanted his inspiration felt, in the Hamlets of the world more than the Horatios. Likewise, this book follows the Hamlets. Rather than label them failures, or locate in them the overlaying of different discourses, I will view them as active philosophers who embody Stoicism as a set of practices, not as an archive of precepts but in the performance of their attempted incorporation. So, too, will I examine how Stoic performance, as it exists in the drama, makes Hamlets and Luciliuses of us all by upending our expectations and forcing considerations of our own comportment and behavior.

The first chapter broadens the claims I have laid out in this introduction. I examine more deeply the circulation of Stoicism in early modern England, including tracts of Neo-Stoicism, such as Justus Lipsius's *De constantia*, as well as translations and adaptations of Seneca, Epictetus, and Marcus Aurelius. Reading these not as containers of knowledge to be transferred but instead as prompts for and residue of embodied action—despite efforts by translators and scholars to flatten this dimension—I explain how Stoicism could be interpreted as a performance, rather than an intellectual pursuit. I also describe more thoroughly what Hadot's notion of a Stoic "way of life" looks like by enumerating the exercises Stoics would do to try to reach this goal, such as meditating on death, questioning intentions, tempting bodily desires, and imagining an audience. Furthermore, the chapter elaborates on how performance works as a useful paradigm for understanding Stoicism because it deemphasizes the figure of the sage (often the actual target of anti-Stoic sentiment) and realizes that actual Stoics were always in training—always, that is, struggling to attain an ideal of control over the passions, rather than successfully doing so. Finally, the chapter introduces the major thinkers who will serve as frequent interlocutors in the case studies that follow.

The second chapter builds on the survey of the first chapter by modeling a way of reading drama as a form of Stoic performance. Specifically, I take up John Marston's Antonio plays, *Antonio and Mellida* and *Antonio's Revenge*. Marston's professed distaste for Stoicism offers recognizably parodic, exaggerated forms of the philosophy in the Antonio plays. However, by repeatedly calling attention to the material conditions of their performance—conditions that, according to satiric convention, promise a kind of failure of dramatic realization—the plays invite a more nuanced understanding of the Stoic ideas they appear to denounce. Stoicism entails a performative grammar that admits to a life lived in a constructed but unknowable world in which one could die at any moment. The acknowledgment of this "violent fate," as Lipsius calls it, finds in Marston's self-aware, continually collapsing, and dramaturgically muddled plays an ideal vehicle.

The third chapter critically analyzes the importance of indifference in *Much Ado about Nothing*, reading Shakespeare's play alongside one of its possible sources, Baldassare Castiglione's massively popular *Book of the Courtier*. I uncover a Stoic connection to Castiglione's work by exploring one of his primary influences, Cicero's *De oratore*. After tracing this dynamic, I closely read *Much Ado* as a work that, when embodied in performance, continually tempts its audience with questions of authenticity only to reveal a deeply held indifference (*apatheia*) to the question of truth. The play thus mobilizes its theatricality to subject its spectators to a Stoic exercise that teaches us to cultivate a radical indifference to epistemological concerns and instead focus on our ability to absorb reason. Throughout, I draw on Michel Foucault's lectures on Stoicism at the Collège de France. These lectures have received considerably less attention than Foucault's more formal published work, particularly as they relate to Stoicism and early modern culture.

The next two chapters shift gears from comedy to tragedy. Chapter 4 reads Cyril Tourneur's *The Atheist's Tragedy* as a demonstration of early modern Christianity's engagement with Stoic physics. I begin with a reading of a paradigmatic encounter of these two belief systems, the speech of Paul at Mars Hill, in Athens, as depicted in Acts 17. Paul's explanation of divine creation as similar to Stoic cosmology renders the philosophy somewhere between faith and apostasy. This ambivalence is reflected in the unsettled ways that Tourneur's play defines its titular term; the supposed atheist, D'Amville, engages in material vitalism akin to Stoic physics, while the nominal hero, Charlemont, is rendered so inert in his dutiful fidelity that he becomes less a realization of Christian mystery than a mild repudiation of it. I propose that the play's theatrical strategy insists on two principles whose opposition reflects the Christian–Stoic tensions of the era: on the one hand, it affirms the energy inherent to materiality; on the other, it continually draws attention to the literal shallowness of its emblematic *mise en scène*.

Chapter 5 takes a critical look at Stoicism's frequent use of "slavery" as a trope to connote an unhealthy tethering to the passions. I place this understanding of slavery in conversation with the legal and material legacy of slavery that attended the philosophy's original incarnation and, in its revival in early modern Europe, began its institutionalization as a global enterprise. I examine *Othello* to propose that the play's frequent invocation of servitude and mastery, coupled with its investment in provoking and interrogating the sources of anger, makes it a profound commentary on how two competing understandings of slavery—moral and legal—can still be intertwined and even codependent, despite the fantasy of contingent bondage put forth by Stoic philosophers. I also examine how Othello's race, the exact contours of which have long been debated by commentators, gains a degree of legibility when we view him as an aspiring Stoic student attempting to control his anger by examining himself as a performer. The perception of his blackness, I argue, withholds him from the proper participation in *askesis*, corrupted as he is by Iago's framing him as overly jealous and "hot," qualities stereotypically associated with his Moorish identity.

Finally, the book's conclusion returns to Hamlet to propose that his shifting sense of identity, murky motivations, and relentless self-examination—all typically seen as markers of his bewildering complexity—all in fact characterize him as an exemplary Stoic pupil, one whose behavior offers a model for how we can think about university teaching today. I then fold this consideration into a reading of Seneca's dismissal of liberal education in his letter 88 in light of our current so-called crisis of the humanities. I explore how Seneca's critique still resonates today by encouraging the incorporation of virtue, in the Stoic sense of a practiced realization of capacity, into the classroom. When thought of as an embodied practice, one typified by Hamlet's behavior, the philosophy gives us resources for thinking through pedagogy. These resources, as articulated in the previous chapters, appear at first blush to be hindrances: unpredictability, indifference, vulnerability, dependence. But if viewed as ways of life that benefit from their practice, rather than as concepts that need to simply be analyzed, these principles gain a beneficial vitality.

We are in a Stoic moment. Silicon Valley CEOs read Marcus Aurelius as a business guru; websites such as the *Daily Stoic* and bestsellers like Ryan Holiday's *Stillness is the Key* purport to find in Stoic philosophy the key to success and happiness; publishers repackage selections of ancient Stoic texts as self-help manuals (*How to Give, How to Keep Your Cool*).[36] It would be easy to dismiss these phenomena as misunderstandings, simplifications, or even outright perversions of actual Stoicism. But I believe that, despite their frequent lack of analytical rigor, such efforts deserve to be taken seriously as, at their root, reviving the real aims of the work of Seneca, Marcus, and Epictetus: to have us live the good life. *Living* is a full-bodied activity; it is not only knowing or thinking. By arguing that this original Stoicism endured in early modern England, a crucial juncture of its global development, I ultimately hope to inspire a broader reevaluation of the inextricability of philosophy and performance, and to provide new ways to study an intellectual tradition as it asked to be studied—suiting its word to its action.

Chapter One

Dining with Lipsius

Imitating Virtue

At the end of the first book of Justus Lipsius's *De constantia*, translated into English by John Stradling in 1595, the stand-in figure for the author—fleeing, like the real Lipsius, from civil strife in his homeland—attempts to put into practice the lessons he has learned over the previous fifty-eight pages. Lipsius's work takes the form of a dialogue between his surrogate and one Langius, an impossibly calm, erudite, and mildly exasperated tutor in the titular subject of constancy: a Stoic sage, in short, of the purely fictional variety mentioned in this book's introduction. Langius has endeavored to convince his skittish guest that his true worries reside not in politics or war, but in his own mind, the one aspect of this world he can exert any control over. "The mind must be changed," he instructs, "not the place."[1]

Though at times resistant to this idea, Lipsius the character also proves eager to absorb and reflect back to his teacher the lessons under discussion. And so as the first book comes to a close, with the two deep in discussion, a servant enters the room "to put us in mind of the hour of supper." Langius takes Lipsius by the hand and begins to follow the servant, but Lipsius has other ideas: "Nay (quoth I) let us sit still a while longer. I account this the best supper of all others, which I may call as the Grecians doe, *The meat of the goddess.* Whiles we are at this banquet, I do alwayes hunger, and am never satisfied." Ostensibly this line of thinking should find a sympathetic ear in Langius, but instead the host gently insists on leaving: "But *Langius* drewe me along with him," Lipsius narrates, "saying, Let us now have regard to our promise made, and that which is behinde our dutie to CONSTANCIE, we will, if it please you, performe tomorrow."[2] Constancy is fine, but a humbler promise to dine together also beckons. Even sages, it seems, have to eat.

The episode marks one of several instances where the text toys with the surprisingly comedic implications of a Stoic encounter. Lipsius attempts what he believes is a version of Langius's creed, and even references proper classical *sententiae*, but his refusal to eat ignores the fact that philosophy, no matter how stringent, must be practiced by humans and located in bodies. Earlier Lipsius similarly responds with self-defeating zeal after Langius finishes a long monologue centered on the popular trope of constancy resembling a boat in a storm. The tranquility of one's mind, Langius claims, resembles "a porte, where is securitie and quietnesse, a refuge and sanctuarie against all turmoyles and troubles"; upon finishing his speech, Lipsius feels "enflamed with a sparke of this good fire."[3] Langius asks his friend if he would like to walk or sit, and Lipsius decides that sitting "would please mee best . . . for I beginne to be hote."[4] Langius's valorization of constancy, of maintaining an inner calm, has so touched Lipsius that it has ironically provoked a distinctly noncalming reaction of overwhelming passion. In the second book the desire undergirding this response becomes explicit when Lipsius cries out, "Oh happie man! (said I) both in tranquilitie and troubles! O more than manly courage in a man which wold to God I were able in some measure to imitate and to creepe after your footsteps, although I came farre behind."[5] Lipsius desperately wants to be Langius, or even a lesser version of him. His motivation is as imitative as it is spiritual, and his desire to be completely singular, blissfully untouched by external forces, results in a need to fashion himself into someone else.

Whether eagerly sputtering his desire to be calm, or blithely ignoring his own need to eat, the Lipsius of *De constantia* shows us that to be a Stoic, one could not forget their material existence. This chapter surveys how this embodiment takes hold in early modern Stoicism. It was not a straightforward process: Stoicism did not demand specific corporeal behaviors so much as require bodily awareness. As mentioned in the introduction, the philosophy encouraged a critical distance from one's environment and self, in order to practice the cultivation of attentive discernment. And yet the Stoics remained disdainful of mere acting; we could say that they emphasized theatricality but disapproved of the theater. After all, the imitation of a person or characteristic constituted a potentially threatening practice, since it created a sense of reliance. How, then, could one imitate but remain independent? The early modern essayist William Cornwallis, one of the more nuanced readers of Stoic texts, makes this distinction in his essay "On Imitation" when he claims that he "will not reject Imitation, yet I will hardly imitate any man living, especially in things apparently his, as his Behaviour, & accustomed Phrases:

In vertue it is very lawfull, for that is neither his, nor mine; it carryes no marke of any owner, but of the reall possessour of Eternity, whom if we could imitate in the least perfection, we are blessed."[6] Cautious of vulgar mimicry, Cornwallis employs legalistic reasoning to deduce that he can imitate only virtue, not behavior or "phrases," as those would qualify as theft. He arrives at this conclusion after dismissing more dangerous modes of imitation, such as the behavior of an Englishman traveling in Italy who forgets his first tongue: such practices are "base imitations begotten betweene the senses, and the fantasie, bastards unknown to the inward true discerning soule."[7] Similarly he rejects the imitators who focus only on physical impersonation, those who hold their necks "awry with *Alexander*"; these are "subtile Apes, which seek to creep into Princes, and great men, with putting on their Habits."[8] Cornwallis's elegant solution to avoid the Platonic pitfalls of base simulation is to call for the imitation of "vertue," which belongs to "Eternity" and thus cannot be stolen, inherent as it is to all humanity. But how does one imitate virtue? As Lipsius's text shows, even the noblest attempts to do so still must take into account the registers of the body, the traces of the "base imitations" that stand in ostensible opposition to virtue. One has to act *like* a Stoic, clumsily so, before one can become a true Stoic. At times, Stoicism embraces a broader understanding of imitation. As discussed in the introduction, Stoicism famously finds in the theater an apposite model for itself, as demonstrated by Epictetus's reminder in his *Enchiridion*—rendered here in English by his early modern translator James Sanford—that "[t]hou must remember that thou arte one of the players in an enterlude, and must plaie ye parte, which the authour thereof shall appoint, thou must play be it long, be it short."[9] Gordon Braden notes that "theatrical language reaches into many corners of Seneca's writing."[10] In a lively essay that helpfully dispels many myths of Stoicism, Andrew Shifflet compares the philosopher's investment in role-playing to the *theatrum mundi* trope epitomized by Jacques's famous "All the world's a stage" speech in *As You Like It*.[11] For Shifflet, the conceptualization of life "as a series of roles in the context of personal and general unhappiness—to do so with the goal of accepting and perhaps assuaging that unhappiness—continues an ethical tradition that stretches from Epictetus to Shakespeare, Ben Jonson, and beyond."[12]

In these examples, we see Stoicism grapple with its inherent ambivalence toward theatricality, which always threatens to devolve into a cheap mode of mimicry. Yet while Stoicism borrows, in its deployment of the *theatrum mundi* trope, a metaphorical sense of theater to explain its ideas, it also demonstrates a more fundamental kinship with the theater in its constitution *as* a mode of performance. The collection of primary classical Stoic texts that have survived today, by Marcus Aurelius, Epictetus, and Seneca, all operate more as byproducts, rather than as central elaborations, of Stoic ideas. *Meditations* exists for private consumption, as a prompt for its author to train habitually his mind and soul; the *Enchiridion* and *Discourses* are remnants of lectures by Epictetus transcribed by his pupil Arrian; Seneca's *Epistles* ostensibly communicates a particularized series of lessons for one individual in specific circumstances. Each text focuses on something other than simple "knowledge transfer," to use a pedagogical phrase popular today; instead, they are necessarily incomplete tools for a specific person (Lucilius, Marcus) or group of people (a classroom) to put to work as they live their lives. These are less explanatory tracts than they are scripts awaiting embodiment.

The formal construction of Stoic texts seems to suggest an inherent theatricality to the philosophy; however, when the actual institution of the theater appears in Stoic texts, it often stands in opposition to the values espoused by the sages, as when Langius scolds Lipsius to "take away these stage-hangings, draw backe the curtain that is afore thee, and without al counterfeiting or dissimulation, acquaint us with the true cause of thy sorrow."[13] Here, the theater uses fakery and deception to distract from the inward truth of the soul. In Guillame Du Vair's version of the *Enchiridion*, translated into English by Thomas James in 1598 as *The Moral Philosophie of the Stoicks*, the author—the selfsame thinker who lends Shakespeare one of his most famous celebrations of the theater—cautions the reader not to frequent the stage, and does so with explicitly theatrical logic:

> Now because a mans wordes and gestures are framed by long custome and imitation of others, we should not sort our selves too much with the common sort of people, or haunt the Theater, and common places of assemblie, or have often recourse to feasts and banquets: for in every one of these places it is not possible but a man should draw some vile humour or other from the common people.[14]

It is precisely because humans depend on imitation that those bent on achieving virtue should avoid the most visible site of imitation's occurrence, the theater. The "vile humour" of the crowd would infect the aspiring Stoic, who would absorb the wrong kind of behavior. Similarly, in *The Golden Boke of Marcus Aurelius*—a spurious, though influential, text by Antonio de Guevara that purported to contain the emperor's *Meditations* but in fact translated a popular biography of him—Marcus evinces distaste toward the stage. "He loved not these counterfattynge players of farces and mummeries," reports Guevara, as translated by John Bourchier Berners in 1535, "and yet lesse trewandes that ben naturall fooles, juglers and gesters for pleasure. The players and gesters suffred great varietie in the empire, accordynge to the diversitie of emperours."[15] Thomas Heywood, in his *Apology for Actors*, similarly labels Marcus hostile to the theater; Heywood, likely drawing on some of the same source material as *The Golden Boke*, foregrounds political dangers of performance familiar to apologists and critics of the theater in the early modern era. Worried that "his owne suspected life should be againe acted by the Comedians, as it before had been by the noble Matrons"—the women allied with his wife, Faustina, who mockingly imitated the emperor—"he profest himself adversary to all of that quality."[16] This is the same Marcus who committed himself to reading Epictetus closely and who himself practiced daily a meditative practice indebted to *Enchiridion*'s rigorous and highly theatrical self-interrogations. Epictetus encouraged his pupils to imagine themselves as playing roles, but his most notable follower punished actual players.

In many ways, this antitheatrical characterization makes sense: the core Stoic virtue of constancy seems to celebrate *in*action, not an ability to find expression through florid representation. The mode of enactment prompted by the scripts of Stoic work persistently carries with it inextricably a sense of stillness, conservatism, and reticence—qualities not usually associated with the kineticism of theater, which is, in Aristotle's famous formula, an "imitation of an action."[17] As Cornwallis idiomatically puts it, "I am my selfe still, though all the world were turned with the wrong side outward."[18] The play on "still" here renders it both geographical and temporal: the same self persists, and that self refuses to leap into the whirl of action that surrounds it. The philosopher Susanne Bobzien, in a thorough survey of early Stoic works, notes that they never employ the Greek word for "freedom." Instead, the Stoic trainee practices a mode of "assent" to those inner sensations and images they determine to be born from reason. It is this act of submission, Bobzien explains, that ensures "freedom from force and external hindrances" because the choice of assenting to appearances is, ironically, "neither forced nor fully externally determined."[19] "Freedom" in its modern and early modern conception of individual action is replaced here by the freedom to submit—freedom from freedom. Martha Nussbaum similarly glosses a central tenet of an early Stoic, Chrysippus, as the thesis "that the passions are forms of false judgment or false belief," which would suggest that they "are not subrational stirrings coming from our animal nature, but modifications of the rational faculty."[20] Because the passions arise from reason, we must employ proper judgment—a function of reason—to cure them. However, it follows that judgment results not from proactive analysis or diagnosis but from "an assent to an appearance."[21] The Stoic executes judgment through the decision to allow (or not) the belief in truthfulness when facing the appearance of feeling. Such a convoluted conception of motivated action has informed the criticism of the Stoics as politically neutered and ultimately more invested in self-centered withdrawal than in liberated agency. Quentin Skinner, in his magisterial study *The Foundations of Modern Political Thought*, assails Lipsius along these lines by claiming that *De constantia*'s attempted treatment of anxiety over civil war stems from a broader distaste. Lipsius's "attacks on religious radicalism are based on the more general claim that all the revolutionary movements of the age are equally and unforgivably destructive, so that the very idea of political resistance, on whatever grounds, deserves to be completely repudiated."[22] Here we can find the DNA of the stock Stoic character that comically graces the early modern stage—a cautious, hesitant, withdrawn figure.

In short, Stoic texts both borrow from and oppose valences of theatricality. A budding philosopher would emphasize in their training a curious mixture of initiative and passivity in curing themselves of the passions and thus living a good life. But they would also always imagine they are on stage and acting out a role. They would train themselves to scrutinize rigorously their own feelings and surroundings, but also to think of this scrutiny as deciding to passively accept, rather than actively interrogate, what they encounter. To read the foundational early modern Stoic works, then, is to encounter not only a pervasive tension between the text-centered demands of the culture that revived Stoicism and the inherent theatricality of the source material, but also a profound, oscillating ambivalence baked into the philosophy to begin with. Was Stoicism performance or not?

Framing Life

I propose that to answer this question, we return to an earlier one. How does one imitate virtue? One possible answer may be simply to indulge in the shallower kind of imitation and hope that virtuous imitation follows. This possible solution is exemplified in the behavior of Marcus in *The Golden Boke*—a figure more mythical than historical, but still one that proved significant in securing the reputation of Stoicism in the early modern era. This Marcus, the same emperor who banished the players from his city, is praised by the author, Antonio Guevara, for his chameleon-like abilities: "He was a childe amonge children: yonge amonge yonge folkes; worldely with them that were worldly; good felowe with good fellowes; A baron among barons; Hardy with hardy men; and finallie olde with olde menne."[23] To imitate virtue here is to be a man for all seasons, a mercurial harmonizer with one's environment. This behavior becomes a motif for Guevara, who elsewhere notes that Marcus "was stronge in vertue, meeke in wordes, attemperate in his excercises, homely with every man, sadde amonge sadde men, hasty amonge hasty men, Mery with mery men, and wise amonge wise men, as it is conveneable for a curious prince to be."[24] In pursuit of an ideal of suitability, though, Guevara paints himself into a telling corner: Marcus, as embodiment of the perfect leader, must both be humble—"meeke in wordes"—yet also express emotions as the situation demands. The implication is that these emotions result from an absolute control of his capacities, which renders them as not entirely real, but perhaps morally justifiable because they arise as symptoms, not causes, of the pursuit of virtue. If we follow this logic, the sad, hasty, merry, and wise Marcuses would not simply be projections of different aspects of himself; they are instead natural outcomes of recognizing the contingent, incidental, and disposable nature the passions possess. Here we see the same principle of constancy that allows for a static character like Langius also authorize a freewheeling array of personalities.

Seneca, in letter 108, suggests a deeper understanding of how one learns virtue in discussing how to learn philosophy. Seneca, we will recall from the introduction, frequently critiqued any mode of learning that focused on memorization and pure demonstrations of knowledge retention. As translated by Thomas Lodge in 1614, the letter avoids any focus on recitation and instead celebrates the ineffable and decidedly nonintellectual transmission of virtue that occurs in the simple act of conversation. For Seneca, when a philosopher speaks,

> some come to heare, not to learne, as we are drawne into a Theater for our pleasures sake, to delight our ears with Oration, Musick, or Comedies. Thou shalt see a great part of the auditors that make the Philosophers Schoole the Inne of their idlenesse. Their intention is not in that place to dispossesse themselves of some vices, or to receive some instruction, or rule of life, whereby they might reforme their manners, but to enjoy some delight that tickleth their eares. Some other there are that come to their tables, not to coate downe matter, but words, which they learne as well without other mens profit, as they heard them without their owne.[25]

Seneca mocks what he sees as improper motivation for hearing a philosopher: on the one hand, those who make school an "Inne of their idlenesse"; on the other, those who focus only on the words rather than the "matter" at hand. Seneca does not fixate on the exact behavior of the pupil: it does not matter if the philosopher expresses a specific demonstration of wit or intelligence. Instead, what matters is the motivation—that one is "drawne" to the philosopher not because they seek mere delight or scholastic pretension, but instead in pursuit of dispossessing vices and receiving "rule of life." Neither lazy nor overly studious, the proper student is defined by their desire to learn. Here, imitating virtue is not a virtuosic display of different personalities, as with Marcus, but instead a route to better understanding one's internal investment.

What is important, then, is that the Stoic *view* their tutelage in a specific way, not that they act in a particular manner. They need to arrive with a sense of openness to what befalls them. And, as Seneca makes clear, they need to be in the presence of human actors.[26] In this sense, all experience can be rendered as learning philosophy, if viewed as a proper training ground for cultivating the self. In *The Diall of Princes*, Guevara's later expansion of *The Golden Boke*, Marcus chastises a military advisor for relying too much on his thoughts and analyses. What is needed for leading an army is "learned by experience of deedes" rather than by "the prating in words."[27] This is an old, somewhat stale duality, but in the context of Marcus—himself a figure proffered by Guevara as a philosopher *par excellence*—the implication is that to *do* philosophy one has to learn from experience; words alone will not suffice.

In order to recognize that experience is translatable into learning, the Stoic needs to situate experience as a set of impressions on the mind that can be studied. Sanford, in his introduction to his translation of *Enchiridion*, echoes this tenet in his praise for the text's ability to provide a "well framing of life."[28] Philosophy lends coherence to experience by "framing" it, by delimiting and thus rendering it significant, and as a result the life itself becomes the philosophy, the actions that constitute its ideas. This definition curiously recalls Heywood's defense of the theater as a place whose "Scenes afford thee store of men to shape your lives by."[29] Both the theater and philosophy teach us to rethink what our lives *are* by giving them shape and purpose. The trope of "framing" here also brings to mind a more modern usage of the word by the sociologist Erving Goffman, whose essay "Frame Analysis," a foundational work for performance studies, proposes thinking of social interactions as having perceptual borders that grant them different rules—as if they were different plays, each with their own dramaturgy. "All social frameworks involve rules, but differently,"

Goffman explains. "For example, a checker move is informed by the rules of the game," while "the physical manipulation of a checker, on the other hand, involves a framework informing small body movements," and so on.[30] Just like the checker game, the checker player has their own set of rules they must follow, according to their social context. In this analogy, Stoicism is not a particular framework—not a genre of performance—but the tool that allows for the imposition of frames onto life. These imaginary lines, like those around a painting, or, more accurately, like the edge of a stage, heighten whatever happens within them and dictate a specific set of behavioral codes and norms. They allow Seneca's student to view a philosopher's lecture *as* a site of betterment. The mindset of the pupil seems to be Seneca's focus, in this letter and elsewhere, more than what is actually said and done. (Chapter 3 will elaborate further on the details of this prioritization of readiness over knowledge.)

This is the mode of "imitation" that Stoicism seizes on, more than the details of copying a specific person or idea: the preparation of a disposition. The philosopher does not have to perform in a particular way; they view life *as* performance. In this way, we can clarify a subtle but important distinction between Stoic performance and the kind of acting elaborated in the protheatrical tracts of Heywood and his colleagues. Both Heywood and Sanford's portrayals of Epictetus presume a value in philosophical work and see the theater as related to that work, but they differ as to what that philosophy actually *is*. Heywood protests that the theater can be a place where philosophical inquiry of a sort can occur, where lives can be shaped in pursuit of the good: theater has value because it is a medium for philosophical ideas. In this way he echoes the most famous apologia for the theater in the early modern era, Philip Sidney's *Defence of Poesy*, which carries a brief for the poetic arts (including theater) by pointing out that ancient philosophy used poetry as a Trojan horse for smuggling in its enlightening content. Sidney singles out one of the theater's historical adversaries, Plato, to make this point, with what must be intentional irony:

> And truly even Plato whosoever well considereth shall find that in the body of his work, though the inside and strength were philosophy, the skin, as it were, and beauty depended most of poetry: for all standeth upon dialogues; wherein he feigneth many honest burgesses of Athens to speak of such matters, that, if they had been set on the rack, they would never have confessed them.[31]

A spoonful of poetry, Sidney suggests, helps the philosophy go down. Had Socrates attempted to torture physically Thrasymachus or Glaucon, he would not have prompted as honest and true reflections as he did by sweetly leading them through rhetorically masterful dialogues.

By contrast, in the case of the Stoics, philosophy was not content transferred by the theater but *was* theatrical by nature. Rendering life as theater is the very work of Stoicism, which gives us the tools by which we can frame our lives as pertinent to the active pursuit of goodness. It allows us to situate the everyday as performance, as self-presentation. In sum, the theater repeatedly finds its defenders claiming it is the medium of philosophy, while the Stoics claim philosophy as already theatrical. Even if this theatricality was not straightforward—it was more conceptual than pragmatic—it still called attention to the use of the body. Looking at the world as theater was not simply a series of mental exercises. One still, like Lipsius's literary avatar, had to try to act like a sage, sometimes with embarrassing results, as when he takes "imitation" too literally. Cornwallis's theory of philosophical imitation helps to explain Stoicism's curious theatricality as a simultaneous engagement with and distance from embodiment. Bodies are needed, he claims, to pursue the good. But focusing on the body alone cannot lead to proper philosophy. In "Of Behavior," Cornwallis argues for the necessity of the body in expressing philosophical ideas to the self in possession of that body: "Philosophies strictest Inquisition of the Soule, dooth not more lively expresse her than Behaviour: for hers are Notions darke, and obscure, too heavy for every head to carry away, but this gives our sences a sight of that Divinity, and is the very picture of the inward minde."[32] The effects of philosophy reside in the body, since otherwise they would be clouded in the obscurity of inaccessible "notions darke"; only in our behavior can the process of philosophy reveal itself to our "sences." We cannot be disembodied philosophers because we need to observe and study our bodies, as repositories of behaviors that we can rigorously analyze and within which we can hope to catch a glimpse of the divine.

Just as the body can reflect divinity, though, so too can it express reason's opposite—opinion, the poisonous conjecture that disguises itself as objective truth. The discernment needed by the philosopher must learn to screen out the body's capacity to be ruled by the passions. A weaker, untrained mind would interpret the reflection of the resulting opinions as truth. Epictetus's declaration, as cited by Hamlet, that "there is no good or bad, but thinking makes it so" provides the most limpid declaration of this principle.[33] The "thinking" here, which assigns moral weight to objects of its scrutiny, is what the proper Stoic must separate from the pure reason of the mind, untainted by the passions. Lipsius, like Cornwallis, suggests that the body acts as the prism through which the beams of thought can be parsed out into separate lines of opinion and truth. As a Neo-Stoic, Lipsius incorporates Christian influences to attenuate the classical belief in opinion's origins in the faculty of reason. Rather than frame opinion as rational, Lipsius offers the more Aristotelian and Platonic gloss that opinion "hath his offspring of the bodie, that is of the earth"; the body furthermore "representeth to the soule the shapes and forms of thinges through the windows of the senses" and thus creates "a communion and societie betwixt the soule and bodie, but a societie (if you respect the ende) not good for the soul."[34] Stradling, the translator, offers the marginal summary that "the original of OPINION is of the earth and the body." Opinion, here, is the image that infects the soul with the pretense of pure reason, but whose origins are outside of the mind and thus should be ignored. While he differs from his classical forebears as to the passion's origins, however, Lipsius retains the quality noted by Nussbaum, the curious *specularity* of Stoicism, one that paradoxically arises from the very passivity and reticence that made it so easily mocked. It is precisely because of the lack of the concept of "freedom" noted by Bobzien and critiqued by Skinner that the Stoic philosopher gains a sort of agency as an audience member to themselves, an onlooker who attempts to discern reason from opinion in the coded behavior of the body. Seneca succinctly connects goodness to virtue to reason to judgment in letter 71:

> there is but onely one good, which is vertue, and that undoubtedly there is not any without vertue. And that vertue is lodged in our better part, which is that, which is reasonable. What shall this vertue be? A true and immoveable judgement from whence shall proceed the heat of the soule, whereby the appearance of things which may move this heate, shall become cleare and certaine.[35]

The theater of the body becomes doubled, in this model, within the reasoning soul, where images arrive like performers on a stage, awaiting critique. If they are derived from the passions, they are to be cast aside, sent on their way. If they arise from reason, and thus—to the early modern Stoic—from divinity, they are to be taken as a projection of the true self.

Cornwallis makes the connection of the spectacle of consciousness to the theater explicit when he, like Hamlet and Richard II, compares the mind to the world that it absorbs and reflects. In "Of Advise" he proposes that the mind is "a magazine [that is, a storehouse] of contentment, it is the mind that can distille the whole world, all Ages, all acts, all humane knowledge within the little, little compasse of a braine, and yet with the force of that little treasure commaund, dispose, censure & determine

States, Actions, kingdoms, warres, overthrowes, and all the Actes, and Actours busied upon our humane Theater."[36] Guillaume Du Vair's preface to his version of *Enchiridion* makes this connection syllogistically. "First of all," he begins, "let us perswade our selves that there is no true honor in the world but that which cometh from vertue. Secondly, that vertue seeks no greater or ampler theater to shew her selfe in, then her own conscience."[37] Like a theater, the mind creates a series of representations based on the world around it, which in turn allows for the control of those representations. The theatrical nature of the faculty of reasoning licenses the seemingly passive role of assent to be reclaimed as one of mastery. And this process of assent does not confine itself to the mind alone; it reflects itself in the body. An episode in *Attic Nights*, a collection of classical philosophy by Aulus Gellius that, while not translated into English until the nineteenth century, still influenced early modern Stoic texts that made reference to it, exemplifies the real-time bodily quality of self-scrutiny needed to train the inner self. Gellius relates that, while on board a ship during a vicious storm, he saw a Stoic philosopher become "frightened and ghastly pale" with a "loss of colour and distracted expression." Later, Gellius asks him why he had acted so scared—weren't Stoics supposed to be restrained and without emotion? The Stoic shares a section of his book of Epictetus that makes a crucial distinction between impression and interpretation:

> The mental visions, which the philosophers call φαντασίαι or "phantasies," by which the mind of man on the very first appearance of an object is impelled to the perception of the object, are neither voluntary nor controlled by the will, but through a certain power of their own they force their recognition upon men; but the expressions of assent, which they call συγκαταθέσεις, by which these visions are recognized, are voluntary and subject to man's will.[38]

Submission to the image relies on willed and controlled expression: one must exercise reason to validate or dismiss an internal picture. But in order to make this crucial decision, one must first register the sensations that bring the image into consciousness. The philosopher in this story first feels the corporeal effects of sickness—he becomes pale, loses color, and changes his expression—before he can properly determine the cause of those effects through his faculty of assent. He is passive insofar as the world acts upon him, but active in his absorption, aestheticization, and critique of the ensuing reflection of what Cornwallis calls the "humane Theater." Like Goffman, we can peel back the layers of this theater, from the author's witnessing of the philosopher's sickness, to the philosopher's own observations of his body, to his internal review of the impressions in his mind. The author watches the philosopher, who watches himself watching.

Thus far I have proposed that Stoic theatricality, rather than indulge in the mimesis of simple imitation, resides in the act of framing experience as a mode of theater that can be studied. In addition, the body itself becomes a key player in this theater; the philosopher trains their eye on their own corporeal sensations. Finally, the mind itself becomes a third stage in which the mental representations of phenomena await judgment as stemming from reason or opinion. Another key quality emerges as a natural symptom of this process: Stoics must work to *distance* themselves in order to frame their lives as worthy of study. In order to see life as a performance subject to judgment, the judge must be separated from the spectacle, even when that spectacle occurs within the body and consciousness of the evaluator. Seneca's *Letters on Ethics* begins with a condensation of this principle in the imperative to Lucilius that he "recover thy selfe to thy selfe."[39] Such is Lodge's translation; a recent rendering by Margaret Graver and A. A. Long has it as "assert your own freedom."[40] Both have a slightly Romantic ring of *carpe diem*, but Seneca shortly undermines this interpretation by clarifying in the second letter that Lucilius is not to attempt to grasp the infinite and savor the sublime, but instead should try to gain happiness only from what he needs—a freedom born from a realization of limits. Ending as he often does with a gloss of Epicurus, Seneca advises, in Lodge's rendering, that "he that contenteth himselfe with his povertie, is a rich man, not that he hath little, but that he desireth the most, is the poor man."[41] Living every day as if it were the last should result not in striving to do more—"He is no where, that is everywhere," Seneca warns—but instead in acknowledging only what is needed to live.[42] Paramount among the skills that Lucilius should learn is his ability to judge what is essential to his life, and this ability can only be honed if Lucilius splices himself in two, one side watching and the other performing. Only upon completing this act of separation can he find his authentic self, his realization of his capacity and thus his virtue. In this sense, I feel Lodge's translation actually captures better the distancing self-observation of the Stoic sentiment: Lucilius needs to rescue himself, to treat himself as his own audience, rather than to burst forth into freedom—assent, not assert.

One potential pitfall in the process described thus far, of crowding out of the observing self from the self under observation in an effort to view it as performance, is that it leads to the abnegation of a sense of individuality at all: if one becomes an audience to oneself, then where is true identity located? Gordon Braden offers a lucid declension of this process. First, Braden explains, the Stoic learns to act indifferent to all political concerns—the civil wars that Langius urges Lipsius to shrug off, say—in cultivating their ability to judge accurately the appearances that crowd the theater of their mind. Braden here recalls Skinner's critique: "Stoicism," he writes, "is not finally a philosophy of political resistance. The essential Stoic strategy for dealing with a tyrant is not interference but indifference . . . Stoicism's central strength is its calculus of adaptation to unchangeable realities."[43] But Braden takes this idea further than Skinner by proposing that this indifference leads, counterintuitively, to obsessive self-surveillance, as exemplified by Marcus's meditations; such practice, in turn, de-interiorizes the self by rendering it entirely an object of study. A natural byproduct of this emptying out is imperial drive—the outward introjection of the punishing and rigorous psychic interrogation. The *thymos*—the element of the soul that, for Plato, is bent toward heroic acts—thus finds that "the ultimate integrity is annihilation."[44] And finally, this annihilation, funneled inwardly to suicide and outwardly to imperial conquest, finds its ultimate purpose in crafting a work of art, something outward-facing and public:

> Consuming itself, his life becomes its own image: if that conversion meets the Stoic need for certainty and self-control, it also commits Seneca, at the last moment, to the care of his friends. An image, whatever its protestations of self-sufficiency, expects to be looked at.[45]

From indifference to cultivation to hyperawareness to self-destruction to spectacle: this is not a Platonic arc of understanding how truth gains aestheticization and representation. We are far from a metaphysical model of ideas guised in the fallible forms that render them understandable, albeit flawed and potentially deceptive. Instead, Stoic performance turns first inward, without an apparent care for other matters. From this obsessive drive inward there arrives an eventual turn outward in crafting a human made to be observed, admired, and—in Marcus's case—feared.

Braden brilliantly traces this connection to draw attention to Stoic influences on early modern imperialist drives. But while he notes the importance of theatrical *language*, he skips past the affinities that this spectacular quality possesses with early modern theater as a material and embodied practice. As I have shown, the way that performance threads its way through Stoic texts is not simply as a metaphor but as the actual manifestation *of* the philosophy. The physical theater is not only "like" virtuous performance, but virtue can only be known *through* behavior that must be heightened, framed, and analyzed. Finally, it is not only the inwardness of consciousness that becomes a space of performance; the Stoic also renders the outward phenomenality of the world as its own theater that constantly cultivates the observer into a state of calm happiness. The *adiaphora*, in other words, do not become discarded and ignored: they constitute an artwork of sorts, manifestations of unknown design that can cause wonder and awe. The atrocities that make Lipsius flee are part of a grander plan, one we cannot comprehend—for early modern philosophers, that plan is God's; for classical Stoics, it is simply fate, unknown perhaps even to divinity—and we, as audience members, should laugh at the ongoing spectacle of horror. (The next chapter draws out in more detail the Stoic conception of fate as a theatrical construction.) Joseph Hall, in exploring the implications of this condition, asks his readers, "how shall wee under this calme & quiet bay laugh at the rough weather & unsteddye motions of the worlde? How shall heaven and earth smile upon us, and we on them; commanding the one; aspiring to the other? How pleasant shall our life be, while neither joies nor sorrows can distemper it with excesse?"[46]

The simultaneous cosmic irrelevance and affirmation spurred by the doubled Stoic gaze, inward and outward—the twinned theaters of mind and world—help further explain the philosophy's ambivalence toward performance. On the one hand, the theater is everywhere; on the other, nothing remains to be offset and analyzed if everything is an artistic object. Consciousness is a theater; the physical body is an actor; the entire world is a play. The risks in the potential for everything to be rendered *as* theater are twofold, each a different extreme. First, the Stoic can become overly individuated as the primary audience member for the world's (and the self's) play; second, the Stoic can be emptied out of any individuality at all, without any interiority to withhold and duped into the false impression of significance. The first has led to a scholarly tradition that positions Stoic philosophy as an inauguration of the modern concept of individuality. A. A. Long's influential essay "Representation and the Self in Stoicism" stakes out this line of thinking. Long notes that, for the Stoics, the "representational faculty"—the component of the mind that renders all objects of awareness as representation—is all-encompassing: "There is no other faculty in virtue of which mental states can appear to the self that has them."[47] By rendering everything as representation, the Stoic self becomes concretized, not dissipated. Long notes the emergence of what he calls the "commanding part" of the soul, or *hegemonikon*, which takes on the role of primary judge that ascertains the validity of each representation brought before it. He elaborates that "the Stoics view the mind, in one of its basic operations, as a receptor which is constantly being occupied by a sequence of representations. They take it that the external world and/or one's internal condition continuously acts upon the mind, and thereby provides it with some definite content or object(s) of awareness."[48] One of Long's primary interlocutors, Charles Taylor's *Sources of the Self*, similarly links the Stoics' assenting faculty to the production of an individual—and the jettisoning of shared capability: "What is morally crucial" about the Stoic, Taylor claims, "is not just the universal nature or rational principle which we share with others, as with Plato and Aristotle, but now also this power of assent, which is essentially in each case *mine*."[49]

At the same time, Stoic performance, by foregrounding assent as a central mechanism of self-assertion, runs the risk of paradoxically invalidating self-importance altogether by indulging in delusion. To assent to representation is an inherently passive behavior, one that foregrounds a lack of action rather than a dynamic assertion of individuality. It is this submissiveness that leads T. S. Eliot infamously to wave away Stoicism as a "philosophy suited to slaves."[50] Eliot's account stems from his reading of Othello's devastating final monologue before his suicide—a speech I will examine (along with further implications of Stoicism's complicity with bondage) in chapter 5—and he sees the Stoic effort to recognize insignificance as, paradoxically, a selfish effort to furnish one's life with the trappings of melodrama. "Stoicism," Eliot declares, "is the refuge for the individual in an indifferent or hostile world too big for him; it is the permanent substratum of a number of versions of cheering oneself up."[51] By *staging* one's status as insignificant in the cosmic scheme, one betrays, in Eliot's reckoning, a desire to be seen and validated as significant. Instead of firming up a sense of self, then, this version of Stoicism peddles a falsely soothing doctrine that only underlines one's desperate failure to achieve actual importance.

Rather than take a stance as to whether the Stoics helped inaugurate or destroy modern individuality, I would like to step back to examine the embodied techniques that one learns to *render* the three spaces of consciousness, body, and public—akin to Hamlet's three "distracted Globes" of mind, stage, and world—*as* containing performance. How does one learn to become an actor, to see others as actors, to see one's head as a theater? As Lipsius demonstrates, the process of learning to distance the self is one of fumbling self-adjustment: one does not immediately become a sage. Training happens in real time. The medium of *On Constancy* demonstrates this best: by reading a dialogue, we experience, with the author's surrogate, the way that Stoic performance attempts, not always successfully, to recognize the performative nature of life without tipping into histrionics. It is as if we could read Lucilius's letters. Langius elaborates on this idea when he compares Lipsius to an improperly motivated actor. The example Lipsius uses—culled, most likely, from Gellius—is the story of Polus, a tragedian in ancient Greece who was said to have brought the bones of his dead son on stage with him to motivate his passions. For Langius, Lipsius's true suffering is private and personal, while the political chaos that surrounds him only *seems* to be the cue for passion. Lipsius needs to admit the true cause of his suffering—to find his son's bones—and so Langius urges him to "examine the matter to the quick, & you shall find many times great difference betwixt the tongue and the heart"; while Lipsius claims that his "countries calamitie affects me," these words "carrie with them more vainglory than veritie." Like Polus, who could "fil the theater with true teares indeed" with his false cause, Lipsius, "under the person of your country," in fact cries because of "private miseries."[52] The sage is reminded of Epictetus's famous comparison: "One saith The whol world is a stage-play," he declares, and then decries "some who crie out, These civil warres torment us, the blood of innocents spilt, the losse of lawes and libertie. Is it so? I see your sorrow indeed, but the cause I must search out more narrowly. Is it for the common-wealths sake? O player, put off thy vizard: thy selfe art the cause thereof."[53] Again, we find a dismissal of the trappings of the stage—Lipsius must cast off his costume—coupled with an embrace of performance as a paradigm for realizing Cornwallis's goal of learning virtue. Lipsius must admit that everything takes place in the scrutinized, artistically intentional world of the theater, but just as Hamlet advises the players, he must perform in a way that suits his *actual* interior motivation to his actions. If you are going to act, he seems to say, do so in a sincere way. Realize that you are the cause of your suffering. Once Lipsius can do so—once he can perform the primal gesture of rendering life as performance, by separating his self from what he is observing, and thus render it theatrical—his suffering shifts into the realm of the changeable and out of the *adiaphora*, and healing can begin.

Reiterating Distances

Lipsius's act of separating himself from his life is aided by an ideal mentor. But one stumbling block for the Stoic student is the dearth of actual sages. Without a real-life Langius or resurrected Cato to supply clear mentorship, or without any secluded gardens into which they can retreat, the philosopher is left in the real world. They can read Stoic texts, but those texts do not offer any systemic overview of what to do. The means of attaining the actual goal, as discussed in the introduction, is hazy, and the mythical figures who lead the way have gained a sense of insubstantiality as a result. The Stoic sage, as Patrick Gray explains, is a "curious cipher," a "mere blank, albeit with praise attached."[54] Readers of Stoicism alive to this ambiguity, such as Hadot, thus switch the focus from the cipher of the sage to the muddling middle of the Stoics-to-be, who live not in rarefied remove but in the thrum of habit and community. In the absence of sages, then, life itself becomes a tutor: a spectacle constantly impressing itself onto perception and demanding evaluation. Yet while this evaluation demands distancing—the self from the self—most Stoic philosophers, Hadot explains, remain irreducibly *within* the world:

> For such a man, daily life, as it is organized and lived in by other men, must necessarily appear abnormal, like a state of madness, unconsciousness, and ignorance of reality. And nonetheless he must live this life every day, in this world in which he feels himself a stranger and in which others perceive him to be one as well . . . the result is perpetual conflict between the philosopher's effort to see things as they are from the standpoint of universal nature and the conventional vision of things underlying human society, a conflict between the life one should live and the customs and conventions of daily life.[55]

For Hadot, a true philosopher cannot help but be in reality, and yet they also must view reality as strange and estranged, as theatrical. The pure distance needed to witness and critically scrutinize life—the distance that allows Hall to laugh in the face of calamity, or Langius to remain calm despite war—is, as a result, less an absolute cut between performer and audience and more a constantly reiterated attempt, a distanc*ing* more than a pure distance. The primal mechanism of the theater, after all, is the reiterated instantiation of a division that allows for a spectator and a performer. In the opening passage of his seminal book on directing, *The Empty Space*, Peter Brook distills the theater to this fundamental split: "I can take any empty space and call it a bare stage. A man walks across this empty space whilst someone else is watching him, and this is all that is needed for an act of theatre to be engaged."[56] Yet Hadot's Stoic must always be caught in the breach, always in the act of distancing rather than cleanly separated. This situation, too, gets to an elemental behavior of the theater: its endlessly reiterative quality, which creates the never-entirely-established distance between performer and watcher. As Samuel Weber suggests, the theater never resolves into a legible break but instead constantly reasserts itself, as if approaching an asymptote: "On the stage, no action is ever fully self-present. As acting, such 'action' is exposed in and through the iterations of a present participle that can never be totalized."[57] The action on a stage is continually under pressure to become absolutely "self-present" but can never yield to this coalescence; its assertions always feel the tug of its own ephemerality and possible disappearance.

Weber, in this passage, specifically addresses the work of the modernist theater innovator Bertolt Brecht, whose celebrated use of *verfremdungseffekt* (distancing-effect) always reminded audiences that they were watching something artificial by challenging the absolute separation of actor and spectator. Martha Nussbaum has noted the affinity between Stoic distancing and Brechtian aesthetics: The pupil who reads Stoic philosophy, Nussbaum claims, must exercise the "critical spectatorship" called for by Brecht because "the main aim" of Stoic advice "must be to create a spectator who is vigilant and probing, active rather than receptive."[58] This vigilant spectatorship should then be carried forth into life, just as Brecht's dispassionate viewer leaves the theater and remains critical of the theatrical illusions in civil society. The Stoic reader must complete the embodied act of reading by reflecting, thinking, and doing; hence the Stoics' frequent use of the exhortative mode as signal of the insufficiency of writing. As Hadot writes,

> the philosophical act is not situated merely on the cognitive level, but on that of the self and of being. It is a progress which causes us to be more fully, and makes us better. It is a conversion which turns our entire life upside down, changing the life of the person who goes through it. It raises the individual from an inauthentic condition of life, darkened by unconsciousness and harassed by worry, to an authentic state of life, in which he attains self-consciousness, an exact vision of the world, inner peace, and freedom.[59]

It is the philosophical *act* that constitutes philosophy, not that which might take place on the "cognitive level." Furthermore, the reward of philosophical practice is authenticity, a reattachment of the self to the world as it actually is, rather than as it inauthentically presents itself in false, passionate imitations of reality. In *The Inner Citadel*, Hadot's study of Marcus's *Meditations*, he elaborates on how the process of training the inward self depends upon rigorously testing the authenticity of the forms that throng to one's consciousness—how one could, like Brecht's spectator, interrogate what is artificial so as to achieve a better grasp of authenticity when it arises. This authenticity, for Marcus, is naturally reason, and the discovery of an inward image's relation to reason and thus divinity allows for the truly philosophical life to take hold. In this sense, Marcus echoes Gellius's notion that, in order to train a Stoic body, one must cultivate the discourses prompted by the *phantasiae* of the world and their inner image-making. And so, for Marcus, one must constantly partake in what he calls "demonstrations." "With the aid of these demonstrations," Hadot writes, "the dogmas imposed themselves upon Marcus with absolute certainty, and he usually restricts himself to formulating them in the form of a simple proposition."[60] Thus the form of the *Meditations*, with its aphoristic sparsity, reflects the propositions that arise from reflection on the absorption of the *phantasiae* of the world. The book, then, is a demonstration when read, as it was in the act of writing it. Hadot elaborates:

> As he wrote the *Meditations*, Marcus was thus practicing Stoic spiritual exercises. He was using writing as a technique or procedure in order to influence himself, and to transform his inner discourse by meditating on the Stoic dogmas and rules of life. This was an exercise of writing day by day, ever-renewed, always taken up again and always needing to be taken up again, since the true philosopher is he who is conscious of not yet having attained wisdom.[61]

For Marcus, as for his Stoic mentors, writing and reading were performances, not transmissions of knowledge. They were technical exercises to reinstate distancing-effects, train inner discourses, and, as a result, lend integrity and purpose to outward motion. The body takes in images and disciplines itself into withholding from pernicious judgment, instead questioning its wider placement. Every ensuing action, for Marcus, prompts a consideration of its situation. As *Meditations* asks its author and reader: "Am I doing something? I relate the act to beneficence to men. Does an accident befall me? I accept it, relating it to the gods and to the source of all things, from which all that comes to pass depends by a common thread."[62]

This passage condenses the constitutive elements of Stoic performance identified in this chapter: it renders the object of its gaze as a performance to be judged; it splits this gaze inward (to its intentions) and outward (to the universe); and it does so through an act of reiterative self-distancing by separating one self (the Marcus reading the text) from an other (the Marcus asking the questions). With these criteria fulfilled, the Stoics could engage in embodied action: they could imitate virtue. They could perform. The ensuing performance was not one of narcissistic, cerebral detachment, as their vilified image would suggest. The Stoics were not against action as such, but, like Hamlet's advice to the players, against its mercurial deployment. If one did not judge the validity of the forms that appeared in the theaters of consciousness, or evaluate the effects in the theater of the world—and if one could not properly separate themselves to conduct this observation to begin with—the action would be fruitless. Epictetus makes this point in his *Manual* with an extended and at times convoluted appeal. He first asks the reader, "Wilt thou conquere at ye playes Olimpia?" Will you, in other words, partake in the competitions of the ancient Olympic Games? While Epictetus grants that it is "a verie honourable thing," he asks, like Marcus, that you "consider wel the beginning, and the sequel and then take the matter in hande." He goes on to distinguish carefully between two modes of desire that could motivate one's participation. If you have properly considered the effects of your action, then "go and fight," but if you have not, "thou wilt be like the little boyes which are now wrestlers, nowe swordplayers, nowe trumpeters, forthwith players in tragedies. So thou also now a fighter, now a swordplayer, afterward an Oratour, at length a Philosopher: but throughly nothing at al." To attempt to do everything renders one as "nothing"; worse still, Epictetus argues, you become a mere counterfeiter: "as an Ape thou doest counterfait and resemble al things, and nowe one thing shall lyke thee, now an other: for thou hast not done thy enterprise advisedly, in foreseeing the circumstances, but adventurouslie following a lighte and colde desire."[63] The dilettantish pupil becomes, in an echo of Cornwallis's "subtile Ape" who indulges in shallow imitations of Alexander, *only* an actor, only a collection of externalized passions, rather than an actor in pursuit of clear-eyed reason and truth.

How can one discern the apish actor from the properly performing philosopher? Through exercise. This is why Hadot's work is essential to best grasp the essentially active nature of Stoicism: rather than pursue the ideal of virtue as a horizon, he recognizes, as the Stoics themselves did, that virtue thrives in the attempt. Thus in *De constantia* Lipsius intuits that the journey toward sagehood involves many bumps along the way, many false starts—as Lipsius histrionically imitates Langius or mistakes the symptom of wisdom for its cause, as when he forgets that he has a body and must eat. Stradling sounds a note of caution in his preface to the reader when he assures them that Lipsius is "none of those subtle sophisticall janglers, that place philosophie in the quirks and quiddities of crabbed questions."[64] Fear not, he seems to say—the purpose is not to get lost in rhetoric and fanciful wordplay, but instead (it is implied) to locate philosophy in the *doing*, in the act of listening, responding, and, as Cornwallis would have it, in properly imitating. Here we have an explanation, too, for the stock Stoic character who mocks the impossible cipher of the stage in so many early modern plays. Langius, at one point, concedes that the difference between a wise Stoic and an unfeeling churl is not readily apparent: Whoever is "not moved with these matters [that is, the Belgian civil wars] nor oppressed with the multitude of so manie and manifold miseries, must eyther be very stayed and wise, or els very hard hearted."[65] Lipsius the character is neither all that wise nor hard-hearted: he is the philosopher-in-training, not the fully realized philosopher, and he admits as much toward the end when he claims, "Neither am I to bee compared as yet to valiant and good men, but perchance am a little better than the most effeminate and worst sort."[66] Lipsius the *author* belies his own wisdom when he demonstrates this real-time and theatrical process of learning, however. (That he doubles himself as a character in the text only realizes more thoroughly the self-separation inherent to Stoicism.)

King James, in his *Basilikon Doron*, inadvertently realizes Lipsius's belief in the impossibility of attaining his work's titular constancy when he insultingly dismisses the "Stoick insensible stupiditie that proud inconstant LIPSIUS persuadeth in his *Constantia*" before issuing a traditional Stoic sentiment that "although yee are not a stock, not to feele calamatie, yet let not the feeling of them over-rule & doazen your reason, as may staie you from taking and using the best resolution for remedie that can be found out."[67] Lipsius's "inconstant" constancy, lambasted by James, does not in fact undermine the Neo-Stoic's work but pays tribute to its complexly staged belief in the impossibility of actually attaining pure constancy, and the bodily and endlessly rehearsed process by which the pupil must strive toward that unattainable goal. Tellingly, it is this same "inconstant" quality that Montaigne, an admirer of Lipsius, finds so compelling in Seneca's brand of Stoicism. Montaigne is more generous than James when he observes that to "see the trouble to which Seneca puts himself to be prepared for death, to see him sweat from the exertion of steeling and reassuring himself, and write about interminably on his perch, would have shaken his reputation with me if he had not very valiantly attained it in dying. His agitation, so burning, so frequent, shows that he was hot and impetuous himself."[68] The perspiration is *needed* for Seneca to attain a state by which he can appear impervious to exertion. Montaigne finds it "valiant" that the philosopher maintained his disposition in dying, and as a result recognizes that the trouble needed to reach that state does not undermine it.

Seneca's sweat returns us to Lipsius's stomach: the Stoic must admit to the body, and all its fallibilities, in attempting to pursue the good life. For all its focus on abstracting the self from itself, in order to observe the mind and the world, Stoicism also admits to the exertion needed to attempt to reach the impossible horizon of pure specularity. The rigorous practice needed to maintain this exertion is not theatrical in any traditional sense. It always shies away from this familiar understanding of outward imitation and instead resides, as I have said, more in the realm of a general state of heightened reality that does not rely on the formal trappings of stagecraft. To perform is to be like Langius's model for Lipsius: bereft of "vizards" that mask one's true self, yet also an actor, like Polus, who needs to understand the true source of his motivation. There is a final element of Stoic performance that naturally follows from these qualities: it is ephemeral. As such, its foundations are unsteady, always threatening to dissolve. The separation of self from self can—and will—blur; the distancing needed to view life as theater can and will collapse, over and over. This wobbly status is, however, an essential component of performance, which always evades a clear definition. In a famous formulation, Richard Schechner, drawing on the anthropological work of Victor Turner, calls the actor "liminal," possessing traces of the performing self and the "actual" self, both and neither. "All effective performances share this 'not—not not' quality," claims Schechner. "Olivier is not Hamlet, but also he is not not Hamlet: his performance is between the denial of being another (= I am me) and a denial of not being another (= I am Hamlet)."[69] To be the self and also *not* the self is to be in the breach between fixed poles of identity. Lipsius is not fully Lipsius, not a realization of his authentic being, but nor is he someone else. To perform is, in its purest form, not so much to *be* something nor simply to *imitate* it, but to fleetingly embody a set of practices, to recognize self-constitution in the recurring moment of the present. That present moment will die away, but so too could it always be rescripted into existence anew. To act is, as Peggy Phelan notes, to be transient and thus to resist codification: "performance becomes itself through disappearance."[70] This essential state of nonessence is an obsessive point of interest for early modern playwrights as well, whether in comedic energies that call attention, with metatheatrical playfulness, to the nothingness at the core of the theatrical endeavor; or the overweening willpower of the tragedies, bent as they are on replicating and critiquing the formation of power and the limits of that power's ability to inflect the actual playhouse.

In the chapters that follow, I study the Stoic performances that revive themselves in the early modern theater. It is to the theater that we must look to find the sweaty, messy, fumbling, brief reality of Stoicism, a philosophy dually founded on the body's enmeshment in and removal from the world. Like Hadot's conjecture that the philosopher is both of and not of the everyday, the theater is both an extension of and removal from its surrounding world. The performance of Stoicism is not coextensive with the aesthetics of the early modern stage, but the theater smuggles in philosophical energies by dint of its own obsessive self-critique. In this sense, to watch a play is to undergo philosophical work, and to philosophize is to perform. As Will D'Addario, a cofounder of the nascent discipline of performance philosophy, puts it, once we think of philosophy as embodied, "thinking no longer refers to an act that faithfully adheres to the criteria of one privileged discipline but now emerges through the doing of artistic and intellectual expression"; philosophy is, D'Addario claims, in terms Hadot would recognize, the "doing of life."[71] The theater, where life of sorts is "done" and redone, provides a perfect reflection of the Stoic's work, permanently poised as it is on the precipice between embodied action and transcendence.

CHAPTER TWO

We Know the World: Stoic Fate in Marston's Antonio Plays

Despite Philosophy

In a brief essay on John Marston, T. S. Eliot attempts to dismiss the playwright's Antonio plays, *Antonio and Mellida* and *Antonio's Revenge*, as mere stylistic throat-clearing that preceded more mature drama. But Eliot cannot entirely abandon these works, try as he may. He finds himself drawn inexplicably to them despite himself because, he confesses, they prompt "bewilderment, that anyone could write plays so bad and that plays so bad could be preserved and reprinted" while refusing to be "plays that one wholly forgets." Their compellingly poor quality, furthermore, "cannot be explained simply by incapacity, or even by plain carelessness. A blockhead could not have written them; a painstaking blockhead would have done better; and a careless master, or a careless dunce, would not have gone out of his way to produce the effects of nonsensicality which we meet."[1] This blockhead-resistant yet undeniably bad artistry is a function of what Eliot terms Marston's "irrelevance" and must, he decides, be a "symptom" of something. He soon lights upon the disease: a quality of poetic drama that Eliot calls a "doubleness" of "dramatic action, as if it took place on two planes at once."[2] The diagnosis complete, Eliot moves on to *The Tragedy of Sophonisba*—in his rare opinion the best example of Marston's genius—with a nearly audible sigh of relief.[3]

This chapter lingers on the Antonio plays' sense of doubleness. There are, appropriately, two doublenesses I want to examine, two dualities that the Antonio plays endeavor, time and again, to link. The first, which Eliot's verdict seems to detect, is the split between actor and character; the second, that between philosophy and action. This latter division marks the gulf between thoughtful withdrawal, named in the play as a form of Stoicism, and a passionate, kinetic embrace of affect. Taken separately, each division conforms to certain well-worn conventions of early modern drama: the cleavage between the performing body and the performed character has long supplied metatheatrical comedic fodder; and the assumption of overwhelming emotion, rather than cool reserve, allows for a handy dramaturgical pivot to rush characters headlong into climactic action.

But the Antonio plays suggest that these dualities are inextricable. More crucially, they suggest that the seemingly clean lines of separation are in fact quite porous. As opposed to its image as purely cerebral, Stoicism operates as dependent on theatrical embodiment; the revelation of theatrical performance's construction, in turn, conducts profound philosophical work. The plays thus portray the specifically performative quality that Stoicism endorsed, as surveyed in chapter 1: as a way of attempting to frame the world so as to render it spectacular and to allow the philosopher to view themselves as both audience and player. In particular, the Antonio plays show how this condition emerges in a consideration and demonstration of Stoic conceptions of fate—and more specifically, of how the early modern era wrestled with the implications of a classical understanding of an unknowable fate within a Christian theological framework that insisted on God's plan circumscribing all action. By repeatedly foregrounding and collapsing the twin doublenesses of philosophy-action and performer-actor, Marston's works *enact*, more than they outright state, the essential condition of the Stoic: adrift in an unknowable world, torn between being and becoming. Furthermore, as I will demonstrate, they suggest a complicity between the genre of comedy and Stoicism. By forcing audiences to laugh at investments in things outside of reason, Marston also forces them to consider comedic playmaking an apt parallel to the folly of believing in mastery over fate—or even, for that matter, over a clear sense of self.

In *Antonio's Revenge*, Pandulpho, grappling with the death of his son, knots together these considerations when he erupts out of his withdrawn and unmoved state. While beforehand Pandulpho has been labeled a "doting stoic" by the vicious Piero (2.2.70), he now boldly suggests that his meditative reserve was simply a form of playacting:

> Man will break out, despite philosophy.
> Why, all this while I ha' but played a part,
> Like to some boy that acts a tragedy,
> Speaks burly words and raves out passion;
> But when he thinks upon his infant weakness,
> He droops his eye. I spake more than a god,
> Yet am less than a man. (4.5.46–52)[4]

On the surface, this passage seems to overlay neatly the binaries of actor-character and philosopher-revenger. But the material conditions of the play's initial performances, conditions of which the text repeatedly demonstrates a keen awareness, unsettle this symmetry. The actor originating the role of Pandulpho was, after all, not "like" some boy who acts a tragedy but, as a member of the Children of Paul's, an actual boy acting a tragedy. The passage, then, implies that the a priori condition of the play is one of comic failure: the mere act of assuming one could "play a part" if one were a little boy acting in a tragedy is a state from which the play cannot escape. "Philosophy," then, operates as an embrace *of* this state of being, and being a man—"breaking out"—is the satirical impossibility.

The philosophy that Pandulpho claims to be leaving behind is named by Piero as Stoicism, and on the surface this seems accurate: Pandulpho frequently recites shopworn Stoic sentiments and even, at times, speaks long passages lifted wholesale from Seneca. Immediately before he "breaks out," in fact, he and Antonio have been faithfully re-creating a scene from a spurious Senecan text, *De remediis fortuitorum*, a dialogue popular in Marston's day.[5] Pandulpho, in voicing these platitudes, joins a formidable roster of fellow unfeeling thinkers, ranging from the nobly perseverant heroine of Elizabeth Cary's *Tragedy of Mariam* to Justice Overdo, Jonson's stock Stoic in the stocks surveyed in the introduction. This brand of Stoicism, conflated as it was with the near-mythical sage figure, often represented the most unrealistically alienated school of thought, one dangerously close to comic humiliation.

Pandulpho's highly exaggerated version of Stoicism belongs in this roster. Many critics have duly found his depiction of a "doting Stoic" to be overly doting: Geoffrey Aggeler notes that in his initial appearances in *Antonio's Revenge*, Pandulpho is "overdrawn [as] an image of Stoic virtue."[6] Michael Higgins goes further, attributing the character's thinly drawn psyche to authorial deficiency:

> The character of Pandulpho is the symbol and proof of a weakness evident in every page which Marston wrote. This man could summon the shapes of villainy and folly and corruption and vice with a remarkable imaginative power: called on to create a figure of positive virtue and living active beauty, he can conjure up only an empty phantom imagined from dry texts and the un-illuminated wisdom of antiquity.[7]

Pandulpho would be recognized by Marston's audience, it seems, not as a noble font of profundity but as a cipher for dated classicism—a caricature of wisdom ill equipped to reckon with the vagaries of life, comically withdrawn and unmoving in the face of unquestionably horrific events. His breaking out of philosophy, then, ties together a *false* sense of Stoicism with the struggles of a boy actor pretending to mature tragedy. As such, I suggest that by shedding not Stoicism but a shallow and crudely approximated version of the sage, a figure as impossible to realize as a boy successfully embodying tragic emotions, Pandulpho inadvertently gives us a picture of Stoicism itself.

It is admittedly counterintuitive to claim that the play endorses a Stoic position at precisely the moment when it is rejected; it is also strange to detect Stoic ideas in Marston given his frequent characterization of the philosophy as ineffective and effete. In *The Scourge of Villainie* he scowls at requests for Stoic calm: "Preach not the Stoickes patience with me, / I hate no man, but mens impietie."[8] In *Antonio and Mellida*, Andrugio voices a similar criticism, anticipating Pandulpho's later fury; as Andrugio is reeling from news of his son's defeat in battle, Andrugio's anger takes the form of a Montaignian digression that once again takes "philosophy" to be synonymous with philosophy's horizon: "Thou liest, Philosophy. / Nature forms things unperfect, useless, vain. / Why made she not the earth with eyes and ears, / That she might see desert and hear men's plaints? / That when a soul is splitted, sunk with grief, / He might fall thus [*He casts himself down.*] upon the breast of the earth" (3.1.35–44).[9] And most elaborately, after Andrugio dies, in *Antonio's Revenge*, his son similarly becomes exasperated in the face of peaceful consolation. Attempting to read Seneca—specifically the essay "On Providence," a text whose citations and translations wind their way through Marston's plays—Antonio tosses it aside in frustration. He aims his invective at Seneca the author; Hamlet's gentle critique of Horatio's "philosophy" becomes magnified, here, as an outright assault on the very notion of thoughtful consolation:

> Pish! Thy mother was not lately widowed,
> Thy dear affied love lately defamed
> With blemish of foul lust when thou wrotest thus.
> Thou, wrapped in furs, beaking thy limbs 'fore fires
> Forbid'st the frozen zone to shudder. Ha, ha! 'tis naught
> But foamy bubbling of a fleamy brain,
> naught else but smoke, O, what dank, marish spirit
> But would be fired with impatience
> At my—
> No more, no more (2.3.49–57)

Antonio claims that Seneca is unsuited to offer solace because he has not lived through what Antonio has; the philosopher can easily advise that one withstand the cold while remaining safely ensconced in warmth. Antonio, here, believes he can refute the Stoic through the intrusion of embodied experience. The lines of Seneca that prompt this outburst suggest that humans face a harder task than God in enduring evil because God is exempt from evil, whereas humans must *choose* not to give in to sin. Thomas Lodge, in his 1614 translation, renders the passage in question as "Suffer manfully, this is the way whereby you may walke before God, he is without the patience of evill, you above the patience."[10] A gloss of this sentiment has, in fact, already been uttered in the play by Pandulpho, who takes it more seriously as a solvent for his woes. Faced with the corpse of his murdered son, Pandulpho, well before he "breaks out" of philosophy, comfortably lives within it. He observes that "This heart in valour even Jove out-goes; / Jove is without, but this 'bove sense of woes; / And such a one, eternity. Behold!" (1.5.99–101). This conclusion follows a long set of instructions to resist succumbing to emotional excess in the face of disaster—precisely the kind of advice that Antonio passionately loathes.

The details of these professed dismissals, however, subtly undermine their potency. Pandulpho, for one, gestures to his son's body as the exemplar of the kind of reserve he summons for himself. "This heart," while perhaps stronger than Jove's, is no longer beating: his ideal Stoic is a corpse. Andrugio's speech prepares us for a skeptical position in which some things are, in fact, simply bad—imperfect, useless, vain—and not suitable for cerebral therapy. But this position is immediately reframed as itself a test of Andrugio's will and character. When Lucio, his servant, instructs him to "abandon passion," Andrugio laments that "there's nothing left / Unto Andrugio but Andrugio" (3.1.48, 61–62). Purged of his passion—and, crucially, purged through comically excessive appropriation—he assumes his new, "mere" self as a foundation for a total self: "Myself, myself will dare all opposites. / I'll muster forces, an unvanquished power" (3.1.75). Finally, what Antonio rejects is less the wholesale philosophy of Stoicism and more its ability to console through mere reading, rather than through practice. Stoicism as isolated theorization alone, his frustration suggests, cannot accurately be called Stoicism. Soon after he tosses aside his pseudo-Senecan consolation, he discovers a despondent Mellida through a grate and rebukes her request that he kill her by rejecting a vulgarly exaggerated version of the *vita activa* he had recently appeared to endorse:

I will not swell like a tragedian
In forced passion of affected strains.
If I had present power of ought but pitying you
I would be as ready to redress your wrongs
As to pursue your love. Throngs of thoughts
Crowd for their passage; somewhat I will do.
Reach me thy hand; think this is honour's bent
To live unslaved, to die innocent. (2.3.104–11)

The version of philosophy offered by reading a text becomes replaced by one as a mode of being, a way of life. As the last line indicates, he assails suicide as sinful: his brand of Stoicism is firmly early modern, in the fashion of Lipsius. But like Lipsius he also imports from the classical Stoics an acute self-awareness, a framing of consciousness as a theater of thoughts that "Crowd for their passage"; his speech offers a real-time process of reason selecting the prudent course and rejecting the possibility of the tragedian's unearned glory. Tellingly, when *De remediis fortuitorum* appears later as a form of consolation of which Antonio approves, it is paired with action, not simply read as comfort: Pandulpho sings its lines as a "dirge" while he, Antonio, and Alberto carry Feliche to his grave. The text works better as an accompaniment to a procession than as a clear program for betterment. Pandulpho, Andrugio, and Antonio, in moments that seem to give voice to their disdain for Stoicism, offer instead a rejection of a simplified, caricatured version of the sage and ironically, in doing so, in giving critiques of false philosophy, ultimately conduct more properly Stoic work than do the sentiments they reject.

In these instances, the false picture of Stoicism that Marston critiques denies any inherent lived quality. What makes the caricature of the sage a ripe target for parody is its refusal to admit to the bodily reality of its surroundings; it lacks an understanding of its condition of embodiment. But as we have seen, the vital quality of experience that each character proffers as antidote to Stoicism comprises, in fact, one of its core qualities—the "art of living" that Pierre Hadot identifies as the explicit aim of Stoicism, which "did not consist in teaching an abstract theory—much less an exegesis of texts" and lived instead in its use of *askesis*.[11] John Sellars has examined this corporeal aspect of classical Stoicism, which, he emphasizes, when "conceived as an art involves both theory and practice."[12] The version of the philosophy proposed and ultimately rejected by Pandulpho and literally tossed aside by Antonio is solely theory, and as such a burlesque, an excessively speculative clone. It is no wonder, then, that Marston's satire criticizes static patience. It is in his plays that we can find the validation, and more critically the *enactment*, of a kind of restive, thoroughly active process of purging excessive versions of selfhood—like Pandulpho shedding the impossible version of the philosopher and vowing to "break out." In doing so, he reveals Stoicism's theatrical essence at precisely the moment when it seems to leave the scene.

This reading runs counter to many analyses of the plays that interpret them as straightforward denunciations of Stoic meditation, as if Pandulpho, Antonio, and others were Marston's mouthpieces and the moment of "breaking out" betrays an un-ironic endorsement of instinctual violence as a more sound, because emotional, way of life. One foundational such reading is by Jonathan Dollimore, who asserts that for Pandulpho, "what is being rejected here is the Christian-stoic view of man as capable of defining himself from within, independently of the world in which he lives and which acts upon him."[13] To be Stoic, for Dollimore, is to be so utterly inward as to be in denial of humanity's social construction. The problem with Stoicism, Dollimore establishes, is that it is

> an attempt to redefine oneself solely from within, to reconstitute one's sense of self by withdrawing from the social reality which has threatened it. As such it is a position precariously attained and incapable of being maintained; attitudes of stoical resistance simply break down . . . faced with a dislocated world, individual consciousness itself becomes dislocated.[14]

As a result, in this interpretation, the importance of Marston's plays is that they detail how false consciousness becomes reintegrated into social reality. This is a powerful Marxist exegesis, and it has influenced more recent analyses, like that of Rebecca Yearling, who notes that "however superficially attractive Stoicism may seem, it is fatally flawed as a guide to life."[15] While there is a critical consensus that Marston was influenced by Stoicism, the precise nature of that influence has been long up for debate. Anthony Caputi labels him a "Neo-stoic" but focuses primarily on his verse, rather than his drama: "As Marston turned from verse satire to the drama, from a genre that required a well-defined persona to one that did not, his explicit concern with intentions naturally diminished."[16] Daniel Finkelpearl believes that the plays are resolutely un-Stoic: "Withdrawal and inner contentment are impossible in a world where evil and folly reign."[17] And George Geckle, echoing Eliot, finds any coherent philosophy impossible in works so thoroughly without intellectual cohesion. Speculating as to the nature of this disjointedness, Geckle posits that Marston, in crafting *Antonio and Mellida*, "wanted to write a comedy, but got carried away with the potential tragedy involving Piero-Andrugio-Antonio. He then divided the play up into alternating comic and tragic scenes, and thereby created a faulty tragicomedy. The play is a failure in any terms, but it is at least an interesting one."[18]

Following the critical pendulum that swings between arguing whether the plays are or are not Stoic misses the larger picture. The Antonio plays are undoubtedly formally and thematically messy, and attempts to align them precisely with any philosophical or cultural structure cannot help but fail. But this failure indexes a simplification of what we mean by "philosophy," rather than a flaw immanent to Marston's works. Gestures such as Pandulpho's "break" and Antonio's dismissal, which occur throughout the two plays, make coherent and potent philosophical claims through their self-reflexive performativity. In particular, as I will explore in the next section, the Antonio plays reflect a core Stoic belief in fate—and a particular early modern twist on this belief—in their depiction of the world's appearance as fundamentally unstable. They do this in markedly different ways: *Antonio and Mellida* models this instability not in its depiction of the world but in its unsteadily theatrical world-making; *Antonio's Revenge* absorbs this chaotic quality into its narrative by thematizing theatrical volatility as political corruption. But for both, the actual process of creating a play "fails," as Geckle observes. And as a result, the apparent instability of the physical world becomes realized. When characters reject philosophy, they actually fall into it: they perform, rather than assert, its claims. They partake in the kind of "art of living" that Sellars and Hadot locate as quintessentially Stoic: a practice that prepares for confrontations with the world's chaotic-seeming nature by cultivating the body.

Little Mites

One peculiar quality of Stoic fate in Marston's day is how, in its absolute unknowability, it both clashed and harmonized with a Christian understanding of divine omnipotence. Senecan and Christian ethics found themselves as often at odds as in harmony.[19] As Richard Strier elaborates, the "psychological and social thinking and feeling of many figures in the Renaissance was deeply and incoherently divided between Stoic ideals of self-sufficiency on the one hand, and Christian and other ideals of mutuality and community on the other ."[20] And yet this tension between self-sufficiency and mutuality, while on the surface an external threat to Stoic thought, is already baked into its beliefs. In "On Tranquility of the

Mind," Seneca suggests that an incoherent breach between the self and its surroundings is an essential component to social and intellectual life—a feature, not a bug. The salient question is more what to do in the face of that incoherence, and in an exemplary section Seneca offers an answer by exhorting his readers to avoid gratuitous worry over social concerns. People who fret about social matters are less than human: "Inconsiderate and vaine is their course, resembling that of the Antes, which creepe along the shrubbes, & now get up to the toppe, and straight runne downe to the bottome, without ought else doing but running."[21] But we can avoid being a frantic ant without completely abandoning society. In fact, complete withdrawal is just as ill-fitting a posture as obsessing over meaningless minutiae, because

> if we renounce all conversation and flie from humane societie, and live only to our private respect, this solitude deprived of all honest occupation will find nothing at last whereto addict her selfe; we shall begin to build some houses, and to over-turne others; we shall turne the sea out of his place; we shall cause the rivers to alter their courses, and dispense the time very evilly, which nature gave us to bestow well.[22]

The repercussions of withdrawal are inflicted on the sea, the rivers, and other houses. Taking leave of society gives one only the illusion of mastery over the natural order, so the correct path seems instead to be an acceptance of that order's unknowability. Here Seneca's prescription plots a careful course between one kind of chaos (the antlike disorder of preoccupation) and another (the seemingly random rhythms of the world that have at their heart divinity and structure). The appropriate behavior that results relies on a careful distinction: "There is a great difference betwixt giving some liberty to a thing, and leaving it wholly at random."[23] Seneca approvingly notes the apparently unnecessary activities undertaken by celebrated philosophers: Socrates played with children, Cato drank wine, and Scipio danced.[24] The reader of Stoic lessons should actually give themselves over to, rather than remove themselves from, the world, so as to "accommodate ourselves to affaires, without presuming over much of our own conceptions" instead of attempting to escape.[25] And part of that giving over is to avoid what Lodge repeatedly translates as "counterfeit" emotions, such as falsely weeping when witnessing the death of a child.[26] The ability to parse out false emotional reactions from appropriately measured responses—just as Andrugio does in his demonstration and rejection of passions—demands a clear mind, but this clarity does not stand in for the emotions themselves. It is, instead, the sieve through which they must pass.

As Charles Bouwsma explains, the apparent pessimism of Stoicism results from an extreme kind of optimism, one that fully trusts a celestial structure governing the seeming random spasms of the universe. Stoicism, then, is the strategy by which, "through a combination of enlightenment and disciplined accommodation, the individual could come to terms with the humanly pessimistic implications of a cosmic optimism. It was a strategy of protection for the isolated self in a thoroughly unsatisfactory world."[27] Accommodation for the possibility of isolation is not the same as *practiced* isolation: the flipside of an inner withdrawal is an acceptance of the changeability of the world—and of one's place as an agent of that changeability. Recall Justus Lipsius's pithy instruction in his *De constantia*: "the mind must be changed, not the place."[28] It is in Lipsius the Neo-Stoic Christian that we find the potential danger of this line of thinking. If the universe is governed by an unknowable force and mapped out onto an unviewable plot, what then is God's role? For the Stoics, God *could* be the master behind the design—the playwright responsible for the play into which, as Epictetus has it, we are cast; however, God could also be subject to fate, and thus changeable: a fundamentally heretical notion to the Christian, early modern or otherwise. Lipsius thus sets to amending, in *De constantia*, Seneca's conception of divine order, which the Flemish author glosses as "violent fate" that absurdly makes "God subject to the wheele of Destiny" and questions "the actions of our will."[29] Lipsius's solution is to propose "Providential fate" as a better version of destiny. The stakes are high enough in this careful rhetorical maneuvering that Lipsius's English translator, John Stradling, confesses to his own uneasiness in his epistle to the reader: "If in writing of destiny & other lik profound matters his tongue (through an ardente and earnest intente of a good meaning mind) hapned anywher to trip or his pen to slide, Be not thou too rigorous towards him for it, he yealdeth to amend whatsoever shal be proved amisse."[30]

Stradling's concerns seem born from the text's confusing insistence, on the one hand, that it condemns Stoic fate, and yet its admission, on the other, that the result ends up sounding much like the classical fate that posed such a problem in the first place. In fact, Langius, the fictional sage figure, approvingly cites Seneca's "On the Good Life" when he clarifies what the proper attitude to providential fate should be: "To obey God is liberty." Lipsius, the character, remains somewhat doubtful, as if anticipating Stradling's anxiety, that Langius is still allowing pagan blasphemy to be "let in afterwards as a postern or backdore," to which Langius simply reiterates that he does not believe the ways of "Stoicall Destinie" as "they make God subject to Destinie."[31] Even the analogy chosen to represent the correct attitude toward fate ends up repeating, consciously or not, the very same picture painted by Seneca:

> As it is lawfull for me to walke up and downe in a shippe and to runne about the hatches or seates, but this stirring of mine cannot hinder the sailing of the ship: So in this fatall vessel wherein we all sayle, let our willes wrangle and wrest as they list, they shal not turne her out of course, nor ane thing hinder the same. That highest will of all willes must holde and rule the raynes, and with the turne of a hande direct this chariot whither soever it pleaseth.[32]

It is fine to take individual action, says Lipsius, without worrying about whether it's your doing or the result of a grander design: our actions are like someone running all over a ship without affecting its journey. The lack of confirmation needed to affirm that someone is steering the boat is a byproduct of proper faith rather than a precondition for accepting an absolute mystery, but for the Stoic and Christian both, the result is the same: an active life that acknowledges its utter lack of understanding or mastery of its surroundings.

In Lipsius's disquisition on fate we find, again, the trope of Stoic "assent" gaining an agential edge as a liberating rather than submissive gesture. Again, too, we can note the harmony between this idea and the Christian valorization of servitude. Seneca's belief in accommodation without presumption—fitting oneself to the world without trying to master it while taking control of one's rational faculty—also appears in his "On Providence," where he defiantly stakes out his humility: "I am not compelled, I suffer nothing unwillingly; neither doe I serve God but assent unto him."[33] One can imagine Lipsius and Stradling flinching at the refusal of serving God, but the distinction between serving and "assenting" intentionally mirrors the assent to imagery taken up in the Stoic's mental theater. The kind of action that results from this mindset risks blind obeisance, in its belief in giving in to a higher power without presuming to understand it, but ultimately affirms just the opposite—the acknowledgment of a meaningful place within a holistic, living system. In the same essay, Seneca asks, "What is it which is proper and becoming in a good man? To commit himselfe to the hands of Destinie. It is great solace to be carried away with the whole world."[34] Giving oneself over to the whole world is to join with it, even if that connection carries no promise of transcendence. In the Stoic mindset, recruitment within the physical confines of the natural environment is sublimity enough, since that environment is framed as, in Andrew Shifflet's words, a "vibrant organism" that allows for the fostering of community, even cosmopolitanism, rather than encouraging total surrender.[35] (Chapter 4 will elaborate further on the theological connotations of Stoic physics.) As John Sellars elaborates, "fate," for the Stoics, is no more (or less) than the complete map of all causes in the universe, causes inextricable from the essence of all the universe's components. In addition, Sellars divides fate into "simple" and "conjoined": the former is a function of essence (Socrates will die; that is his fate *as* a human), and the second is contingent and not directly related to essence (Socrates will die tomorrow).[36] Philosophical training thus focuses on both ensuring that one's happiness does not rely on fate *and* aligning one's desires with those of the universe, thus ensuring that one assents to the fate given them but does not attach themselves in what they cannot control, which is the result of—fate. The Stoic is inextricably part of the universe but not invested in it.

This surprising conclusion arises from Stoicism's paradoxical capacity to remain focused on the everyday, banal qualities of one's being—to resist believing in anything beyond the material world—while training oneself to remember always the larger picture, in which that being is nearly nothing.[37] In particular, the recuperation of meaningfulness in a world that denies affirmations of purpose results from theatricalizing oneself, from framing one's life as a performance—but not a performance that allows for escape into a new identity or control over one's stagecraft. Instead, Stoics imagined themselves as both inescapably themselves *and* a trivial speck in a vast universe. In Lipsius's work, this duality reaches its literal apex when Langius asks Lipsius to imagine traveling to the highest mountain and gazing down at all humanity: "O marvelous and miserable spectacle! . . . My mind and toong both do faile me (*Lipsius*) in recounting these matters: And I see al our stirs in comparison of those, to bee nothing else but small fragments of straw, or as the Comicke Poet saith, *Little mites*."[38] This recurring Stoic "view from above" exercise—the extreme zooming-out of perspective only to return to the mere body, the "little mite" of our personal inconsequence—is picked up by Michel Foucault in his lectures on Stoicism at the Collège de France. When Seneca asks us to watch everyone scrambling like ants, or when Langius tells us to gaze down at little mites, we are confronted with the impossibility of being anything more than we are:

> What is involved is not an uprooting from this world into another world. It is not a matter of freeing oneself from one reality in order to arrive at a different reality. It is not a matter of leaving a world

> of appearances so as finally to reach a sphere of the truth. What is involved is a movement of the subject that is carried out and effectuated within the world—really going towards the point from which the light comes, really gaining a form that is the same form of divine reason—and which places us, inasmuch as we are in the *consortium Dei*, at the very peak, the highest point (*altum*) of this universe. However, we do not leave this universe and this world, and at the very moment we are at the summit of this world, and by virtue of this, the inner recesses, secrets, and very heart of nature are opened to us . . . At the very moment that, participating in divine reason, we grasp the secret of nature, we can grasp how small we are.[39]

Foucault's careful reading avoids the simplification of Stoicism as antagonistic misanthropy or sublime interiority. The proper Stoic, here, parses out what is trivial from what is necessary. Notably, again, the Stoic does not withdraw from life altogether after determining, like Harry Lime in *The Third Man*, that all life is merely expendable when viewed from a distance. The process of imagining a high vantage point does not supply an escape into the kind of total misanthropy despised by the liberated Pandulpho and Antonio. To remove oneself absolutely, under the veil of mystical exile from the material plane, is to become the deathly parody of ideal Stoicism that Pandulpho improperly admires.

Balancing the impulse to situate the world as a theater is, as discussed in chapter 1, the realization that one is being watched by others—that one is a performer. The Stoics understood, as Shifflett puts it, that "the afflictions of good and bad men make for excellent theater."[40] And they realized that positioning themselves as audience members does not remove them absolutely from the proceedings: the fourth wall is not a barrier. Instead, the distancing of self from self encourages recognition of our own complicity in the ongoing procession of activity. Seneca, in "On Providence," is careful to delineate different modes of gamesmanship, in an effort to specify what kind of action is meaningful and what smacks of folly, of overattachment. One should beware of merely entertaining pastimes, such as watching someone hunt; instead, he asks us if one can have the wherewithal to be trained to "see a spectacle that meriteth, that God should intentively behold the worke," so that they can "fix thine eye upon it, behold a couple of combatants worthy the presence of God?" This worthy spectacle is, Seneca specifies, "a generous man planted before adverse Fortune, challenging her hand to hand."[41] In letter 25, Seneca acknowledges the potential for us to become members of this spectacle when he instructs Lucilius to follow Epicurus's advice and "doe all things (saith he) as if another man looked on."[42] By imagining—and thus empathetically becoming—a spectator observing us, we take on the dignity of someone planting themselves in front of the vagaries of chance.

Foucault, too, picks up on this element of theatricality in his reading of another Stoic exercise, the meditation on death, which trains the mind to accept seemingly inconsequential aspects of life. Accepting death does not lead to the hardened, isolating position Dollimore and others imagine, however. It is instead, Foucault insists, the act of "placing yourself, in thought, in the situation of someone who is in the process of dying, or who is about to die, or who is living his last days . . . [it is] not a game the subject plays with his own thought or thoughts, but a game that thought performs on the subject himself. It is becoming, through thought, the person who is dying or whose death is imminent."[43] It is, in short, performative—precisely what actor, character, and audience go through in these moments. Ben Golder elaborates in his analysis of Foucault that "via a notion of an aesthetics of existence, the Greeks proposed that life become the object of conscious elaboration and self-critique."[44] Jamey Graham finds the death meditation explicitly theatrical, noting that Stoic self-discipline creates "a model of theatricality stressing the activity of the audience, making unobstructed spectatorship of one's own performance prerequisite for effective performance."[45] One must "audience" themselves to be aware of their own performance, to permit evaluation of the spectacle of the self. Yet this process of becoming one's own audience must paradoxically return consciousness to itself instead of jettisoning it to another, distant way of being. Rather than simply disciplining the self, Stoic exercise allows for us to virtualize the impossibility of our own full transcendence.

We are, in this understanding, both audiences to the unknowable vastness of cosmic theater and actors performing for a hypothetical audience that keeps us oriented toward ethical action. Crucially, for Seneca, the imagined audience to our actions serves as a corrective to solitude, which "induceth us to all evill."[46] The act of opposing impulses becomes thwarted: we must withdraw enough to gain a vantage point, but remain present and capable of interaction; we must perform without the hope of becoming something else. We are irreducibly ourselves. Lipsius, too, seizes on the communal potential of realizing our inconsequence by having Langius chide Lipsius, at the end of book 1, that he cannot "simply sit with thy hands in thy bottome," as destiny does not work "alone without coadjutant and meane causes"; if Lipsius is to gain a sense of divinity, if he is to "attain to the haven," then he must "ply the oares, and hoste thy sayles, and not idly expect winde at will from heaven."[47] The purpose of Stoic activity is not to seclude oneself from life, as with stock Stoic characters like the Pandulpho of the early scenes of *Antonio's Revenge*, but instead to realize one's capacity for a responsible—or, in the case of Langius's dinner, physically necessary—form of action.

In their attitude toward an uncaring fate, the Stoic is poised between essential selfhood and universal triviality. One way to stage a Stoic drama, it follows, is to depict the excesses of affect that defy attempts to discipline the body and soul. This is the technique favored by Seneca himself, who in his dramas shows the overweening passions of, for instance, Atreus (who is quoted directly by the bloodthirsty Piero in *Antonio's Revenge*) as a cautionary example of violent cupidity. Atrocities are staged as a test of our own potential to partake in them; as Lipsius has it, "Even we ourselves that thus complaine of tyranny, do beare in our brestes some seede thereof, and many of us doe not want wil to performe it, but ability."[48] All that keeps us back is capacity, not desire. Marston flirts with this dramaturgical mode in the induction to *Antonio's Revenge* by pleading for the audience to let loose their passion, as if testing them to become overwhelmed with affect:

> If any spirit breathes within this round
> Uncapable of weighty passion
> (As from his birth being hugged in the arms
> And nuzzled twixt the breasts of happiness)
> Who winks and shuts his apprehension up
>
> Form common sense of what men were, and are,
> Who would not know what men must be—let such
> Hurry amain from our black-visaged shows;
> We shall affright their eyes. (ll. 13–21)

Marston further identifies who his audience should be: those with "blood whose heat is choked / And stifled with true sense of misery," for if "ought of those strains fill this consort up, / Th'arrive most welcome" (ll. 24–27). Drawing from a humoral lexicon, Marston seems to want only those who have broken out of philosophy, who know the overwhelming pain that can cloud true judgment, to witness his dramas, which should, it seems, stage humankind's inherent tendency toward tyranny as actuality.

Many paratextual elements of the Antonio plays, however, keep them from simply becoming *Thyestes Redux*. The texts, unlike tragic classical models, seem typologically aware of their eventual realization as fleshed-out occasions acted by a boys' company.[49] Rebecca Yearling points out that the play's audience would have been intelligent enough to pick up on "metatheatrical references" that would not simply be "in-jokes for the (reputedly) knowing and sophisticated Saint Paul's audience: they also work to concentrate the audience's attention on the artifice behind the play-making, leading them to consider the way in which effects of genre are created, and the way in which the playwright works to conceal dramatic loose ends."[50] It is this concentration on their own modes of representation that marks the plays as Stoic in their execution, not merely in their thematic underpinnings. Many plays, early modern or otherwise, comment on their own theatricality, but Marston's dramatic works excel at combining this awareness with a recurrent self-collapsing quality, as if forces outside their control could at any time overcome the actors, overdetermined as underqualified, and lead to disaster.

This carefully constructed messiness is precisely the "doubleness" that Eliot detects, an extension of what Joseph Loewenstein calls Marston's tendency, as exemplified in his touchy rivalry with Ben Jonson, to become "addicted to defensive self-inspection."[51] When this defensiveness, Loewenstein argues, translates from satire into the corporeal realm of the stage, it becomes a mode of "somatic dysfunction."[52] It is precisely this dysfunction, as I will elaborate, that realizes powerfully Stoicism's resolute antitranscendence and fixation on material limitation. In other words, the plays *do* what they cannot simply *say*: we should not conflate any one character's anti-Stoic sentiment with Marston's thoroughly Stoic theater. An awareness of the theater's simultaneous limitation and possibility haunts both *Antonio and Mellida* and *Antonio's Revenge*, and the irreconcilability of these two impulses leaves the plays trapped in the histrionic present, deeply aware of what they are unable to do.

"Do Something!"

The "irrelevance" detected by Eliot as a formal flaw with the plays emerges from their recognition that they fail as successful works of theater. But recognizing the gratuity of *adiaphora*, the "things indifferent" in which we should not invest ourselves, is a key Stoic tenet. And so I read Marston's collapsing theatricality as the embodied demonstration of this recognition and rejection, a natural byproduct of his Stoic focus on his characters' condition as both irreducibly their "real" selves, as actors, and cosmically insignificant, as ignorant participants in a cosmic scheme. As such, this irrelevance is, as Marston establishes it, in fact highly relevant, as signaled in the first moments of *Antonio and Mellida*. The induction features the actors fretting over their incapacity to act as their assigned characters. These actors are, of course, characters themselves, hyperrealized versions of the boy actors who made up the Saint Paul's troupe, and as these characters prepare for the representational labor at hand, they offer advice and mockery while handily introducing themselves to the audience. The actor who plays Antonio seems especially confused that he will also play Antonio *playing* Florizel, the Amazon princess: "I take this feigned presence of an Amazon, calling myself Florizel and I know not what" (ll. 73–74). Meanwhile, the actor playing the noble Felice has "a part allotted me which I have neither able apprehension to conceit nor what I conceit gracious ability to utter" (ll. 105–7). And in an especially layered explanation, Antonio answers for Galeazzo when the latter is asked about his part; the Antonio actor seems dumbfounded by the demands placed upon Galeazzo's performer:

> For sometimes he must take austere state as for the person of Galeazzo, the son of the Duke of Florence, and possess his exterior presence with a formal majesty, keep popularity in distance and, on the sudden, fling his honour so prodigally into a common arm that he may seem to give up his indiscretion to the mercy of vulgar censure; now as solemn as a traveler and as grave as a puritan's ruff. (ll. 122–36)

Galeazzo is an absurd character, Antonio reasons, because he demands violent swings of affect, from restraint to incontinent passion. Of course, changes in affect are traditionally what *constitute* character, but here these shifts are rendered into seams. "Character" as a result becomes a horizon, stitched together insufficiently by what Antonio calls "signs and tokens" but without any coalescence into believable subjectivity. And knowledge of this insufficiency supplies the doubleness that in turn leads to the failure of *Antonio and Mellida* to function on the most basic level of dramatic narrative.

Taken as a Stoic exercise, the induction offers a comic realization of Lipsius's and Seneca's repeated injunctions to become aware of our complicity in spectatorship. The performers are consumed with being watched and infect themselves with the realization of the social fictions they must necessarily ineffectively embody. The induction directly suggests a connection between the failure to become characters effortlessly and the presumption, scorned by the Stoics, that one can master fate when Alberto lends his advice to the actor playing Piero as to how he should carry himself: "Then thus frame your exterior shape / To haughty form of elate majesty, / As if you held the palsy-shaking head / Of reeling Chance under your fortune's belt / In strictest vassalage" (ll. 7–11). To play Piero properly, one must act as if they could control chance, in a reversal of the process of assent praised by Seneca. In this formulation, instead, fate must play the crippled vassal to the individual. That this character never fully becomes realized—indeed, *cannot* fully become realized, circumscribed as he is by the limitations of the actor—only further ordains the actors' enterprise as a necessary failure.

Their failure, though, is not limited to a consciousness of the play's status as performed. The disorder runs deeper, on the level of structure. At times the plot seems simply to be a collection of haphazardly assembled sketches and citations, placed in the mouths of interchangeable characters who alternate between inarticulate emotion and intellectual showmanship. G. K. Hunter, in the preface of his edition of the play, is vexed by this threadbare construction: "Characters veer from insensate stupidity to diabolical cunning without warning and apparently without cause; attitudes are assumed and dropped at the merest whim of the author; situations are laboriously built up and then abandoned."[53] For Hunter, as for Eliot, this madness must conceal a hidden method—but while the play's ramshackle nature might disguise hidden hermeneutical payoffs, it also embodies a struggle to theatricalize any action at all. Take, for instance, the moment in *Antonio and Mellida* when the villainous Piero realizes that Antonio is alive and attempts to assemble his forces; he demands that Felice stay in court and the "rest stand still, or run, or go, or shout, or search, or scud, or call, or hang, or do—do—do, su—su—su, something. I know now who—who—who, what I do—do—do, not who—who—wo, where I am" (3.2.181–85). The stuttering, incomplete demand to the assembled characters doubles as a frantic engine for the actors to keep the physical play going: Do this! Or that! Or something! Just do something to emulate movement!

The constant revelations of the artifice of the stage, so explicitly rendered in *Antonio and Mellida*, become compressed into more cohesively integrated aspects of *Antonio's Revenge*. Here, to the relief of formalists like Hunter, metatheatricality becomes a motif rather than a technique: the characters stage their own dramas, don their own masks, and put on shows within a show already revealed, in the first play, to be within a bigger spectacle. A loose thread, though, remains in the figure of Balurdo, the fool who occasionally punctures the nesting dolls of narratives. In *Antonio and Mellida* he satirizes corrupt courtiers, but in the sequel he realizes his absurd nature by calling attention to the play's theatrical mechanics even after the other characters have stopped doing so. After Antonio's long speech about his prophetic and horrifying dream—a rhetorically knotted, melodramatic exegesis that betrays uncanny awareness of his father's death—Balurdo responds with a dream monologue of his own. "Veryily, Sir Geoffrey had a monstrous strange dream the last night," he begins; in his dream, it had appeared that

> the ground yawned and belked up the abominable ghost of a misshapen Simile, with two ugly pages, the one called Master *Even as*, going before, and the other Mounser *Even-so*, following after, whilst Signior Simile stalked most prodigiously in the midst. At which I bewrayed the fearfulness of my nature, and—being ready to forsake the fortress of my wit—start up, called for a clean shirt, eat a mess of broth, and with that I awaked. (1.3.61–71)[54]

Like Spenser's grotesque, ink-spewing Errour, the monstrosity here is not simply literary but a physicalization of literariness itself, belching out embodied rhetorical devices.[55] These gentlemen are so terrifying because they are analogies, pretenses to comparison. Balurdo exposes the sheer work needed to render successfully any speech, any vision, thus immediately reminding the audience how elaborately Antonio constructs his lament. The fool figures Stoicism's nontranscendence by grounding words in the body, text in the theater.[56]

Balurdo also smuggles into the play its predecessor's awareness of the boys performing the drama. Responding to a beckoning call from Piero, Balurdo enters as if an actor unprepared for his cue, with his beard "half off, half on" (2.1.20.1). When Piero inquires as to this appearance, Balurdo responds with a surreal speech about fish, mermaids, and wit; the monologue threatens to crystallize into an allegory, and Piero, perhaps hoping for illumination, asks, "Does thou know what thou hast spoken all this while?" (2.1.33). But Balurdo's response indicates his capacity to say nothing at all: "O Lord, Duke, I would be sorry of that. Many men can utter that which no man but themselves can conceive; but I thank a good wit, I have the gift to speak that which neither any man else nor myself understands" (2.1.34–37). As a disrupting force in the drama, Balurdo refuses resolution into either pure comic nonsense or clear meaning-making. Instead, he confounds even his own efforts to clarify his purpose and strips his words of signification.

Over and over, the plays repeat Balurdo's gesture of hemming in any attempt to allow for dramatic transportation. Speeches almost tip into sense-making, like costumes that remain half off, poised on the edge of correct disguise. Just as Pandulpho and Antonio cast aside exaggerated forms of themselves, and as the induction to *Antonio and Mellida* refuses the simple connection of character to actor, Balurdo screens out the impossible ideal of lyrical communication. What results is a form of Stoic embodiment that gives the lie to the image of the withdrawn and antisocial hermit warming his feet by the fire while consoling others who shiver in the cold. The two depict Stoicism more deeply by corrupting their environments, both represented and real; as Gordon Braden puts it, Marston "moulds traditional techniques to create a dramatic world out of touch with traditional drama, which in turn mirrors a real world larger and more grotesque than reality."[57] The cracks and fissures in the appearance of smoothly operating theatrical illusion indicate a wider force at play, one toying with structure and dramaturgy just as God (or, for a classical Stoic, a force outside of God) alters the universe without betraying clear reasoning. The mirroring noted by Braden could be extended further: it is not only the plays' dramatic world that differs from traditional drama but the traces of theatrical reality that seemingly hobble the drama and, in turn, mirror more deeply the inability to capture the entirety of existence as a cohesive whole.

One key quality of the plays' theory of embodied meaning—that is, their processes of parsing out which elements of their own material realization constitute their production of meaning—results from their status as satires. This genre would seem far removed from our inherited image of Stoicism as resistant to aesthetic playfulness, but as Balurdo demonstrates, humor can model Stoicism more specifically by calling attention to and disrupting theatrical and social conventions. While skepticism, the philosophical school most often associated with satire, similarly revels in turning a critical eye to the follies of collective behavior, it lacks Stoicism's belief in a more fundamental normative goodness; Sextus Empiricus, the founder of classical skepticism, critiques Stoicism's belief in an unknowable cosmic plan and instead calls for a suspension of all judgment as the only true rational response to moral struggle.[58] What makes Marston's satires particularly Stoic is that, while they mount a skeptical attack on the stability of social and theatrical decorum, they also gesture sincerely at the possibility of a higher purpose. This belief is explicitly—and, this being Marston, grotesquely—imaged in *Antonio and Mellida* by the noble newcomer Felice, Andrugio's son, as a kind of light. Upon seeing a candle in his predawn wanderings, Felice imagines that "if that candlelight were made a poet, / he would prove a rare firking satirist / And draw the core forth of impostumed sin. / Why I thank heaven yet that my content / can envy nothing but poor candlelight. / As for the other glistering copper spangs / that glisten in the tire of the court, / Praise God, I either hate or pity them" (3.2.12–19). For Felice, the "firking," or striking, satirist must attack the "impostumed sin"—the abscess that needs to be lanced and purified. The satirist's goal is to drain the body of its abject waste, to strain artifice from one's core, a mission not unlike that of the Stoic, who must always remain within the confines of the body while (*pace* the skeptics) admitting to the unknowable power of the wider world. Felice aims his powers of satirical purification at the glittering excesses of the court, but he also critiques, with equal vigor, the aesthetic fakery that floridly surrounds him, equating a courtier's airs to the pretense of boy actors that structures his entire theatrical surroundings: "Fut, what treble manikin squeaks here, ha? 'Good, very good, very very good' " (3.2.31–32). The comedic parsing out of performed character from actor mimics, then, the therapeutic parsing out of unnecessary distraction from life.

This understanding of satire as a Stoic exercise returns us to the doting Pandulpho, who denounces his own archetypal nature as poorly performed. He has, at the point of his breaking, compared philosophical posturing to acting before. But in the previous case he had criticized emotional outbursts, the selfsame eruptions he will later embrace as more authentic. Early in *Antonio's Revenge*, he questions the appropriate reaction to his son's death. The speech reads like a philosophically ironic echo of Hamlet's advice to the players:

> Wouldst have me cry, run raving up and down
> For my son's loss? Wouldst have me turn rank mad,
> Or wring my face with mimic action,
> Stamp, curse, weep, rage, and then my bosom strike?
> Away, 'tis apish action, player-like.
> If he is guiltless, why should tears be spent?
> Thrice blessed soul that dieth innocent.
> If he is lepered with so foul a guilt,
> Why should a sigh be lent, a tear be spilt? (1.5.76–84)

The intricacy of this speech, in relation to his later confession that "man will break out," is worth teasing out carefully. Here, early in the play, Pandulpho embraces what he sees as the philosopher's position: maintain solitude and emotional control; condemn outbursts of passion and affection as useless and fake—mere "Apish action, player-like." (Pandulpho's description echoes the "apish" topos of unnecessary action noted by Epictetus and invoked in the previous chapter: "as an Ape thou doest counterfeit and resemble al things.") But later on, Pandulpho admits to the impossibility of maintaining the performance of apparent Stoicism. What is performative turns out to be the resistance to performance. Both characterological extremes—cerebral withdrawal and zealous emotion—ring false, and what is needed instead seems to be an admission of the impossibility of acting at all, an admission that both plays make repeatedly.

This realization, in turn, resonates deeply with the Senecan imperative to accommodate life without attempting to contain it, to have no presumptions but to be receptive to the shifting events of the world. And this is why Marston's plays excel at showing, rather than explaining, Stoic thought. By constantly calling attention to the foolishness inherent in staging action at all, Marston reflects on the Stoic condemnation of calcifying one's character into a heightened figure of confidence, rather than a humble embodiment of performance's ruse. It seems appropriate, then, that at the play's end, when the revengers face the surprising clemency of the senators who refuse to condemn them for their deeds, Pandulpho's confession takes the form of an admission of experiential knowledge:

> We know the world, and did we know no more
> We would not live to know; but since constraint
> Of holy bands forceth us keep this lodge
> Of dirt's corruption till dread power calls
> Our souls' appearance, we will live enclosed
> In holy verge of some religious order,
> Most constant votaries. (5.6.30–36)

In a straightforward sense, knowledge of the world keeps them from killing themselves and motivates religious retreat.[59] Pandulpho's epigram marks the limit of proper Christian action but also, in the highly metatheatrical context of the plays, speaks to the larger "world" that the theater itself knows but cannot contain. This is the world that has edged its way into the representational structure and expectations of the works and disrupted attempts at clear communication. Marston finds satire an apt vehicle for demonstrating knowledge of this world because the form is, paradoxically, less effectively mimetic: he shows the cracks in the theatrical vehicle itself and renders it incapable of self-presentation but capable of staging its own incapacity. The theater acknowledges its own impossibility and in doing so acknowledges the unsteadiness of reality and—in the satirical turn—contaminates its plot with the conditions of its production. It zooms out continuously to reveal its triviality but refuses escape into the known totality of a wider structure. Theatrical performance itself, the play argues, creates the knowledge of an inaccessible but ultimately constructed world, and this knowledge takes on the appearance Eliot dreads and fixates on. But the resulting air of irrelevance is a symptom of something more than doubleness; it belies the plays' stubborn awareness of the precise limits of their expression and, as a result, accommodates the possibility of something bigger.

CHAPTER THREE

Acting Indifferently: *Apatheia* in *Much Ado about Nothing*

This chapter takes *Much Ado about Nothing* at its word. The play's bemused title announces a diagnosis of unnecessary behavior, presumably aimed at the characters' flurry of rash actions born from their misunderstandings. Another valence of this phrase comes into focus, however, when analyzed alongside the plot's repeated instances of characters deflecting and deflating their pursuit of knowledge. The title invites us to consider not only the lack of real dramatic stakes underneath layers of apparent suspense but also the deeper question of why discerning the truth at its core even matters in the first place. *Much Ado about Nothing* journeys toward a romantic-comic resolution while frequently swerving into possible tragedy, and it reaffirms at its close that in reality these near-collapses resulted from deception, the "nothing" of its title. But it also stages a rigorous interrogation of our motivations for wanting to savor the revelation of this nothingness. The "nothing" in this reading is not the lack of genuinely tragic events but instead the emptiness of framing the play strictly in terms of knowledge. In this sense, *Much Ado* proffers a radical and intractable form of indifference.

In what follows, I focus on two related features that characterize how this form of indifference is practiced. The first is that it is practiced at all. Indifference in *Much Ado* arises not as a lack of activity, nor as blithe ennui or disregard, but as a fully realized performance, one with an articulated physical grammar aimed toward a defined goal. The second is that this embodied and performed indifference conducts philosophical work. These two points cohere around the Stoic tradition, which provides *Much Ado* with both historical and dramaturgical inspiration. As discussed in chapter 1, Stoicism was in its ancient practice not simply a set of doctrines to be absorbed but primarily a practice or way of life. And as demonstrated by Marston's fantastically self-collapsing theatricality, examined in chapter 2, this "way of life" can be realized through the staged manifestation of drama that purports to demonize Stoicism as inactive and static. In *Much Ado*, Stoicism's vitality resides in the play's careful cultivation of *apatheia*, or indifference to things not dependent on reason. It is this mode of indifference that colors the play and distinguishes it from other, more prosaic forms of "nothingness" that appear to constitute its thematic focus.

The play professes explicit hostility toward philosophy in general and implicit mockery of Stoicism in particular. One of the more florid gestures of rejecting Stoicism, mentioned in the introduction—and in this book's title—occurs when Leonato, in the throes of false mourning for his daughter, Hero, waves away consolation with a dismissal of philosophy's efficacy: "there was never yet philosopher / That could endure the toothache patiently" (5.1.34–35).[1] As with Antonio, philosophy apparently crumbles in the face of embodied experience; as with Pandulpho, the philosophy Leonato takes aim at is not named, but once again is clearly Stoicism, rendered in its familiar stereotype of unrealistically unfeeling withdrawal. Leonato's critique aligns with the play's frequently expressed disdain for conceptual systems that attempt to explain away irrational feelings, violent turns of circumstance, and erotic affectations. Moments before his dismissal, Leonato had railed against those who would "patch grief with proverbs" (5.1.34–38). In a more minor key, *Much Ado* frequently satirizes as inefficient the "paper bullets" that litter its plot with witticisms and idioms. "Dost thou think I care for satire or an epigram?" asks Benedick at the close, in an apparent show of his redeemed belief in the virtue of dealing with emotional realities head on (5.4.99). And Don John, wallowing in his melancholy, acts offended at the comforts of philosophy proffered by Borachio: "I wonder that thou—being as thou sayst thou art, born under Saturn—goest about to apply a moral medicine to a mortifying mischief" (1.3.10–12). These instances supply variations of Leonato's lament. Like a coolly leveled epigram, the reasoning goes, Stoic consolation sounds lovely but cannot survive a toothache or heartache.

One argument against this characterization is offered by Michel Foucault, who suggests that Stoicism is not "philosophical" at all because it does not determine "that there is and can be truth and falsehood and whether or not we can separate the true and the false."[2] Nor is it spiritual, as Stoic practice does not act "in the form of losing oneself in god or of a movement which plunges deep into God, but in the form that allows us to find ourselves again."[3] Instead of aiming toward truth or godliness, Stoic *askesis* promotes existence in the continuous present by focusing only on one's capacity for reason and to everything else professing indifference, a word activated as both the philosopher's disposition and the *adiaphora*, or "things indifferent," with which the Stoic was unconcerned. Pierre Hadot, in an inspired passage, plays with this double meaning when he claims that the task of Stoicism is to educate people to know only "the goods they are able to obtain" and to know the difference between good and evil:

> In order for something good to be always obtainable, or an evil always avoidable, they must depend exclusively on man's freedom; but the only things which fulfil these conditions are *moral* good and evil. They alone depend on us; everything else does *not* depend on us. Here, "everything else," which does not depend on us, refers to the necessary linkage of cause and effect, which is not subject to our freedom. It must be indifferent to us: that is, we must not introduce any differences into it, but accept it in its entirety, as willed by fate. This is the domain of nature.[4]

To be a Stoic, for Hadot, is to practice the dictum with which Epictetus begins his *Encheiridion*: "Some things are up to us and some things are not up to us."[5] Epictetus's limpid proclamation finds moral resonance in the day-to-day and moment-to-moment upkeep of attentiveness needed to separate things derived from reason from Hadot's "everything else," the domain of nature that need not invite our curiosity, much less mastery, nor have differences introduced. It is indifferent to us, and we resist layering differences upon it. In order to develop the attentiveness that allows for indifference to be practiced, one did not, *pace* Leonato, shut oneself off from the messy reality of life but instead focused intensely on it so as to cultivate the self, to use the self as if it were an instrument.

This chapter explores how *Much Ado about Nothing* practices this kind of performed *apatheia*. I will examine how, as indicated by Shakespeare's comedy, early modern culture complicated Stoicism's performative dimensions. Specifically, I propose that one mode of classical Stoic *askesis* survived in early modernity more tacitly but no less vividly in one of the most influential texts of the era, Baldassare Castiglione's *The Book of the Courtier*. I will trace the transmission of this form of Stoic practice from its origins in Cicero's *De oratore* to Castiglione and eventually to Shakespeare's comedy. First, though, I will elaborate briefly on Foucault's theorization of Stoicism, as developed in his lectures, to define how indifference becomes an active practice. While I draw on *Much Ado about Nothing* throughout this exploration, I will return at the end of this chapter to a more sustained reading of Shakespeare's comedy as a meditation on and realization of Stoic indifference.

Why Truth?

For Foucault, the Stoic refutation of philosophical and spiritual claims allows the subject, as theorized in Epictetus's constantly imagined theater, as living only in the captivation of the here and now, as only presenting itself. In *The Hermeneutics of the Subject*, during a discussion of Seneca's *Letters on Ethics*, Foucault observes that in letter 65, where Seneca exhorts his friend Lucilius to examine the world around him, "there is no question of the soul withdrawing into itself and questioning itself in order to discover within itself the memory of the pure forms it had once seen. Rather, what is involved is really seeing the things of the world, of really grasping their details and organization."[6] The conclusion Seneca urges Lucilius to reach here is humble. It resolves into neither the transformative recollection of *anamnesis*—the immortal soul's ability to remember previous incarnations—nor the self-abnegating force of religious conversion. Seneca acknowledges the transcendence of the truth but forecloses on the possibility of that transcendence transforming the subject. Lucilius need only focus on one element, reason, both within himself and in the world, because, as Seneca puts it, everything has a cause, and that cause is reason. Like Marcus's meditations, distinction supplies its own end. We distinguish byproducts of our reason from things indifferent and cultivate the attentiveness characteristic of spiritual exercise. If we are not ever-vigilant in ascertaining reason's role in the universe, we may, Martha Nussbaum reminds us, "confuse the *instrumenta*—for example, wealth and status—with that life itself."[7] Seneca's process of examination, then, may appear to be outward-facing, but in fact the primary site of his practice is the same as Marcus's: the interior subject. The Stoic refocuses inward the energy otherwise spent on the metaphysical possibilities of externalities, which results in an ethical tradeoff. "If declaring worldly activity external and unnecessary eases the agent's ethical burden in one way," claims Nussbaum, "in another way it increases it, by focusing all ethical attention on the internal doings of the heart."[8]

Foucault pushes his conclusions further than this. Stoicism, for Foucault, represents the embryonic version of the self-care regimes that would eventually lead to the biopolitical operations of the state.[9] But Stoicism also contains a refreshing rejection of one of the basic assumptions of Western metaphysics: a pursuit of truth. As such, Stoicism, while linked genealogically to the disciplinary modes Foucault famously explores elsewhere, also presents a radical undoing of civilization's aims when taken on its own terms and divorced from teleology. In a 1981 lecture, Foucault hints at these liberating possibilities. After a long section of closely reading manuals of marriage and proper sexual conduct, Foucault notes that Stoic exercises result in no "developed relationship of knowledge" and have "nothing like those subtle and suspicious decipherments that will be found, for example, in Christians with regard to the flesh." He does allow the faint premonition of the nearly pathological focus on corporeality that, in his telling, Christian morality inaugurates. While not a site of knowledge production, the Stoic practices of the self contain a "kernel, the primordial and elementary form of a relationship of self to self that is at the same time a relationship of objectivation."[10] The Stoics etch the bare outline of a relationship one has to one's own body by staking out the more elemental relationship of self to self, the very relationship Seneca urges Lucilius to take up in his practice.

Foucault himself seemed eager to stay focused on Stoicism's capacity to divorce the self from concerns of knowledge and power. In an interview concerning his lectures, published under the title "The Ethics of the Concern of the Self as a Practice of Freedom," the interlocutors repeatedly ask questions about power and knowledge while Foucault returns, time and again, to the more fine-grained details of Stoic care. "After all," he begins in response to a question about politics, "why truth? Why are we concerned with truth, and more so than with the care of the self? And why must the care of the self occur only through the concern for truth?"[11] These questions, on their face, have the ring of self-caricature: who cares about the truth? But with knowledge of Foucault's careful extrication of Stoic practices from dominant epistemological traditions, the query becomes more radical. Why, the Stoics seem to ask, do we begin with any desire for attaining the truth at all? Instead, what if we, like Lucilius and Epictetus's friend, aimed to turn our gaze inward, to study *how* we responded to something, to try and access our own capacities? Unlike Hadot, who similarly distinguishes Stoic practice as divorced from a clear telos, Foucault's fascination in part relates to the distinctly non-Christian and nonsoteriological quality of this dynamic. Stoic exercise offers preparation for the subject—but, Foucault asks, "Preparation for what?"[12] The answer he offers is again tautological. For the Stoics, as Foucault puts it, salvation is not a promised end but "an activity" that "ensures an access to the self that is inseparable from the work one carries out on oneself within the time of one's life and in life itself."[13] Again, the reward is the work itself, because the work allows us to be attentive to how we relate to ourselves in our responses to the life we live.[14]

Foucault's readings help us add a political resonance to the non-Platonic and non-Aristotelian grammar of performance that coalesces around Stoicism. To behave in a Stoic manner is not to concern oneself with the truth of forms or even with the possibility of representation; it is not to follow the genealogies of mimesis that dominate considerations of Western theater. It is instead to embody self-scrutiny as a continuous process that supplies its own end, to profess and corporeally effect total indifference toward that which *is* indifferent. It is to view life as a constant theatrical enactment—not strictly the *theatrum mundi* that analogizes character as social role, but a pressurizing force that sharpens one's faculties of discernment. By denying the importance of epistemology, Stoicism creates a form of performance that resists cooption into the systems of power that depend on the creation of knowledge.

In its focus on interior virtue and disregard of authenticity, the Stoic mindset seems somehow both antiquated and vulgarly poststructuralist. But here Shakespeare's *Much Ado about Nothing* is instructive in its recuperation of Stoicism as a vital practice. *Much Ado* is concerned, even obsessed, with examining different scenes of interaction and evaluating their content. We might be tempted to think that such evaluations hinge on questions of authenticity (do characters "really" see what they think they see?), and most critical traditions focus on this question, tempted as they are by the play's interest in acting and theatricality. It has indeed become a commonplace to situate the play's dramatic action in a context of truth that needs to be discovered. The play's titular interest in "nothing," for many, signals a preoccupation with the presence or absence of truth, or an interrogation of what kind of truth the play really pursues. In a particularly rhapsodic example, Harold Goddard launches into associative meditations on the nature of the "nothing" that is or is not discovered: pondering a thought exercise where he draws a circle in the sand, he imagines that "however immense it be conceived to be, beyond it extends not merely the infinite but the infinitely infinite realm of what might have been but was not, of what may be but is not.[15] This image, Goddard maintains, is a natural line of thinking for those "who seek a deeper meaning in the title" of Shakespeare's comedy.[16] Nothingness, with its dual registers of absence and the infinite, affords Goddard a consideration on the play's Christian and metaphysical themes, and his reading, while uniquely poetic, duly falls into a long tradition of placing the withholding and acquisition of knowledge as *Much Ado*'s primary themes. The history of this mode of criticism follows the wider pattern of Shakespeare scholarship more broadly: after the character criticism of the eighteenth century, readers of *Much Ado* began foregrounding analyses that note how patterns of linguistic imagery braid into wider themes. The German critic Hermann Ulrici sparked this interest in the nineteenth century and largely established the importance, for critics, of knowledge in *Much Ado*. Shakespeare, writes Ulrici, "rather seems to have drawn his ground-idea from a contemplation of the contrasts which human life presents between the reality of outward objects, and the perceptions of the inward subject."[17] The contrast noted here, which presumes a difference between the outward reality and the inward subject, splits perception from truth, a gesture that gains prominence as criticism of *Much Ado* develops. In a 1956 lecture, A. P. Rossiter pinpoints "imperfect self-knowledge" as the comic heart of the play.[18] Ralph Berry, in a 1971 reading that trains its eye on the play's structure, still foregrounds its central theme as the "knowledge" that differentiates between levels of perceptual reality by proposing "that we conceive of the theme of *Much Ado* as an exploration of the limits and methods of humanly-acquired knowledge."[19]

It may seem obvious to say that *Much Ado* consists of a series of scenes in which characters do not know what they need to know, and that the play proceeds by revealing, at times with a perverse slowness abetted by misapprehension, the "truth" of the situations held at bay. Don John orchestrates the scene that Claudio mistakes for Hero's seduction; Benedick and Beatrice are not aware of each other's, or their own, romantic feelings. But the play also continually shifts its focus away from concerns for the truth and instead tracks the ways in which the characters *prepare* themselves for the truth to arrive. In this way, *Much Ado* plays with the expectations of its audience to assume the centrality of epistemological revelation to the plot. Seneca, in letter 108, anticipates the desires of the play's characters—and observers—who hunger to gain knowledge, self- or otherwise. After citing a passage of Virgil ("The best times of our lives, poor mortal creatures, / first fly away") Seneca asks Lucilius to consider different ways one could approach an understanding of the text.

> The one who reads with the eye of a literary scholar does not consider why the best times of our lives come first—that in their place comes illness, that old age looms over us even while we are still intent on our youth. Instead, he says that Virgil always uses the words "illness" and "old age" together. So he does, and with good reason! For old age is an illness that has no cure.[20]

Later in the letter, after another example of a literary scholar reading a text, this time by Cicero, only to obsess again over the words and references, Seneca claims that he does not want to turn into someone who spends his time "trying to track down archaic words, neologisms, peculiar metaphors, and figures of speech"; instead, he wants to "listen to the philosophers" so as to direct "attention to our goal, which is happiness."[21] The literary scholar, for Seneca, wishes to find the truth behind the words: their references, histories, and how they create distinct meanings in different combinations. But Seneca reads texts differently by asking himself how he can become better as a result of what he encounters. This reorientation strikes me as instructive for readers of *Much Ado*. If we view its characters not as literary scholars who scour the text for clues and interpretations, but instead as philosophers-in-training who wish to become better, we can reframe the play as a spiritual exercise of self-care. Rather than think of the play's rhythms of deception and revelation as epistemological in nature, we can detect a different current in the narrative, one in which characters turn away from the act of looking outward as a worthwhile activity. This latter mode is a more properly Stoic one, and it is one to which the play frequently turns. We might say that *Much Ado* twists Foucault's "why truth?" into "why representation?" and in doing so swerves away from the adoption of a critical framework that assumes a premium placed on knowledge. Why care in the first place if things we see stand for other things? In addition to its playful attitude toward epistemology and revelation, then, *Much Ado* exercises a more fundamental (for the Stoic) concern over care, over modes of self-inquiry that attempt to ensure the capacity to receive knowledge in the first place.

The play reflects an investment in this concern in its opening scenes, which tempt its audience to fit the dramatic action into a scheme of knowledge and revelation, only to veer into the more Stoic preoccupations of self-examination, capacity, and preparation. After seeing Hero for the first time since his return from the war, Claudio appeals to Benedick for confirmation of his smitten reaction, first asking if Benedick "noted" her, and then if she is "not a modest young lady?" (1.1.154, 157). This latter question hangs in the air but is never quite answered. Instead, Benedick responds by considering the nature of the inquiry: "Do you question me as an honest man should do, for my simple true judgement? Or would you have me speak after my custom, as being a professed tyrant to their sex?" (1.1.158–61). The quality of the questioner preoccupies the questioned more than what was originally asked. Like Seneca or Epictetus, Benedick takes on the role of Stoic mentor consoling his pupil, but the consolation he offers demands first to know what priorities inform the inquiry. Even when pressed to answer sincerely, Benedick responds to a different query entirely as to whether he likes her: "Why, i'faith methinks she's too low for a high praise, too brown for a fair praise and too little for a great praise. Only this commendation I can afford her: that were she other than she is, she were unhandsome; and being no other but as she is, I do not like her" (1.1.163–67). His string of litotes performs a comic function by avoiding a direct description of Hero, but the mechanics of this comedic trope uncannily match those of Stoic *apatheia*.

Benedick is far from a Stoic sage here. As blinkered as Claudio is in his lack of comprehension of Hero, Benedick has fallen prey to his own false judgments. These men, incapable of clear reflection, practice a form of Stoic care sutured onto a comic structure that relies on the endlessly prismatic reflections of self-regard crowding out consideration of the ostensible object of discussion. Hero herself becomes lost in a sea of investigations of intention. Benedick responds again by asking if Claudio speaks "with a sad brow? Or do you play the flouting jack, to tell us Cupid is a good hare-finder and Vulcan a rare carpenter? Come, in what key shall a man take you to go in the song?" (1.1.172–76). Much as Benedick makes sure he knows what role he is to play in responding to Claudio, he also wonders what role Claudio takes on in asking. This metatheatrical playfulness calls attention to the mechanics of the scene, but it also hints at the audience demanded by their behavior, a fun-house version of Epictetus's theatrical attentiveness. Claudio responds by not acknowledging Benedick's answer—which still isn't about the actual topic of discussion, Hero's modesty—and instead reports that "I can see yet without spectacles, and I see no such matter"; for Claudio, Hero is the "[s]weetest lady that ever I looked on" (1.1.177–80).

Claudio now begins to mirror Benedick's concerns, rather than returning to the question of Hero's worth. He claims he "would scarce trust myself, though I had sworn the contrary, if Hero would be my wife" (1.184–85). The formulation of the statement, that he would scarce trust himself, is idiomatic, but also belies the real theme of the dialogue thus far, buried under an apparent interest in whether Hero is modest: is Claudio fit to judge whether Hero is modest in the first place? Even when confronted with the possibility that he loves Hero, Claudio admits that "[i]f my passion change not shortly, God forbid it should be otherwise" (1.1.205–6). The evocation of "passion" here acts as a shorthand of affectation, but it also recalls the Stoic understanding, originally put forth by Chrysippus, of false judgment. By explicitly linking affectation to judgment, Claudio prioritizes the nature of his faculties of perception over the actual understanding of Hero's worth. Following his admission, more conditional "ifs" begin to carbonate the exchange. Don Pedro, entering the scene, claims that "if you love her, for the lady is very well worthy"

(1.1.207–8); later, he again proposes that "[i]f thou dost love fair Hero, cherish it, / And I will break with her and with her father, / And thou shalt have her. Was't not to this end / that thou began'st to twist so fine a story?" (1.1.289–92). The persistent conditional tense reroutes focus onto the internal circumstances that would give birth to action and delays judgment on the actions themselves.

Claudio's response once again turns (prophetically, as it happens) on his own anxiety over the authenticity of words, rather than their content: "You speak this to fetch me in, my lord" (1.1.209). It is not until sixty lines after Claudio begins to question Benedick that any kind of conclusion arrives, and yet again the answer foregrounds the status of Hero within Claudio's consciousness, rather than an assessment of Hero herself: "That I love, her, I feel," Claudio reports, which sets up the assent of Don Pedro, who has entered the scene: "That she is worthy, I know" (1.1.214–15). Only Don Pedro explicitly links judgment to knowledge. Every other exchange zeroes in on the condition of the speaker or teases out a hypothetical situation that could emerge from the present situation. The dialogue sets up Benedick's fateful profession of romantic obstinacy, articulated in a confessional mode; he is so set in his opinion of women that "fire cannot melt out of me; I will die in it at the stake" (1.1.218). Even this affirmation of constancy protects a stance that is negatively defined: Benedick passionately believes that he does *not* know nor care to know the true nature of Hero's character. Don Pedro then offers the wager that springs the romantic plot into action: "I shall see thee, ere I die, look pale with love" (1.1.231).

The rapid rhythms of this scene clearly satirize the men's reliance on linguistic trickery at the expense of honesty, patriarchal ignorance of Hero's humanity, and solipsism in insisting on interrogating the topic at hand through their own experiences. These habits all present vast opportunity for producing political and sociological implications, but as the previous chapter demonstrates, the scene's comic status should not prevent its potential to conduct philosophical work. As Nussbaum elaborates, comedy and Stoicism in fact make natural, if strange, bedfellows:

> as a further weapon against excessive involvement with tragic characters, the Stoic uses humour and satire. The topic of Stoic humor sounds rather unpromising. But I believe it is not, and that one could do interesting research along those lines . . . the spectator is urged to find (his own or another's) excessive involvement in trivial things foolish, to laugh at the weepers. Such laughter cements the distance between hero and audience.[22]

Comedy can distance the reader from the text—or, in this scene, the player from the part. Benedick's repeated turn to question what roles he and Claudio play allows for a distancing-effect that encourages critical spectatorship for both the characters and the actual audience to the play. The Stoic seeks to distance the viewer from the hero; Benedick distances Claudio from Hero. He does so to discourage attachment and instead allow for self-satire, a mode that encourages reflection on Claudio's motive and temperament.

There is a danger in this line of thinking. If we simply view the play as charting the course of a group of gentlemen who improve themselves through exploiting women, we expose Stoicism's deeply misogynistic potential.[23] *Much Ado* counters this charge by exhibiting its most successful Stoic practices in Beatrice's self-cultivation. At the close of the celebrated scene of her overhearing the staged scene of her friends recounting (and perhaps creating) Benedick's amorous feelings for her, Beatrice seems less concerned with the veracity of what was said and more with her own responses:

> What fire is in mine ears? Can this be true?
> Stand I condemned for pride and scorn so much?
> Contempt, farewell; and maiden pride, adieu;
> No glory lives behind the back of such.
> And Benedick, love on, I will requite thee,
> Taming my wild heart to thy loving hand.
> If thou dost love, my kindness shall incite thee
> To bind our loves up in a holy band.
> For others say thou dost deserve, and I
> Believe it better than reportingly. (3.1.107–16)

Beatrice renders what could be a display of solipsism into a program for self-attentiveness. She first notes her own affective response—"What fire is in mine ears?"—and moves to weigh the potential veracity of the overheard scene: "Can this be true?" The speech then steers away from examining evidence as she instead prepares herself for truth's possibility, marked with another persistent "if." Her prescribed regimen intends to rid herself of contempt and embrace kindness, and her decision to "requite" Benedick's love arrives through the clarification of her own opinion. The final paradoxical lines free the monologue from the charge of deception by claiming that her belief stems solely from within herself, that which is "better than" mere report. Beatrice more closely embodies the ideal toward which Claudio and Benedick, in the earlier scene, stumble: an introspection that fine-tunes the ability to discern right from wrong brought about by alertness to and genuine feeling of embodied sensations. Furthermore, she is careful to recognize the anchor of her emotional responses within herself, activated but not created by the contingent performance she witnesses. Using reason to parse out her own internal psychological landsape, she decides to love Benedick only once she discerns the causes of her reaction.

The two scenes surveyed thus far—the opening scene of the gentlemen discussing Claudio's intentions toward Hero, and Beatrice's reflection on overhearing Benedick's feelings—allow the audience to resist the temptation to find a semblance of the truth (for the men, who is the real Hero? for Beatrice, do these people report accurately?). Instead, they invite a profoundly different set of questions that cannot help but sound, potentially, embarrassingly dated: How are these characters becoming better people? That is, how are they gaining access to virtue by questioning their inner selves? How can they realize their natures, their capacities? These questions lack any interest in or anxiety over the truth and instead bypass concerns with knowledge altogether. Claudio, Benedick, and Don Pedro exhibit more interest in how the self can absorb reality and how they could evaluate what kind of person Hero actually is. Beatrice, too, realizes she must recast herself in a different mold and reorient her judgments to match inward reason. There is no interest in the sublime nothingness that Goddard locates in the play's fascination with artifice. Instead, illusion functions as an agent for identifying which deceptions internally prevent the viewer from understanding the integrity of appearances at all. In this way the scenes twist away from Socratic molds. Rather than reduce forms to their origins, the discussants obsessively try to reduce their own perception to an exercise of reason. The scenes thus bear a close resemblance to exactly the kind of consolation that Leonato mocks in his fury at offers to soothe his false mourning.

Before continuing to analyze the play along these lines, I want to examine the context of the mode of Stoicism that these scenes practice. Foucault develops his model of Stoic self-care as indifference to truth from classical sources. But Stoicism arrives in *Much Ado* with the particular texture of early modern culture. Even though early modern appropriations of Stoicism attempted to wring their texts dry of any trace of theatricality, the performative dimension survived in the era in less obvious ways. For *Much Ado*, the cosmic goals of Stoic exercise ground themselves in the play's complex choreography of social power, negotiated through the more humble vehicles of humor, flirtation, and deception. Philosophical inquiry becomes repurposed as courtly decorum.

A Certain Recklessness

Much has been made of how *Much Ado about Nothing* both celebrates wit as a medium of disruption and weaponizes wit as a vehicle of dominance; in Ian Munro's words, wit is *Much Ado*'s "common currency" and the "means by which social and cultural relationships in the play are negotiated."[24] With its capacities to efface any trace of labor and to demonstrate a winkingly naturalized ability to undermine or highlight currents of social capital, wit affords its practitioners opportunities to show off a dazzling mind or, if misused, it can belie a character's desperation for approval and acceptance. Before examining instances of wit in *Much Ado*, I will detour into an exploration of early modern wit's subterranean, but palpable, Stoic engagement, as traced from its classical origins and translated into courtly behavior—the selfsame behavior lampooned and celebrated in equal measure in Shakespeare's comedy.

The Stoics seem highly unlikely allies with practitioners of wit. In reckoning with the Stoics, Cicero professed profound ambivalence—exemplified most strongly, perhaps, in his *Stoic Paradoxes*—in large part because the Stoics tended to disdain oratory and other modes of self-expression. For Cicero, the Stoics had admirable philosophical aims: a valorization of wisdom, a belief in the interconnectedness of the universe. But they lacked the ability to convey this wisdom effectively. In *De oratore*, the Stoics appear as a both admired and castigated school of thought that had potential but needed a clearer medium. *De oratore* takes the form of a dialogue, and in book 2, one of its main interlocutors, Antonius, surveys various philosophical schools of thought and weighs each by the Ciceronian criterion of how they can synthesize communicability and profundity. The Stoic, he proposes, is "of no help whatsoever here" because Stoic speech is "neither clear, nor expansive and steadily flowing, but meager, dry, cramped, and disjoined."[25] Antonius's charge complements Cicero's praise of theatrical skill in his introduction to *De oratore*. Cicero proclaims that oration

> must be regulated by the movement of the body, by gesture, by facial expression, and by inflecting and varying the voice. Just how much effort this requires, even by itself, is indicated by the trivial art of actors on the stage. For although every one of them strives to regulate his facial expression, voice, and movement, we all know how really few actors there are, and have been, whom we can watch without irritation.[26]

The Stoics lack the ability to communicate properly, while actors lack the ability to transcend the triviality of their sole mastery of delivery. The implication is that the Stoics provide the profundity that actors lack, and conversely, stage performers could lend to the Stoics the craft of delivery to realize better their philosophical potential. Both trivial performer and obfuscating philosopher serve as extremes in need of moderation.

Cicero's suggested potential for Stoicism to benefit from theatricality has largely been scrubbed from early modern adaptations of Stoic works, but it remains in a more tacit way in one of the most influential pieces of performance theory in the era, Baldassare Castiglione's *The Book of the Courtier*. Castiglione's manual patterns itself on *De oratore* in ways explicit and elusive. One of Castiglione's more coy references to Cicero's work occurs in perhaps its most famous section, a debate between Canossa, the primary speaker in book 1, and a few of his interlocutors about whether grace is learned. The group has just settled on the topic of discussion that will preoccupy them for the rest of the text: enumerating the criteria of a "perfect Courtyer" (I quote here from Thomas Hoby's 1561 translation). The question at hand is whether the perfect courtier could learn grace as he would other skills, such as archery or horsemanship. Canossa, whose disquisitions occupy much of book 1, answers that grace cannot emerge from simple emulation. He first relays a brief anecdote about a colleague who imitates a peculiar physical tic of the Prince of Aragon. "And manye such there are," Canossa continues, "that thynke they doe much, so they resemble a great man in somewhat, and take many tymes the thynge in hym that woorst becommeth hym." But if grace cannot be emulated, it still can be practiced through the paradoxical concealment of the effort needed to attain it. One must, Canossa claims, "eschew as much as a man may, and as a sharp and daungerous rock, Affectation or curiosity and (to speak a new word) to use in every thing a certain Reckelesness, to cover art withal." The "new word" here is the Italian *sprezzatura*, the famously untranslatable sense of aristocratic nonchalance that signals power while effacing any betrayal of power's exercise. Canossa nimbly escapes the trap set up by the premise of the question of learning grace—if one cannot, then one cannot learn to be a courtier; if one can, then grace becomes sullied by the whiff of labor—by claiming that the courtier learns "a very art that appeereth not to be art."[27]

The roots of *sprezzatura* can be found in Castiglione's source material. As much as it has become a metonymic quality of early modern subjectivity, *sprezzatura* does not so much amend its classical source as it does move one of *De oratore*'s topics from the margins to the center. What is grace for Castiglione was, for Cicero, an example of wit. *Dissimulatio*, translated as "irony" or "dissembling," arrives in book 2 of *De oratore* as a possible technique of persuasion through gentle jesting. After appeals from his conversation partners, Caesar, an orator renowned for his cleverness, begins anatomizing various forms of rhetorical humor that could be used to win over an audience. He first provides examples of *dissimulatio*, a kind of dissembling that is "a bit trivial" and more "suitable for actors in mimes" than for the orator.[28] Cicero proceeds to provide several humorous stories of people pretending not to know important information—often information that is plainly and self-evidently available. As noted by scholars such as Rebecca Helfer, this mode of humor, dependent as it is on undermining knowledge as an exercise of social leverage, slyly anticipates Castiglione's valorization of an "art that conceals itself."[29] Jennifer Richards has further illuminated ways that Cicero himself practices a fundamental form of *dissimulatio* by repeatedly couching his speakers' ideas in self-effacing asides, thus concealing the actual importance of deception in oratory.[30] The primary participants in *De oratore*, then, couch their virtuosity in the kind of careful rhetorical camouflage that Castiglione will later feature as the signal quality of the courtier.[31]

Another subtle, though less noticed, link to Castiglione's source material is his acknowledgment of Stoicism as an ambivalent patron. In book 2 of *The Courtier*, a new figure, Frederick, takes center stage to begin crafting the means by which the ideals Canossa has sketched out could be realized in practice. This section acts as a rough analogue to Crassus's efforts in *De oratore* to implement a stylistic execution of Antonius's outline of oration's goals. Frederick evokes the Stoics in a fashion similar to Crassus. For both, Stoicism offers ideal versions of harmony by which the subject at hand—oration, courtiership—can be inspired. It "behoverth oure Courtier," Frederick notes, to

> order the tenour of his life after suche a trade, that the whole may be answerable unto these partes, and see the selfe same to bee always and in every thing suche, that it disagree not from it selfe, but make one body of all these good qualities, so that everye deede of his may be compact and framed of al the vertues, as the Stoikes say the duetie of a wiseman is: although not withstanding alwaies one virtue is the principall, but all are so knit and linked one to an other, that they tende to one ende, and all may bee applied and serve to every purpose.[32]

The vision of universally expanding harmony imagined as the model of proper speech by Crassus becomes, in an early modern context, both explicitly named as Stoic and relocated from oration back into its original context of "virtue." Here the principal virtue, unnamed but undoubtedly that of reason, is that to which all other qualities are tethered. At stake here, though, is not something as lofty as the Stoic goal of harmony with nature, but rather the execution of social power. The section that begins with an excursus on Stoicism ends with a conclusion that regrounds the discussion in the practicalities of the courtier's art. Frederick finishes by deducing that "little speaking muche doing, and not praising a mannes owne selfe in commendable deedes, dissemblyng them after an honeste sorte, dooeth increase both the one vertue and the other in a person that can discreatly use this trade."[33] Stoicism's preoccupation with cosmic order becomes converted into a recommendation that ironically echoes the characteristic of Stoicism that Cicero critiqued, its lack of oration. Here, though, "little speaking" becomes instrumentalized as the means by which the courtier can better "discreately use this trade"—how, in other words, the courtier can once again cover the tracks of labor, not as a fanciful meditation on grace but instead as a valuable aspect of a craft, a technique.

Stoicism operates as an example of this performative skill. It functions in *The Courtier* as an ideal of witty self-concealment, effaced textually in its own concealment via authorial *dissimulatio*. In its near-disappearance it models both the ideal, in terms of unity, and negative example, in terms of execution, of rhetoric. The Stoics lacked the ability to let speech gain the same cosmic balance with which they imbued the world. And yet the proper technique for achieving the Stoic's goals is *not* rhetorical excess. Instead, the aspiring student would learn a mode of being that, for Castiglione at least, is resolutely corporeal. Though this kind of Stoic theatricality is relegated to the margins of *The Courtier* and *De oratore*, its textual minimization does not attenuate its influence. Instead, for texts so obsessively circuitous and evasive in mapping their own heritage, Stoicism's occlusion becomes an ironic mark of its importance. We find here a way that Stoicism survived in the early modern era closer to the bodily, experiential way of life that more straightforward scholarly modifications of Stoicism attempted to scrub clean in translations of the primary texts. To act as a Stoic was to turn away from knowledge, from even caring about truth, and instead to conceal its importance. In particular, *wit* affords the student of Cicero or Castiglione the means of this mode of performance that avoids pomposity, on the one hand, and misanthropic stupor, on the other. Wit allows a disposition suited for civil conditions, a realization of *sprezzatura* that bestows grace, sans any trace of labor, onto its successful practitioner.

If wit provides a means for Stoicism to survive as a mode of performance, I would suggest that *Much Ado* stages occasions of Stoic theatricality within its traditionally comic structure. It does so through its direct and well-documented engagement with Castiglione,[34] but it also acts as its own kind of exercise where we join Claudio, Benedick, and Beatrice as pupils, unwilling or not, who learn to look away from knowledge and fine-tune our sense of attentiveness.

No More Than Reason

Much Ado clearly foregrounds wit in its use of proverbs and epigrams, those nuggets of wisdom so disliked by Leonato, to stand in for the seemingly more vital knowledge gained from experience. This disdain for shallow wit, I would argue, also acts as its own dramaturgical *dissimulatio* by distracting from the more subtle methods by which it proffers wit as a Stoic performance of indifference, as Shakespeare's writerly *sprezzatura* that willfully evinces a lack of interest in knowledge. Witness, for instance, the way that Beatrice uses epigrammatic speech in her reply to her uncle lightly urging her toward marriage. "You may light upon a husband that hath no beard," suggests Leonato, to which Beatrice replies:

> What should I do with him? Dress him in my apparel and make him my waiting-gentlewoman? He that hath a beard is more than a youth, and he that hath no beard is less than a man; and he that is more than a youth is not for me, and he that is less than a man, I am not for him. Therefore I will even take sixpence in earnest of the bearward and lead his apes into hell. (2.1.28–35)

The speech begins with Beatrice, who has just mocked beards as uncomfortable and scratchy, swiftly switching positions to reference the common belief that a lack of facial hair connotes effeminacy. She then expounds on her conundrum by offering a jesting proof, which possibly satirizes the Aristotelian belief in virtue as a mean between extremes, before aurally linking "beard" to "bearward," one who takes care of bears, and connecting this image of animal husbandry to the contemporary belief that spinsters lead apes into hell, presumably because they lacked children to lead them to heaven. Leonato, bearlike, takes the bait, asking, "Well then, go you into hell?" and Beatrice answers with another sequence of imbricated references:

> No, but to the gate, and there will the devil meet me like an old cuckold with horns on his head, and say, "get you to heaven, Beatrice, get you to heaven. Here's no place for you maids!" So deliver

> I up my apes and away to saint Peter fore the heavens. He shows me where the bachelors sit, and there live we as merry as the day is long. (2.1.3743)

A pattern becomes discernible in this stream of imagery. The sonic or semantic logic of one phrase links partially to another, which in turn offers a connection to another agreed-upon convention, which in turn becomes an exemplary sinew to entangle a new idiom, and so on. In this case, the devil appears at the gates of the hell into which the apes lead spinsters, and, in an aside offered purely for the spontaneous discovery of imagistic overlap, Beatrice notes that the devil's horns echo the cuckold's horns. She then proceeds to heaven, which recognizes her maidenhead as virtuous and sits her next to bachelors. Having mocked beardless men as effeminate, she now anoints herself as masculine to possess the freedoms afforded to men, the very kind she will later lament not having, in a moment of vengeful anger against Claudio: "O God, that I were a man! I would eat his heart in the marketplace" (4.1.304–5).

In these early scenes, Beatrice's intentions are more generous. She means in part to confuse and ultimately deter her uncle from questioning her lack of a husband. She also demonstrates a kind of intelligence missing from other epigram-wielding wits. Rather than attempt to "patch grief with proverbs," she patches the proverbs themselves by building a veritable world with its own internal logic, as such demonstrating a distinctly early modern use of wit that carries forth the classical Stoic goal of learning: to mobilize and cohere sayings into something new, rather than to collect them as individual signifiers of status. Lodge's translation of Seneca's imperative in letter 88 makes this goal clear: "both command and say what shall be committed to memorie, and produce something of thine owne."[35] Beatrice's celebration of wit realizes this mission. Her use of popular tropes, not simply in citation but in their instrumentality, recalls as well Foucault's lectures on Marcus's *Meditations*. The "effect expected" from reading this text, Foucault suggests, is "not to have understood what an author meant, but the creation of an equipment of true propositions for yourself, which really is your own"; furthermore, this process "is not a matter of putting together a hodgepodge of propositions from different places, but of building a solid framework of propositions that are valid as prescriptions, of true discourses that are at the same time principles of behavior."[36] The repurposing of what is read into an active, world-making way of life is thus "a kind of habit for the body."[37] Adopting Diana Taylor's distinction, we might say that Beatrice translates from the archive into the repertoire, from the static textuality of recitation to the organic vitality of experience. Thomas Hoby, in his preface to *The Courtier*, similarly likens his own adaptation of Castiglione—and Castiglione's adaptation of Cicero—to a movement beyond the text and into the curation of corporeal behavior, since translation creates "a gap for others to folow their steppes, and a vertuous exercise for the unlatined to come by learning, and to fill their minde with the morall vertues, *and their body with civyll condicions*."[38] In this way, Beatrice's wit translates her learning into behavior, a way of being.

The play opens with a comparison between these two paradigms of learning. When the messenger arrives to tell Leonato that Claudio has performed bravely in the war, and that Claudio's uncle (never mentioned again in the play) has felt so much joy "that joy could not show itself modest enough without a badge of bitterness," Leonato responds with a chiasmic platitude: "How much better it is to weep at joy than to joy at weeping!" (1.1.21–22, 26–27). The two exchange expressions without any of the playful mutability exhibited by Beatrice, a contrast made clearer moments later, when she questions the messenger while using a nickname for Benedick. "I pray you," she asks, "is Signor Mountanto returned from the wars or no?" (1.1.28–29). The more literal-minded messenger does not follow, responding that he knows "none of that name." After being corrected, the messenger replies that Benedick has returned, which prompts Beatrice to weave another complex account out of aphorism and resonance:

> He set up bills here in Messina and challenged Cupid at the flight and my uncle's fool, reading the challenge, subscribed for Cupid and challenged him at the bird-bolt. I pray you, how many hath he killed and eaten in these wars? But how many hath he killed? For indeed I promised to eat all of his killing. (1.1.36–43)

The raw materials for this complex description consist of a set of commonplaces: handbills announce archery contests, archery contests require longer arrows, Cupid fires bird-bolts, fools subvert the rules, and so on; the charge to eat all of Benedick's "killing" mocks him for his inefficacy as a warrior and thus overlays his military skills onto his amorous abilities. The messenger, moments before comfortably lobbing sayings as a means of approximating proper emotional conduct, remains confused: "He hath done good service, lady, in these wars" (1.1.45–46). Unable to use his proverbs as equipment, he concerns himself only with discovering the truth, while Beatrice floridly demonstrates her witty indifference to even the question of Benedick's service and instead fine-tunes her own ability to evince a "principle of behavior," a way of cultivating a proper disposition toward the world rather than validating the authenticity of what inhabits it.

The play also tests our own capacity, as audience members, to rely on knowledge as the proper criterion for experiencing the drama. *Much Ado* tempts us into thinking its plot depends solely upon access to knowledge, but continually prioritizes the cultivation of dispositions over the revelation of facts. It presses us to make ethical valuations based on how characters respond to representations rather than how they interrogate them as real. One such technique by which it challenges our outlook is to play with the convention of bystanders gaining access, intentionally or not, to privileged knowledge that it would benefit someone else to hear. The major turn on which the main plot hangs, the revelation of Don John's second, more serious scheme to fool Claudio, seems to relate necessary information. However, before this revelation takes place, the audience has been trained to cultivate its own critical indifference to epistemological inquiry. One of the first instances of the overhearing convention takes place when we learn, in the second scene, that an earlier exchange between Claudio and Don Pedro had been misapprehended by "a man" of Antonio's. Leonato's brother relates to him that "the prince discovered to Claudio that he loved my niece your daughter, and meant to acknowledge it this night in a dance, and if he found her accordant, he meant to take the present time by the top and instantly break with you of it" (1.2.19014). We know that, despite Antonio's insistence that his spy is a "good sharp fellow," he has mistakenly heard only some of Don Pedro's plan to "tell fair Hero I am Claudio; / and in her bosom I'll unclasp my heart / And take her hearing prisoner with the force / And strong encounter of my amorous tale" (1.1.303–6). Presumably he has solely heard the description of what he will do as Claudio, not that he will then break the news to Leonato that Claudio in fact loves Hero, not him. Leonato's response is not to question the sharp fellow but instead to "hold it as a dream till it appear itself," to hold the mental image as true without investigating its correspondence with reason.

This is the first layer of misunderstanding, onto which is mapped another disclosure that, along with Antonio's servant, Borachio had similarly overheard Don Pedro's plan. "I whipped me behind the arras," Borachio excitedly reports to Don John in a parallel scene, "and there heard it agreed upon that the prince should woo Hero for himself, and having obtained her, give her to Count Claudio" (1.3.56–59). Borachio's news leads to Don John swiftly misleading Claudio into thinking that Don Pedro *actually is* wooing Hero, which Claudio believes. But no real secrets exist in Claudio's gulling. There is no plot to deceive anyone except, perhaps, the hapless Hero, who is supposed to believe that Don Pedro is Claudio before Claudio himself appears. Claudio's misunderstanding arises not because of a withheld truth but because of improper attitudes toward the importance of truth. Borachio's deception relies on telling Claudio *what he already knows*. Don Pedro has already claimed, to Claudio, that he will unclasp his heart and "take her hearing prisoner." What Don John tells Claudio, later, is that Don Pedro "is enamoured on Hero," which he knows because he "heard him swear his affection"; Borachio confirms that Don Pedro "swore he would marry her tonight" (2.1.149, 153–54). No change of knowledge actually occurs. What differs in Claudio from his initial conference with Don Pedro to his later discussion with Don John is his capacity to judge, his ability to evaluate what the criteria for truth are rather than the truth itself or even the truth's misrepresentation. Claudio must assume that Don John's version of the same story given to him by Don Pedro is more worthy to be deemed accurate. The many aesthetic misdirections at play—Claudio dresses as Benedick; Leonato mishears one account of what occurred; Don John promises to woo as Claudio; and so on—practice a kind of *sprezzatura* on the audience by disguising the rigor of what is essentially an exercise of our judgment alongside a test of Claudio, which he fails. These early scenes suggest that we witness a straightforward revelation of knowledge, an Aristotelian *peripeteia* by which the unknown becomes known, but instead they wittily retreat from the elevation of knowledge as criterion for suspense.

It is telling that shortly after hearing Claudio morosely confess his unhappiness at Don Pedro claiming Hero, Benedick laments hearing Beatrice call him a fool by expressing anger at her "disposition": "It may be I go under that title because I am merry. Yea, but so I am apt to do myself wrong. I am not so reputed; it is the base, though bitter, disposition of Beatrice that puts the world into her person and so gives me out. Well, I'll be revenged as I may" (2.1.187–91). Benedick focuses less on the truth behind what Beatrice says and more on how Beatrice positions herself relative to the world. And Claudio himself, before the nondeception exercised by Don John, frames his love for Hero as an inward-looking evaluation of his passions, in the Stoic sense of judgment, rather than as any objective change in Hero herself: "But now I am returned, and that war-thoughts / have left their places vacant, in their rooms / Come thronging soft and delicate desires, / All prompting me how fair young Hero is, / Saying I liked her ere I went to wars" (1.1.282–86). The characterological shift from war hero to lover depends on Claudio processing and inwardly curating the placement of desire, personified here as a tenant in his cognitive faculties. Claudio is not particularly witty; the Stoic performance of humor demonstrated by Beatrice finds no purchase in his use of language. But the play executes its own performative wit in the comic effortlessness with which it distracts its audience and readers from the importance of truth. This pattern becomes perfectly emblematized in the moment of Hero's own "revelation" to Claudio, which is withheld from the audience by that simplest of theatrical concealments, the whisper: "My cousin tells him in his ear that he is in her heart," reports Beatrice (2.1.289–90). It is not difficult to know what she says; it is impossible. The audience does not become surrogate detectives, as in a modern novel, sifting for clues.[39] Instead we become critical spectators left only to examine our own expectations for what we think *should* be said, and thus we bear witness to our own processes of judgment. In the early modern milieu of the comedy of manners, the Stoic philosophical attitude, so scorned by Leonato, appears as a viable mode of dramaturgy for the play in which he resides.

Despite its aversion to the revelation of knowledge, the effect of *Much Ado*'s dramaturgy, which diverts epistemological inquiry through its deployment of wit and deliberate plot confusion, is not an agon over the terror of meaninglessness. It is instead, to recall Foucault's salient question, to wonder why truth matters at all. Why should truth determine certainty? In this sense, Stoic indifference is closer to what James Kuzner labels "epistemological humility," the ability to be uncertain and in that uncertainty allow for political community.[40] But I believe Stoicism is getting at something even stranger to our sensibilities: the notion that we cannot exist in humility of our knowledge if we never cared about knowledge in the first place. And yet indifference does not connote a lack of concern over virtue. Indeed, the practice of *apatheia* in the play seizes on a particular virtue, reason, that makes no appeal to knowledge and constitutes the one principle we can actually control. The version of Stoicism that survives through its adaptation in *The Courtier*, inherited by way of Cicero, still retains this focus even if—especially if—it professes a *sprezzatura* of nonchalance toward the truth.

And so I take seriously a conversation in *Much Ado* usually played for laughs: the exchange of assurances practiced by Beatrice and Benedick at the conclusion of the play that asserts reason as the impetus for their mutual affection. "Do you not love me?" asks Benedick. Beatrice responds: "Why, no, no more than reason." She asks the same question of him, to which he replies, "Troth no, no more than reason" (5.4.73, 77). Benedick's reflection upon his engagement lingers less on any evaluation of Beatrice. Instead, he thinks of love as a matter of discernment, of separating judgments: "In brief, since I do purpose to marry, I will think nothing to any purpose that the world can say against it; and therefore never flout at me for what I have said against it" (5.4.103–6). Beatrice's and Benedick's vows to follow reason promise that they will engage with the present in acts of mutual predisposition. They make no appeals to knowledge of their affection, instead identifying the potential of communality in the application of discernment to the moment. In doing so they recall the lines of Marcus Aurelius, written as one of his daily reminders:

> Everywhere and at all times, it is up to you to rejoice piously at what is occurring *at the present moment*, to conduct yourself with justice towards the people who are *present here and now*, and to apply rules of discernment to your *present* prepresentations, so that nothing slips in that is not objective.[41]

Theirs is not a love of austere self-discipline, as the echo of Marcus would suggest. It celebrates their bond in a distinctly early modern fashion, through their mutual use of wit, an ability to synthesize material beyond their fragmentations, to defer knowledge and thus to realize comically Stoicism's goals. Although the knowledge that they love one another has been fabricated by conspiring friends, their comportments have echoed one another through the play. Like Beatrice, Benedick continuously engages with wit as the reconstruction of idiom, as critical playfulness that demonstrates Senecan learning. In the first scene of the play, confronted with Don Pedro's straightforward recitation of an old saying—"In time the savage bull doth bear the yoke"—Benedick responds by narrating an expansive picture similar to Beatrice's flights of images: "the savage bull may, but if ever the sensible Benedick bear it, pluck off the bull's horns and set them in my forehead; and let me be vilely painted, and in such great letters as they write 'Here is good horse to hire', let them signify under my sign, 'Here you may see Benedick, the married man' " (1.1.244–49). The audience has been primed to see their commitment to reason as linked to their wit, and their wit to their judgment.

To an ear trained on the post-Romanticist equation of passion with abandon, a love born from reason carries a touch of the paradoxical. For the Stoics, however, the truest sense of love results only from a pursuit of absolute reason. In letter 23, Seneca urges Lucilius to "learne to rejoice"; this imperative precedes a knowing acknowledgment of the supposed self-seriousness of Stoic practice, as Lucilius "thinkest now that I take many of thy pleasures from thee, who drive from thee those that are gotten by casualtie, who suppose that these hopes and sweetest delights are to be avoyded, nay, it is quite the contrarie. I will not that at any time thou be without joy."[42] Rather than try to wring pleasure from life, Seneca here attempts to strain unnecessary and distracting delights so as to focus on a purer form of happiness. He quips, wryly, "joy is a severe thing."[43] Pierre Hadot notes that this passage distinguishes between *hedone* (pleasure) and *eupathia* (joy): pleasures, those contingent and enticing vices, only undermine the pursuit of joy. And joy, for Seneca, can only result from a focus *inward*, a plunge into consciousness that paradoxically results in the reward of a bond with the transcendental: "Seneca does not find joy in 'Seneca,' but by transcending 'Seneca'; by discovering that there is within him—within all human beings, that is, and within the cosmos itself—a reason which is part of universal reason."[44] With this amalgam—of self and universe, joy and reason—in mind, we can revise Benedick and Beatrice's union, born from their mutual capacities to reason, as a mode of Stoic love that avoids the derogatory aspects of eros (while allowing for amatory playfulness in their language) and instead finds compassion and empathy in a shared journey within their innermost selves in pursuit of a wider, enmeshed network of being. No more, and no less, than reason.

If we follow this line of thinking, we release the play from the many interpretations of their engagement that ironize their affection. In the preface to the Norton edition of the play, Stephen Greenblatt casts its central depiction of courtship as an ideal plaintiff for New Historicism: "Beatrice and Benedict constantly tantalize us with the possibility of an identity quite different from that of Claudio and Hero, an identity deliberately fashioned to resist the constant pressure of society. But that pressure finally prevails. Marriage is a social conspiracy."[45] Greenblatt's view is challenged in a footnote in the third Arden edition that appends Don Pedro's declaration to "fashion" the love between Beatrice and Benedick. Claire McEachern, the Arden editor, notes that for "some heartless critics," such as Greenblatt, "this language of artifice is proof that the ultimate union of Beatrice and Benedick is more indebted to social convention and machination than voluntary feeling."[46] But the Stoic would ask: why do we care so much about what is real or what is fashioned? Greenblatt and other New Historicists are deeply inspired by the work of Foucault, who is in turn deeply influenced by the Stoics, but their analysis relies on Foucault's ultimate endpoint of the care of the self—technologies of power—rather than dwelling on the narrower (but no less complex) understanding of "fashioning" that takes place in the Stoic texts that help pave the way for, but are ultimately independent of, the processes of objectivation taken up by modernity. The Stoics train their eyes on how the self relates to the self without recourse to wondering whether either self is authentic. The question at hand would instead be how Beatrice and Benedick relate to their own response to the courtship, not to the courtship itself.

Their responses stand in stark contrast to the misuse of reason, figured as a *lack* of proper indifference to knowledge, as exercised by Claudio and Leonato, whose entangled misjudgments in the first two acts compound into near-tragedy in the failed wedding between Claudio and Hero. We could view the events of this scene as the result of deception, and of course, this is partly true: Claudio has been "deceived" insofar as a false scene has apparently stood in for a real one as he believes he has seen Hero sexually engaged with someone else. But *Much Ado* once again steers us away from thinking of Platonic knowledge, and with it Platonic and Aristotelian models of mimetic performance, as the primary medium for dramatic action. In other words, it is not simply that one person (Margaret) has stood in for another (Hero), therefore deceiving Claudio in the manner Plato laments in his *Republic* and to which Aristotle accedes in his *Poetics*.[47] Instead, what preoccupies these scenes is how Claudio disposes himself in preparation for what the truth may be. When Don John relays to Claudio and Don Pedro that Hero may be unfaithful, he frames the accusation in terms of Claudio's *reaction* to the news. After Claudio repeats Don John's accusation, "Disloyal?" Don John clarifies: "Think you of a worse title, and I will fit her to it. Wonder not till further warrant" (3.2.97, 99–100). Even though no evidence has yet been given for any scandal, Claudio immediately prepares to humiliate Hero: "If I see anything tonight why I should not marry her, tomorrow in the congregation where I should wed, there will I shame her" (3.3.111–13). The scene ends with a burst of stichomythia that adds tragic portent to the scene, as Hero's guilt becomes overdetermined:

> DON PEDRO: O day untowardly turned!
> CLAUDIO: O mischief strangely thwarting!
> DON JOHN: O plague right well prevented! So will you say when
> you have seen the sequel. (3.3.119–21)

With a hiss of sibilants, Don John exits the scene, a serpentine figure leaving Don Pedro and Claudio to experience their Fall preemptively, before gaining any real information. They have already marked the day as "turned" and conjured up thwarting mischiefs that have not yet come to be. Tellingly, and despite the intervention of many directors, the actual scene of deception does not occur for us to witness. The play blinks. We miss what should be a key deliberation on the gullibility of Claudio and the deceptive prowess of Don John, Borachio, and Margaret. Much like

Hero's whispered profession of love, this scene too denies us knowledge, and we must judge instead without an appeal to the truth. Of course, we know what this truth is, but the play calls attention to our ability to deduce this based upon our evaluations. Claudio, by contrast, lifts himself out of the present and prepares himself for what he *will* do. He loses the sense of critical indifference that would allow him to acclimate himself to the present with the proper clinical sense of reason.

There is admittedly something perverse in attempting to recover Claudio as a pupil who trains himself to recognize virtue with Stoic exercises. He is a rash, sexist, self-obsessed character who does not nearly reach enlightenment, much less sagacity. But the truly Stoic approach would be to recognize even Claudio's capacity for growth—*especially* his. Throughout the play, Shakespeare insists on language that favors judgment over knowledge, reason over truth, and inward cultivation over outward assurances. He centers this language in part on someone who seems barely redeemable; most critics have found him excessively and implausibly foolish. But if we resituate our own criteria for evaluating Claudio outside of what we think we know about him and instead chart his own capacity to reason, his virtue, we find that *Much Ado* documents a radical performance practice plucked from antiquity and laundered through early modern social codes. In doing so the play challenges our *own* capacity to reason. We are not asked to sympathize and are kept at a distance from the proceedings, as cemented in Benedick's jarring final line, a schoolyard riposte aimed at Don Pedro: "Prince, thou art sad—get thee a wife, get thee a wife! / There is no staff more reverend than one tipped with horn" (5.4.120–21). This bizarre and obscure jape plays on cuckoldry imagery while suggesting that one's staff—wife?—may become "tipped" or "tupped" and thus gain a form of ironic reverence. Recalling Nussbaum's novel observation of Stoicism's Brechtian affinities, we can view the bawdiness of this line as a distancing-device that ensures we do not overly invest ourselves in the fate of the personae on stage and instead commit to a response guided with "no more than reason." Sympathy would connote an attachment to the passions, to our judgments, rather than to our rational selves, and the humor the play exercises in this moment attempts to keep that rationality alive.

Rather than prompt Brecht's revolutionary response, in which the audience questions otherwise invisible social forces, what the play ultimately demands is our indifference, figured as an audit of our own reason and thus our own capacity. In *Much Ado*'s deployment of wit, dazzling displays of creative reading and repurposing of idiom, persistent favoring of introspection over external investigation, and obstinate refusal of sympathy, indifference breaks free from the image of the unfeeling Stoic Leonato mocks in his faux passion. Rather, the indifferent spectator remains a highly theatrical one, removed from the lure of prediction or knowledge but attentive to the action on display. The play makes good on its title and gives us nothing, and in doing so, it teaches a kind of grace.

CHAPTER FOUR

Unbrace the Air: Stoic Cosmology in *The Atheist's Tragedy*

To the Unknown God

Who is the atheist of *The Atheist's Tragedy*? At first blush, the answer is obviously the villainous D'Amville, who spends much of Cyril Tourneur's 1611 play openly spurning the Christian God in the name of personal advancement. D'Amville specifically names his false, surrogate deity as *reason*, a treasured quality that separates him from lesser creatures. He gives voice to this apparently corrupt worldview when he declares that "in my reason dwells the providence / To add to life as of much happiness" (1.1.126–27).[1] In this act of idolatry he echoes an archetype of atheism from Thomas Nashe's *Christ's Teares over Jerusalem* known as the "outward Atheist," a dissembling figure who cloaks their heresy in the appearance of innocent rational inquiry. This person, warns Nashe, "establisheth reason as his God, and will not be perswaded that God (the true God) is, except he make him privie to all the secrecies of his beginning & government. Straightly he will examine hym where hee was, what he did before he created Heaven and Earth; how is it possible he shoulde have his beeing from before all beginnings?" The outward atheist's questions pile up, each with the veneer of intellectual curiosity: "Every circumstance of his providence he will runne through, and question why he did not thys thing, and that thing, and the other thing, according to theyr humors?"[2] With each supposedly reasonable inquiry, God becomes more human, more material and changeable rather than beyond time and space, until by the end He is simply a person acting on the capriciousness of His "humors."

Like Nashe's atheist, D'Amville relentlessly materializes and demystifies the ineffable. The mysteries of God, fate, kingship, family, and romantic love become reduced to agency, choice, politics, alliance, and eros.

D'Amville rehearses this signal maneuver in the play's opening moments as he sketches out motivations for conspiring against his brother and nephew. He laments that

> even in that sufficiency of state
> A man has reason to provide and add,
> For what is he hath such a present eye
> And so prepar'd a strength that can foresee
> And fortify his substance and himself
> Against those accidents, the least whereof
> May rob him of an age's husbandry?
> And for my children, they are as near to me
> As branches to the tree whereon they grow,
> And may as numerously be multiplied.
> As they increase, so should my providence. (1.1.46–56)

The justification for murder is presented here mathematically: He must add to his state to fortify against accidents, as if hedging against fate, and his offspring must be "multiplied"; as a result, his "husbandry," or management, can properly take the place of any other forces that may control his life. As a result the reach of his economic power—his "providence"—will grow. The implied mirroring of religious zeal becomes explicit when, later, he surveys the gravel pit where his brother, the baron Montferrers, has been murdered. Borachio, his loyal servant, describes how he has laid Montferrers's skull "upo' the ground / For's pillow, against the which they thought he fell / And perish'd" (2.4.96–98). He then deliberately mirrors Jesus's famous proclamation to Peter ("on this rock I will build my church") in announcing, "Upon this ground I'll build my manor house, /And this shall be the chiefest corner-stone" (2.4.99). "This," for Borachio, is the rock used to murder his brother; instead of declaring the foundation of the Christian church, D'Amville plans his "manor house"; much like his doubling of "providence" to mean individual wealth, rather than divine power, he alchemizes spiritual language into personal, material self-advancement.

Along with recalling an archetypal atheist, however, D'Amville, by stripping away the possibility of transcendence existing outside of the material world, and in his worship of rationality as a surrogate God, also mirrors the Stoic valorization of reason.[3] In Christian thought, Stoic belief could either shade into nonbelief or provide a classical blueprint for proper worship. As surveyed in my introduction, Saint Augustine condemns the Stoic insistence on reason alone as the means of realizing virtue. The Stoic, Augustine argues, blinds themselves to the miraculous workings of God's grace—invisible and undetectable to mere reason, beyond our capacities to discern in this world—and, bereft of faith, becomes subjected to torture, disease, and eventually suicide. Yet as we have seen throughout the book so far, some Stoic teachings found harmony with the church. The Christian valorization of humility echoes the Stoic emphasis on constancy; likewise, Christians approved of the Stoic understanding of joy elevated above mere bodily pleasure and impassivity in the face of worldly desires. Saint Jerome observes, in his commentary on Isaiah, that the Stoics "agree with our teaching in many particulars" when he approvingly notes their dismissal of earthly possessions as mere *adiaphora*, "things indifferent."[4] The stubborn nontranscendence of the Stoic worldview, as explored in chapter 2, prevented it from neatly overlaying Christian ethos as seamlessly as Platonism. At the same time, the Stoics were not Epicureans, easily dismissed as nonbelievers who thought of God as outside the world. They did believe in God, after all—or at least *a* God, named frequently enough in philosophical writings to appear broadly similar to the Christian deity. And yet they also seemed resolutely of the world, focused, like D'Amville, on the here and now, on inner faculties rather than on outward divinity.[5]

This amorphous, neither-apostasy-nor-doctrine quality finds its signal demonstration in the Stoics' appearance in the New Testament. In Acts 17, Paul travels to Athens, where he is met by some local philosophers who demand he defend his faith:

> Then certain philosophers of the Epicureans, and of the Stoicks, encountered him. And some said, What will this babbler say? other some, He seemeth to be a setter forth of strange gods: because he preached unto them Jesus, and the resurrection. And they took him, and brought him unto Areopagus, saying, May we know what this new doctrine, whereof you speakest, is?[6]

Paul proceeds to give a speech on Mars Hill that explains what he sees as the fundamental innovations of his religion, but does so with a nod to local tradition. He begins by observing that in Athens he noticed "an altar with this inscription, *to the unknown god*," which he takes as a marker of the worshippers being "too superstitious."[7] Rather than believe in a faraway, unknown deity, one whose existence is taken on delusion and who sustains himself on prayer, Paul advocates for a God free from any particular place—one who "dwelleth not in temples made with hands"—and who through grace instead resides in life itself, "seeing he giveth to all life, and breath, and all thing."[8] In explaining that "in him we live, and move, and have our being," Paul draws on the words of a local writer to help weave his beliefs into those of his audience: "as certain also of your own poets have said, 'For we are also his offspring.' "[9]

The local poet in question is Aratus, a Stoic, and the brief passage of his in the Areopagus sermon appears in his only surviving work, the *Phaenomena*. But the words cited by the apostle are not a central part of Aratus's poem, which primarily deals with the weather. Instead, they appear in the very beginning, as a preliminary incantation that divinely authorizes the natural theories that follow:

> From Zeus let us begin; him do we mortals never leave unnamed; full of Zeus are all the streets and all the market-places of men; full is the sea and the havens thereof; always we all have need of Zeus. For we are also his offspring; and he in his kindness unto men giveth favourable signs and wakeneth the people to work, reminding them of livelihood.[10]

It is only because God created the world, asserts Aratus, that it can be legible to us and worthy of study. Furthermore, prayer serves as a way to affirm the divine connection between humans and the heavens. Paul marshals these words to a markedly different effect, imbuing them with a sense of urgency as he warns his audience of the oncoming judgment that awaits them when Jesus returns. He also implicitly yokes Aratus's Stoic cosmology to the Christian doctrine of creation, as both believe in the miraculous coexistence of the divine and the physical. Aratus's doxology reads, in this sense, as a pagan version of the first chapter of the Gospel of John, which itself knowingly rehearses the opening lines of Genesis with the addition of the typological knowledge of Jesus's birth. Before Jesus's arrival on earth, the narrator of John asserts, God "was in the world, and the world was made by him, and the world knew him not."[11] Aratus's praise is less grandiose but similarly finds Zeus not an "unknown God" outside of the world but all around, in the streets and the marketplaces; because he created us, we can locate his signs in nature. J. E. Atkinson notes a resonance between Paul's address and the *Hymn to Zeus* of Cleanthes, another early Stoic.[12] Cleanthes's work, like Aratus's, proffers Zeus as its addressee but, because Zeus exists in all of creation, takes this topic as license to survey natural wonders: "Most glorious of immortals, mighty God, / Invoked by many a name, O sovereign King / Of universal Nature, piloting / This world in harmony with Law—all hail!"[13] The limitless nature of Zeus's power becomes the true subject at hand, and expands, like Paul's gloss of Aratus, to the animating forces of humankind: "No work is wrought apart from Thee, O God, / Or in the world, or in the heaven above."[14]

It may seem jarring to us today that Paul borrows from a work of "science," as we would now term it, rather than a work of philosophy or theology, to offer a charitable point of overlap between his own and his audience's beliefs. But for the Stoics, no such disciplinary division existed. Rather, their ethical practice, centered on the realization of virtue, could only exist because of their understanding of physics. As reported by Diogenes Laertius, in his *Lives of the Eminent Philosophers*, early Stoics believed that the universe was not simply inert and insignificant, but instead a vibrant and interconnected whole:

> That the cosmos is a living being, rational, endowed with a soul, and intelligent is asserted by Chrysippus in the first book of his work *On Providence*, by Apollodorus in his *Physics*, and by Posidonius. It is a living being in that it is a substance endowed with a soul and sensation. For the living being is better than the nonliving; and there is nothing better than the cosmos; therefore the cosmos is a living being. And it is endowed with a soul, as is clear from the fact that each of our souls is a fragment of it.[15]

The cosmos is alive and possesses its own consciousness, its own soul; furthermore, the Stoic conception of God is no more or less than the holistic, unified totality of this cosmos. "For the Stoics," John Sellars puts it, "God simply *is* Nature."[16] Michael White concurs, noting that the Stoics believed both that God *created* the universe and that God *is* the universe; He is "immanent in the cosmos as its active, rational, and corporeal principle."[17]

If we follow this line of thinking, then worshipping the tangibility of the world and refusing to locate divinity outside of the universe—obscured though its unknown vastness may be—can realize, rather than undermine, a sense of spiritual belief. *The Atheist's Tragedy* certainly lacks any clear profession of an animated and vibrantly incarnated material ecology, but it does curiously deny any claims to a metaphysical "other" outside of the strictly literalized confines of its theatricalized setting. As Bruce Boehrer notes, this lack of interest in conceptualization extends to political concerns as well; despite the strict morality supposedly augured by the play's title—its "traditional Christianity," as Irving Ribner has it—*The Atheist's Tragedy* in fact "consists almost entirely in a mystification of the forms and concerns of kingship."[18] Rather than link monarchical and divine power,

Tourneur obscures the former by ignoring the latter. The play dodges any real political meditation in place of a vague sense that kingship exists and must be upheld, and that D'Amville's forced succession to the throne perverts whatever that proper mode of rule is. D'Amville, Boehrer elaborates, is "literally unnatural: operating within circumstances into which he was not born and aspiring to a 'state' that is not his by birth. He becomes not simply an atheist but a sort of social antichrist, acting like a king, talking like a king, and thinking like a king—all in the name of fundamentally bourgeois aspiration."[19] As "antichrist," D'Amville furthers the atheist imperative to attack the foundations of divine rule by aping the mannerisms of kingship to advance its opposing set of values. Kingship becomes an extension of proto-capitalist desires rather than an ideological terrain that can be explored or even interrogated, in the manner of Shakespeare's plays. There is none of Prince Hal's or Richard II's ruminative questioning of the foundations of rule; *The Atheist's Tragedy* forgoes skepticism and analysis in favor of weakly opposing vague platitudes against ruthless self-advancement. As such it is not subversive, or even faux-subversive, in the New Historicist sense, so much as a priori deflating its representations of power right out of the gate.

The effect of this lack of interest in exploring the metaphysics of rule is a nearly comic quantification of abstractions. Even many of the play's supposedly virtuous characters articulate the drive to attain a lofty sense of honor while employing the rhetoric of monarchical principles—yet they betray any rarefied sense of these ideas by echoing D'Amville's insistence on the accrual of divine qualities as if they were apprehensible things. Montferrers, Charlemont's father and the target of D'Amville's machinations, balks at the prospect of his son going to war because he believes Charlemont already has enough honor: "And all the honour thou canst get by arms / Will give but vain addition to thy name, / Since from thy ancestors thou dost derive / A dignity sufficient, and as great / As thou hast substance to maintain and bear. / I prithee stay at home" (1.1.5–10). Charlemont's retort similarly relies on an understanding of honor as a commodity that needs to surpass a certain level; he bemoans that he should "serve / For nothing but a vain parenthesis / I'th'honour'd story of your family, / Or hang but like an empty scutcheon / Between the trophies of my predecessors / And the rich arms of my posterity?" (1.1.18–23). Following this response, D'Amville, desirous of Charlemont's death so that he can obtain his brother's inheritance, offers a closing argument that most legibly quantifies honor: "What to the father of a gentleman / Should be more tender than the maintenance / And the increase of honour to his house?" (1.2.36–38). What is striking about this exchange is what *isn't* mentioned: there is no discussion of the broader institution of royalty or the court, no mention of God, no deferral to even military history or expertise. The only question that matters is: does Charlemont already have enough honor, or does he need more? D'Amville's argument wins the day, and Charlemont ships off to bolster his résumé by collecting more of this precious resource. The dialogue essentially acts as an extension of D'Amville's devious soliloquy about his "providence" and legacy, albeit cloaked more effectively in properly noble rhetoric.

This same shift from conceptuality to materiality occurs in Tourneur's comic subplots. The absurd Languebeau Snuffe, a candle-holder posing as a Puritan, continually offers wrongheaded explanations and interpretations that reduce any pieties and abstractions into bodily, concrete phenomena. After Charlemont and Castabella exchange a faithful and chaste kiss to import "by the joining of our mutual and incorporated breaths / That we should breathe but one contracted life," Languebeau enters the scene to immediately deflate any such high-mindedness (1.2.91–93). Charlemont naïvely recruits Languebeau to be a "witness to the contract of our vows," to which Languebeau replies, "I salute you both with the spirit of copulation. I am already informed of your matrimonial purposes and will be a testimony to the integrity of your promises" (1.2.101, 103–5). These lines, reminiscent of Balurdo's dream in *Antonio's Revenge*, read as a sort of source code of a speech more than as actual language; Languebeau translates love to copulation—he must mean the antiquated sense of "union" rather than sexual generation, though both senses resonate—and vows to mere "matrimonial purposes." The stilted awkwardness of the prose makes the lovers' verses screech to a halt; while one effect of this interruption is surely to shorthand Languebeau's status as comic relief, it also more subtly rehearses D'Amville's orientation, expressed just before, toward delegitimizing more abstract principles and ideals.

These materializing gestures are not explicitly Stoic, though they recall the anxious fulcrum point that Stoic physics occupies between atheism and incarnation. If honor, love, and kingship exist *here*, in bodies and objects, rather than out there, in the ineffable beyond, does that imbue concrete things with a sense of divinity, or does it rob us of the possibility of acknowledging something outside of our reality? In a similar way, spiritual valences in Christianity have more material, yet still divine, referents in Stoic spirituality. One particularly fraught contact point between Stoic and Pauline cosmologies is the concept of *pneuma*, a term that Paul uses to mean "spirit" and that for the Stoics denotes a blended material of fire and air elements that, while invisible, binds together the perceptible world. Troels Engberg-Pederson has suggested that Paul's use of the term draws significantly from Stoic origins, even if the intervening years of commentary have given it more of a Platonic cast. Engberg-Pederson notes that Paul's understanding of *pneuma* is in fact a resolutely material and bodily one. It is specifically "apocalyptic" in the sense that the *pneuma* that threads through human beings is the selfsame substance that will rise at the resurrection. As such, when this "physical pneuma, which has been received in baptism, is in operation in believers, their physical bodies of flesh and blood are literally in the process of dying away: atrophying. The takeover by the physical pneuma that will be completed at the resurrection is already under way."[20] The rituals exalted by Paul as signal events of Christian spiritual growth are, in this understanding, not simply symbolic but actual reactions that catalyze the fallen body into a pneumatic body ready for the Rapture. *Pneuma* is thus physical, yet also a component of Godliness; as Christopher Crosbie puts it, the Stoic understanding of *pneuma* "stresses the substance's cosmological, rather than merely physiological, role."[21]

This understanding of Stoic physics, as irreducibly physical but also part of a heavenly schema, further exposes the philosophy's potential for both harmony and friction with Christianity. Paul seizes on the possibility of Aratus's hymn to Zeus acting as a primer for the incarnation and all it entails—the hypostatic union of Jesus, the holy spirit, and God; the presence of God in all things; the trace of the divine given to the passible human form—but he would, one imagines, stop short of endorsing a vision where the stuff of the world *composes* God rather than being animated *by* an unseen and incomprehensible being. This latter model of divinity can, perhaps, still be the "unknown god" of the altar: unknown not because God is outside of the world, but because He *is* the world, the sum totality of which will always be outside our grasp and which possesses a superior intelligence. Even in a properly Stoic mindset, this conception of divinity can seem odd, if not outright contradictory: if the Stoics, as Jerome points out, dismiss most matter as *adiaphora* and instead hold up a clear moral vision of goodness, how can they also believe that all things compose God? Is materiality trivial and not worth our attention, or is it imbued with a universal soul? This potential contradiction is noticed by Plutarch, a contemporary of both Paul and Seneca, who observes in book 13 of his *Morals*:

> I think also that this is said by [the Stoics] against common sense, that Nature herself is indifferent, and yet that it is good to agree with Nature . . . if, as Chrysippus has written in his First Book

> concerning Exhortation, a happy life consists only in living according to virtue, other things (as he says) being nothing to us, nor co-operating any ways towards it, Nature is not only indifferent, but foolish also and stupid, in inclining us to such things as belong nothing to us; and we also are fools in thinking felicity to be an agreeing with Nature, which draws us after such things as contribute nothing to happiness.[22]

It would be foolish to live in accordance with something that deserves at best a shrug in our philosophical considerations. So, then, which is it: are all the material trappings of the world filled with divine energy and part of a larger whole that is God? or are they to be dismissed entirely in the pursuit of virtue, which focuses only on what can be controlled through our unique human capacity? When viewed through a Christian lens, this problem takes on a new valence: are Stoics idolatrous in their worship of mere materiality, or do they anticipate Jesus's innovation of the Word made flesh? Do they mistakenly dismiss the possibility of transcendence—again, we see here why Plato, with his chain of being, provides a more favorable syncretic model—or do they uphold a version of proper morality in their reverence for creation?

These concerns become foregrounded in *The Atheist's Tragedy*, published in 1611 and at that point already "acted," as its title page relates, "in diverse places." Tourneur's work, in many ways a stock narrative of revenge and corruption, implicitly and explicitly features—despite or because of its hackneyed dramaturgy—a particularly early modern entanglement of beliefs, with various understandings of Stoicism, Christianity, and atheism at play in its thematic and theatrical concerns. Characters evince Stoic behavior as index of both villainy and heroism; Christian faithfulness emerges as morally correct but dramatically feeble; atheism is readily denounced, and yet the play tacitly leaves open the possibility of a Godless world. Furthermore, *The Atheist's Tragedy* repeatedly grounds these ideas in bodies and things. Its relentlessly materialist vision helps identify not just the discourses of its belief-systems but also their embodied practice. As such, rather than simply cite Stoicism as a malleable cultural text, it conducts a Stoic exercise, albeit one enmeshed in Christian ethos: the audience must confront the possibility of a world that does not stretch beyond perception, but must also consider that a universe of things can still harness a spiritual, even divine, power, and how that power can be sustained through theatrical and religious belief.

Before diving more deeply into the strategies Tourneur employs to conduct this task, I will examine how early modern Stoicism relates to the play's titular term, "atheism," by further exploring Stoicism's uneasy place in Christian thought. With Paul's Mars Hill speech as a *locus classicus* for this dynamic, I expand beyond patristic commentary on that episode into early modern appropriations of Stoicism in anti-atheist tracts and in the cautious translator prefaces to adaptations of Stoic works. Viewed one way, the Stoic was clearly a nefarious atheist, who resisted the salvation offered by Jesus and absurdly believed in their own internally cultivated ability to pave the way to the good life—and yet, as Paul intuited, this faith in materiality can resemble the all-encompassing grace of the Incarnation. I will then seek to enrich the understanding of "belief" by examining contemporary theological and philosophical understandings of belief in contrast to knowledge; this contrast, in turn, opens up a consideration of the more secular (but equally nonepistemological) mode of belief needed to sustain the self-aware illusion of the theater. Finally, I will read *The Atheist's Tragedy* itself at length, in light of these concerns, to suggest that its qualities that have led to critical derision and dismissal—its dramatic flatness, lack of character interiority, and appropriation of an antiquated emblematic visual language—all in fact steer its audience to consider an interpretation of the play that is Stoic, Christian, *and* atheist at once. This of course is an unsustainable coexistence of doctrines, but Tourneur's dramaturgy and stagecraft imply that the process of attempting to balance these contradictory ideas ultimately operates as its own spiritual exercise that tests us to reframe our lives as more virtuous by weighing competing claims to our goodness.

Moved Withal

Often, when Stoics appear in early modern religious tracts, they make manifest idolatrous and dangerously self-reliant conceptions of selfhood. In the 1560 version of the Geneva Bible, the Stoics, when they approach Paul in Athens, are described in the commentary as having "taught that vertue was onely mans felicitie, which notwithstanding they never attained unto."[23] The revised notes by Laurence Tomson in 1583 assert that the Stoics "determine upon matters of religion according to their owne braines."[24] Tomson rehearses, here, a tamer version of Augustine's and Nashe's critiques: the Stoics fail to place faith in something outside their own reason, and thereby close themselves off from the mystery of faith. In the numerous early modern tracts against atheism, reason-worship similarly masks more blasphemous beliefs. In Jeremy Corderoy's 1608 dialogue *A Warning for Worldlings*, a D'Amville-like "traveler" figure sneeringly challenges the faith of a devout student, who calmly deflects the attack with passages from scripture and fawning descriptions of the miracle of creation. At one point the traveler claims that "in *reason* no man ought to take in hand anything, but to some good end and purpose, whereby in the end hee may reape some pleasure, and commoditie."[25] It is telling that the traveler sees the ultimate end of his life as "pleasure and commoditie" rather than the true joy espoused by the Stoics as the achievement of *eudaimonia*; the idolatrous worship of worldly goods here once again replaces a more spiritually fruitful investment in the unknown and immaterial—in the "evidence of things not seen," to quote Paul's famous definition of faith in his Letter to the Hebrews.

At times, though, authors of atheist literature detect a nascent Christian impulse in ancient philosophy, even as they assail the heathenish implications of classical thinkers who claimed to know true wisdom before the birth of Jesus. For Philippe de Mornay, whose *Woorke concerning the Trewnesse of the Christian Religion* was translated into English by Philip Sidney and Arthur Golding in 1587, the answer to the vexing question of the potential apostasy of Stoic reason-worship is a qualified endorsement: "Schooles of the Stoickes, Academikes, and Peripatetikes, and all other schooles that florished in old time" number among those many ancient philosophers who could not recognize God but who found themselves instinctually drawn to prayer; they felt "ashamed to denie God."[26] Paul's more charitable vision of bridging the two worldviews, a model that recognizes their shared interest in the vitalism of materiality, also tinges the atheist literature of the era. In *The Gallants Burden* Thomas Adams specifically names the Mars Hill episode as *not* an example of false belief:

> Atheists, such as have voluntarily, violently, extinguished to themselves, the Sun-light of the Scripture, Moone-light of the Creature; nay, the sparkes and cinders of Nature, that the more securely (as unseen and unchidden of their own heartes) they might prodigally act the works of darknesse; not *Athenian*-like, dedicating an Altar to an unknown God, but annihilating to themselves, and vilipending to others, Altar, Religion, God; and suffocating the breath of all Motions, Argumentes, manifest Convictions, that heaven & earth have produced.[27]

Adams's vision of atheism is totalizing: more than mistakenly aiming devotion at the incorrect deity, the atheist "violently" destroys the possibility of grace. They do this by blotting out the sun (God), the moon (the miracle of mankind's creation), and the "sparkes and cinders of Nature," a poetic turn of phrase that gives a sense of the world's fallen nature but also of its retention of divine light. The Athenians of Acts 17 fulfill the role of the counterexample, a people who implicitly *do* understand that God exists, but simply do not know what He is. With a harsher tone, John Dove, in *A Confutation of Atheisme*, similarly holds out hope for the Athenians, even as he chastises those who built the altar as aware of their own path of heresy. "There is a God besides all those Gods which you superstitiouslye doe worship," he exhorts, "and is yet unknown unto you, witnes your selves and your own Altar, Doe not think it absurd that I preach unto you such a God for if there be not, why do you then create an Altar unto him & write this superstition upon it?"[28] Dove at least admits that they *do* worship a God, or gods; they just do not know that it is the Christian God. By stamping their own deity as not known, they damn themselves as sinners who have not been—but could be—saved.

The era's most famous atheist, Christopher Marlowe, was labeled as such because he—like Corderoy's traveler and Nashe's outward atheist—focused an apparently scholarly inquiry onto the truth of the Bible. The infamous "Baines Note," supposedly discovered among the possessions of the informer Richard Baines, paints a picture of at times wild notoriety (he loved "Tobacco & Boies") but also of a figure obsessed with transforming the insubstantial and transcendental qualities of Christianity into material and quotidian matters. Thus Moses is a "juggler," Christ a "bastard," the apostles "fisherman and base fellowes neyther of wit nor worth, that Paull only had wit but he was a timerous fellow in bidding men to be subject to magistrates against his conscience."[29] This version of religion is one doomed to be forever tied to the familiar vagaries of everyday life—fishermen, tricksters, illegitimate marriages, and nervous apparatchiks carrying out their boss's orders. Marlowe's gruesome and untimely death is recounted in Thomas Beard's *Theatre of God's Judgments* as the climactic episode in a long list of atheists who die as a result of God's punishment. In one case, after someone makes a blasphemous set of accusations against the Christian faith, a sudden earthquake causes the building to collapse onto him; Beard recounts this episode and muses that

> it is most likely that God by that accident would give us to understand both how monstrous and detestable all such speeches are, as also how men ought to feare & abhorre them, seeing that the dumbe & senslesse creatures & wood, beams, planckes, and stones, and the earth itselfe (by nature steadfast and fixed) are so farre from enduring them that they are moved withal.[30]

Rocks suddenly fall, rooftops collapse: ordinarily static *things* become instruments of God's justice—and, in Beard's telling, they almost gain a sort of agency themselves, being "moved withal," like indignant spectators. When Beard arrives at the case of Marlowe, he recounts how the playwright and spy, who was "by profession a scholler," attempts to stab "one whom hee ought to grudge unto" with his dagger only to "stabbe his owne dagger into his owne head" when his opponent catches his wrist. Beard introduces the story as a homily, cautioning his reader to "see what a hooke the Lorde put in the nothrils of this barking dogge."[31] In this framing, Marlowe, tempted by his own wrath and propensity for vengeance, falls for a trap set by God and becomes a symbol of atheism's self-destructive ways. The anecdote is perhaps too perfect to be true, not least because of its uncannily, bloodily Marlovian elements, but its harrowing events are rehearsed in *The Atheist's Tragedy* when D'Amville meets his own violent end. In the final act, the dutiful and pure young lovers, Charlemont and Castabella, stand trial for their supposed crimes; D'Amville asks to do the deed himself and takes the axe from the executioner. However, in an absurd turn of events, he bashes his own skull when he lifts the axe; the executioner immediately notes with comic understatement that "[i]n lifting up the axe, I think h'has knock'd / His brains out" (5.2.242–43).

Divine providence or horrifying mistake? The play does not quite resolve this tension, but its recollection of Beard's self-destructive Marlowe also suggests a third option: is the axe, as a divine ember of creation, possessed of its own sense of justice? is D'Amville's death not the result of God's hand nudging the weapon back toward his forehead, but instead of the world, as its own vibrant and spiritual organism, taking action? This is the more Stoic understanding, and—as I will elaborate later—one the play sponsors more readily than it might first appear. Beard himself tacitly brings in Paul's Stoic-Christian symbiosis when he lambastes "voluptuous Epicures and Atheists"—not, tellingly, Stoics—as denying "the providence of God" and other tenets of Christianity (the immortality of the soul, Heaven, judgment day, and so on) and as a result "living in this world like brute beasts, & like dogs and swines, wallowing in all sensuality." What these blasphemers fail to understand, Beard emphasizes, is that "there is a God, by *whom we live, move, and have our being*; who although in his essence is invisible, yet maketh he himselfe knowne and as it were seene by his workes and creatures, and mighty government of the world, that he that would seeke after him, may (as one might say) handle and feele him."[32] In the margins he notes the source of this sense of divinity: Acts 17:28, Paul's Mars Hill speech, and specifically, the citation of Aratus. Beard thus brings in Stoicism, though not labeled as such, through a Pauline recognition of a God who cannot be limned or faced head-on and instead is revealed in the creation. His language is hesitantly tactile: we might even *handle* or *feel* God, as if He were tangible.

A recognition of the vitality of things, works, humans—of the world—acts as evidence of God, even though it can quickly shade into animism or even atheism if it were to be limited to one *specific* place or material (the altar to the unknown God). Hence one man's divine materialism can also be apprehended as *mere* materialism, as with Augustine's commentary on Acts 17 in his *On the Trinity*. For Augustine, when Paul states that God is "close even when we are far away," his reassurance transcends place itself:

> If this were spoken in a material sense, it could be understood of our material world: for in it too, so far as our body is concerned, we lie and move and are. We must take the text, then, as spoken of the mind, which is made in his image, and of a manner of being more excellent, not visible but spiritual. What is there indeed that is not 'in him,' of whom Holy Scripture says, 'for from him and through him and in him are all things?' (Rom. 11.36) if in him are all thing, in whom, save in him in whom they are, can the living live or the moving move? Yet all people are not with him after the manner of the saying 'I am always with you.' Nor is he with all after the manner of our own saying, 'the Lord be with you.' It is a person's great misery not to be with him without whom people cannot be. Certainly, people are never without him, in whom he is; yet if a person does not remember him, does not understand him or love him, he is not with him.[33]

In this reckoning, a mental cartography of salvation replaces a cosmic picture of divine presence. To be "far" from God is to place Him outside of memory and comprehension—even though, reassures Augustine, God will always technically be *in* all people as we are part of the creation; we are "never without him, in whom he is." Augustine believes the folly of Paul's audience, which included Stoics, was that they did not mentally accept the truth of their creation; they did not remember their divine origin. And yet Augustine also critiques the Stoics for their overly inward focus in cultivating the mind: the deification of reason at the expense of God. The Stoics could be seen as either overly inward *or* outward, mental *or* material; they had to walk a careful line between the idolatrous, hubristic worship of reason and the typological recognition of divine works. They could be solipsistic or worshipful, helpless pagans or proto-Christians, atheists or believers.

For their early modern translators, then, the task was to recognize the Stoics' potential for complementing and anticipating Christian teaching while also reassuring their readers that they were not being led away from the truth by corrupt heathens. In doing so, though, translators actually made the Stoics less dynamic, less invested in the world, and, strangely, less Christian. In order to justify the translation of Stoic philosophy, the early modern Christian writer had to acknowledge that their source material could not be conscious of the existence of Jesus but still uncannily anticipated Jesus's arrival as part of God's plan. This is a familiar archetype: think of the rueful ancient thinkers perched in limbo in Dante's *Inferno*, or the Christlike Socrates in Neo-Platonists' revisions of Plato's dialogues. The Stoic, as we have established, provides a more difficult case. Without the clear metaphysical investment of the Platonists, which would easily translate into a Christian hierarchy, the Stoics could fall into Augustine's model of the reason-worshipping, overly material apostate. Yet this figure of hermetic isolation also, strangely, resembled a good Christian—recall that Epictetus's *Manual* became adapted into monastic guidebooks. Thus, a potential Marcus Aurelius could easily turn into a Pandulpho or Horatio. The difference between the dynamic and engaged philosopher who attunes to the divine spark in the world due to their social extrication, on the one hand, and the materially invested solipsist blind to salvation, on the other, is difficult to grasp, and as a result early modern adaptations of classical works betray a sense of tentativeness in recognizing the Pauline vision of Stoic dynamism. Instead, the Stoics that emerge are typically once again stultifying caricatures of sages—stock Stoics. The curious condition that results from this revisionist process is that in attempting to salvage Stoics as more Christian, translators actually make them closer to the anti-Christian, atheistic figure described by Augustine or Nashe.

John Sanford, the translator of the 1567 English version of Epictetus's *Manual*, first assures Queen Elizabeth in his dedicatory epistle that the original author, "although he were an Ethnicke, yet he were very godly & Christian."[34] But shortly thereafter, in describing Epictetus's life, Sanford invokes the Justice Overdo-esque figure of isolated stasis:

> [H]e properly and verily was a man, whose substance altogether did consiste in the reasonable mynde, accompting the mind only to be man, and ye body but an instrument . . . he did so withdrawe himselfe from the care & love of outward things, so litle regarding hys body, or any thing there to belonging, that at *Rome* his house had no dore, for there was nothing at all but a beggarly bed of little value.[35]

Both Christian *avant la lettre* and overly cerebral, Epictetus exists for Sanford as a prefiguration of proper religion and an inactive misanthrope, part Saint Anthony and part Diogenes. Thomas James, another English translator, prefaced his 1598 translation of Guillame Du Vair's version of the *Manual, The Moral Philosophie of the Stoicks*, with an even more vituperative jab at his source material: "The Stoicks are as odious unto some men, as they themselves are hated of others: they call themselves professors hereof in their gibing manner stockes, and not Stoickes, because of the affinitie of their names."[36] James, like Jonson, invents an "affinitie" both phonetic and epistemological between the Stoics and "stocks," the contemporary term of derision that signals senselessness and stupidity.

Seneca's works, in Lodge's 1614 translation, similarly become robbed of any potential to harmonize with the supposed vibrancy of Christian life and instead become dry, rote, and lifeless tasks for memorization—all in the name of rendering Seneca into more of a Christian thinker. In his preface, Lodge addresses the spiritually beneficial effects of reading the fruits of his labors: "Would God Christians would endeavour to practice his good precepts, to reform their owne in seeing his errours; and perceiving so great of learning from a Pagan's pen, ayme at the true light of devotion and pietie, which becometh Christians. Learne him in these good lessons, and commit them to memory."[37] Seneca's paganism will prove instructive to the good Christian, suggests Lodge, not because of any possibility of recognition but because of the philosopher's "errours" and simultaneous "good learning." Lodge's "good lessons" recalls the memorization of Seneca's "sentences," or *sententiae*: nuggets of wisdom that can be tucked away and recited at will. Roughly 250 pages after Lodge makes this point, his directive is contradicted by Seneca himself. Letter 33 from *Letters on Ethics* mostly consists of a substantial critique of memorization and learning. Seneca notes, in Lodge's translation, that children are given "sentences" to memorize because

> a childish wit can comprehend them, being as yet uncapable of a more certaine and solid science. A complete man hath no honour to gather nose-gayes, to stay him selfe and build on certain usuall or few wordes, and to trust unto his memorie, hee ought to trust himselfe. Let him speake these but not retaine them: for it is a base thing for an olde man, or such a one as is stept in yeares to be wise in nothing but his note-booke. This said *Zeno*, what sayest thou? This *Cleanthes*, but what thou? How long art thou directed by others? both command and say what shall be committed to memorie, and produce something of thine owne.[38]

The authors Seneca selects as examples of rote, childish learning are telling. Both Zeno and Cleanthes are Greek Stoics, antecedents to the philosophy as developed by Seneca and other Romans. In warning against simply regurgitating the words of these thinkers, Seneca affords a reflection of his own project. His version of Stoicism cannot be simplified as a reiteration of classical precedent, and neither should the student of Stoicism treat philosophical texts as mere "nose-gayes" to be collected—even though Lodge encourages readers to do precisely that. Instead, like Beatrice, they should exhibit a lively sense of interplay and originality in their learning. The disdain on display here links to a sustained critique of learning that Seneca maintains throughout the *Letters*; most famous, perhaps is letter 88, which begins with a blunt dismissal of liberal studies: "Thou desirest to know what I thinke concerning liberal studies. I admire none, I number none among those things to be good, whose end is for gaine. Hired workmanships they are, so farre profitable, as they prepare, and not determine the wit."[39] Lipsius, who provided brief prefaces to each of the letters in Lodge's edition, lightly amends Seneca's distaste in his opening gloss: "But although they doe not leade, yet they helpe: that is, they further and prepare."[40] Seneca assuredly does not state, here, that the liberal arts "helpe" anything; his point is that focus on the liberal arts as their own end distracts from the pursuit of wisdom through philosophy. The model of learning that Seneca does advocate—open, creative, and critical of learning "whose end is for gaine"—more closely resembles a charitable and humble spirit of Christianity than does the supposedly Christian purpose that Lodge reads into the text: the memorization of apothegms to help prepare students.

In attempting to make Stoicism more doctrinal, systematic, and textual, early modern translations and adaptations suppress the more dynamic elements that demand bodily engagement. They neglect, in short, the "way of life" that Pierre Hadot sees as the Stoic project. Paul's Mars Hill speech, attuned to this dimension, invites a more generous offer of sympathies that extend beyond surface similarities. I would argue, furthermore, that the specific quality of Stoicism robbed by these translators is the selfsame element that actually makes the philosophy closer to Christianity: belief. This slippery idea also links Stoic faith to the medium in which it would become actualized in a way that escapes textual efforts of recuperation: the theater, a site sustained by, perhaps even coextensive with, belief. To believe in the theater is to make it dynamic, even alive; it grants, through the power of attention, an allowance for its capacity to move and act in ways unexpected in everyday life. It is more broadly the signal element of performance, as discussed in chapter 1: the frame that allows everything within it to gain a sort of dignity—and divinity.

Beyond Belief

Thus far I have identified how Stoic physics proposes a model of embodiment that, seen one way, anticipates Christian incarnation, but, seen another, denies the philosopher an understanding of the transcendence of the Christian God. At stake in this distinction is how we comprehend the materiality of the world. Are we to see it as cast within a larger, unknowable plan, an ember with a divine spark? Or is it mere *adiaphora*, to be dismissed as unnecessary to the more important focus inward, toward the soul's ability to reason? Despite the best efforts of the Christian translators of Stoic texts, their primary sources end up becoming more, not less, a picture of the stereotypical heretical Stoic, bereft of the potential dynamism Paul identifies in his Mars Hill speech. It is this dynamism that protects the Stoic from the claims of atheism in the early modern literature devoted to assailing unbelievers. Instead, Stoics exist in a gray zone between its dual capacities.

D'Amville, the supposed atheist of *The Atheist's Tragedy*, frequently practices the vulgar Stoic's fetishization of reason in place of proper piety. And yet this idolatry always threatens to transform into a belief in natural divinity akin to the sacred hymns of Aratus and Cleanthes.[41] The play begins with a dialogue between him and his servant, Borachio, about the primacy of nature in determining the worth of humankind. "Borachio," he asks, "thou are read / In Nature and her large philosophy. / Observs't thou not the very self same course / of revolution in man and beast?" Borachio responds that this revolution is "[t]he same, for birth, growth, state, decay, and death; / Only a man's beholding to his Nature / For th'better composition o' the two" (1.1.3–9). Tourneur establishes the pattern, noted earlier, that will repeat throughout his play: the dissolution of apparently mystical social and political properties into material and bodily sources, named "Nature" here and elsewhere. In this sense D'Amville and Borachio's dialogue recalls the Baines letter's charges against Marlowe, who (allegedly) preached the humble and decidedly nonspiritual causes for the miracles of the Bible. The trope is a common one in drama of the period—recall Edmund's paean to nature, "my Goddess," in *King Lear*—but D'Amville specifically identifies Nature as a "large philosophy" that can be read, rather than simply as a substitute God to be worshipped. Borachio's assessment that men and beasts have the same "revolution" of birth, life, and death is qualified by humankind's debt to nature for giving it a "better composition." Nature is both deity and rejection of deity, a democratizing force that unites humans and "beasts" and guarantor of humans' advantage over all else.

Is this Stoic or atheist? Or does it expose the complicity of the two systems, or even, following this logic, the complicity of atheism with the Christianity it supposedly attacks? Carlo Tibiletti and Luigi Longobardo enumerate a version of D'Amville's theory of nature—they call it the "doctrine of cosmic anthropocentrism"—as a point of agreement with, not conflict between, early Christians and Stoics. "God has created the things of the world for the benefit (not in view of) of human beings," they observe, and find echoes of this sentiment in Justin Martyr, Theophilus of Antioch, and Tertullian, among others.[42] The Christian thinker would not call the creator-figure "Nature," but the Stoics would see no difference between the two; God, after all, is simply the conscious, rational, cosmic sum of all materiality. This being reveals itself to humans, the sole reason-possessing creatures, as theirs over which to practice dominion. Recall Augustine's warning that an overly material understanding of Paul's address on Mars Hill leads to an absurd abandonment of God's transcendent life in the minds, not bodies, of his followers. Augustine dismisses even Paul's use of *pneuma* as a material embodiment of spirit and takes up instead the more abstract understanding of God's love as invisible and immaterial, something to be believed in despite or because of its essential lack of tangible symptoms—the evidence of things not seen.

Adam Miller, a theologian influenced by the recently formed discipline of object-oriented ontology, has posited the Stoic-like assertion that religion is "objective"; that is, it is "made of objects, practiced by objects, and practiced for the revelation of objects. When estranged from its objective character, religion plays as a ridiculous parody."[43] Borrowing from the work of the sociologist Bruno Latour, Miller uses the term "object" here to simply mean anything irreducible: holistic things, not vague concepts or notions. His project is in part to reclaim "belief" as something less Augustinian—the faith that an unknowable God exists outside our comprehension—and instead to reorient away from a focus on knowledge altogether. The epistemological model of belief, wherein followers believe in something despite its apparent lack of existence, leads to the mischaracterization of religion as hopelessly naïve. Instead, Miller advocates for a kind of "grace" in the interplay between objects' withdrawal from total understanding and giving-over to others. This is not entirely a Stoic view, in the sense that it certainly denies a doctrine of cosmic anthropocentrism, but it is instructive in giving us an understanding of belief that evades the charge of misguided worship in need of enlightenment. Instead, belief lives in the interaction among components of the world.

The reclamation of belief from the clutches of knowledge also occupies a contemporary realm of philosophy pioneered by Neil van Leeuwen, whose work attempts to separate the oft-conflated paradigms of "fact" and "belief." For van Leeuwen, religious beliefs, or credences, "(a) have perceived normative orientation, (b) are susceptible to free elaboration, and (c) are vulnerable to special authority."[44] Facts, by contrast, are susceptible to evidence, exist independent of normative orientation, and govern attitudes. Beliefs exist in the believer's orientation and dynamic with other believers, rather than in their commitment to evidence: no evidence can outweigh a firm belief in a religious doctrine. Rather, the *elaboration* of belief—its subjectively articulated expounding and expression—changes its contours. Like Miller, van Leeuwen unhooks belief from knowledge, not as a dismissal of spirituality but just the opposite—as a liberation of belief as a different model of engagement altogether.

This endeavor, while resonant with certain radical trends in contemporary philosophy, has long been a tenet of Christian theology as well. Alvin Plantinga, a Catholic theologian, has long critiqued the misunderstandings that he sees in debates of religions "against" science or other fact-based systems. To hold religion accountable to the demands of science is to conduct an overdetermined battle wherein Christianity cannot help but seem foolish and delusional. Plantinga proposes what he calls the "Aquinas/Calvin" model: a way of understanding religious belief as the revelation of what is *already* within the human. Plantinga elaborates that

> this natural knowledge of god is not arrived at by inference or argument (for example, the famous theistic proofs of natural theology) but in a much more immediate way. The deliverances of the *sensus divinitatis* are not quick and *sotto voce* inferences from the circumstances that trigger its operation. It isn't that one beholds the night sky, notes that it is grand, and concludes that there must be such a person as God: an argument like that would be ridiculously weak . . . It is rather that, upon perception of the night sky or the mountain vista or the tiny flower, these beliefs just arise within us. They are *occasioned* by the circumstances: they are not conclusions from them.[45]

Like Miller, Plantinga sees belief not as the logical deduction based on evidence (though confusingly Aquinas's beliefs are often stated as just that) but as the natural consequence of circumstances that reveal the divinity *that is already there*. His careful use of the verb "occasioned" adds a temporal and even performative dimension to this. For Plantinga, our environment sparks the emergence of an affective sense within us, and we call this sense "belief." This belief is still a form of knowledge—it constitutes a deeply held conviction—but it is not a "fact" as van Leeuwen uses the term: it is not derived from and susceptible to observed evidentiary criteria. Plantinga draws on Paul's Letter to the Romans to expound further that, if belief is natural—if it is the logical circumstance of harmony found between two aspects of creation, the human actor and the surrounding world—then denying this uprising of feeling is *un*natural. "According to Saint Paul," Plantinga explains, "it is *unbelief* that is a result of dysfunction, brokenness, failure to function properly, or impedance of rational faculties. Unbelief, he says, is a result of sin; it originates in an effort, as Romans 1 puts it, to 'suppress the truth in unrighteousness.' "[46] In this reckoning, if our natural predisposition is to allow recognition of a sense of a greater plan, then the atheist is not necessarily one who simply transfers this sense to something else—that would be idolatry. Or it would be idolatry if it *limited* itself to a particular material object, such as a golden calf, or painted crucifix, or altar to an unknown God. To partake in what D'Amville does, the worship of "Nature" as a powerful entity that grants him a capacity to reason, is closer to the Stoics and, as Plantinga indicates, to the Christians that D'Amville supposedly spurns.

To characterize one's own belief as beyond evidence provides a key maneuver in many intra-Christian conflicts. To take just one salient example, Thomas More, in *A Dialogue concerning Heresies*, attacks those who would "mystrust and deny the miracles bycause reason and nature telle hym that they cannot be done" and compares this attitude to the doubt against one's own parents.[47] "Thus may every man reken him selfe unsure of his owne father," More elaborates, "if he believe no man or because all ye profe thereof standyth but upon one woman . . . and lett us see yf we beleve nothynge but that we see our self, who can reken him self sure of hys own mother."[48] The denial of the miracles through appeals to reason and nature, for More, turns into an absurd doubt that one's mother is their own; one imagines a Leontes-like trial of familial bonds, demanding evidence for something that exists—at the time—as beyond verification. More anticipates the arguments of much of the atheist literature of Tourneur's day: the absurdity of the atheist's bad-faith intellectual argument is that they apply a limiting criterion onto a limitless phenomenon. *Belief* stands as the relation that distinguishes itself from factuality but that strengthens, rather than attenuates, its power as a result.

The performance of religious belief invites a comparison to the theater, a place that also thrives on, and is even constituted by, the affective relations of observers. The shared attentiveness of an audience confers authenticity upon the actions framed by a specific physical or conventional set of strictures (a stage or an imagined line demarcating the audience). This belief is not factual in de Leeuwen's or Plantinga's sense; theatrical audiences do not demand to know whether performed proceedings might not be "real" if contradictory evidence arises. Instead, they are invested in through communal orientation and elaborated on in terms of normative adherence. More broadly, religion and performance, a wider conceptualization of observed action, both have the capacity to determine identity. Lance Ghavari observes that, apart from their historical affinities born through dithyrambic and other ritualistic events, theater and religion share the performative quality of constituting that which they represent: "Religion, whatever else it might or might not be, is a common marker of identity, and it should thus be no great leap to suggest that, consonant with other theories of identity performance, religious identity is constituted through performance."[49] Drawing on the work of Judith Butler, Ghavari finds that the practice of religion, like the "doing" of gender (to use Butler's famous phrase), is not an external and incidental behavior but key to the very existence of the participant. If religion is constituted by belief, and belief by performance, and if belief tissues the very being of the believer, then the continual actions of belief that the theater contains sustain not just the reality of staged scenes but reality itself. (To call these realities "illusions" would be to fall prey to the appeal to factuality that Christian theology and object-oriented ontology both resist.)

According to Tracy Davis, this conferral of belief, which she identifies as the defining property of what is commonly called "dramatic license," can be clearly observed in one of the popular theater's most famous scenes—the near-death of the fairy Tinker Bell in J. M. Barrie's 1904 children's play, *Peter Pan*. To quickly recap: Tinker Bell has nobly swallowed the poison intended for Peter Pan and can only be revived if the children in the audience believe in fairies. The children then demonstrate their belief by clapping; Tinker Bell is revived, and the plot proper carries on. For Davis, this moment conducts two seemingly contradictory tasks: first, it exposes the artifice of the presentation of the play; second, it demands that the audience reaffirm their commitment to believing this artifice to be real. Davis elaborates that "in precisely the moment when the apparatus of theater is laid bare—when the presence of an audience made emotionally vulnerable by the swooning of an erstwhile lively and sassy fist of light is called upon—the question of belief is foregrounded."[50] The clapping thus "exemplifies the active creation of belief."[51] As if shooting a radioactive dye into the bloodstream, the clapping illuminates a process that occurs at all times invisibly and silently: the upholding of the ostension of the performed world through the communal focus of attention. This sense of "belief" recalls Plantinga's: neither depends on verification; instead, they rely on the occasioning of a sense of commitment through mutual engagement.

Belief, then, connects religious practice to theatrical experience. Both are sets of coded behaviors sustained not by empirical verification but by the emergence of a sense of allowing for a preexisting natural inclination to lend credence to phenomena—whether we call this resulting affect wonder, or awe, or simply attention. This understanding of belief helps square the circle of Stoicism as it relates to atheism: the difference, it seems, is not necessarily whether the *object* of belief is material or not, so much as what that object evokes in the beholder. The Stoic's resolutely materialist view of the world can become closer to a Christian one if it results from a naturally occurring wonderment at the pieces of the cosmological whole that we witness. If that belief were to turn into an epistemological inquiry, it would transform the Stoic into the skeptical, misanthropic atheist who populates the anti-atheist literature of the era. The key is that Stoic belief must be, as Plantinga intimates and Davis asserts, *performed*. It must be constituted through the interaction of entities in space and time. In the remainder of this chapter, I explore how *The Atheist's Tragedy*, even though it appears to be a simple and straightforward endorsement of a Christian worldview, at a closer look actually contains, in its performance, a distinctly Stoic quality. It asks the audience to confer belief upon the theatrical world it creates and links this belief to the form occasioned by Stoic physics—and dangerously close to the form voiced by D'Amville. The play's title may imply that the work consists of a Christian set of principles, and yet for all its professed belief in spiritual, otherworldly ideas, *The Atheist's Tragedy* is a determinedly physical work that never entirely quells the doubts raised by its foil. The audience has to animate the events on the stage in an act of faith similar to the Stoic belief in a dynamic and tangible world without becoming the nonbeliever of the title.

The World's Example

In his Letter to the Romans, Saint Paul famously urges his addressees not to take revenge: "Dearly beloved, avenge not your selves, but give place unto wrath: for it is written, Vengeance is mine, I will repaye, saith the Lord" (Rom 12:19). Paul repurposes the eschatological warning of Deuteronomy (32:35) as a therapeutic salve: allow God to exercise vengeance, and your anger will dissipate. This advice haunts early modern revenge drama as the eternal road not taken. Over and over, characters take up the mantle of revenge themselves, hubristically bypassing divine intervention and summarily paying the consequences for their rash actions.[52] One of the few exceptions to this principle is Charlemont, who self-consciously elects *not* to take action and thus reveals how ethical righteousness can so easily turn into narrative insipidity. The problem is that Charlemont possesses such resolve and faith that he is rendered inert and unmoving; *The Atheist's Tragedy* has commonly been labeled an "antirevenge play" as a result of this static quality. Fredson Bowers, in his foundational study *Elizabethan Revenge Tragedy, 1587–1642*, finds that, compared to other examples of the vengeful hero, Charlemont "is a motionless and undramatic figure and the greater part of the dramatic conflict is never realized."[53] Gordon Braden notes that the "relentless passivity of Tourneur's Charlemont finally allows the villain D'Amville to engineer his own fall"—in other words, Charlemont is less an active character than a moral measuring stick with which D'Amville's pursuits can be gauged.[54] Herschel Baker identifies Charlemont's unmoving quality as Stoic by nature, noting that "Charlemont is the *reductio ad absurdum* of the Stoic hero: he accepts the universe, but his acquiescence is indistinguishable from a tearful Christian sentimentality; his resignation reflects less of a philosophic policy than an incapacity for action, and he seems to be the death-wish made articulate. Yet he mouths the Stoic formularies glibly enough."[55]

In fact, Charlemont mouths the very Stoic formulary that gives the play its subtitle: after D'Amville's death, he announces that "*patience is the honest man's revenge* (5.2.278, emphasis in original). The ghost of his father, an anti–Hamlet Sr., duly warns Charlemont to "leave revenge unto the King of kings" (2.6.24) and Charlemont readily takes his father's advice and returns to the court of his killer, content to wait for God to intervene. No Hieronimo-like madness seizes him, much less grief. The closest he arrives at taking action against his divine instructions occurs in prison, when he briefly questions the fairness of his punishment. He first addresses heaven to grant that "thy goodness doth command / Our punishments, but yet no further than / The measure of our sins" before swelling to a confession delivered to his own soul: "O my afflicted soul, how torment swells / Thy apprehension with profane conceit / Against the sacred justice of my God!" (3.3.1–3, 12–14). The setup has the ring of a theological debate: how are humans to interpret suffering if it exceeds any possible crime? Yet his conclusion to this inquiry is not to favor one interpretation over the other but instead to find interpretation itself at fault:

Our own constructions are the authors of
Our misery. We never measure our
Conditions but with men above us in
Estate, so while our spirits labour to
Be higher than our fortunes, th'are more base.
Since all those attributes which make men seem
Superior to us are man's subjects and
Were made to serve him, the repining man
Is of a servile spirit to deject
The value of himself below their estimation. (3.3.15–24)

Charlemont backs away from analysis as readily as he does from kinetic action. He rues that humans are fated to compare themselves to others of higher station, which in turn makes our spirits "more base"; the "repining man" must remind himself that flashy accoutrements of wealth are ultimately "made to serve" and not to dictate one's wealth. Rather than lower himself by indulging in any comparison, he implies that he must forgo such thoughts altogether and find resolve in the knowledge of a bigger providential plan.

Baker is correct to note Stoic ideas at play in Charlemont's speechifying and (in)actions. But like Pandulpho and Leonato, Charlemont acts as nothing more than a repository of Stoic doctrine unyoked from the essentially performative nature of Stoic practice. He is another caricature of a sage, placed in the dramatic action like a boulder in a river. He lacks any investment in Stoic *practice*, in particular the model of Stoic-Christian cosmology that celebrates the embodied dynamism and divinity of the universe. The play hints that its *sententiae* are not to be taken seriously; one of its recurring jokes features Belforest, the cuckolded baron, self-seriously holding forth on matters of constancy and acceptance. "Recollect yourself," he orders D'Amville, who has pretended to swoon at the news of his brother's death, "lament him not. Whether our deaths be good / Or bad, it is not death but life that tries. / He liv'd well, therefore questionless well he dies" (2.4.43–46). Yet it is Belforest who, despite his avowed commitment to steadfastness, falls into a fury at the news of his wife's serial adultery, accosting Fresco (who has been helping Cataplasma run a brothel out of her residence) with frenzied charges: "You are the pander to her pleasure, you varlet, are you not? You know the conveyances between Sebastian and my wife. Tell me the truth, or by this hand I'll nail thy bosom to the earth" (4.4.39–42). He proceeds to challenge Sebastian to a duel and die.

Even Charlemont's seemingly Stoic fixity feels the gravitational pull toward shallow materialism, passions, and desires.[56] When Sebastian offers to pay his bond and free him from prison, Charlemont does not exercise patience; he absorbs the favor as the play of fate. First, upon seeing his apparent rival, Charlemont, fueled by the momentum of his meditative soliloquy on justice, expresses to Sebastian—with whom he had recently dueled—that he is now beyond the influence of his passions: "No, sir. I have a heart above the reach / Of thy most violent maliciousness, / A fortitude in scorn of thy contempt— / Since Fate is pleas'd to have me suffer it— / That can bear more than thou hast power t'inflict" (3.3.34–38). Fate has decided to inflict him with suffering, so he will bravely withstand it. Yet immediately when Sebastian offers to pay for his freedom, Charlemont marshals the rhetoric of fate to justify his acceptance: "Since I must submit myself to Fate, / I never will neglect the offer of / One benefit, but entertain them as / Her favours and th'inductions to some end / Of better fortune, as whose instrument / I thank thy courtesy" (3.3.55–61). Here, we see Stoicism mobilized in precisely the same fashion as "honor" and "providence" have been by Charlemont's antagonists: as rhetorical capital that guises self-interest in the language of spiritual or political authenticity. Declaring something to be fate nominates it as foretold and obscures the agency necessary in manipulating its operation.

Throughout the play, Stoic sentiment becomes cheaply employed as a horizon of impossibility. Despite any effort to purge their souls of passions, characters in *The Atheist's Tragedy* either nakedly reject the possibility of attaining virtue or cite virtuous rhetoric as a means to advance themselves. And yet this does not mean that the play secretly, ironically props up the very quality—atheism—that it purports to denounce. It may practice a compulsive push toward materialism, but that materialism is closer to that of the Stoic than to that of the nonbeliever. I agree, then, with Alison Shell's observation that while the play invites us to share "Charlemont's belief in divine judgment," it does not "endorse easy assumptions of a hand of heaven."[57] But I would push this observation further: Rather than hedge its Christianity with a dose of atheistic naturalism, it encourages a belief that materiality can still be enlivened with a sense of divinity. That divinity, however, is coextensive with, not transcendently accessed through, the sum total of its worldly forms. The play thus practices a specifically Stoic-Christian sense of matter. Instead of subscribing to a Platonic understanding of the play, in which its world is no more than a fallen set of physical things awaiting unseen and unknown deliverance, the Stoic would view God as within the materiality of the theater, as it is everywhere else. A *Christian* Stoic would furthermore attempt to distance themselves from the heretical implications of this view while retaining the promise of the incarnation, which attests to the Word made flesh. Both Paul's God and Aratus's God remain viable.

The play upholds this viability through various strategies, many involving characters who forthrightly espouse seemingly cheap sentiments of materialistic desire. One recurring characterization depicts bodies as possessing an inherent animating force divorced from the soul and inherent to its materiality. In the bawdy subplot involving the affairs of Levidulca, the wife of the baron Belforest, any ideas of sublime love become rendered as resolutely bodily desires.[58] Yet this focus on bodies pushes beyond the selfish desires that other characters exhibit. Tourneur amplifies the basic structure of this hoary setpiece (the wife's overpowering sexual desire tempts her to step outside the confines of her marriage) into an absurd conclusion: she simply desires any body, any flesh, any*thing* at all, regardless of the particularities of character or form. In fact, she does not limit her erotic imaginings to substance. When she views the forced marriage of Castabella and the sickly Rousard, she declares that "[w]hen my affection even with their cold bloods, / As snow rubb'd through an active hand does make / the flesh to burn, by agitation is / Inflam'd! I could unbrace and entertain / The air to cool it" (2.3.40–44). Such is her affection that even if she had the "cold" passions of the two would-be partners, it would be enough to enflame her "blood." The startling imagery that ends her speculation conjures the image of undressed and sexually aroused air: even the absence of bodies or, really, of anything sensible could stir her desires and prompt her to embrace the emptiness around her. Shortly thereafter she makes plans for an illicit meeting with Sebastian, but proclaims after he leaves that she could "clasp with any man" (2.3.63). The trope of the amorous housewife becomes overheated into a caricature of desire as all-consuming, but the depths of her attraction render even the air as possessing a bodily quality.

The play repeatedly suggests that bodies are *coextensive* with subjectivity, not mere shells of selfhood. Even the chaste and faithful Castabella, when she swoons over the return of her beloved Charlemont, believed dead at the siege of Ostend, celebrates his identity as a resolutely bodily phenomenon. "I feel a substance warm and soft and moist," she reports, "[s]ubject to the capacity of sense" (3.1.83–84). She has confirmed that he is not a ghost, but also celebrates his ability to be "subject to the capacity of sense"—curiously reminiscent of the Stoic definition of a body as anything that can be acted upon—and implies his identity as dependent on his physical manifestation. The ailing Rousard, when he initially forces himself on Castabella, announces as he kisses her that she is "so witty now and so sensible," to which she replies, "Tush, I would I wanted one o'my senses now" (1.3.28–29). Cheap humor such as this, reliant as it is on the ambivalence of meanings in puns, often lingers on words whose definitions diverge into physical and spiritual definitions. Thus, the "wit" that Castabella possesses recalls the now-obsolete meaning of "wit" as "sense," which Rousard employs to mean "capable of feeling," but which in her retort takes the meaning of "one of the five senses." Once we are attuned to this small rhetorical move, we see it appear everywhere in the play, often with the word "spirit" splitting into "spirit" as "ethereal being" and as "corporeal life-force." When Sebastian sees Charlemont apparently returning from the dead, to take one example, he announces, "The spirit of Charlemont? I'll try that"; after Charlemont returns his blow, he wryly notes, "'Fore God, thou sayest true; th'art all spirit" (3.2.19–26).

Another formal ambivalence centers on the word "blood," which stands both for literal, tangible blood and intemperate passions. The play, however, continually conflates them into one materialist-symbolic whole. D'Amville is frequently the source of this concatenation. Standing over Montferrers's body, he observes "the lively tincture of his blood! / Neither the dropsy nor the jaundice in't / But the true freshness of a sanguine red, / For all the fog of this black murd'rous night / has mix'd with it" (2.4.55–64). Clearly manipulating the others' eagerness for interpretation, he translates the clear blood into a sign of purity in spite of the dark happenings—which he has engineered—that have taken place. Yet elsewhere D'Amville seems to believe in the vitalist power of blood as an extension of the soul, as if literalizing the analogy into graspable reality. After he thinks he sees a ghost of Montferrers, he wishes to kill anew, so that he could gain humoral balance: "I could now commit a murder, were / It but to drink the fresh warm blood of him / I murder'd, to supply the want and weakness / O'mine own, 'tis grown so cold and phlegmatic" (4.3.240–43). The image of drinking blood, redolent of Boehrer's description of D'Amville as an antichrist, untransubstantiates into his wish to drink wine at the end of the play, a perhaps fatal decision that leads to his wobbly executioner's hand. Blood also signifies lust; again, this is a common enough metaphor, but Tourneur pursues the similarity as if it could be actualized in his staging. When Cataplasma is sentenced for running a brothel out of her house, the judge determines that "[s]ince from the spring of lust which you preserv'd / And nourish'd ran th'effusion of that blood, / Your punishment shall come as near to death / As life can bear it" (5.2.24–27). As a wellspring of passions, her home is a site of blood; so will her own actual blood, like that of her apparent victims, be threatened. Finally, Levidulca ominously advises Languebeau, who is fruitlessly trying to convince Castabella that Charlemont is unfaithful, that "you mistake the way into a woman; / The passage lies not through her reason but her blood" (1.4.65–66).

These examples all traffic in common wordplay and hardly constitute a holistic proposal of philosophical vision. But when coupled with the absence of any sign or even straightforward belief in divinity, they subtly question what inherent powers the body might possess. In addition, *The Atheist's Tragedy*, through the mouthpiece of its apparent antagonists, invokes nature as something more powerful than simply an areligious denunciation of God. In a humorous demonstration of this phenomenon, D'Amville gloats to Borachio, after Montferrers's murder, that the "power of rule philosophers ascribe / To him they call the supreme of the stars, / making their influences governors / Of sublunary creatures, when their selves / Are senseless of their operations—" only to be interrupted by thunder (2.4.136–40). Has a divine force answered his denunciation of the "philosophers' " stellar God? D'Amville quickly answers with a naturalist explanation: " 'Tis a mere effect of Nature, / An exhalation hot and dry, involv'd / Within a wat'ry vapour i'the middle / Region of the air" (2.4.141–45). Yet he does not settle entirely on a purely empiricist explanation either; instead, he decides to interpret the thunder as an omen put forth not by a God but by nature:

> 'Tis a brave noise,
> And methinks graces our accomplished
> Project as a peal of ordnance
> Does a triumph; it speaks encouragement.
> Now Nature shows thee how it favour'd our
> Performance, to forbear this noise when we
> Set forth because it should not terrify
> My brother's going home, which would have dash'd
> Our purpose. (2.4.152–64)

Like his declaration at the beginning of the play that nature is a philosophy that can be read, here D'Amville practices a kind of conspiratorial reading that allows the thunder to signify a larger approval of his plan, without tilting into spirituality or religious hermeneutics.

Of course, D'Amville does not articulate a Stoic understanding of the cosmos; his is far too solipsistic a worldview (the thunder is *for him*) to harbor a view of peaceful incomprehension in the face of an unknowable cosmic order. While D'Amville may orient our attention to the capacity for nature to carry divine properties, the play's more Stoic model of materiality occurs not in the voice or consciousness of any particular character, but in the manner of its overall presentation. It is paradoxically the thinness, in every sense, of the play's construction that calls attention to how the materiality of the stage itself becomes animated, even incarnated, by the belief of the audience.[59] This line of thinking runs dangerously close to a typical antitheatricalist attack; Anthony Munday, in "A Second and Third Blast of Retreat," suggests that the blasphemy of the theater lies in its idolatrous replacement of the church with the tiring house, since "in shows there is a certain apostasy from the faith, and a deadly declining from our belief and the heavenly sacraments. For what is the first profession of Christians at their baptism? They protest they will renounce the devil, and all his works, his pomps, and vanities."[60] Munday implies that the stage, a sort of devil's theater, rechannels the belief of the Christian away from God and onto the mere vanities that pretend to have authority. Stephen Gosson goes even further in "The School of Abuse," protesting—perhaps too much—that those vanities literally seduce the audience and replace the proper workings of their souls with a kind of sickness. In theaters, writes Gosson, poets

> abroach strange consorts of melody, to tickle the ear; costly apparel, to flatter the sight; effeminate gesture, to ravish the sense; and wanton speech, to whet desire to inordinate lust . . . these by the privy entries of the ear slip down into the heart, and with gunshot of affection gall the mind, where reason and virtue should rule the roost.[61]

In a reversal of the holy spirit's entrance into Mary's ears, the desires manufactured by the theaters slip into "the privy entries of the ear" and drive out reason and virtue. The plays produce a mode of madness, as a result, that resembles a perverted faith.

And yet, as we have seen, reason is not necessary for proper faith, nor must faith necessarily disavow materialism. Gosson and Munday avoid the considerations of materiality espoused by Paul and the Stoics and equate the mimicry of the stage with outright idolatry. But Tourneur invites a continual meditation on his play's bodies—those same bodies that become the devil's workings—as leading neither to spiritual deliverance *nor* to decline. The play, in short, can be forthrightly obvious and dramatically simple, by our standards—and by those of the time—but this does not necessarily make it inferior, despite its array of critical dismissals. Even more charitable readers, like Algernon Charles Swinburne, conceded that aspects of the play were "painted, though rapidly and slightly," with a "firmness of hand and tenderness of touch."[62] The verb is telling—the play does occasionally feel painted, as if bent on flattening its figures and *mise-en-scène* into straightforwardly digestible allegories or thematic pictures. Katharine Eisaman Maus identifies this as a deliberate dramaturgical strategy, noting that "*The Atheist's Tragedy* prominently features emblematic or allegorical moments that assert the correspondence between spiritual and material truths, between heavenly and mundane realms, between God and human beings."[63] The play's employment of exemplarity, its insistence on lucid visual declarations of moral purpose, compensates, in some estimations, for its lack of complexity or intellectual demands placed on the audience. Irving Ribner assesses the play along these lines in his introduction to the Revels edition, declaring that if the play is

> seen in terms of a moral *exemplum* by which Tourneur seeks to embody certain Christian principles . . . the structure and meaning of *The Atheist's Tragedy* are very clear, and what otherwise might appear as a play about mechanical, lifeless characters involved in absurd situations comes to have some artistic merit in terms of its dramatic medium.[64]

The merit of the play arises from Tourneur's deliberate choice to favor the embodiment of principle over dramatic propulsion. Alison Shell takes this estimation further by suggesting that "one needs to understand exemplarity not as failed individuation but as a legitimate choice for a dramatist to make: one which maximizes the clarity of artifice, and points towards the power of types to affect real-life behavior."[65] She compares this device to those of medieval morality plays, which by definition resist granularity by employing allegory and attempt to invoke spiritual reverence from their audiences.

In a play that specifically questions belief, and which gives surprisingly no forthright endorsement of a belief system reliant on an immaterial power, the use of exemplarity gains another salutary effect. It demands a reckoning with the materiality of its staging. One salient method by which it makes this demand is its continual use of bodies as props to create emblematic tableaux that emphasize the lack of interiority to both its characters or its themes. The "emblematic" scenes, which actualize Swinburne's vision of painted characters, accrue largely in the play's second half and are clearly delineated in the stage directions. When Charlemont, in the graveyard, attempts to hide in the charnel house because he hears Languebeau approaching, he "*takes hold of a death's head; it slips and staggers him*"; he immediately offers a homiletic gloss: "Death's head, deceiv'st my hold? / Such is the trust to all mortality" (4.3.78–80). Soon after, when he and Castabella decide to sleep in the graveyard, they "*lie down with either of them a death's head for a pillow*" and once again elicit interpretation from D'Amville when he discovers them: "Stay. Asleep? So soundly? And so sweetly upon death's heads? And in a place so full of fear and horror? Sure there is some other happiness within the freedom of the conscience than my knowledge e'er attained to" (4.3.204sd, 4.3.284–87). The stage pictures pile up; act 5 opens with D'Amville's servant sleeping in front of a pile of gold, in front of which his dead sons will soon be wheeled—one can almost imagine the caption to an engraving: "*The wages of avarice.*"

Aural emblems abound, as well, as with Sebastian's extended ekphrasis on the needlework in Cataplasma's house. He sees a pear tree next to a plum tree, each suggestive of genitalia, and expounds on the extensive details while he weaves together his interpretation, replete with a snail that stands for sexual potency and laziness, whose horns suggest cuckoldry, a tree bending toward the river out of narcissistic love, and a stream flowing "like a strumpet" (4.1.23–42). When the "strumpet" of the play, Levidulca, dies, she bemoans her metatheatrical fate: "Must my life / Be made the world's example?" The watch, when they discover her, answer with a resounding yes by immediately translating her body into visual signification: "O with what virtue lust should be withstood, / Since 'tis a fire quench'd seldom without blood" (4.5.90–91). When Charlemont, in prison, questions the operations of divine justice, he wonders if his suffering is disproportionate to his crime because he is tasked with teaching "the barb'rous world / Examples that extend her cruelties / Beyond their own dimensions" (3.3.8–10). Like the plants in the needlework composition, he realizes his body's fate to be translated into meaning.

Tourneur foregrounds, again and again, a flattened scene, all while demonstrating how meaning can still be—*must* be—extracted. Yet this game of visual interpretation takes place within the broader visual field of the theater. The constant attempt to read meaning into the material world thus doubles the efforts of the audience to sustain attention and, more abstractly, to sustain the entire artifice *of* the theater—not an artifice of licentious devilry, as Munday would have it, but a material manifestation of their belief. And as a work of theater, rather than prose or illustration, the play demands that its material world act as an overcharged cosmos of objects that resists epistemological challenge and instead relies on the awakening of faith, occasioned by attention, of its audience. This is true, surely, of any work of theater, but Tourneur constantly calls our attention to his use of artifice, example, and emblematization while simultaneously reminding us of the stage's irreducible tangibility. The result is a play that savors the power of its materiality by charting a middle way between the atheist's dismantling of divinity and the Platonist's investment in the insubstantial. We are trained to see the world as the Stoic does—interconnected, holistic, and energized, as if it were an ongoing performance playing out before our eyes.

Chapter Five

Othello's Slave

In a notorious 2018 interview with the gossip website *TMZ*, the rapper and producer Kanye West opined that the 400-year history of slavery in the United States could have been curtailed, had the slaves simply freed themselves:

> 400 years? That sounds like a choice. You was there for 400 years and it's all of y'all. It's like we're mentally in prison. I like the word prison because slavery goes too direct to the idea of blacks. Slavery is to blacks as the Holocaust is to Jews. Prison is something that unites as one race, blacks and whites, that we're the human race.[1]

West's comments, which immediately sparked widespread disgust and rebuke, hinge on the conflation of two senses of the word "slavery"—on the one hand, the abstract sense of enslavement to a particular mindset, ideology, or object; on the other, the legal and historical enslavement that renders a subject as property through involuntary labor and submission. By imagining chattel slavery as a byproduct of conceptual slavery, West engages in a fantasy of contingency wherein one need only break out of their "mental" imprisonment to escape from their forced servitude. Thus his aversion to even the word "slavery," and his preference for "prison," a term he deems more suitable as it encompasses a more universal experience.

This egregious misunderstanding has classical roots. Epictetus, in his *Discourses*, observes that "whenever you see someone groveling to another person or flattering him insincerely, you can confidently say that this man is also not free"; he advises his interlocutor to label "people who act like this for small things petty slaves, and call the others, as they deserve, slaves on a grand scale." In short, he asserts that "freedom is something in one's own power and self-determined."[2] This opinion is both natural when viewed against Stoic principles—if slavery is outside of one's control, it is mere *adiaphora*, to be shrugged off as with all such hindrances—and striking, given Epictetus's own history as a freed slave. In John Sanford's translation of the *Manual*, Epictetus's thoughts on freedom gain a Christian gloss. Borrowing an ancient metaphor, the philosopher equates life with a voyage on a ship: "I understand the shippe, either to be Philosophie, or the trade of our life: the ruler and maister of the Shippe to be GOD: to whom when he calleth, who so obeyeth not either is entreted as a slave, or else is utterly forsaken."[3] With language that anticipates Saint Paul's endorsement of spiritual bondage, Epictetus calls for a proper mode of slavery that yokes one's personhood to a higher power rather than to any quotidian concern. Elsewhere, he clarifies this sense of freedom untethered to material oppression: "He is Master and Lord of any man, to whome (nil he will he) he maye either give or take awaye. He then which will be free, let him neither desire, nor flee any thing, which is in an other man hys hande, and power, otherwise of necessitie he shal be constrained to serve."[4]

But West's version of Stoicism touches on the particular history of Black Americans, insofar as he views the terms as inextricable: slavery "goes too direct to the idea of blacks." He seizes on a particularly racialized understanding of slavery, one irreducible to a universal condition of bondage and whose afterlife powerfully contributes to the social and economic structures that stubbornly linger in American life. This conception of slavery as inseparable from Blackness finds its elegant and haunting formulation in the journalist Nikole Hannah-Jones's observation that, aboard the slave ships headed toward Jamestown, Virginia, in 1619, the captured West Africans "had been made black."[5] The middle passage, as Hortense Spillers puts it, is not so much a geographical or temporal phenomenon as an ontological one that burrows into the subjectivity of Black American life by rendering bodies as "flesh," a "zero degree of social conceptualization."[6] Slavery, in this view, is less a merely historical instance than it is a building block of civil society dependent on the disenfranchisement and dehumanization of Black subjects into mere flesh. By invoking slavery, then, in an American context, as a Black American, and at a time in which slavery's inheritance has been linked to discriminatory policing, unjust housing practices, and numerous efforts of economic bias, West yokes an Epictetan liberatory gesture to a racialized reality incapable of liberation from mere mental rearrangement. The Stoic conception of slavery as freedom from desire, alongside its Neo-Stoic adaptation as a favorable slavery to God, becomes toxic when combined with a mode of slavery that cannot be shrugged away.

This chapter examines a different site of this collision of mental and physical servitude: Shakespeare's *Othello*, which steeps itself in debates about slavery's multiple valences as a form of service, a function of race, and a giving-over to emotional volatility. The play's conception of race is famously slippery: Othello himself has been framed as "monstrous," as akin to an aristocratic Mediterranean ambassador, as foremost an Islamic convert, as a mercenary whose skin color is secondary to his military rank.[7] Critical debates have long concerned how these multiple categories overlap or fail to intersect: can we think of slavery, or servitude, in the play as coextensive with race? Is Othello's status overdetermined as a Northern African, or is his tragedy rooted in his overweening passions and fomenting sexual envy? Complicating matters is Othello's own self-conscious staging of his exoticism, as found in his stories, so enticing to Desdemona and Brabantio, that position him among the pseudo-mythological travel literature of the era, though the precise border between his racial performativity and the racial status imposed by others remains vaguely defined.[8] But it is this self-aestheticization that opens up *Othello* to consideration as a Stoic drama, concerned as it is with rendering the self as spectacle in order to master the passions. This Stoic conception of mastery, then, also threads through the play alongside its other understandings of bondage, though its inclusion is less noted. Othello, I contend, embarks on a doomed arc of Stoic consolation, modeled on early modern adaptations of Seneca and Epictetus, and Christianized by its focus on spiritual bondage and rebirth; this trajectory, far from remaining separate from the play's other modes of slavery—race and servitude—provides a sticking-point for both. In other words, reading the play as a failed Stoic exercise of control allows us to reconsider how the fantasy of contingent slavery imagined by West and Epictetus *still* entails material slavery, and a racialized mode of slavery at that, despite its aspirations toward a universalism of cognitive liberation. Othello believes he can learn to perform Stoic self-mastery, but his status as an apparently redeemed slave, alongside the Blackness that attends this designation both tacitly and legibly, prevents the successful completion of this program and allows instead for his corruption and submission to his passions—and, more tellingly, to the erasure of his history.

The Curse of Service

What is the difference between a slave and a servant? In Shakespeare's time, the former could simply be an extreme example of the latter. John Baret's 1580 dictionary, *An Alvearie*, defines a "bondman" as anyone "that is borne in our owne house, of our servaunt and slave."[9] Michael Neill points out that the Latin *servus* could refer to either term. The greater distinction for early modern era understandings of service, Neill posits, is between involuntary service and the virtuous enactment of service as a realization of duty; one could serve as an expression of "the sublime virtue of voluntary obedience" and thus be a liberal, or "free," servant, as opposed to a "servile" one taken through war or ransom."[10] In the Venice of *Othello*, servitude of all stripes would be a common sight. Gaspar Contrareno's *The Commonwealth and Government of Venice*, a text thought to have been consulted by Shakespeare in writing the play, describes servitude in relation to proper citizenship. Venice, Contrareno explains, "standeth in neede of artificers [that is, artisans] and many mercenarie people, and hired servants, of which none can bee truely tearmed a citizen: for a citizen is a free man, but those are all servile, eyther privately or publickly: for mercenarie men & artificers, are to be accounted as publique servants."[11]

For Contrareno, the servant—those who are, echoing Neill's terminology, "servile," in distinction to the liberal servitude of the soldier or statesman—are withheld from citizenship because they are not "free," as opposed to those potential limit cases, the mercenary and the artisan. While he does not employ the term "slave" in his text, slavery in the modern sense would be an everyday phenomenon, as Virginia Mason Vaughan points out: "By the early sixteenth century, the presence of black servants in Venice would have been commonplace."[12] Are these Black slaves subsumed here under the sign of "servitude," or are they invisible in Contrareno's reckoning, unmentioned because so obviously noncitizens, nonsubjects? The further question of whether, at this time, "slave" operates as a racialized term is complicated by the geographic differences in slavery's implementation as an institution. England prided itself on not having slaves, as noted in William Harrison's famous account in *The Description of England*:

> As for slaves and bondsman, we have none; nay, such is the privilege of our country by the especial grace of God and bounty of our princes that if any come hither from other realms, so soon as they set foot on land they become so free of condition as their masters, whereby all note of servile bondage is utterly removed from them.[13]

Such, at least, was the self-mythologizing story. According to Vaughan, however, slaves certainly inhabited England, if not technically, then practically speaking, as "household servants, prostitutes, and court entertainers."[14] One imagines that an early modern English audience could have a generalized immediate reference to the slaves referred to by Shylock, in Shakespeare's *The Merchant of Venice*, who in the trial scene spitefully denies offers of supposed "mercy" by noting that "You have among you many a purchased slave, / Which, like your asses, and your dogs and mules, / You use in abject and slavish parts, / Because you bought them."[15] Alive to the potentially violent implications of Christian mercy and empathy, Shylock equates his potential "liberation" from the terms of his bond—itself another valence of servitude—to the unthinkable liberation of his tormentors' slaves. Here, we have a startlingly contemporary understanding of slavery, one that anticipates Spillers's distinction of body and flesh; by claiming he would no sooner give up his promised pound than the Duke would give up his slaves, Shylock gives us a glimpse of a moral calculus—one that he imagines operant within the souls of the Christians—that equates slave to mere matter, as dehumanized and inanimate as a severed piece of human meat.

While Black slaves may not officially have lived in England until a century after the slave trade began on the Iberian Peninsula, England began partaking in slavery as a profiteering enterprise overseas as early as the reign of Henry VIII. Imtiaz Habib, in his monumental study *Black Lives in the English Archives, 1500–1677*, suggests that, while the term "slave" grew more specifically racialized in continental practice (he points out that in Portuguese it became nearly synonymous with "blackamore"), early modern English slavery was "a shadowy terrain, denied in contemporary accounts, contradictorily treated in legal rulings of the time, and, in consequence, uncertainly regarded in current historical scholarship." Historical records are filled with "official denials of English slavery" like Harrison's, which were in fact "fed by an anxious national English Protestant culture straining to differentiate itself from what it holds to be corrupt Catholic cultural practices."[16] During Shakespeare's day, then, slavery and Blackness were not necessarily coextensive, though neither were they epistemologically divorced.

Othello appears in this "shadowy" time of English slavery and servitude, where the terms began forking into more concrete and specifically racial connotations, but still retained traces of their classical kinship.[17] The enslavement of Black Africans occurred at the edges of English cultural consciousness, palpable in its presence but unmarked in the official archive. One could be a "slave" because they were robbed of their humanity, or because they served a particular household—or simply because they earned a term of derision. The England of *Othello*'s initial performances, then, stood on the brink of Blackness and slavery's semantic entwinement; the play thus registers not a definitive statement as to their relation so much as an embodiment of the shifting cultural forces at play. As Ian Smith puts it, *Othello* "not only registers changing notions of race, but also presents them simultaneously, holding them in tension for the audience to grasp the trending shifts and developments in racial thinking."[18] Furthermore, the drama of the era, drawing on Roman dramaturgical models, retains the nonracialized sense of slavery as bond service, a conditional state of servitude that gave birth to the archetypal "clever slave" of city comedy. It is Iago, of course, who takes up this mantle, as noted by Stephen Greenblatt, who claims that Iago, though nominally below Othello in rank, practices a "mastery invisible to the servant, a mastery, that is, whose character is essentially ideological"; in this way his "subordination is a kind of protection, for it conceals his power and enables him to play upon the ambivalence of Othello's relation to Christian society: the Moor at once represents the institution and the alien, the conqueror and the infidel."[19] Iago is, in this formulation, the patient zero of Greenblatt's New Historicism, and he makes an ideal standard-bearer—a cipher constructing himself from a patchwork of extant identities, he represents a heightened version of the ways by which subjectivity itself, in Greenblatt's influential reckoning, always reinscribes itself in dominant discursive regimes. Like Mosca, in Ben Jonson's Venetian comedy *Volpone*, Iago finds in servitude a trickster-like grammar of manipulation and subversion, couched in behavior coded as inferior and in anticipation of a liberation into subjectivity that depends only on a change of economic or meritorious circumstance.

Othello, in contrast, is a servant to the state, a former slave, and, when the play opens, an official master of sorts to Iago. But the play troubles any neat categorizations of Othello and Iago along the lines of servitude or slavery, just as it refuses to declare any clear relation of race to bondage. In its first two scenes, we witness Iago ruing his condition of undeserved service and Othello proclaiming his worth as husband to Desdemona. And yet Iago's servitude depends, as Greenblatt notes, on a coiled sense of mastery, and Othello's superiority was born from his narrative as a freed slave. The dialogue between Roderigo and Iago that opens *Othello* introduces the unsteady flicker by which subservience can turn into power; Iago, after complaining to Roderigo of Cassio's advancement, critiques a social order that fails to honor individual natures. Announcing that he will obey Othello only "to serve my turn upon him," he then notes that "[w]e cannot all be masters, nor all masters / Cannot be truly followed. You shall mark / Many a duteous and knee-crooking knave / That, doting on his own obsequious bondage, / Wears out his time much like his master's ass / For nought but provender, and, when he's old, cashiered" (1.1.41–47).[20] Iago's rebellion, in his eyes, acts as a form of justice: rather than serve his whole life only for "provender," for mere sustenance, he will take on the role of the devious servant in order to effect righteous change. In his worldview, mastery is not something open to all, though the arbitrary nature of advancement, ignorant of merit, shunts natural masters like Iago into roles of servitude, while rewarding those not naturally inclined to lead—the implication is that Othello is such an impostor—with prestige. It is this condition that he sneeringly calls "the curse of service": one may work to deserve recognition, but ultimately such attention depends on the whims of someone who may not be fit to calculate it (1.1.34). In finishing his taxonomy, he clarifies his deceptive role and frames it as both natural and virtuous:

> Others there are / Who, trimmed in forms and visages of duty, / Keep yet their hearts attending on themselves / And, throwing but shows of service on their lords, / Do well thrive by them, and, when they have lined their coats, / Do themselves homage: these fellows have some soul / And such a one do I profess myself (1.1.48–54).

In wordplay reminiscent of the "spirit" that snakes its way through *The Atheist's Tragedy*, Iago claims that with the spark of "soul," an animating force that impels them beyond the inertia of knee-crooking knavery, the deceptive servant who looks after themselves while performing an artificial brand of duty embodies the proper mode of servitude when societal reward fails to align with nature.

Iago thus repurposes the wily Plautine slave as an agent bent on the reinstantiation of a just order. And yet he appears to deny the naked self-advancement that motivates the classically comedic model of servitude. Instead, he obscures the motives of his deception, explaining cryptically that

> Were I the Moor, I would not be Iago.
> In following him I follow but myself:
> Heaven is my judge, not I for love and duty
> But seeming so, for my peculiar end,
> For when my outward action doth demonstrate
> The native act and figure of my heart
> In complement extern, 'tis not long after
> But I will wear my heart upon my sleeve
> For daws to peck at: I am not what I am. (1.1.56–64)

The first lines, hinting at chiasmus but denying any neat rhetorical symmetry, echo the lack of order that Iago perceives in his station. Were Iago

Othello, he would not want to be Iago; the currents of desire only run upward in the chain of command. But when he *does* follow Othello, he follows himself, as he follows his own plan to attain the deserved compensation denied by the role he has been assigned—so effectively he actually *is* the Moor, at least in this scheme, even though he professes he is not. Curiously, it is "heaven" that will judge him, not himself—or, at least, this is the narrative he tells Roderigo. The description of his deception occurs within the frame of a confession, a testimony that privileges Roderigo as the sole possessor of a conspiratorial truth: only *you* know how I really feel; you may see me behave one way in "outward action," but in fact I feel another in the "native act and figure of my heart." The ending claim "I am not what I am" infamously profanes the statement by God in Exodus, "I am that I am"; Iago here colors the classical model of servitude with the blasphemous character of Vice, the tempter.

We learn shortly that this confession is itself a gulling device to prompt Roderigo to accost Brabantio's household with news of Desdemona's marriage. It is telling that Iago frames this disruptive act as an act of service, aimed at avoiding a further perversion of the natural order. "Zounds, sir," he shouts to Brabantio, "you are one of those that will not serve God, if the devil bid you. Because we come to do you service, and you think we are ruffians, you'll have your daughter covered with a Barbary horse; you'll have your nephews neigh to you, you'll have coursers for cousins and jennets for germans!" (1.1.107–12). As with his rueful description of false masters and deserving servants, Iago here frames "service" as something dependent on will, while naturalizing that will as the result of proper fealty to a higher power—heaven, nature, God. Brabantio would not do something proper and faithful (serve God) if he distrusted the figure encouraging him to do so (the "devil"); likewise he refuses the noble service of Iago and Roderigo simply because he believes they are "ruffians."

Iago's mock-confidential conversation with Roderigo foresees freedom from Othello's supposedly feckless rule and the inheritance of deserved liberation. In this sense, Iago's speech operates, in broad strokes, as a blueprint for the story we will shortly hear about Othello's emancipation—or, more accurately, the story about the stories *about* his emancipation. Like Iago's carefully crafted confession of deception, which engineers confidence on Roderigo's part, Othello reassures the senators of Venice that he seduced Desdemona with tales of his background culled liberally from popular and fantastic early modern travel narratives. In the speech that precedes this defense, however, Othello confides to Iago that his own "service" will counter Brabantio's slander—and that by sharing his service, he avoids imprisonment:

> My services, which I have done the signiory,
> Shall out-tongue his complaints. 'Tis yet to know—
> Which, when I know that boasting is an honour,
> I shall promulgate—I fetch my life and being
> From men of royal siege, and my demerits
> May speak unbonneted to as proud a fortune
> As this that I have reached. For know, Iago,
> But that I love the gentle Desdemona
> I would not my unhoused free condition
> Put into circumscription and confine
> For the sea's worth. (1.2.18–28)

The logic on display here hinges on service as a commodity, like honor to D'Amville in *The Atheist's Tragedy*, a resource that Othello hoards for the sake of appearing humble but can reveal strategically to balance the damage of "complaints." At stake in sharing these services—which we shortly learn are the stories of Othello's capture, freedom, and travels—is nothing less than Othello's freedom; here, one sense of "service" (conscription, imprisonment) threatens to replace another (noble and selfless favors). Like Iago, Othello instrumentalizes service as a means of maintaining liberty, though he betrays more faith in the clear correlation of that service to its reward.

Slavery, however, hovers over Othello's use of the word, in a way that it fails to do in Iago's disquisitions. The term appears when Othello recounts the stories he told Brabantio—which Desdemona overheard in "parcels"—and describes "moving accidents by flood and field, / Of hair-breadth scapes i'th' imminent deadly breach, / Of being taken by the insolent foe / And sold to slavery; of my redemption hence / And portance in my travailous history" (1.3.135–40). Yet while the story climaxes in liberation and "redemption," the language of bondage persists in the play's portrait of Othello's love of Desdemona—precisely the condition that Othello sees as a celebration of an "unhoused free condition." When Brabantio accuses Othello of having "enchanted" Desdemona, he borrows the language of enslavement, justifying his pronouncement by claiming that if "she in chains of magic were not bound, / Whether a maid so tender, fair and happy, / So opposite to marriage that she shunned / The wealthy, curled darlings of our nation, / Would ever have, t'incur a general mock, / Run from her guardage to the sooty bosom / Of such a things as thou? to fear, not to delight" (1.2.63–71). Othello, the former slave, is now in Brabantio's eyes the enslaver, the devilish, "sooty" demon who enchained her with a curse. Desdemona, then, in Brabantio's telling, lives out Othello's tale of redemption in reverse: rather than being redeemed out of slavery, she is corrupted into it. Later, in an aside, Iago observes that Othello's "soul is so enfettered to her love / That she may make, unmake, do what she list" (2.3.340–41). Thus, Othello's marriage, as Urvashi Chakravarty observes, "*returns* him to a state of slavery," at least metaphorically.[21] Brabantio's damning couplet, issued to dismiss the Duke's summons of Othello after the news of the Turkish fleet, further perpetuates the link between Othello and slavery: if "actions" like his daughter's marriage "may have passage free, / Bond-slaves and pagans shall our statesmen be" (1.2.98–99). Borrowing from Iago's slanderous "Barbary horse" formulation, Brabantio lays out what he sees as the monstrous consequences of normalizing this coupling. Bond-slaves, denied citizenship by the state, shall become equal to nobility; one mode of service, as practiced by slaves—involuntary, coerced, unrecompensed—will be made equivalent to its opposite and dignified sense, as practiced by statesmen—liberally enacted, virtuous.

These opening scenes render "service" as a multivalent term while highlighting its many semantic fissures and contradictions. For Iago, proper service operates as an extension of will, a corrective against the capricious nature of socially determined placement. Othello, by contrast, frames service as a check against the ever-present threat of returning to slavery, which is itself a more pernicious sense of the word that attends Othello despite or because of his apparent liberation. *Othello*, then, begins with a profound investigation of how "proper" service, freely conducted and nobly intended, constitutes more of a horizon than an actual civic element. In practical terms, servitude and mastery are skills, practices to be perfected, rather than reflections of a natural or just world. Furthermore, the play suggests, while never directly naming it as such, that service cryptically relates to race. As Smith and others have pointed out, the play lacks a stable reference point for the nature of Othello's Blackness, while also refusing to discount race as a vital factor in its designation of humanity and social power. Othello's status as, in Roderigo's words, an "extravagant and wheeling stranger / Of here and everywhere" both places and displaces him as other, non-Venetian, while also establishing his humanistic potential as a self-made man (1.1.134–35). Yet his Christianized language and military experience vault him into authoritative ranks. While Brabantio refuses to see Othello as a peer to statesmen, he is nonetheless accepted by them, at least professionally—and yet hateful language, demonizing him and rendering him bestial, doggedly follows him.

The subterranean ways that Othello's servitude entails race operate as an offshoot of the "shadowy" ways that the play both insists on and obscures his exact racial identity. As such, as difficult as it is to pinpoint his race, as surveyed earlier, it has proven harder still to link that race to his status as freed slave. On the one hand, as Habib points out, the connection of Blackness to slavery existed in the cultural ambience, if not—as Harrison protests—forthrightly as a part of English political identity. Jonathan Gil Harris points out that slavery could, in Shakespearean drama, operate as metonym of Blackness, as when Aaron the Moor addresses his son as a "black slave" in *Titus Andronicus*.[22] Emily Weissbourd, in a comparative study of *Othello* and early modern Spanish drama, notes that while "blackness on the Elizabethan and Jacobean stage is often linked to evil, in the Spanish *comedia* it is most frequently associated with slavery."[23] This creeping continental association of race to slavery seems at the fringes of *Othello*'s drama, tacitly operating while never legibly stated. Many scholars, such as Neill, Emily Bartels, and Camille Wells Slights, have staged persuasive, skeptical critiques of this connection; in Slights's words, slavery in the play "is represented not as a manifestation of individual or racial inferiority but as a result of military and financial exigencies."[24] With an attentive ear to the many ways slavery could act as simply an extension of, rather than threat to, service, Slights and others expand slavery to encompass less a clear racial designation and more a contingent mode of bondage that anyone could experience.[25] Another narrative of mastery and slavery, however, weaves through the play—a narrative borrowed from Stoicism, which depends heavily on notions of mastering the passions and thus mastering the self. This framework seems metaphorical, and indeed frames itself in Stoic writing as loftily removed from actual slavery; however, when on display in *Othello*, Stoic practices of slavery and mastery cannot help but bring to the fore a connection to race missing from accounts of servitude that focus solely on military and civic duty.

The Cursed Slave

What binds together Iago's and Othello's visions of service, different though they may be, is their conviction that service does not follow a natural order. It must instead be manipulated, commodified, enacted. By proposing this vision of servitude, both Iago and Othello share in Stoicism's rejection of Aristotle's vision—shocking to our contemporary sensibilities—of slavery as an organic state of being, one necessary to the function of any proper society. In contrast, according to Peter Garnsey, the Stoics sought to dissociate slavery as a material practice and instead abstract it into a philosophical concept. The Stoics, explains Garnsey, "far from continuing the debate over natural slavery" that characterized Plato and Aristotle, "redefined slavery and freedom as properties of the mind or soul, thereby removing at a stroke the 'need' to justify or question legal slavery, or investigate its origins."[26] As a result, in "the post-classical period moral slavery, or slavery of the soul, is given priority," though simultaneously the actual practice of slavery is "never far away," since the Stoic "needed legal slavery to show what 'true' slavery was *not*."[27] Here we return to Epictetus's distinction of physical slavery as an indifferent and focus the philosopher's attention instead on slavery to the passions, a form of bondage that can be broken by anyone, should they commit themselves to rigorous *askesis*. The legal institution of slavery needed to exist to demonstrate to the Stoic that it was not real slavery at all. Instead, as an extreme negative example, it provides a limit case for what the soul should withstand in the name of pursuing sagacity.

It is this belief—that freedom can be achieved by anyone—that provides the fodder for Cicero's fifth entry in *Stoic Paradoxes*, which states, in Thomas Newton's 1569 translation, that "only a wyse man" who "doth nothinge agaynste hys wil, nothing grudgingly, nothyng by compulsion" can be truly liberated: "no man is free but hee whiche is thus disposed and affected: and therfore all naughty persons are slaues and bondmen."[28] Iago, by stating his conviction that his deception provides a necessary means for the realization of proper reward, proposes a similar justification: the real slave is not the person whose lot in life is cast as subservient, but instead he who accepts that destiny without fully achieving his potential. In fact, Iago and Roderigo's discussion of merit, which opens the play, draws not only on the Ciceronian paradox of "the curse of service" but on a debate Seneca stages in his *On Benefits* over several entries. Framed as a debate, Seneca's piece takes up the question as to whether a slave can properly do a favor for their master. The precise distinction made by Lodge, in his early modern translation, is among "benefits," "duty," and "service," even though lines of separation wobble as he attempts to delineate them:

> That certaine thinges are benefits; certaine, duties; and certain, services. They say that we ought to call that a benefit which we receive from a stranger, and we terme him a stranger that is not borne to doe us any pleasure, except he please. They name that, dutie, which appertaineth properly to a Sonne, a Wife, and those persons who are provoked by alliance, and tied by office, to assist. They terme that, service, which belongeth to a slave or bondman, who is

> brought to this exigent by the condition of his fortune, so that he cannot in any sort challenge his Superior for any thing, whatsoever hee hath done unto him.[29]

"Benefits," Seneca maintains, must be performed by a stranger, one who stands to gain nothing from their actions. "Duties," in contrast, name the due fulfillment of expected assistance by a family member or associate. Finally, "service" is simply the behavior by a slave who performs his function under threat from his superior. What characterizes different modes of giving, then, is not anything inherent to the action; rather, they are contingent on the performer. Slaves cannot truly give freely; thus, they cannot perform service. But after some debate the interlocutor challenges this view, claiming that the slave's position of inferiority in fact valorizes their attempts at benefits all the more. Thus, when a slave "surpasseth the termes of his miserable fortune, and performeth some extraordinairie and brave enterprise, which might bee held honorable in one more happily borne, and surmounteth the hope and expectation of his Master, then is it a benefit."[30] The slave, then, can still be free: in fact, their service is *superior* because of its apparent lack of necessity. It is the slave's a priori status of "stranger"—realized in Othello's free-wheeling estrangement, of here and there—that entitles them to the purity of beneficial acts. When a slave serves their master extraordinarily well, beyond what is expected, the service must be freely given, as it is without expectation of recompense. Seneca does not propose a proto-Hegelian account of dialectic emancipation, but instead redefines what constitutes slavery at all. A true slave, one of the speakers announces at the close of the debate, is not one forced into labor but one tempted into passion: "Doest thou call any one a servant, thou being a servant of lust and of gluttonie, and of an adulteresse, yea a common slave of adulteresses? Callest thou any one a servant?"[31]

Lipsius, slightly recontextualizing this classical debate as one concerned with the more early modern topic of free speech, places Seneca's closing sentiment in the mouth of Langius, once again chiding the literary Lipsius for allowing his temperament to be shaken by external circumstances. Langius offers a declension of freedoms that constricts the frame of subjectivity inward to the sole faculty of the mind that no outward force can ever touch—judgment. "A man may have power upon this bonde or fetter of the minde, but not over the mind it self," he explains; while a tyrant may have "power to loose it from the body, but not unloose the nature therof. Such things as bee pure, everlasting, and of fierie nature, set nought by al external & violent handling. But (saist thou) it is not lawfull for mee to expresse my mind freely. Be it so: herein thy tongue alone is bridled, not thy mind. Thy judgment is not restrained, but thy acts."[32] A tyrant or master can restrict the expression of the mind and the body, but judgment, that crucial faculty to exercising reason, will not be corrupted. Physical and legal slavery, as Garnsey explains, becomes a repeated motif in these Stoic discussions as an example of false slavery, an entrapment of only the body.

Othello takes place perched on the tectonic line between enforced servitude and enslaved reason, often weaving the two modes of slavery together, as when Iago protests to Othello, while the latter presses further on whether Iago believes Desdemona is unfaithful, that "[t]hough I am bound to every act of duty / I am not bound to that all slaves are free to—Utter my thoughts?" (3.3.136–39). For Iago, one form of bondage, the "duty" of an ancient, chafes against another, the freedom of thinking. So, too, does Lodovico compact these modes of slavery in his lamentation upon witnessing the ruination at the close of the play: "O thou Othello, that wert once so good, / Fallen in practice of a cursed slave, / What shall be said to thee?" (5.2.288–90). Othello is, to Lodovico, both slave to his overweening rage and—as hinted at by the evocation of his formerly "good" and redeemed self—fallen back into his slavery as subjugated property. Seen in this light, the opening debates on servitude and slavery mirror the Stoic discussions of mastery while mobilizing their philosophical conclusions to different ends. Neither Iago nor Othello remains content to possess freedom of their reason while living under subservience—this is the dutiful life, sneered at by Iago, of the servant, content for only provender. Othello, likewise, refuses to have Desdemona taken from him and instead exchanges his service to Brabantio for the maintenance of his freedom from the Duke—helped, no doubt, by the sudden need for his military expertise in Cyprus. And yet the impetus to take action, to fight against forced servitude, also externalizes the Stoic impulse toward mastering the passions. Both Iago and Othello see their liberation as an extension of their inward progression toward reason: for Othello, his "unhoused free condition" is one where he can pursue his love, not one where he merely attaches himself to false affection; according to Iago, his ultimate judge is heaven, not his own sense of satisfaction or accomplishment.

The question of race and slavery—the question that Othello's scenes nearly bring into consciousness without ever rendering completely visible—gains more clarity when viewed alongside a Stoic understanding of freedom. If true slavery is slavery to the passions, then an early modern understanding of slavery gains firmer reference to race, and particularly to Blackness; by binding Othello's anger to his identity as a Moor—or, more accurately, by articulating the ways in which this linkage is enforced by the other characters—the play proposes that Othello, in his attempts to gain mastery over his passions, is overdetermined to fail because of the naturally "hot" temperament of his ethnicity. The paradigmatic account of this trope arises in Leo Africanus's *Geographical Historie of Africa*, where he notes of the "Arabians which inhabit in Barbarie or upon the Mediterran sea" that "[n]o nation in the world is so subiect vnto iealousie; for they will rather leese their liues, then put vp any disgrace in the behalfe of their women. So desirous they are of riches and honour, that therein no other people can goe beyonde them."[33] Robert Burton references this passage in the section "Causes of Jealousy" of his *Anatomy of Melancholy*, first noting that "southern men are more hot, lascivious, and jealous than such as live in the north; they can hardly contain themselves in those hotter climes, but are most subject to prodigious lust," before invoking the "incredible things" told by "Leo Afer" concerning the "lust and jealousy of his countrymen of Africa, and especially as live about Carthage, and so doth every geographer of them in Asia, Turkey, Spaniards, Italians."[34] Burton's praise of Africanus as a purveyor of tales links the travel writer to Othello, whose tales enrapture Brabantio and move Desdemona to pity; as Ania Loomba notes, Africanus, a Moor, may have been similarly indulging in the self-conscious typing of his experience as a way to gain the confidence of his audience. Othello, Loomba writes, "consolidates his own position in Venice by establishing his distance from cannibals and monsters whom he has overcome, and Turks whom he has fought and will continue to combat; similarly, Africanus establishes himself as a reliable historiographer by reproducing dominant notions about dark-skinned 'negroes' as well as African women."[35] Yet even as the play is sensitive to the ways that Othello fashions his own travel narrative as a socially permissible projection of himself, it also teeters close to validating a vision of naturalized jealousy. Over and over, we are told of Othello's passion and his inability to conquer it. In the climactic moment before he strangles Desdemona, she notes, horrified, "[s]ome bloody passion" that "shakes your very frame" (5.2.44). The description realizes the vision put forth by Lodovico, who, shocked to see Othello strike his wife, wonders rhetorically. is "this the noble Moor whom our full senate / Call all in all sufficient? This is the nature / Whom passion could not shake? whose solid virtue / The shot of accident nor dart of chance / Could neither graze nor pierce? (4.1.265–68). Lodovico had been told—reassured, more likely—that Othello could not be shaken by passion; by slapping Desdemona he has betrayed the first tremor. When Lodovico finally names this passion as enslavement, at the play's end, and tacitly relates this enslavement to Othello's former condition, he articulates the pseudo-ethnographic logic that insists on this linkage.

Othello's anger, furthermore, is often voiced in specifically Senecan language. In an explosion of fury at Cassio, Othello analogizes his vengeful rage to a demonic awakening: "Arise, black vengeance, from the hollow hell, / Yield up, O love, thy crown and hearted throne / To tyrannous hate! Swell, bosom, with thy fraught, / For 'tis of aspics' tongues! (3.3.445–53). He continues, in an outburst that nearly parodies classical revenge tragedy: "O blood, blood, blood!" (3.3.454). Along with the fraught repetition of plosives and heightened apostrophes to roiling emotions, the passage is notable for its link of Blackness to anger. Surely, this Blackness plays on the traditional association of evil with darkness, one familiar in medieval pageantry and iconography; however, by overlaying that association with a racialized evocation of jealousy, Othello's speech links his own Blackness to the hellish personification of vengeance, which he beckons in richly allegorical language. Earlier, Othello has similarly Blackened his passion when reporting on his internal state after the conflict between Cassio and Montano: "Now, by heaven, / My blood begins my safer guides to rule / And passion, having my best judgement collied, / Assays to lead the way" (2.3.200–203). From Blackness to passion to clouding judgment, Othello's rage serves as a locus of multiple competing discourses on enslavement—enslavement to the passions, to the ingrained destiny of one's race, and to the historical practice of chattel slavery. Rather than parse out one from the other with the neat formulation of Seneca and Cicero, *Othello* demonstrates how the naturalization of jealousy to a specific race forces a consideration of moral slavery's material manifestation on a Black and formerly enslaved body. Iago magnifies this vision further when he reflects on Othello's rage; as if anticipating Lodovico's stunned rhetorical questioning, he asks, "Can he be angry? I have seen the cannon /When it hath blown his ranks into the air / And like the devil, from his very arm, / Puffed his own brother—and can he be angry? / Something of moment then. I will go meet him, / There's matter in't indeed, if he be angry" (3.4.135–40). Iago paints the false portrait of a typically composed commander suddenly losing his temper, with the aim to render his fury as singular, a curious event for someone who has seen his own brother blown up by a cannon and, he implies, remained calm. Tacitly drawing on the association of Africanus, Iago implies that jealousy, more so than the bloody and devilish chaos of battle, has the ability to provoke true anger and add "matter" to the cause.

Othello, then, joins this book's roster of failed Stoics. In attempting to rein in his rage, he only further clouds his judgment, and as a result loses his capacity to reason. It may seem odd to think of him as a Stoic at all, due to his capitulation to passion, but while he ultimately fails to become his own master—at least, arguably until the final, harrowing seconds of his life—Othello does attempt to frame his struggle in Stoic terms. In particular, he partakes in a specifically early modern brand of Stoicism, one mingled with a Christian sense of slavery to God. But Othello cannot successfully complete this program, not necessarily because he is consumed by passion, but because he is not granted proper dominion over the representation of his own consciousness. Othello's tragedy is thus not only his doomed actions but his incapacity to access a mode of salvation barred to him. He is ironically unable to become a slave—at least, not the right kind.

The Missing Double

In viewing Othello as a Stoic, I recall one of the more maligned readings of the play, by T. S. Eliot, who in his essay "Shakespeare and the Stoicism of Seneca" interprets Othello's final monologue before his suicide, in which he recalls "some service" he has done to the state and bloodily reenacts his murder of a "turbaned Turk," as a delusional ploy for self-importance:

> What Othello seems to me to be doing in making this speech is *cheering himself up*. He is endeavouring to escape reality, he has ceased to think about Desdemona, and is thinking about himself. Humility is the most difficult of all virtues to achieve; nothing dies harder than the desire to think well of oneself. Othello succeeds in turning himself into a pathetic figure, by adopting an *aesthetic* rather than a moral attitude, dramatizing himself against the environment. He takes in the spectator, but the human motive is primarily to take in himself.[36]

Eliot views this moment as proof of Othello's narcissism but also of Shakespeare's genius, his capacity to expose the determination of a doomed figure to deflect attention away from their transgressions and create an artificial air of theatrical grandeur. Stoicism furnishes Othello with a grammar for expressing his worthlessness, and paradoxically in doing so transforms him into a spectacle. Leaving aside the calculatedly breezy tastelessness with which Eliot dismisses Othello's speech—he is simply "cheering himself up"—this reading captures something of the subtlety of Othello's self-aestheticization, his ability to render his actions as if on a stage, and connect this behavior to his Stoicism. For Eliot,

Othello's bastardized Stoicism portends a false belief in connecting to the universal, a proto-Nietzschean grammar for a weak and powerless figure to feel an outsized importance. As mentioned in my introduction, Eliot muses in the same essay that Stoicism is a "philosophy suited to slaves."[37] As we have seen with Stoic physics in chapter 4, this belief in connecting to a universal, material energy was indeed fundamental to Stoic thought, though often countered by, if not in outright conflict with, Stoicism's insistence on the relative insignificance of the individual when faced with unknowable fate.

Eliot is careful not to dismiss Stoicism as a whole as merely a façade of profundity. Rather, he sees its potential for unearned melodrama as an outgrowth of the philosophy's particularly Roman character. In "Seneca in Elizabethan Translation," Eliot proposes that the Roman form of Stoicism, as opposed to its earlier Greek incarnation, results from the Roman "devotion to the State" that renders "virtues as public virtues" as opposed to the Greek "traditional morality" that, unhindered by a devotion to civic duty, focused more on a direct, unmediated relationship to the gods and thus "a skeptical and heterodox intelligence."[38] As a philosophy yoked inexorably to the relation of an individual consciousness to public good, Stoicism, in Eliot's estimation, cannot help but have a declamatory style unconcerned with dramatic tension. As such, Stoicism, as filtered through Seneca's closet dramas, results in a slack narrative devoid of suspense and laden instead with portentous rhetoric. Indeed, "the ethic of Seneca is a matter of postures," and the posture that "gives the greatest opportunity for effect, hence for the Senecan morality, is the posture of dying: death gives his characters the opportunity for their most sententious aphorisms."[39] In dying, the Senecan hero, incapable of wrestling with the interior struggles of Greek morality, merely performs a superficial, mock-epic swan song that hypocritically declaims its own humility. As Eliot notes, such a critique was commonplace in his day; he follows the footsteps of other classicists who wave away Seneca's tragedies, such as F. L. Lucas, who derides Seneca's "ego-centric altruism."[40] But Eliot lays his charge at the feet of Roman culture—and at times more perniciously of the Roman "race"—rather than in Stoicism as a philosophical system.

I agree, then, that Othello literally stages himself in this moment, and I too see this as a particularly Stoic maneuver. I also see Othello's speech in conversation with a particularly public understanding of virtue, one entangled with notions of obligation to the state, and also intimately related to notions of slavery. But these elements do not diminish his words as simply a pathetic attempt at becoming a tragic hero; Eliot believes so because his primary interlocutor is Senecan *drama*, not philosophy.

If we view Othello's speech as an updated version of Roman revenge tragedy, then it does risk diminishing the power of his words as simply an attempt at classical grandeur, as with his histrionic address to "black vengeance." However, here and throughout the play, Othello attempts to enact Stoic exercise, not merely cite Stoic-influenced plays, by staging and distancing himself while viewing his performing body as both an extension and theatricalization of his soul. Furthermore, the play, like early modern Stoic literature, continually links this self-distancing to servitude. Recall Seneca's letter 25, discussed in chapter 2, which urges Lucilius to "do all things as if another man looked on." Following this injunction, Seneca goes on to characterize this specular relationship as akin to a proper mode of slavery: "But it is far better to live as if one were a slave to some one good man, who should be alwayes at his heeles. I likewise holde my selfe content provided alwayes that that which thou doest, thou doest it as if a man had an eye upon thee. Solitude induceth us to all evill."[41] Slavery to an imagined audience—an audience of "some one good man"—constitutes for Seneca an acceptable mode of bondage; implicit in this description is that Seneca himself, as the mentor, could be the spectral onlooker to Lucilius's every action. Substituting slavery to the passions with slavery to the spectator, Seneca recommends a program of servitude that maintains disdain for the indifferents that characterize physical enslavement. The imagined "good man" doubles the consciousness of the aspiring sage and audits the passions that arise in the soul.

Seneca returns to this therapeutic doubling gesture throughout his writings. In *Of Natural Questions*, he observes that a free man is one who has "discharged himselfe from himselfe," since "to be a subject to mans passion is a continuall servitude, from which it is impossible to escape, a slaverie that presseth with an equal waight"; the recommended course of action, to liberate oneself from this condition, is to

> set before thy eyes thy weakenesse and age, and say unto thy selfe, Why am I mad? Why puff I? Why sweat I? Why change I places? Why haunt I the courts and places of conference? I haue neyther neede of much, nor of long time. Moreouer, it shall be good to consider the nature of things: this will first of all cause us to retire our selves from shamefull matters, and afterwards will separate the bodie very far from the minde, which should be great and sublime.[42]

Here, the proper audience is the enslaved person himself, who must set themselves "before thy eyes" and speak to themselves, interrogating the cause of the physical manifestations of their passions: the sweat, "puffing," and—in a turn of phrase that must have resonated with the courtier class in Lodge's time—the "courts and places of conference" that presumably preoccupy attention better spent on cultivating virtue. In *De ira* Seneca orients this process toward rage in particular, a passion deserving of its own treatise due to its potential to cloud fully the reasonable faculty. In book 3 of *De ira*, Seneca addresses techniques for pacifying anger; chief among these approaches is effecting a "delay" of action by embarking on a deep investigation, as in *Natural Questions*. In this case, the process takes on a more aesthetic and even legal language, which Seneca frames as a form of trial:

> We shall subdue Anger, if from time to time we represent unto ourselves those vices that are hatched under this passion, and if we consider the same as we ought, with all her dependences and appurtenances; we must accuse her before our selves, condemne her, examine her infirmities, and lay her open to view; then compare her with the most detestable vices, to the end that as yet we may be better instructed what she is.[43]

Feminized and criminal, anger takes on the form of a parasitical force that can be subdued if it gains "representation." The *askesis* quarantines rage and lends it form as legible and capable of comparison and, as a result, extirpation. An inward trial of passion allows for the removal of its root and accessories, all while creating the delay needed to attenuate its effects.

Beyond simply questioning the causes of passion, however, the Stoic is to imagine their own death. The pupil must picture their end as a way to render insignificant all the trivial matters that preoccupy them; this aspect of meditation provides a common trope in Stoic writing and was received by early modern translators as a noble practice. Lipsius, providing prefatory remarks on each of Lodge's translations of the *Epistles*, notes before letter 24 that this one is "ranked among the best" because the author "exhorteth not to feare evils to come, although they threaten. But rather to propose them to happen, and so to forme a mans selfe by examining or extenuating them. For what are all these feares? The last of them is death, and contemne that by reason. Great men have done it. Plebeians and Slaves have done it. Why shouldest thou not aspire? Take the vizard from things."[44] The language is nearly artisanal: the philosopher must "forme" their very self through examining fears, most saliently death, the democratizing force that consumes slave, plebeian, and noble alike. The letter itself echoes the imperative of *Natural Questions* while bearing Lodge's careful rendering of the language to avoid an endorsement of suicide, a Christian sin that the ancient Stoics believed could be a morally correct result of proper meditation. "It is an excellent thing to learne to die," begins Seneca, again linking this practice to liberation from slavery:

> Meditate on death, who saith thus, commandeth to meditate on libertie: he that hath learned to die, hath forgotten to serve, it is above all power, undoubtedly beyond all. What careth he for prisons, holds, or restraints? He hath alwayes free passage. There is but one chaine that holdeth us bound, that is the love of life, which as it is not to be rejected, so is it to be diminished, to the end that if occasion so fall out, nothing may detaine or hinder us, but what we may be ready to do that presently, which at some other time hereafter we must needs doe.[45]

The proper course of action is to meditate on death to realize the "one chaine" that remains after other modes of service are shed: the "love of life," which cannot be "rejected" through suicide but can at least be "diminished" in case fate threatens to sever it entirely. In what is at once a vitalizing call to live in the present and a morbid admission that death could strike at any time, Seneca here calls on Lucilius to purify his internal composition in preparation for his inevitable end.

In his laudatory preamble, Lipsius, a Neo-Stoic intent on synthesizing Stoic thought with his contemporary religious ethos, implicitly endorses this purification as akin to the mortification of the flesh, the means by which a Christian would purge themselves of sin to prepare for death. This connection becomes more explicit in Sanford's translation of Epictetus's *Manual*, where the chapter "How to learne, and set our minde to highe things" echoes Seneca in its instruction to "[s]et before thy eyes, deathe, banishment, and all things which seeme terrible, but especially death: in so doing, thou shalt not thinke upon base and vile things, and shalte never be exceeding covetous."[46] By projecting a spectacle of the worst circumstances, the soul purges itself of its attachments to indifferents and instead focuses on what is in its control—its ability to reason and judge.

Pierre Hadot notes that in early Christianity, influenced as it was by Stoic thought, the practice of penitence, "inspired by the fear and love of God, could take the form of extremely severe self-mortification. The remembrance of death was intended not only to make people realize the urgency of conversion, but also to develop the fear of God."[47] Hadot connects this adaptation of the Stoic death meditation to Paul's pronouncement in Corinthians 15:31 that, as the Geneva translation succinctly puts it, "I dye daily." For Paul, the daily enactment of death is an effort not merely to purge himself of passions, but also to prepare himself for the Second Coming, to ensure his soul is ready for a radical transformation of his personhood. Elsewhere in the same chapter of Corinthians he espouses the affirmation of his new identity as both a realization of his absolute selfhood and the abnegation of his personhood as a mere vessel for God's graces: "But by the grace of God I am what I am: and his grace which was bestowed upon me was not in vain; but I labored more abundantly than they all: yet not I, but the grace of God which was with me. Therefore whether it were I or they, so we preach, and so ye believed."[48] The ultimate servitude to God—the absolute version of Seneca's "good man," or sagacious audience—is to enact the Stoic meditation on death without extending it to the bloody period of suicide by killing a *version* of the self attached to the superfluity of the surrounding world. Instead of actually dying, the properly prepared subject braces to serve a new master, God—or, for the Stoics, reason. The rhythms of Senecan therapy become repurposed as divine ritual.

With this complex overlaying of servitude, death, and simultaneous self-abnegation and self-realization in mind, we can turn in full to Othello's final monologue, which so fascinated and repelled Eliot. Confronted with the truth of Iago's betrayal, Othello tarries briefly before being escorted from his chambers:

> Soft you, a word or two before you go.
> I have done the state some service, and they know't.
> No more of that. I pray you, in your letters,
> When you shall these unlucky deeds relate,
> Speak of me as I am. Nothing extenuate,
> Nor set down aught in malice. Then must you speak
> Of one that loved not wisely, but too well;
> Of one not easily jealous, but, being wrought,
> Perplexed in the extreme; of one whose hand,
> Like the base Indian, threw a pearl away
> Richer than all his tribe; of one whose subdued eyes,
> Albeit unused to the melting mood,
> Drops tears as fast as Arabian trees
> Their medicinable gum. Set you down this,
> And say besides that in Aleppo once,
> Where a malignant and a turbaned Turk
> beat a Venetian and traduced the state,
> I took by th'throat the circumcised dog
> And smote him—thus! (5.2.336–54)

As Daniel Vitkus notes, this haunting passage engages with early modern understandings of conversion and spiritual infidelity by serving as a perverse act of self-civilization: "Othello enacts his own punishment and damns himself by killing the Turk he has become."[49] But the outward projection of an inner manifestation of monstrosity also recalls traditions of philosophical exercise bent on eliminating passions. In this vein, Eliot correctly identifies the structure of this passage as Stoic in nature, but it is not, as Gordon Braden has it, simply "devious cover," a captivating story meant to distract his onlookers from his suicide and prevent their intervention.[50] Seen as an externalized and corporealized adaptation of the Stoic meditation on death, Othello's self-sacrifice instead takes the shape of therapy beyond Eliot's facile rendering of "cheering himself up." Instead, Othello, in destroying the "Turk he has become," also attempts to conquer the anger, racialized and essentialized in the contemporary imagination, by paring away the component of himself that cathects to the passions. Externalizing and, as Epictetus exhorts, setting before his eyes this exaggerated and vengeful character, he situates it rhetorically onto the "turbaned Turk" and physically onto his own body. In a passage that recalls the paradox of Stoic freedom cited in chapter 1, Othello furthermore *assents* to what he judges as the correct appearance of himself—the loyal soldier who protects the state—while pruning the aspect deemed unnecessary and ineffective, that is, the enraged and jealous Moor turned Turk. But unlike the psychological terrain of *De ira*, Othello actualizes this process outwardly and theatrically by finding the sign of anger on body rather than soul; thus, the purge of jealousy is a purge of the self, a suicide, a corporealized version of spiritual Stoic training.

Julia Reinhard Lupton has observed that Othello's death acts as "a kind of circumcision, a gesture that constitutes at once a means of social reinscription and a subjectivizing gaze."[51] Circumcision functions as a covenantal act that both alienates and reinscribes its signatory into a community; in this case Othello both becomes and destroys the "circumcised Turk" of his libidinal threat. He is, in Lupton's words, "ultimately reincorporated into the body politic, in his case by dying into the citizenship that before he had claimed through intermarriage and public service."[52] Inducing both birth and death, servitude and mastery, pagan suicide and Christian attainment of grace, the fatal cut of the sword allows Othello to murder Othello's slave, his passion—but the price of this severing is his life, because his Blackness essentializes him to that passion. Urvashi Chakravarty reads the circumcision as an act of mortification inherent to an act of natality, or birth into a particular identity.[53] The cut, for Chakravarty, "registers a physical mark on the body that denotes both a proto-racial designation as well as an irreversible and unchangeable sign of the fundamental problem of natality: that it embodies the 'promise of grace' even as it reaffirms the innate 'corruption' of all begotten children, so that the promise of natality also always incorporates the prospect of death."[54] As Chakravarty observes, the promise of circumcision also entails the death of the prior subject while ensuring a permanent marker of the transformation that renders the circumcised as corrupt, other.

Both Chakravarty and Lupton see Othello's bloody act as the uncanny return of the "redemption" out of slavery that constitutes an element of his stories to Brabantio; similarly, Othello figures his second, more tragic act of redemption as a form of service, conditional to his status as vassal. His fatal mistake, if his actions are to be evaluated as a Stoic exercise, is believing he could separate the two modes of slavery—legal and moral—that so often remain parallel in the philosophical literature. By contrast, Iago proves capable of doubling himself easily, without the conflation of modes of slavery that stubbornly attends Othello. This act of doubling does not merely confine itself to Iago, either: the play is filled with acts of imaginative projection, hypothetical self-scrutiny, and struggles to maintain specular focus while buffeted by distractions. Christopher Pye links *Othello*'s persistent emphasis on the visual with its self-conscious formalization of political identity; thus the play, which imagines the containment of its own vanishing-point (literally so, in the scene where Desdemona, Iago, and Montano await sight of Othello's ship on the horizon), possesses an "autochthonic character" that gives it the "capacity to constitute itself as a self-grounding and limitlessly inscribing form."[55] Within this limitless world, vision becomes thematized as a means of attempting to script one's formal construction: characters watch, witness, eavesdrop, strain their eyes, and, most iconically, demand "ocular proof." Desdemona, in singing Othello's praises, notes that she "saw Othello's visage in my mind" (1.3.253) and projects herself as "[s]uch as she said my lord did say I was" (4.2.121); Iago, as has been noted, imagines himself performing for "heaven"; Cassio rues the phantasmic version of himself captured by his "reputation," ruined after his impassioned, drunken brawl. More broadly, as Matthew Steggle observes, the play features recurring instances of "doubleness" in its genre and *mise en scène*; the play possesses an "ability to be both a story of exuberantly exotic, highly political geography, and one of detailed domestic tragedy set off by rows over mundane objects such as bed sheets and handkerchiefs."[56]

This compulsive visualization and scopic oscillation between intense scrutiny and wide-angled observation acutely recalls the processes of self-investigation on which Stoic exercise thrives; Jamey Graham observes, as mentioned in chapter 2, that Stoic philosophy, particularly its meditation on death, furnishes Shakespeare's dramas "with a model of theatricality stressing the activity of the audience, making unobstructed spectatorship of one's own performance prerequisite for effective performance."[57] Graham's "audience" is the actual theatrical audience, which *Othello* certainly hails with frequency, but so too does it draw attention to the audiences within the characters themselves as they investigate—or in some cases manipulate—their passions. Othello nearly paraphrases Seneca when he performs both the man possessed by passion and the viewer diagnosing its causes:

> Lie with her? lie on her? We say lie on her when they belie her! Lie with her, zounds, that's fulsome!—Handkerchief! Confessions! Handkerchief!—To confess, and be hanged for his labour! First to be hanged, and then to confess: I tremble at it. Nature would not invest herself in such a shadowing passion without some instruction. It is not words that shakes me thus. Pish! Noses, ears, and lips. Is't possible? Confess! Handkerchief! O devil!
> *[He] falls in a trance.* (4.1.35–44)

At once in thrall to the sputtering images that claim his imagination and curious as to the "instruction" that Nature has embedded within his own performance, Othello offers here a tamer version of the split self that he takes on at the play's end; however, by falling into a trance at the conclusion of his investigation, he also demonstrates his fragility, his inability to harbor within him his split into both observer ("I tremble at it . . . It is not words that shake me thus") and impassioned victim of the passions ("Handkerchief!" . . . "Pish!" . . . Confess! Handkerchief! O devil!"). This unsustainable split symptomizes his inability to project effectively an externalized and imaginary figure of himself to analyze and, hopefully, cure. As such, Othello also needs Iago to help him create his own spectator: his "good man" is not himself nor God but his supposedly trusted ancient and ensign, whom he praises as his mentor: "thou teachest me" (5.1.33). The "marriage" of Othello to Iago cements this dynamic through a ritual that, like his redemption out of slavery and suicide, binds him as an initiate who becomes both familial and liminal. Like Iago, he recruits heaven as his judge: "Now by yond marble heaven / In the due reverence of a sacred vow / I here engage my words" (3.3.462–64). Iago, of course, is more corrupter than sage, one who profanes Stoic meditation and Pauline mortification into the emergence of an internal demon: "By heaven," exclaims Othello, "thou echo'st me / as if there were some monster in thy thought / Too hideous to be shown" (3.3.109–11). Othello outsources his specularity to Iago, as a Senecan mentor, only to find that instead of a drive to strain out his passions, he only gains the full embodiment—the "monstrous birth"—of those passions.

If the other plays discussed in this book model Stoic exercises for their audiences, by which they train spectators to become better attuned to their faculties of reason, *Othello* reverses the formula: here, the audiences—actual, fictional, purely imagined *within* fiction—are the masters, and the characters nakedly appeal to these onlookers for the validation of a proper image of themselves through which they can properly mediate the functions of their souls. Seen this way, the real tragedy of Othello is his lack of ability to have his doubled self gain dignity and significance. His self-aesheticization, his attempted therapy, fails as both medicine and theater: there is no identification, no catharsis, no mentorship. After his final, desperate plea to record the story of his service to the state, his narrative is silenced, scrubbed from the official record. Lodovico announces instead that he will report only the murder of Desdemona: "Myself will straight aboard, and to the state / This heavy act with heavy heart relate" (5.2.368–69). This is the same "state" for which Othello has done "some service," and his demand to be remembered not as an instrument in a "heavy act" but "as I am" has been ignored, overshadowed by the "bloody period" of his stabbing. Ian Smith compares Othello's request to be remembered to the favor asked by the dying Hamlet, who is, by contrast, immediately rewarded with Horatio's assembly of listeners to hear his tale. For Smith, the repercussions extend beyond the play and into its critical reception; while Hamlet has come to stand in for a universal humanist subject, no throng of scholars clamor to identify with Othello's story. The different receptions, Smith avers, result from the different races of the protagonists: "Hamlet and Othello—one white, the other black—desire to have their stories told, and it is perhaps the singular racial distinction that affects the telling, offering an insight into contemporary critical practice as it relates to matters of race."[58] We can think of this lack of critical identification as yet another lost double, another audience Othello is denied. Like Hamlet, whose "distracted globe" identifies theaters of his mind, the playhouse, and the world, Othello attempts to imagine being seen by himself, the theatergoing audience, and the scholarly community; however, unlike Hamlet, the seats in these structures remain empty, the performance invalidated.

The theft of representational capacity, alongside the more violently inscribed theft of bodily integrity, has a long history rooted in colonial acts of disenfranchisement. Miles Grier, in a study of the relation of ink to Blackness in early modern culture, notes that the persistent white rendering of Black bodies as inked, etched, and scrawled upon results from the ingrained belief in Black subjects' inability to control their own representation:

> Doubting the objectivity, reliability, the representative capacity of "blacks," is an intransigent habit. Indeed, it is often the very mechanism for parading one's own apparent lack of bias, one's intellectual independence. It will be difficult to show people that what they have called "thinking" is not an encounter with the world but instead, a "recognition" of the imaginary types they had already been told they would find.[59]

Grier concludes that "one of those white privileges—seldom mentioned but fundamental to the status—is the ability to dream, to produce a representation."[60] In *Othello*, the substitution that Grier identifies as constitutive of white privilege—the twin beliefs that the imaginary figure of Blackness is the Black subject itself *and* that those subjects are incapable of self-representation—staggers any attempts at successful philosophical consolation and the accretion of virtuous self-realization. By cross-hatching its meditations on service and mastery with its scenes of therapeutic self-staging, while simultaneously holding race as both an illegible and omnipresent determinination, *Othello* shows the price of the fantasy of contingency put forth by Kanye West and anticipated, millennia before, by Stoic and Christian thinkers: that slavery, for a Black subject, can be a choice, a mere extension of servitude that can be substituted out for a greater slavery to a divine or wise audience. Instead, Othello is robbed of the very quality that allowed him entry into citizenry—his narrative—because he dared to purge it from himself as gratuitous and indifferent. His indifferent qualities remain, to everyone else, his essence.

Conclusion

The Dust of the Humanities

I conclude this book with a reiteration of the question posed at its beginning: how can you teach virtue? This question might be accompanied, today, with a reasonable follow-up: *why* teach virtue at all? Our current educational system, allergic to vagueness and abstractions, compulsively attaches itself to outcome statements, grading rubrics, career viability, and the potential for monetary gain. These are not, in and of themselves, qualities deserving of scorn. But they form an uneasy grid to place atop the values long associated with humanistic inquiry: self-realization, public responsibility, an understanding of one's place in history, a critical apparatus capable of challenging assumptions. By way of a conclusion I want to consider how our current "crisis of the humanities," stuck as it is between the poles of objective evaluation and conceptual engagement, might benefit from a return to the Stoic ethos of pedagogy as rediscovered and, as I have been arguing, literally staged in the early modern era. Before doing so, however, I first bring back the wayward Stoic pupil from this book's introduction: Hamlet.

I return to Hamlet to propose something perhaps counterintuitive: that we regard him not only as a Stoic student but also as a model for students in humanities classes today. As established earlier, the dejected prince of Denmark presents not a "failed Stoic" but someone closer to the vast majority of philosophers in Stoicism's classical beginnings: a stumbling, muddling figure who continually attempts to train his actions toward what he perceives as good, only to fall prey to distraction, digression, and delusion. Hamlet presents a particularly apt figure with which to explore Stoicism's implications for today's education because he helps expose the precise border between doctrinal learning—knowledge transfer, textual study, memorization—and virtue as a way of life. Fresh from Wittenberg, the young student must find a way to translate his dry intellectual pursuits into behavioral action. He finds, understandably, that this is a difficult task. Witness, for instance, his soliloquy as he observes

Fortinbras's forces advance to Denmark in act 4. First, Hamlet notes a philosophical commonplace: that humans distinguish themselves among living creatures because of divine reason. "Sure he that made us with such large discourse, / Looking before and after, gave us not / That capability and godlike reason / To fust in us unus'd" (4.4.36–39). He then chastises himself for ignoring the "Examples gross as earth" that urge him to take action, like Fortinbras (4.4.46). How, muses Hamlet, can he not respond to the horrifying events of his father's death and his mother's marriage to a murderous uncle—how, especially, when someone like Fortinbras risks the lives of thousands of men over a patch of land? The conclusion cannot help but strike us as wrongheaded; indeed, the newly assumed role of the revenger will, for Hamlet, lead him to a rush of melodramatic and fateful behavior when he returns to Denmark. But in inquiring as to his own motives, in trying to latch onto reason as a guiding principle, in locating a double—here, Fortinbras—to use as a double of his own psychic landscape, Hamlet attempts to give life to what for him has been, up until this point, a matter of philosophical piety. He embodies a kind of lived, performed learning, one that Stoicism encourages in the face of today's press for marketable outcomes.

To be clear, I am not advocating that our students pervert logic to become murderous revengers. Rather, I believe that Hamlet's misguided explorations symptomatize a recurring effort on his part to focus a pedagogical gaze toward embodied action, and to think of that action as a kind of philosophizing. Stoicism's value, as I have established throughout this book, rests in its performance, not its doctrine; that performance, I believe, provides a powerful paradigm for the classroom. I thus take Hamlet's advice seriously when he tells Gertrude, "Assume a virtue if you have it not" (3.4.162). This charge may seem ironized and feeble right out of the gate, since virtue, in the common understanding, resists the mere assumption of a role. But the plays I have surveyed in this book view virtue not as a naturalized quality but, hearkening back to its classical definition, as something that must be culled, crafted, and tested out. Their characters all attempt, with various degrees of success, to explore their own capacities for proper action, and they engage in modes of inquiry that challenge inherited wisdoms and locate their moral development in the performed evaluation of their own perception of value. Beatrice, through her wit, refashions sentiment as an expression of the novelty of her mind; Othello, while meeting a horrific end, embarks on a program of self-interrogation that takes on a theatrical form in its final demonstration; Pandulpho casts away dull *sententiae* and locates knowledge at the limit of perceiving fate's unknowability; and, for *The Atheist's Tragedy*, the pupil is us, the audience, asked to ponder the possibility of divine materiality. Thinking of these behaviors as acts of learning threatens to shade them into catchphrases familiar to any educator today—they demonstrate *critical thinking*, or *self-discovery*. But what is refreshing about Stoic education is its expressed distaste of principle itself, its location of learning in the lived spaces between the hypothetical class of the syllabus and the finalized experience of the outcome statement. Instead, the Stoic lives in the present, in the sweaty and fumbling realm of the everyday—the realm, in short, of *actual* education, which takes place in actual classrooms replete with awkward pauses, wayward distractions, and moments of sublimity alternating with moments of disappointment or misunderstanding.

Hamlet pushes this understanding of lived philosophy to its breaking point: his self-inquiry shades, at times, into narcissistic paralysis; his pointed indifference often resembles sociopathy. And most crucially, his focus on finding meaning in performance, in the embodied doubles and projections of his self, turns the larger play into a theatrical hall of mirrors. After meeting the ghost of his father, Hamlet answers its charge to "Remember me" with a promise to a form of fidelity that nearly negates his own identity:

> Remember thee?
> Ay, thou poor ghost, whiles memory holds a seat
> in this distracted globe. Remember thee?
> Yea, from the table of my memory
> I'll wipe away all trivial fond records,
> All saws of books, all forms, all pressures past
> That youth and observation copied there,
> And thy commandment all alone shall live
> Within the book and volume of my brain,
> Unmix'd with baser matter. (1.5.95–104)

Not only will Hamlet remember the imperative of the ghost, he will cleanse his mind—stuffed, one imagines, with *sententiae*, translations, rhetorical exercises, grammar, and historical lessons—and replace the impressions of the "tables" (waxen pages) of his mind with only the commandment of the ghost residing in their stead. This clean slate presumably allows for Hamlet to take on the "antic disposition" he warns Horatio about, wherein the prince will act "strange or odd" but which should not prompt his classmate to say he knows "aught of me" (1.4.180, 178, 187). And this disposition takes hold of Hamlet for the next two acts, gripping him in the comic frenzy that puzzles Rosencrantz and Guildenstern and leads to Ophelia's agonized demand that we see in his psychic volatility "that noble and most sovereign reason / Like sweet bells jangled out of tune and harsh, / That unmatch'd form and feature of blown youth / Blasted with ecstasy" (3.1.157–62).

Of course, the "sovereign reason" that Hamlet has "blasted with ecstasy" has been evacuated from his contrived aspect, not—so it appears—from his deeper, truest self. Hamlet, like Othello, engages in a version of Seneca's advice in *De ira* to surrogate an impassioned version of the self so as to anatomize its effects. For Hamlet, this is a moving target: his plan to distract the court with madness alternates with bewilderment at humanity's capacity to act at all. When the players visit, and he hears the impassioned speech of Hecuba's lament, Hamlet finds yet another double, this one outside of himself completely, and begins to wonder how "this player here, / But in a fiction, in a dream of passion, Could fore his soul so to his own conceit / That from her working all his visage wann'd, / Tears in his eyes, distraction in his aspect, / A broken voice, and his whole function suiting / With forms to his conceit? And all for nothing! For Hecuba!" (545–52) Hamlet's reflection, while well known, remains dizzyingly complicated. While Hamlet has engaged in diversionary performances of madness, theoretically to disguise his *actual* impassioned soul, spurred by the ghost to seek vengeance, he now begins to wonder if that truer repository of righteous anger is itself "real" at all—because he has so successfully prevented it from translating into action. How could it be real, when this actor so completely gives themselves over to a wounded pain in the face of the "nothing" of a mere fictional character? This theory is put to the test with *The Mousetrap*, the play whose characters—whose "nothings"—seek to prompt real passion on the part of Claudius, the guilty creature. Later, in the speech surveyed above, he locates Fortinbras as yet another example of passion, this one properly aligned with reason and apparently oriented to justice. Finally, in the final act, Hamlet assumes the role he has thus far feigned, crafted, observed, and idolized, by seeking to become the character of the revenger he has watched from afar.

This bricolage of identities may seem far afield from Stoicism, on the surface. Yet in his deep ambivalence to theater—both as constituting disposition and illusory aesthetic—Hamlet mirrors the curious role of the stage in Stoic thought, as symbol of distracting *adiaphora* and motivating condition of life, wherein we must act as if we are observed at all times. How can one be both always watched, always on display, and yet not devolve into a mere simulacrum of a self, a lackluster John-a-dreams?

For Hamlet, the attempt at taking on or observing a new self accompanies a deep internal questioning of motive and an attempted reorientation toward reason, and while he never seems to find even a fraction of the divine reason so praised by the Stoics, his endless struggle ends up less a Sisyphean demonstration of absurdism and more an ultimate acknowledgment of something grander beyond his understanding but still, somehow, reaffirming: "Rashly— / And prais'd be rashness for it: let us know / Our indiscretion sometime serves us well / When our deep plots do pall; and that should learn us / There's a divinity that shapes our ends, / Rough-hew them how we will" (5.2.6–11). Like the hapless, foolishly played characters of the Antonio plays, Hamlet takes the outrageous and bewildering power of theater, a medium always collapsing into itself, as a symptom of a grander design. For Hamlet, in fact, it is such indiscretion and rashness, not solitude and meditation, that better index the evidence of divinity.

In a recent, deeply considered, and influential study of *Hamlet*, Rhodri Lewis similarly finds the prince as nothing more—or less—than an endless assumption of roles, characters, and dispositions. But Lewis sees this constant playacting as symptomatic of the prince's inability to make manifest the promise of humanist education and, more fundamentally, of the deep, incurable rottenness of humanism at all. This critique depends upon an assumed opposition, on Lewis's part, of performance to authenticity; thus, when Hamlet asks "questions of performance and self-display," he actually "further calls into question the existence of the inner authenticity by which he had earlier set such store."[1] Lewis levels this charge repeatedly: because Hamlet merely "seems" to take on the inquisitive modes of poet, historian, and philosopher, he exposes the play as having "no realm of inner integrity or authenticity against which to measure trifles, contingency, or mendaciousness of the *persona*" (31).[2] The classical topoi of *theatrum mundi* that such personae evoke are themselves also, for Lewis, delusional; Cicero's frequent reliance on the theater as metaphor, for instance, only confirms "that one can only act, only fabricate, only pretend to be oneself."[3] As far as the charge that Hamlet exhibits Stoic tendencies or beliefs, Lewis shrugs off the possibility by pointing out that Hamlet's language "is *designedly* incoherent, and reveals a character whose philosophical reach exceeds his grasp"; as such, the critic's responsibility, when confronted with such an inchoate assemblage of shallow posturing, is "not to make Hamlet more decorous by squeezing his language into some sort of *discursive* corset, but to understand what the dramatic significance of his philosophical incoherence might be."[4]

Hamlet cannot be properly philosophical—and certainly not Stoic—in this reckoning because he is incoherent and overly imitative, and he resists discursive apprehension. And yet Stoic philosophy, as I have labored to demonstrate, *is* mimetic, *does* admit to a necessary engagement with incoherence, and *purposefully* resists the "corset" of discursive structure. Lewis apprehends Stoicism just as the majority of early moderns did: as a cache of *sententiae* that advocated for an impossible ideal of stodgy remove. What is remarkable about Hamlet is that by shedding such a musty misinterpretation, he ends up literally embodying Stoicism in perhaps its purest form, as a way of life. Furthermore, he does so not in the confines of his university but back in Elsinore, among people: his scholarship is, we might say today, public-facing. Hamlet resists the removal from civic life that characterizes Epicurean and Cynic habituation; by remaining in the public eye, he insists that his philosophical work must be done in the quotidian (for him) grain of his familial and political worlds, not removed from them. In fact, by leaving the isolated intellectual haven of his school, he signals complicity between political and personal engagement, on the one hand, and serious inquiry, on the other. He flees from the stuffy moralism of strictly discursive learning and enters the philosophical laboratory of performative play.

We can learn something from this young pupil, tragically misguided though he may be. I suggest that Hamlet offers a way to think about Stoicism in our classrooms, not simply because he may resemble a certain archetype of college student (though he certainly does), but because he fixes our eye on the value of attending to the present, to the interactions of bodies and things that constitutes our immediate reality. As Michael Dobson points out, in a critique of Lewis's book, "in *Hamlet* Shakespeare deliberately withholds certain key pieces of information from his audience (such as the nature of Gertrude's relationship with Claudius in Old Hamlet's lifetime), obliging us to listen intently to the way his characters interact from one moment to the next instead of fitting their behaviour into a single conveniently explicated schema."[5] In other words, the play cultivates our own mode of learning akin to the kind Hamlet takes on after he wipes clean the tables of his memory: trained on what we see before us, aware of a grander design, questioning our own ability to absorb the truth, and partially resigned to the realization that we can never truly know everything.

I turn now to the question of how Hamlet's Stoic learning can inform the kinds of learning that currently take place in humanities classrooms. What if we think of Hamlet's experience as virtue, rather than elevate virtue into the ethereal heights of intellectual pursuit? For the Stoic, virtue is simply—and impossibly—the realization of one's complete potential.

Stoic practice thus exists in the long gap between the actual and the ideal. A recognition of this, of education's dependence on (and perhaps coextensiveness with) performance, characterizes Seneca's famous dismissal of the liberal arts in his letter 88, evoked already in chapter 3 as a model for Beatrice's wordplay. Like Hamlet, Seneca dismisses the kind of rote learning that has plagued both the prince and those who seek to fit him into a clear, textually coherent theoretical container. The letter takes up, one by one, each of the classical liberal arts—literature, geometry, music, astronomy—and mocks their pretenses to teach virtue. Most of the letter consists of critique, rather than an articulation of what the proper mode of learning would be. Even the glimpses it affords of how virtue *can* be learned are still phrased in the negative. "Wisdom is vast and expansive; it needs room," he declares. And so one "must learn about things human and divine, things past and yet to come, things transitory and things eternal. One must learn about time—and see how many questions there are about that alone." Seneca proceeds to list productive questions along these lines—did anything precede time? is the mind incorporeal?—before extolling this form of learning as infinitely better than a focus on facts and memorization: "With so many big questions waiting to occupy our minds, we must make room for them by evicting those others that are superfluous. Virtue will not take up residence within such narrow confines: so large a guest needs elbow room. So let everything be driven out, and let the whole heart be open to virtue."[6] What seems to characterize the difference between an appropriate question and one relegated to the triviality of mere knowledge-hoarding is, for Seneca, the open-endedness that attends it—the lack of any clear answer. We should train ourselves to ask questions without knowing where they will take us—"To be or not to be," say—and indeed, we should ask them *because* we do not know where they will take us.

How, though, would one learn to ask these questions? How can we train our minds to know the correct questions to ask? Seneca supplies answers, but they resist incorporation into methodology: "There is just one way our minds attain their full stature," he declaims, "and that is by unalterable knowledge of what things are good and what are bad."[7] The absolutism of this knowledge is startling, especially read alongside the capaciousness of the questions he deems appropriate. As with Hamlet equating rashness and indiscretion as proof, not a refutation, of a grand design, Seneca casts aside simplified attempts at marshaling education into programmatic exercises and instead revels in the tension between acknowledging mystery and affirming cosmic order. The implied conclusion seems to be that the most difficult questions, the ones that should preoccupy us, may not have answers—at least not yet—but they *can* be answered, and were they to be, the knowledge gained would be absolute, unshakable in its morality. In order to approach these truths we must pursue philosophy, which resides at the foundation of all other studies: it provides the blank slate onto which the disciplines of the liberal arts scrawl themselves. Seneca never prescribes a precise regimen for how his pupil can discipline themselves to ask these questions, but while a curriculum is never given in words, I believe the very medium of the letter supplies a metatextual solution. In its digressive way, so characteristic of all the messages to Lucilius, letter 88 marks itself with traces of its own embodiment, its real-time and performed quality. At one point Seneca remarks that, in his haste to express his distaste for traditional studies, he has not proceeded in the order he has proposed, because when he should have discussed music, he was confronted with his own complete disgust:

> You must bear with me if I don't keep to the regular sequence: I can't bring myself to count painters among the practitioners of the liberal arts, any more than I could statue makers, marble workers, and all the other ministers of luxury. Likewise, I reject wrestlers and every sort of knowledge that consists merely of oil and dirt. Otherwise I would have to count masseurs, cooks, and all the others who accommodate their talents to our pleasures. What, pray tell, is the liberal arts of those starving vomiters who keep the body at the feeding trough while the mind grows feeble for lack of nourishment? Shall we believe today's young people when they call *that* a liberal arts education?[8]

I quote this seemingly unimportant digression at length *because* it is a digression: that is, its formal properties mirror the mounting frustrations effected by a conversation on the matter. Over and over, Seneca replicates precisely the sensation of talking in real time; he quickly jettisons his promise not to talk about music by talking at length about *why* he will not talk about it. "Shall I linger," he asks sneeringly, "over the dust of geometry?"[9]

Perhaps not, but I believe it is to the humanities' "dust," those incidental fragments and shavings, that we can aim our study. It is the inchoate, conversational, and literary quality that hints at how education can proceed between live, embodied people, in time and space. Martha Nussbaum identifies the smudges and traces of orality in Stoic writings as essential to their philosophical aims, not simply an incidental quality or mere "voice." For the Stoics, writes Nussbaum, "the rhetorical and literary dimensions of an argument are not incidental frills: they are part and parcel of what the business of arguing is all about."[10] John Schafer takes this proposition further by suggesting that we think of Seneca's epistles generically as a form of drama. It is through the conventions of drama that we find the temporal and characterological features of the letters unify with their content. The "dramatic reading" of the letters, Schafer posits, explains their inherent "disorder" because disorder is an essential feature of any educational process:

> Learning philosophy involves wrestling with the intricacies of theory, but it also includes protreptic, exhortation, and in general the full battery of (respectable) persuasive technique. What method to use at a given moment, for pupils at different stages in their training, is a matter of expertise and is subject to great situational variability. There is sure to be no small amount of repetition, both in form and in content. Actual human relationships, moreover, whether face-to-face or epistolary, involve randomness. Events intervene: friends die, the correspondence is slowed by tardy couriers, people get sick, natural disasters strike. Thought proceeds by association, cannot be scripted in advance; friends share their thoughts.[11]

The letters carry with them marks of their live engagement. Of course, these marks result from a formal effect; they are not actual fossils of a person-to-person encounter. But like any work of drama they anticipate the liveness of their encounter with the *present* reader, who cannot help but take up the role of Lucilius, marked in his absence by the many hiccups that attend any actual processes of reading: the distractions, interruptions, and sudden moments of revelation all interleaving into an experience we retroactively call "reading."

Too often these are the aspects of education that are wished away, if they are mentioned at all: teachers exchange stories, perhaps, of classes that are "not that into it" or "really engaged" or "in over their heads" and so on. The presumption in these framings—a natural outgrowth of the model of learning as "knowledge transfer"—is that what happens in the class is merely the transmission of learning, not the learning itself. Stoicism, by contrast, focuses and refocuses itself on the creak of a chair, the clamor of construction out the window, the mispronunciation by the teacher, the sudden realization with five minutes left that an entire section of the lesson plan has been ignored. So too would it train our attention to the individual experiences from outside of the classroom that cannot help but enter the room despite any fantasy of a hermetically sealed-off space:

the student who fights back tears, or who falls asleep, or who leaves suddenly, or who empathizes deeply with a particular character. Far from mere ambience, these constitute grace notes in the learning process, nearly absent though they may be from most mainstream theorizations of pedagogy.[12] Like Hamlet and *Hamlet*, when we abandon the hope of a perceptible "reality" governing the play from behind the scenes, we start to focus more on what is *actually* happening before us.

Of course, knowledge still matters. It is the responsibility of instructors to impart facts, traditions, and truths, just as it is our responsibility to teach students the tools to dismantle the apparent stability *of* all those facts, traditions, and truths. Scott Newstok ably identifies this dialectic as one essential to teaching and reminiscent of Shakespeare, the great "upstart crow" who assembled originality and innovative critique out of the texts he ravenously consumed: "You simply cannot transform tradition (a creative ideal) without first knowing it (a conserving ideal). Making an inventory must precede making an invention."[13] I would adapt this observation to the binary of text and body, simplistic though it is: you cannot engage with texts, much less transform them, without admitting to the ongoing lived performance in which that text exists.

The observation that one can find traces of live interaction abounding in the Stoic philosophical literature, and the secondary observation that the implied liveness of the text constitutes, rather than diminishes, its pedagogy, hearkens again to the essentially public quality of virtue. It resides in Elsinore more than in Wittenberg. The Stoics critiqued many aspects of Aristotelian thought, but they held onto its conviction of virtue's communal nature.[14] Far from being hermits, Stoics were engaged in a shared life: they simply had to learn how to evaluate what constituted the proper motivation for that participation, and gauge whether the effects would lead them to the good. In *Nicomachean Ethics* Aristotle also identifies this as a key feature of his prescribed course of training. The pursuit of virtue makes it, in his view, "architectonic"; it is the fundamental art determinative of all others. The study of capacities "might be held to belong to the most authoritative and most architectonic one, and as such appears to be the political art. For it ordains what sciences there must be in cities and what kinds each person in turn must learn and up to what point."[15] He uses the term "political" to mean that it exists among people in civic life—that it is public, in short; thus the cultivation of virtue constitutes the root of all other studies, which emerge from this primary discipline.

Nussbaum, alongside Amartya Sen, has developed a political system that honors Aristotle's belief, along with that of the Stoics, that virtue must be public. The "capabilities approach" stems from the axiom that all humans naturally seek justice through the achievement of their potential. This set of claims is designed to offset the more coldly calculated utilitarianist approaches, systematized in many global programs, that reduce human goodness purely to an index of economic growth. Nussbaum explains that the capabilities approach believes that "the connection of human opportunities with ideas of basic entitlement and justice" is a "ubiquitous" and universal condition and thus can be applied globally in place of models of political economy.[16] She credits the Stoics as a major influence on this line of thinking, in particular the debt that nascent republican systems owe to the Stoic belief in individual dignity. As antimonarchical political orders became historically ascendant, "it came to seem more and more reasonable for Stoic thought to ally itself firmly with the idea of accountable republican institutions: only within them can human beings live lives worthy of human dignity."[17] Thus Stoicism, in its belief in the capacity for freedom among all humans, is best realized and celebrated when it upholds political systems that grant agency to all of its members.

Throughout Nussbaum's work, she looks to the humanities, not the sciences, to render democratic institutions viable. Following the Stoics, she locates political power in conceptual terrains long thought ineffective or trivial: emotions, self-scrutiny, and above all the unshakable presence of live human beings, in all their unsteadiness and unpredictability, in affairs of the state. In *Poetic Justice* she locates literature as an apt model for this worldview. She directs her focus away from measurements like GDP and "on the characteristics of the literary imagination as a public imagination, an imagination that will steer judges in their judging, legislators in their legislating, policy makers in measuring the quality of life of people near and far."[18] Careful study of literature, with its mimetic reproductions of life, helps occasion the self-reflection necessary for responsible action. Beyond just attending to the thematic and formal qualities of literature, however, Nussbaum wants us to learn through tracing "what sense of life" literature's "forms themselves embody: not only how the characters feel and imagine, but what sort of feeling and imagining is enacted in the telling of the story itself, in the shape and texture of the sentences, the pattern of the narrative, the sense of life that animates the text as a whole."[19] In sum, she asks us to keep an eye on the stubborn fact of liveness, of bodies that animate what appears to be a static formal construction—the repertoire that always doggedly pulses under the archive.

It is this Stoic education that early modern drama enacts, and it does so with all the peculiarities of its era, one marked with profound spiritual and aesthetic ambivalence. On the early modern stage live all the theatrical traces of Stoicism wrung out of the texts, and as teachers, we can turn to this site as a model of our own practices. We can be virtuous instructors if we thrive in the inherent liveness of the class and the inherent liveness of reading. Rather than shut out the everyday theater of pedagogy, we can find in that theater the very stuff *of* pedagogy. An aspiration toward virtue alone is an impossible goal, as Julia Annas articulates:

> We can't teach the virtues in isolation, one by one, since they can't be learnt that way. Generosity gives us a good example here. A child doesn't learn to be generous by just giving her things away, or sharing things whether they belong to her or not. Generosity involves consideration of fairness and justice . . . Generosity requires intelligence about what people both need and want, and also about appropriate ways, times, and manners of giving, avoiding obtrusiveness and condescension.[20]

In other words, if we want to learn generosity, we must pay attention to the granular, quotidian decisions that constitute it; generosity does not become taught simply through the maneuvering of a particular set of knowledge from one cerebral space to another. In attending to the performances that take place in the classroom, we can reframe it not as an incubator for the public but as a particular corner *of* the public sphere.

The theater, too, stands as a heightened extension of the public: it is a place of communal exchange, of embodied interaction. Like the classroom, the theater is political in the classical sense, and when we visit either place, we are left with a sense of responsibility. It is a common feature of early modern drama that its final moments gesture toward the wider world, as if connecting their internal plots to the happenings outside of fiction. The plot leans toward an event that will not happen on stage—a wedding, a war, a coronation. The staged Stoic exercises surveyed herein take this turn as a means to include their spectators as the public that will be incorporated into the training regimen. It is we who provide the marks of live interaction throughout the performance, through our entrances and exits, coughing, laughter, tears, and more imperceptibly through the ineffable but palpable energy of our attention. And at the close of the dramas, we are cut adrift from our mentor, hopefully wiser and more virtuous, now actors of our own.

NOTES

Introduction

The epigraph is drawn from Seneca (Lucius Annaeus Seneca), *Letters on Ethics*, trans. Margaret Graver and A. A. Long (Chicago: University of Chicago Press, 2015), 20.2. A note is in order as to how I utilize translations throughout this book. When I seek to make a point about Stoicism in general, as a philosophy, I draw from the most recent and acclaimed English translations to ensure clarity and rigor. When I want to give a sense of the particular early modern texture of Stoicism, I use translations contemporary to the works of drama under examination. As this book is, for the most part, historically situated in its analyses, the latter mode will be the dominant one.

1. Seneca, *Letters on Ethics*, trans. Graver and Long, 20.1.

2. Pierre Hadot, *Philosophy as a Way of Life*, trans. Michael Chase, ed. Arnold I. Davidson (Malden, MA: Blackwell, 1995), passim. Another notable apprehension of Stoicism's performed and embodied quality was that of Edith Hamilton, the classicist who achieved popularity with a general audience in the mid-twentieth century. In her 1960 book *The Roman Way* (New York: W. W. Norton, 2017), she posits curiously that the "Stoic's eyes were fixed on life, not on intellectual truth. Right and wrong had to do not with the reason, but with the will. All virtue was vain that did not result in virtuous doing. It was a doctrine fitted to the deepest-depth demands of Roman nature. They wanted not philosophy, which is for understanding, but religion, which is for action" (197). While the Stoics might not approve of her dismissal of "intellectual truth," such an objection would result from the belief that it was coextensive with, not separate from, life.

3. Hadot, *The Inner Citadel: The* Meditations *of Marcus Aurelius* (Cambridge, MA: Harvard University Press, 1998), 35, emphasis mine.

4. Hadot, *Philosophy as a Way of Life*, 58–59.

5. Hadot, *Philosophy as a Way of Life*, 69.

6. Hadot, *The Inner Citadel*, 79.

7. Martin Puchner, *The Drama of Ideas: Platonic Provocations in Theater and Philosophy* (Oxford: Oxford University Press, 2010), 13.

8. Martha Nussbaum, *The Therapy of Desire: Theory and Practice in Hellenistic Ethics* (Princeton, NJ: Princeton University Press, 1994), 328.

9. The translation is Pierre Hadot's, in *The Inner Citadel*, 44–45.

10. Epictetus, *The Handbook (The Encheiridion)*, trans. Nicholas P. White (Indianapolis, 1983), 16.

11. Julia Annas, in *The Morality of Happiness* (Oxford: Oxford University Press, 2009), succinctly explains the Stoic link of virtue to practice: "Virtue is a skill, a disposition to do the right thing for the right reason" (162).

12. William Baldwin, *A Treatise of Morall Philosophie* (London, 1600), 35.

13. Ben Jonson, "Bartholomew Faire," in *The Alchemist and Other Plays*, ed. Gordon Campbell (Oxford: Oxford University Press), 1995, 4.6.100–101.

14. Augustine (Saint Augustine of Hippo), *The City of God*, trans. Gerald G. Walsh and Daniel J. Honan (Washington, DC: Catholic University of America Press, 1954), 198.

15. John Calvin, *Institutes of the Christian Religion*, trans. Henry Beveridge (Peabody, MA: Hendrickson Publishers, 2008), 3.8.9.

16. Joseph Hall, *Heaven on Earth: Or, True Peace, and Tranquilitie of Minde* (London, 1606), 5.

17. Joseph Campana, *The Pain of Reformation: Spenser, Vulnerability, and the Ethics of Masculinity* (New York: Fordham University Press, 2012), 244.

18. Seneca, *Letters on Ethics*, trans. Graver and Long, 20.1.

19. William Irvine, *A Guide to the Good Life: The Ancient Art of Stoic Joy* (Oxford: Oxford University Press, 2009), 37.

20. Cicero (Marcus Tullius Cicero), *Tusculan Disputations*, trans. J. E. King (Cambridge, MA: Harvard University Press, 1945), 3.24.

21. Michel de Montaigne, "Of Constancy," in *The Complete Essays of Montaigne*, trans. Donald Frame (Stanford, CA: Stanford University Press, 1957), 59–68.

22. Nussbaum, *The Therapy of Desire*, 387.

23. Nussbaum, *The Therapy of Desire*, 421.

24. William Shakespeare, *Much Ado about Nothing*, ed. Claire McEachern (Boston: Thomson, 2006), 5.1.34–38.

25. Diana Taylor, *The Archive and the Repertoire: Performing Cultural Memory in the Americas* (Durham, NC: Duke University Press, 2003), 3.

26. Richard Schechner, *Performance Studies: An Introduction* (New York: Routledge, 2002), 28.

27. Michel Foucault, *The Hermeneutics of the Subject: Lectures at the Collège de France 1981–1982*, ed. Frédéric Gros, trans. Graham Burchell (New York: Picador, 2005), 185.

28. William Shakespeare, *Hamlet*, ed. Harold Jenkins (London: Methuen, 1997), 3.2.16–24. All further citations noted parenthetically in text.

29. Alan Sinfield, *Faultlines: Cultural Materialism and the Politics of Dissident Reading* (Berkeley: University of California Press, 1992), 223. For another paradigmatic account of Hamlet the failed Stoic, see A. D. Nuttall, *Shakespeare the Thinker* (New Haven, CT: Yale University Press, 2008). Nuttall, in a philosophically probing and idiosyncratic account, finds Hamlet both a potential student of Stoicism and someone constitutionally unfit for such a program of study; in Nuttall's words, "Hamlet is more like Sartre's man than he is like Seneca's" (199). Part of Nuttall's critique, however, is that Stoicism anticipates the anchorless morality of existentialism. In this way he recalls both Eliot and Alisdair MacIntyre, the former of whom is discussed later in the book.

30. Joshua Scodel, "Finding Freedom in *Hamlet*," *Modern Language Quarterly* 72, no. 2 (2011): 182, 184.

31. Geoffrey Aggeler, "Hamlet and the Stoic Sage," *Hamlet Studies* 9 (1987): 21.

32. Seneca, *Letters on Ethics*, trans. Graver and Long, 70.12.

33. Plato, *Phaedo, The Last Days of Socrates*, trans. Hugh Tredennick and Harold Tarrant (New York: Penguin, 1993), 121.

34. Andrew Fitzmaurice links Stoicism to Christian mystery in a similar way by claiming that Stoicism's purchase in Shakespeare's day results from the deep

epistemological and theological challenge of the Reformation. In this provocative if perhaps historically simplistic telling, Stoicism sounds more like skepticism or even cynicism in challenging the fundamental precepts of humanism (even though it arose from humanism's investment in classical forms): "The Reformation prepared the reception of Tacitus and Seneca in a further way: namely, through an insistence upon the inherent sinfulness and misery of man. Hamlet follows this transition from the optimistic emphasis upon the dignity of man in the early Renaissance to the misery of man in the post-Reformation Renaissance, making an ironic speech on the dignity of man" (148). See "The Corruption of Hamlet," in *Shakespeare and Early Modern Political Thought*, ed. David Armitage, Conal Condren, and Andrew Fitzmaurice (Cambridge: Cambridge University Press, 2009).

35. G. M. Ross, "Seneca's Philosophical Influence," in *Seneca*, ed. C. D. N. Costa (London: Routledge, 1974), 117.

36. For a survey of Stoicism's current popularity, see Gregory Hays, "Tune Out & Lean In," *New York Review of Books* (March 11, 2021)."

Chapter One

1. Justus Lipsius, *Two Bookes of Constancie*, trans. John Stradling (London, 1595), 7.

2. Lipsius, *Two Bookes of Constancie*, trans. Stradling, 58.

3. Lipsius, *Two Bookes of Constancie*, trans. Stradling, 14.

4. Lipsius, *Two Bookes of Constancie*, trans. Stradling, 15.

5. Lipsius, *Two Bookes of Constancie*, trans. Stradling, 67.

6. William Cornwallis, *Essayes* (London, 1600), sig. M1r.

7. Cornwallis, *Essayes*, sig. M1v.

8. Cornwallis, *Essayes*, sig. M1v.

9. Epictetus, *The Manuell of Epictetus*, trans. John Sanford (London, 1567), sig. C2r–C3v.

10. Gordon Braden, *Anger's Privilege: Renaissance Tragedy and the Senecan Tradition* (New Haven, CT: Yale University Press, 1985), 26.

11. William Shakespeare, *As You Like It* (London: Arden Shakespeare, 2006), 2.7.140–67.

12. Andrew Shifflet, "Shakespeare and Early Modern English Literature," in *The Routledge Handbook of the Stoic Tradition*, ed. John Sellars (New York: Routledge, 2016), 175.

13. Lipsius, *Two Bookes of Constancie*, trans. Stradling, 21.

14. Guillame Du Vair, *The Moral Philosophie of the Stoicks*, trans. Thomas James (London, 1598), 193.

15. Antonio de Guevara, *The Golden Boke of Marcus Aurelius Emperor and Eloquent Oratour*, trans. John Bourchier Berners (London, 1535), sig. H1v. The provenance of this text is, as I explain, highly corrupted. It is clearly not a work by Marcus, though I believe it important in understanding how the *impression* of Stoicism was received in the early modern era. Ada Palmer names it a flat-out "forgery" in "The Recovery of Stoicism in the Renaissance," in *The Routledge Handbook of the Stoic Tradition*, ed. John Sellars (New York: Routledge, 2016). For a nuanced reading of its relation to the actual Marcus as well as the early modern genre of the princely manual, see Michael P. Mezzatesta, "Marcus

Aurelius, Fray Antonio de Guevara, and the Ideal of the Perfect Prince in the Sixteenth Century," *Art Bulletin* 66 (December 1984): 620–33.

16. Thomas Heywood, *An Apology for Actors* (London, 1612), sig. C2r.

17. Aristotle, *Aristotle's Poetics*, trans. Hippocrates G. Apostle, Elizabeth Dobbs, and Morris A. Parslow (Grinnell, IA: Peripatetic Press, 1990), 6.

18. Cornwallis, *Essayes*, sig. B5v.

19. Susan Bobzien, *Determinism and Freedom in Stoic Philosophy* (Oxford: Oxford University Press, 1998), 330.

20. Nussbaum, *The Therapy of Desire*, 366–67.

21. Nussbaum, *The Therapy of Desire*, 374.

22. Quentin Skinner, *The Foundations of Modern Political Thought, Vol. 2: The Age of Reformation* (Cambridge: Cambridge University Press, 1978), 282.

23. Guevara, *The Golden Boke*, sig. G4v.

24. Guevara, *The Golden Boke*, sig. H2v.

25. Seneca, *The Workes of Lucius Annaeus Seneca, Both Morall and Naturall*, trans. Thomas Lodge (London, 1614), 442–43.

26. One of the ironies of Seneca's epistles is that, insistent as they are about human contact, they seem to have almost certainly been fictitious. There may not have been a Lucilius at all, or if there were, he may be independent of the figure depicted by Seneca. Brad Inwood summarizes this accepted opinion by remarking that "like the dialogues of Plato, Seneca's letters are a literary representation of a philosophical exchange which is to some extent imaginary" (346). However, Inwood seems to give little credence to the sense that all of our "selves" are literary, nor to the possibility that literature can still make philosophical claims: "This sense of 'self' that we get, then, is in one way a mere artefact of literary technique. What is not yet clear to me—and perhaps it will remain unclear—is when we may reasonably regard such literary artefacts as philosophical innovations" (352). See "The Will in Seneca," in *Reading Seneca: Stoic Philosophy at Rome* (Oxford: Oxford University Press, 2005).

27. Antonio de Guevara, *The Diall of Princes*, trans. Thomas North (London, 1568), n.p.

28. Epictetus, *Manuell*, trans. Sanford, sig. A2v.

29. Heywood, *Apology for Actors*, sig. G1v.

30. Erving Goffman, *Frame Analysis: An Essay on the Organization of Experience* (Boston: Northeastern University Press, 1974), 24.

31. Philip Sidney, "The Defence of Poesy," in *The Major Works*, ed. Katherine Duncan-Jones (Oxford: Oxford University Press), 213.

32. Cornwallis, "Of Behavior," in *Essayes*, sig. M3v.

33. William Shakespeare, *Hamlet*, 2.2.249–50.

34. Lipsius, *Two Bookes of Constancie*, trans. Stradling, 12.

35. Seneca, *Workes*, trans. Lodge, 294.

36. Cornwallis, "Of Advice," in *Essayes*, sig. C4r.

37. Du Vair, *Moral Philosophie*, 78.

38. Aulus Gellius, *The Attic Nights of Aulus Gellius*, trans. John C. Rolfe (Cambridge, MA: Harvard University Press, 1927), 351.

39. Seneca, *Workes*, trans. Lodge, 163.

40. Seneca, *Letters on Ethics*, trans. Graver and Long, 1.1.

41. Seneca, *Workes*, trans. Lodge, 165.

42. Seneca, *Workes*, trans. Lodge, 164.

43. Gordon Braden, *Anger's Privilege: Renaissance Tragedy and the Senecan Tradition* (New Haven, CT: Yale University Press, 1985), 17.

44. Braden, *Anger's Privilege*, 25.

45. Braden, *Anger's Privilege*, 26.

46. Joseph Hall, *Heaven upon Earth*, 219–20.

47. A. A. Long, "Representation of the Self in Stoicism," in *Stoic Studies* (Cambridge: Cambridge University Press, 1996), 270–71.

48. Long, "Representation of the Self in Stoicism," 272.

49. Charles Taylor, *Sources of the Self: The Making of the Modern Identity* (Cambridge, MA: Harvard University Press, 1989), 137, emphasis added.

50. T. S. Eliot, "Shakespeare and the Stoicism of Seneca," in *Selected Essays* (London: Faber & Faber, 1932), 131.

51. Eliot, "Shakespeare and the Stoicism of Seneca," 132.

52. Lipsius, *Two Bookes of Constancie*, trans. Stradling, 17.

53. Lipsius, *Two Bookes of Constancie*, trans. Stradling, 18.

54. Patrick Gray, *Shakespeare and the Fall of the Roman Republic: Selfhood, Stoicism, and Civil War* (Edinburgh: Edinburgh University Press, 2019), 54.

55. Hadot, *Philosophy as a Way of Life*, 58.

56. Peter Brook, *The Empty Space* (New York: Simon & Schuster, 1968), 9.

57. Samuel Weber, *Theatricality as Medium* (New York: Fordham University Press, 2004), 116.

58. Martha Nussbaum, "Poetry and the Passions: Two Stoic Views," in *Passions and Perceptions: Studies in Hellenistic Philosophy of Mind*, ed. Jacques Brunschwig and Martha Nussbaum (Cambridge: Cambridge University Press, 1993), 138. Brecht was a voluminous theorizer of his own theater and remains the ideal starting point for research into his techniques; see the excellent collection *Brecht on Theatre: The Development of an Aesthetic*, trans. and ed. John Willet (New York: Hill & Wang, 1977).

59. Hadot, *Philosophy as a Way of Life*, 83.

60. Hadot, *The Inner Citadel*, 83.

61. Hadot, *The Inner Citadel*, 51.

62. Marcus Aurelius, *Meditations*, trans. A. S. L. Farquharson (Oxford: Oxford University Press, 1944), 71.

63. Epictetus, *Manuell*, trans. Sanford, sig. D3r–v.

64. John Stradling, "The Epistle to the Reader," in Lipsius, *Two Bookes of Constancie*, trans. Stradling, A3r.

65. Lipsius, *Two Bookes of Constancie*, trans. Stradling, 17.

66. Lipsius, *Two Bookes of Constancie*, trans. Stradling, 67.

67. James Stuart (King James I), *Basilikon Doron* (Edinburgh, 1599), 117–18.

68. Montaigne, "Of Physiognomy," in *Essays*, 795.

69. Richard Schechner, *Between Theatre and Anthropology* (Philadelphia: University of Pennsylvania Press, 1985), 123.

70. Peggy Phelan, *Unmarked: The Politics of Performance* (New York: Routledge, 1993), 146. For a rich critique of and engagement with Phelan's influential belief in absence paradoxically making manifest performance's power, see the work of Rebecca Schneider, particularly *The Explicit Body in Performance* (New York: Routledge, 1997).

71. Will D'Addario, "Doing Life Is That Which We Must Think," *Performance Philosophy* 1 (2015): 169–70.

Chapter Two

1. T. S. Eliot, "John Marston," in *Essays on Elizabethan Drama* (New York: Harcourt, Brace & World, 1960), 165–66.
2. Eliot, "Marston," 173.
3. For a genealogy of Seneca's influence that takes into account more nuanced inheritances and phases than Eliot's important, though generalized, account, see Jessica Winston, "Seneca in Early Elizabethan England," *Renaissance Quarterly* 59 (2006): 29–58. The absorption of Senecan modes, Winston persuasively argues, occurs in two major phases, one in which Seneca's plays are copied wholesale (like *Gorboduc*), and a latter one in which Seneca survives in fragmentary *sententiae*. The Antonio plays seem poised precisely between these modes, laced as they are with quotations and long passages but resisting complete structural mimicry.
4. All in-text citations from the Antonio plays are from the Revels editions: *Antonio and Mellida*, ed. W. Reavley Gair (Manchester: Manchester University Press, 2004); and *Antonio's Revenge*, ed. W. Reavley Gair (Manchester: Manchester University Press, 1999).
5. The provenance of *De remediis fortuitorum* has long been a subject of debate. Although it was believed in the early modern period to be by Seneca, this claim of authorship became scrutinized and ultimately rejected. For a relatively recent attempt to rehabilitate Seneca as the author, along with a helpful history of the matter, see Robert. J. Newman, "Rediscovering the *De Remediis Fortuitorum*," *American Journal of Philology* 109 (1988): 92–107. See also Ralph Graham Parker, *Seneca's "De Remediis Fortuitorum" and the Elizabethans: An Essay* (Chicago: Institute of Elizabethan Studies, 1953), which helpfully includes side-by-side versions in Latin and in the translation Marston apparently knew, by Robert Whittington.
6. Geoffrey Aggeler, *Nobler in the Mind: The Stoic-Skeptic Dialectic in English Renaissance Tragedy* (Newark: University of Delaware Press, 1998), 84.
7. Michael Higgins, "The Convention of the Stoic Hero as Handled by Marston," *Modern Language Review* 39 (1944): 346.
8. John Marston, *The Scourge of Villainie* (London, 1599), 2.5–6.
9. The Montaigne passage in question appears in his essay "On the Useful and the Honourable." Montaigne's point is that imperfection can still carry with it purpose—a critique of scholasticism's notion of a perfectly purposed universe—though this deeper humanism is lost to Andrugio.
10. Seneca, *Workes*, trans. Lodge, 508.
11. Hadot, *Philosophy as a Way of Life*, 82–83.
12. John Sellars, *The Art of Living: The Stoics on the Nature and Function of Philosophy* (Burlington, VT: Ashgate, 2003), 108.
13. Jonathan Dollimore, *Radical Tragedy: Religion, Ideology and Power in the Drama of Shakespeare and His Contemporaries*, 3d ed. (New York: Palgrave Macmillan, 1984), 33.
14. Dollimore, *Radical Tragedy*, 31.
15. Rebecca Yearling, "John Marston, Stoic? *Sophonisba* and the Early Modern Stoic Ideal," *Ben Jonson Journal* 18 (2011): 94.

16. Anthony Caputi, *John Marston, Satirist* (New York: Octagon Books, 1976), 78.

17. Daniel Finkelpearl, *John Marston of the Middle Temple: An Elizabethan Dramatist in His Social Setting* (Cambridge, MA: Harvard University Press, 1969), 142.

18. George Geckle, *John Marston's Drama: Themes, Images, Sources* (Rutherford, NJ: Fairleigh Dickinson University Press, 1980), 78.

19. The terms of Christianity's awkward partnership with Stoicism have been the subject of many compelling discussions. See, for instance, J. H. M. Salmon, "Stoicism and Roman Example: Seneca and Tacitus in Jacobean England," *Journal of the History of Ideas* 50 (1989): 199–225. Why is Stoicism looked at unfavorably by the English in particular? "The sour note sounded by the English avatars of Seneca and Tacitus," claims Salmon, "signified the failure of the royal court to contain and reconcile the competing forces within it, and heralded the advent of a wider forum for conflict" (202). Salmon focuses, too, on Lipsius's amendments to Seneca as indicative of the wider philosophical-theological tensions. Lipsius took umbrage with several aspects of Seneca's work: the placement of fate (God, says Lipsius, is above fate, not prey to it); the difference among venial and mortal sins (Lipsius maintains this hierarchy rather than flattening it as Seneca would hold); the ethics of suicide; and most prominently, the conflict between Christian dependence on divine charity and the Stoic's use of reason (204).

20. Richard Strier, *Resistant Structures: Particularity, Radicalism, and Renaissance Texts* (Berkeley: University of California Press, 1995), 34.

21. Seneca, *Workes*, trans. Lodge, 648.

22. Seneca, *Workes*, trans. Lodge, 639.

23. Seneca, *Workes*, trans. Lodge, 653.

24. Seneca, *Workes*, trans. Lodge, 652.

25. Seneca, *Workes*, trans. Lodge, 649.

26. Seneca, *Workes*, trans. Lodge, 651.

27. Charles Bouwsma, "The Two Faces of Humanism: Stoicism and Augustinianism in the Renaissance," in *A Usable Past: Essays in Contemporary European Cultural History* (Berkeley: University of California Press, 1990), 38.

28. Lipsius, *Two Bookes of Constancie*, trans. Stradling, 7.

29. Lipsius, *Two Bookes of Constancie*, trans. Stradling, 45.

30. Lipsius, *Two Bookes of Constancie*, trans. Stradling, A3r–v.

31. Lipsius, *Two Bookes of Constancie*, trans. Stradling, 50.

32. Lipsius, *Two Bookes of Constancie*, trans. Stradling, 53.

33. Seneca, Workes, trans. Lodge, 506.

34. Seneca, Workes, trans. Lodge, 507.

35. Andrew Shifflet, *Stoicism, Politics, and Literature in the Age of Milton: War and Peace Reconciled* (Cambridge: Cambridge University Press, 1998), 2. For Stoics, the world was infused with *pneuma*, or life-force—the same energy that made up both the human soul and divinity. See chapter 4 for more on this concept.

36. Sellars, *The Art of Living*, 138.

37. This set of claims carries clear political repercussions, which Shifflet analyzes brilliantly; in addition, see Gerhard Oestrich, *Neostoicism and the Early Modern State* (Cambridge: Cambridge University Press, 1982), which argues that

Neo-Stoicism's aim was to "increase the power and efficiency of the state by an acceptance of the central role of force in the army" while at the same time demanding "self-discipline and the extension of the duties of the ruler and the moral education of the army, the officials, and indeed the whole people, to a life of work, frugality, dutifulness and obedience" (7).

38. Lipsius, *Two Bookes of Constancie*, trans. Stradling, 115.

39. Michel Foucault, *The Hermeneutics of the Subject*, trans. Graham Burchell, ed. Frederic Gros (New York: Picador Press, 2001), 276.

40. Shifflet, *Stoicism, Politics, and Literature*, 32.

41. Seneca, *Workes*, trans. Lodge, 500.

42. Seneca, *Workes*, trans. Lodge, 208.

43. Foucault, *The Hermeneutics of the Subject*, 358.

44. Ben Golder, *Foucault and the Politics of Rights* (Stanford, CA: Stanford University Press, 2015), 136.

45. Jamey Graham, "Consciousness, Self-Spectatorship, and Will to Power: Shakespeare's Stoic Conscience," *English Literary Renaissance* 44 (2014): 268.

46. Seneca, *Workes*, trans. Lodge, 208.

47. Lipsius, *Two Bookes of Constancie*, trans. Stradling, 56.

48. Lipsius, *Two Bookes of Constancie*, trans. Stradling, 121.

49. The literature on boys' companies in early modern England is extensive; to cite only a few indicative works, see Michael Shapiro, *Children of the Revels: The Boy Companies of Shakespeare's Time and Their Plays* (New York: Columbia University Press, 1977); Stephen Orgel, *Impersonations: The Performance of Gender in Early Modern England* (Cambridge: Cambridge University Press, 1996); and Richard Dutton, "The Revels Office and the Boys Companies, 1600–1613: New Perspectives," *English Literary Renaissance* (32): 324–51.

50. Rebecca Yearling, *Ben Jonson, John Marston, and Early Modern Drama: Satire and the Audience* (New York, 2016), 95.

51. Joseph Loewenstein, "Marston's Gorge and the Question of Formalism," in *Renaissance Literature and Its Formal Engagement*, ed. Mark David Rasmussen (New York: Palgrave, 2016), 92.

52. Loewenstein, "Marston's Gorge," 93.

53. G. K. Hunter, introduction to *Antonio and Mellida* (Lincoln: University of Nebraska Press, 1965), xii.

54. Balurdo rehearses here a signature bodily function for Marston: the belk, or belch. Ben Jonson, in his parody of Marston in *Poetaster*, plays on this obsession with oral projection when he has the Marston stand-in, Crispinus, vomit up a slurry of neologisms: "Oh—*retrograde—reciprocal—incubus* . . . Oh—*glibbery—lubrical—defunct*—Oh—" and so on (*The Devil Is an Ass and Other Plays*, ed. Margaret Jane Kidnie [New York: Oxford University Press, 2000], 5.3.427–31). Scatological though it may be, Marston's fixation on reminding the listener of the complicity of physical musculature in producing words—and Jonson's keenly observed satire thereof—has a certain Stoic resonance not dissimilar from Balurdo's ramblings.

55. See Edmund Spenser, *The Faerie Queene (New York: Penguin Classics, 1978)*, 1.1.20.

56. While Piero is largely puzzled by Balurdo, Antonio ends up mimicking the fool's techniques when he disguises himself clownishly at the end of *Antonio's*

Revenge; for Antonio, the fool is also precisely the kind of Stoic he had despised at the beginning of the play: a fool, he tells us, is "not capable of passion; / Wanting the power of distinction, / he bears an unturned sail with every wind; / Blow east, blow west, he stirs his course alike" (4.1.37–41).

57. Braden, *Anger's Privilege*, 53.

58. See Sellars, *The Art of Living*, 86–106, especially 95. For an exemplary analysis of the affinities between skepticism and early modern comedy, see Matthew R. Martin, *Between Theater and Philosophy: Skepticism in the Major City Comedies of Ben Jonson and Thomas Middleton* (Newark: University of Delaware Press, 2001); the paradigmatic account of skepticism and comedy may be Stanley Cavell, *Pursuits of Happiness: The Hollywood Comedy of Remarriage* (Cambridge, MA: Harvard University Press, 1984).

59. The exaggerated Stoic version of Pandulpho had no qualms about suicide—in fact, he found solace in remembering that he could always die and thus remove the power of mortal threat from his nemeses. "The portholes / Of sheathed spirit are ne'er corbed up, / But still stand open, ready to discharge. / Their precious shot into the shrouds of heaven" (2.2.85–88). We might view his shift into suicide-fearing as a theatricalized version of Lipsius's Christian changes to Seneca's Stoic ethics.

Chapter Three

1. William Shakespeare, *Much Ado about Nothing*, ed. Claire McEachern (Boston: Thomson, 2006), 5.1.34–35. All subsequent citations made parenthetically in text.

2. Foucault, *The Hermeneutics of the Subject*, 15.

3. Foucault, *The Hermeneutics of the Subject*, 275.

4. Hadot, *Philosophy as a Way of Life*, 83, emphasis in original.

5. Epictetus, *The Handbook (The Encheiridion)*, 11.

6. Foucault, *The Hermeneutics of the Subject*, 281.

7. Nussbaum, *The Therapy of Desire*, 356.

8. Nussbaum, *The Therapy of Desire*, 364.

9. For an overview of the field of biopolitics as derived from Foucault, see Timothy Campbell and Adam Sitze, eds., *Biopolitics: A Reader* (Durham, NC: Duke University Press, 2013). For an exemplary discussion of biopolitics and early modern drama, see Russ Leo, "Michel Foucault and Digger Politics," *Studies in English Literature, 1500–1900* 58, no. 1 (2018): 169–94.

10. Michel Foucault, *Subjectivity and Truth: Lectures at the Collège de France 1980–1981*, trans. Graham Burchell (New York: Palgrave Macmillan, 2017), 285.

11. Michel Foucault, "The Ethics of the Concern of the Self as a Practice of Freedom," trans. P. Aranov and D. McGrawth, in *The Essential Foucault: Selections from the Essential Works of Foucault, 1954–1984*, ed. Paul Rabinow and Nikolas Rose (New York: New Press, 1994), 37.

12. Foucault, *The Hermeneutics of the Subject*, 445.

13. Foucault, *The Hermeneutics of the Subject*, 184–85.

14. In a particularly self-referential moment in the lectures collected in *The Hermeneutics of the Subject*, Foucault points out that as a result of its insistent focus inward, on the self's relationship to the self, Stoicism resists its own

theorization: "It is as if this theme of the technique of the self, of the culture of the self, had an autonomy with regard to the theoretical problems that we feel hover around this practice" (445). What happens, the Stoics ask, if we live our lives within a question and do not feel compelled to answer it—not in terms of philosophical truth or spiritual transformation?

15. Harold Goddard, "Much Ado about Nothing," in *The Meaning of Shakespeare* (Chicago: University of Chicago Press, 1951), 1:271–72.

16. Goddard, "Much Ado about Nothing," 271.

17. Hermann Ulrici, "Much Ado about Nothing—Taming of the Shrew," in *Shakespeare's Dramatic Art and His Relation to Calderon and Goethe*, trans. Dora Schmitz (London: Chapman Brothers, 1876), 289.

18. A. P. Rossiter, "Much Ado about Nothing," in *Angels with Horns and Other Shakespeare Lectures*, ed. Graham Storey (London: Longman, 1961), 65.

19. Ralph Berry, "*Much Ado about Nothing*: Structure and Texture," *English Studies* 52, no. 1 (1971): 213.

20. Seneca, *Letters on Ethics*, trans. Graver and Long, 108.28.

21. Seneca, *Letters on Ethics*, trans. Graver and Long, 108.35.

22. Nussbaum, "Poetry and the Passions," 141.

23. Foucault points out in *The Hermeneutics of the Subject* that *stultitia*, the form of foolish restlessness that Seneca seeks to eliminate in his pupils, "has its moral version in the bearing of the *effeminatus*, of the man who is effeminate in the sense of being passive in relation to himself, unable to exercise *egkrateia*, mastery or sovereignty, over the self" (344). For treatments of gender in *Much Ado*, see Carol Cook, "'The Sign and Semblance of Her Honor': Reading Gender Difference in *Much Ado about Nothing*," *PMLA* 101, no. 2 (1986): 186–202; and Janice Hays, "'Those 'soft and delicate' Desires: *Much Ado* and the Distrust of Women," in *The Woman's Part: Feminist Criticism of Shakespeare*, ed. Carolyn Ruth Swift Lenz, Gayle Greene, and Carol Thomas Neely (Champaign: University of Illinois Press, 1983), 79–99.

24. Ian Munro, "Shakespeare's Jestbook: Wit, Print, Performance," *ELH* 71, no. 1 (2004): 90.

25. Cicero, *On the Ideal Orator (De Oratore)*, trans. James M. May and Jakob Wisse (Oxford: Oxford University Press, 2001), 164–65.

26. Cicero, *On the Ideal Orator (De Oratore)*, trans. May and Wisse, 61.

27. Baldassare Castiglione, *The Book of the Courtier*, trans. Thomas Hoby (London: Everyman, 1994), 53.

28. Castiglione, *The Book of the Courtier*, trans. Hoby, 200.

29. See Rebecca Helfer, "Wit and the Art of Memory in Nashe's *Unfortunate Traveler*," *English Literary Renaissance* 47, no. 3 (2017).

30. See Jennifer Richards, "Assumed Simplicity and the Critique of Nobility; Or, How Castiglione Read Cicero," *Renaissance Quarterly* 54, no. 2 (2001): 460–84.

31. Philip Sidney, in his "Defence of Poesy," seizes on deception as the primary characteristic of the two orators in *De oratore*. Sidney, though, leaves no doubt as to whether their lack of learning itself constituted a performed skill by noting that Antonius "pretended not to know art" and Crassus "not to set by it, because with a plain sensibleness they might win credit of popular ears" (247).

32. Castiglione, *The Book of the Courtier*, trans. Hoby, 107–8.

33. Castiglione, *The Book of the Courtier*, trans. Hoby, 108.

34. See Phillip D. Collington, "'Stuffed with Honorable Virtues': *Much Ado about Nothing* and *The Book of the Courtier*," *Studies in Philology* 103, no. 3 (2006): 281–312; and Mary Augusta Scott, "*The Book of the Courtier*: A Possible Source of Benedick and Beatrice," *PMLA* 16, no. 4 (1901): 475–502.

35. Seneca, *Workes*, trans. Lodge, 221.

36. Foucault, *The Hermeneutics of the Subject*, 358.

37. Foucault, *The Hermeneutics of the Subject*, 359.

38. Thomas Hoby, preface, in Castiglione, *The Book of the Courtier*, trans. Hoby, 5.

39. For the elaboration of metaphor, which ties together the reader's experience with the sleuthing figure at the core of many modern novels, see D. A. Miller, *The Novel and the Police* (Berkeley: University of California Press, 1989). Miller is in turn influenced by the later Foucault of *Discipline and Punish*.

40. James Kuzner, *Shakespeare as a Way of Life: Skeptical Practice and the Politics of Weakness* (New York: Fordham University Press, 2016), 8.

41. Translated by Pierre Hadot, quoted in *Philosophy as a Way of Life*, 84.

42. Seneca, *Workes*, 202.

43. Seneca, *Workes*, 202.

44. Hadot, *Philosophy as a Way of Life*, 207. Hadot's reading appears in his response to Michel Foucault's treatment of Stoic attitudes toward pleasure in *The Care of the Self*. Hadot critiques what he sees as Foucault's elision of Seneca's careful distinction between pleasure and joy, and with it the absence of any discussion of Stoic transcendence. Foucault's treatment offers a secularized and simplified account of the philosophy. It is because of Foucault's tendency to make such sweeping and thinly researched claims in his published work that I draw instead, in this chapter, on his much more considered and nuanced readings of the Stoics in his lectures.

45. Stephen Greenblatt, "Much Ado about Nothing," in *The Norton Shakespeare*, ed. Greenblatt et al. (New York: W. W. Norton, 2016), 342–43.

46. Claire McEachern, in *Much Ado about Nothing*, 2.1.340n.

47. For a critique of mimesis and gender, see Elin Diamond, *Unmaking Mimesis: Essays on Feminism and Theatre* (Abington-on-Thames: Routledge, 1997).

Chapter Four

1. All in-text citations of the play are from Cyril Tourneur, *The Atheist's Tragedy*, ed. Irving Ribner (Cambridge, MA: Harvard University Press, 1964).

2. Thomas Nashe, *Christ's Teares over Jerusalem* (London, 1594), 59–60.

3. A note is in order to explain what I mean, exactly, by "atheism." While Nashe supplies one definition, his taxonomy is far wider; furthermore, his was only one guide of many. In Tourneur's day, "atheism" could signal anything from political dissent to Catholicism to improperly directed intellectual curiosity. Atheists could believe in God but not believe in God's involvement in His world; they could disavow a specific facet of Christian doctrine, such as the immortality of the soul; or they could be confidence artists who appropriated religious language for personal gain; or they could be devout Christians who simply angered powerful people. Ada Palmer defines one salient category of atheism as believing "doctrines that do not themselves directly attack belief in the divine, but

that nonetheless had the potential to do so in the early modern period, either by weakening traditional proofs of the existence of God or by facilitating the development of new atheist arguments" (*Reading Lucretius in the Renaissance* [Cambridge, MA: Harvard University Press, 2014], 23). For other treatments of atheism, see Michael Hunter, "The Problem of 'Atheism' in Early Modern England," *Transactions of the Royal Historical Society* 35 (1985): 135–57; and perhaps most paradigmatically Stephen Greenblatt, "Invisible Bullets," in *Shakespearean Negotiations: The Circulation of Social Energy in Renaissance England* (Berkeley: University of California Press, 1988). Palmer notes wryly that Milton makes use of this more pliable definition when he calls the demons in *Paradise Lost* "the atheist crew."

Clearly these fallen angels believe in the existence of God, as they have fought against Him and actively plot against Him.

4. Saint Jerome, *Commentary on Isaiah*, trans. Thomas P. Scheck (New York: Newman Press, 2015), 218.

5. Matthew Kendrick, too, views D'Amville as a potential Stoic, though his analysis hinges on positioning Lipsius's philosophy as a precursor to the logic of global capitalism. Such a reading echoes Braden in locating Stoicism's self-reliance as a proto-tyrannical impulse, but Kendrick tempers this by highlighting the inherent conservatism of the philosophy and its early modern variants. See "Neostoicism and the Economics of Revenge in Cyril Tourneur's *The Atheist's Tragedy*," *College Literature* 41, no. 3 (Summer 2014): 8–26.

6. *The English Bible King James Version: The New Testament and the Apocrypha*, ed. Gerald Hammond and Austin Busch (New York: W. W. Norton, 2012), Acts 17:18–19. I turn to this version as a default for early modern biblical citations, while evoking the Geneva Bible (and noting as such) to consider its particularized commentaries.

7. Acts 17:22–23 (KJV).

8. Acts 17:25 (KJV).

9. Acts 17:28 (KJV).

10. Aratus, "Phaenomena," in *Hymns and Epigrams*, trans. A. W. Mair and G. R. Mair (Cambridge, MA: Harvard University Press, 2014), 207.

11. John 1:10 (KJV).

12. J. E. Atkinson. "St. Paul's Encounter with Athenian Stoics and Epicureans." *Akroterion* 61 (2016): 53.

13. Cleanthes, *The Hymn of Cleanthes*, trans. E. H. Blakeney (London: Macmillan, 1921), ll. 1–4.

14. Cleanthes, *The Hymn of Cleanthes*, trans. Blakeney, ll. 22–24.

15. Diogenes Laertius, *Lives of the Eminent Philosophers*, trans. Pamela Mensch, ed. James Miller (Oxford: Oxford University Press, 2018), 7.142–46.

16. John Sellars, *Stoicism* (New York: Routledge, 2006), 93.

17. Michael J. White, "Stoic Natural Philosophy (Physics and Cosmology)," in *The Cambridge Companion to the Stoics*, ed. Brad Inwood (Cambridge: Cambridge University Press, 2003), 129–30. For a more extensive study of classical philosophy's belief in an integrated (to our contemporary eyes) system of thought, one that incorporates natural philosophy and moral philosophy, see White's *The Continuous and the Discrete: Ancient Physical Theories from a Contemporary Perspective* (Oxford: Oxford University Press, 1992).

18. Bruce Boehrer, *Monarchy and Incest in Renaissance England: Literature, Culture, Kinship, and Kingship* (Philadelphia: University of Pennsylvania Press, 1992), 95.

19. Boehrer, *Monarchy and Incest in Renaissance England*, 96.

20. Troels Engberg-Pederson, *Cosmology and Self in the Apostle Paul: The Material Spirit* (Oxford: Oxford University Press, 2010), 55.

21. Christopher Crosbie, *Revenge Tragedy and Classical Philosophy on the Early Modern Stage* (Edinburgh: Edinburgh University Press, 2019), 203.

22. Plutarch, *Morals*, trans. William W. Goodwin (Boston: Little, Brown, 1878), 376.

23. *The Geneva Bible: A Facsimile of the 1560 Edition* (Peabody, MA: Hendrickson, 2007), Acts 17:18 (marginalia).

24. *The Newe Testament of Our Lord Jesus Christ*, trans. Theodore Beza (London, 1583), Acts 17:18 (marginalia).

25. Jeremy Corderoy, *A Warning for Worldlings* (London, 1608), 10.

26. Philippe de Mornay, *A Woorke concerning the trewnesse of the Christian Religion*, trans. Philip Sidney and Arthur Golding (London, 1587), 10.

27. Thomas Adams, *The Gallants Burden* (London, 1612), sig. 16v.

28. John Dove, *A Confutation of Atheisme* (London, 1605), 18.

29. "Richard Baines on Marlowe," in Park Honan, *Christopher Marlowe: Poet and Spy* (Oxford: Oxford University Press, 2005), 375.

30. Thomas Beard, *The Theatre of God's Judgements* (London, 1597), 145.

31. Beard, *The Theatre of God's Judgements*, 148.

32. Beard, *The Theatre of God's Judgements*, 139.

33. Quoted in *Ancient Christian Commentary on Scripture, New Testament V: Acts*, ed. Francis Martin and Evan Smith (Downers Grove, IL: IVP Academic, 2006), 219–20.

34. Sanford, "To the Most High and Vertuous Princesse, Elizabeth," in Epictetus, *Manuell*, trans. Sanford, sig. A4v.

35. Sanford, "To the Most High and Vertuous Princesse, Elizabeth," in Epictetus, *Manuell*, trans. Sanford, sig. A7v–A8r.

36. Thomas James, "To the Right Honorable Sir Charles Blunt," in Du Vair, *The Moral Philosophie of the Stoicks*, trans. James, sig. A6v.

37. Thomas Lodge, "To the Courteous Reader," in Seneca, *Workes*, trans. Lodge, sig. B4r.

38. Seneca, *Workes*, trans. Lodge, 221.

39. Seneca, *Workes*, trans. Lodge, 365.

40. Seneca, *Workes*, trans. Lodge, 365.

41. A more traditional and conservative view of the play is that the devout Tourneur tests the audience's faith by challenging us to see through the obviously heretical beliefs of the atheistic antagonist. For this reading, see Peter Murray, *A Study of Cyril Tourneur* (Philadelphia: University of Pennsylvania Press, 1964). Murray's reading is not necessarily incompatible with my understanding of Tourneur's possibly inadvertent Stoic/Christian cosmology, as it simply demonstrates how closely atheism brushes up against a materialist expression of belief.

42. Carlo Tibiletti and Luigi Longobardo,"Stoicism," in *Encyclopedia of Ancient Christianity*, ed. Angelo Di Berardino (Downers Grove, IL: IVP Press, 2014), 3:642.

43. Adam Miller, *Speculative Grace: Bruno Latour and Object-Oriented Theology* (New York: Fordham University Press, 2013), 123. The field of object-oriented ontology has quickly established itself as a vital discourse across humanistic disciplines, with particular purchase in medieval and early modern studies. It has also forked into many subsets of related, though at times subtly theoretically opposed, subfields, such as flat ontology, vibrant materialism, alien phenomenology, and dark ecology. For a generalist overview of object-oriented ontology, see Graham Harman, *Object-Oriented Ontology: A New Theory of Everything* (New York: Pelican, 2018); for a "vibrant materialist" philosophy, see Jane Bennett, *Vibrant Matter: A Political Ecology of Things* (Durham, NC: Duke University Press, 2010); for a "dark ecological" view, see Timothy Morton, *Dark Ecology: For a Logic of Future Coexistence* (New York: Columbia University Press, 2016).

44. Neil van Leeuwen, "Religious Credence Is Not Factual Belief," *Cognition* 133 (2014): 699.

45. Alvin Plantinga, *Warranted Christian Belief* (Oxford: Oxford University Press, 2004), 175.

46. Plantinga, *Warranted Christian Belief*, 198.

47. Thomas More, *A Dialogue of Sir Thomas More knyghte* (London, 1529), xi.

48. More, *A Dialogue of Sir Thomas More knyghte*, xii.

49. Lance Ghavari, introduction to *Religion, Theatre, and Performance: Acts of Faith*, ed. Lance Ghavari (New York: Routledge, 2012), 18.

50. Tracy Davis, "Do You Believe in Fairies? The Hiss of Dramatic License," *Theatre Journal* 57, no. 1 (March 2005); 65.

51. Davis, "Do You Believe in Fairies?" 79.

52. Perhaps the most famous example of a revenge hero ignoring Paul's caution is Hieronimo, in *The Spanish Tragedy*, who reads from Romans only to change his mind suddenly when his eyes light upon Seneca; concluding that his dead son will be protected by God's grace regardless of his actions, he announces his freedom to pursue bloodletting a mere nineteen lines after hearing the Christian case for peace (3.13.1–19).

53. Fredson Bowers, *Elizabethan Revenge Tragedy, 1587–1642* (Princeton, NJ: Princeton University Press, 1972), 144.

54. Braden, *Anger's Privilege*, 203.

55. Herschel Baker, *The Wars of Truth: Studies in the Decay of Christian Humanism in the Earlier Seventeenth Century* (Cambridge, MA: Harvard University Press, 1952), 113.

56. Charlemont and Castabella may be so thinly drawn as to inadequately serve as surrogates for a properly faithful Christianity, according to Doug Swartz; see his "Profit and Pleasure in *The Atheist's Tragedy*," *Medieval and Renaissance Drama in England* 30 (2017): 76–104. Rather than see, as Shell does (see below), the lack of divinity as indicative of a medieval sense of mystery, he rejects a straightforwardly "Christian" reading of the play, especially the end, which is notable for "an absence of wonder or fear or any sense of the presence of the divine" (99).

57. Alison Shell, "Tragedy and Religion," in *The Cambridge Companion to English Renaissance Tragedy*, ed. Emma Smith and Garret Sullivan Jr. (Cambridge: Cambridge University Press, 2010), 48.

58. For a detailed reading of Levidulca's suicide scene, which abruptly transitions out of a comic setpiece into a tragic morality play, see William E. Gruber, "Building a Scene: The Text and Its Representation in *The Atheist's Tragedy*," *Comparative Drama* 19, no. 3 (1985): 193–208. Gruber sees the usage of a boy actor in the role (customary at the time) as inherent to the Brechtian way the staging mingles metaphorical and literal hermeneutics: "Within such a context, *mimesis* does not necessarily represent what is 'natural,' but begins to embody complex interchanges between signification and metaphorization, all of which can figure in the production of meaning for an audience. In the particular case of *The Atheist's Tragedy*, what emerges when the role of Levidulca is played by a boy is a generic portrait of female sexual behavior which has been partly turned inside out, heightened ironically for some kind of critical or possibly parodic exposure" (197).

59. The theory of materiality that, in my reading, the play advances resonates with the theatrical ideas of Antonin Artaud, who proposed a "theatre of cruelty" in his manifesto, *The Theatre and Its Double* (trans. Mary Caroline Richards [New York: Grove, 1958]). Artaud's complex and poetic writings resist reduction into a programmatic methodology (as opposed to his frequent theoretical foil, Bertolt Brecht), but he does proffer a sense of "cruelty" that both opposes "forms"—cultural representations, historically contingent and falsely psychological—and instead attempts to regain a sense of primal, shared ritual that operates beyond language. In his "First Letter" in *The Theatre and Its Double*, in which he elaborates on his use of the word "cruelty," he insists this access to fundamental spirituality is also resolutely concrete: "The word 'cruelty' must be taken in a broad sense, and not in the rapacious physical sense that it is customarily given. And I claim, in doing this, the right to break with the usual sense of language, to crack the armature once and for all, to get the iron collar off its neck, in short to return to the etymological origins of speech which, in the midst of abstract concepts, always evoke a concrete element" (101).

60. Anthony Munday, "A Second and Third Blast of Retreat from Plays and Theaters," in *Shakespeare's Theater: A Sourcebook*, ed. Tanya Pollard (Malden, MA: Blackwell, 2004), 67.

61. Stephen Gosson, "The School of Abuse," in *Shakespeare's Theater*, ed. Pollard, 25.

62. Algernon Charles Swinburne, *The Age of Shakespeare* (New York: Harper & Brothers, 1908), 265.

63. Katharine Eisaman Maus, introduction to *Four Revenge Tragedies*, ed. Katharine Eisaman Maus (Oxford: Oxford University Press, 1995), xxxi.

64. Irving Ribner, introduction to *The Atheist's Tragedy*, xxxv.

65. Shell, "Tragedy and Religion," 51.

Chapter Five

1. "Kanye West Stirs Up TMZ Newsroom Over Trump, Slavery, Free Thought," *TMZ* (2018), https://www.tmz.com/2018/05/01/kanye-west-tmz-live-slavery-trump. One of the more thorough and lucid critiques of West's absurd proposition is by Ta-Nahesi Coates; see "I'm Not Black—I'm Kanye," *Atlantic Monthly* (May 2018), https://www.theatlantic.com/entertainment/archive/2018/05/im-not-black-im-kanye/559763.

2. Epictetus, *How to Be Free*, trans. A. A. Long (Princeton, NJ: Princeton University Press, 2018), 113.

3. Epictetus, *Manuell*, trans. Sanford, 5v.

4. Epictetus, *Manuell*, trans. Sanford, 9r.

5. Nikole Hannah-Jones, "The Fight for a True Democracy," *1619*, podcast audio, August 23, 2019, https://www.nytimes.com/2020/01/23/podcasts/1619-podcast.html.

6. Hortense Spillers, "Mama's Baby, Papa's Maybe: An American Grammar Book," in *Black, White, and in Color: Essays in American Literature and Culture* (Chicago: University of Chicago Press, 2003), 206. Spillers's work has been named as one of the key texts in the field of Afro-pessimism, which proposes that the enslavement of and violence against Black bodies is *constitutive* of civil society itself, and that nothing short of a complete political revolution would alter the ensuing fundamental nonbeing of Black subjects. For a manifesto of sorts of this important set of discourses, see Frank Wilderson III, "Gramsci's Black Marx: Whither the Slave in Civil Society?" *Social Identities* 9, no. 2 (2003): 225–40. Along with Spillers, Wilderson names as foundational to Afro-pessimism the work of Frantz Fanon, in particular *Black Skin, White Masks* (trans. Richard Philcox [New York: Grove, 2008]). For an Afro-pessimist account of early modern literature, see Matthieu Chapman, *Anti-Black Racism in Early Modern English Drama: The Other 'Other'* (New York: Routledge, 2016).

7. Samuel Taylor Coleridge issued the notorious and noxious charge of Othello's monstrosity; see his lecture on *Othello* in *Lectures on Shakespeare (1811–1819)* (Edinburgh: Edinburgh University Press, 2018).

8. Othello's own self-conscious performance, coupled with *Othello*'s status as a performed work of art, has led to many scholarly explorations of how racial and theatrical performance collide. Ayanna Thompson has been a leading voice in this fascinating conversation; see *Passing Strange: Shakespeare, Race, and Contemporary America* (Oxford: Oxford University Press, 2013).

9. John Baret, *An Alvearie or, Quadruple Dictionarie, Containing Foure Sundrie Tongues* (London, 1580), entry 919.

10. Michael Neill, "'His master's ass': Slavery, Service, and Subordination in *Othello*," in *Shakespeare and the Mediterranean: The Selected Proceedings of the International Shakespeare Association World Congress, Valencia, 2001*, ed. Tom Clayton, Susan Brock, and Vicente Forés (Newark: University of Delaware Press, 2004), 217.

11. Contrareno, Gaspar, *The Commonwealth and Government of Venice*, trans. Louis Lewkenor (London, 1599), 16.

12. Virginia Mason Vaughan, *Performing Blackness on English Stages, 1500–1800* (Cambridge: Cambridge University Press, 2005), 76.

13. William Harrison, *A Description of England*, ed. Georges Edelen (Washington, DC: Folger Shakespeare Library, 1968), 118.

14. Vaughan, *Performing Blackness*, 77.

15. William Shakespeare, *The Merchant of Venice*, ed. John Drakakis (New York: Bloomsbury, 2011), 4.1.89–92.

16. Imtiaz Habib, *Black Lives in the English Archives, 1500–1677: Imprints of the Invisible* (Burlington, VT: Ashgate, 2008), 54.

17. In discussing the ever-shifting entanglement of references, mythologies, and structural politics that defined early modern concepts of race, Sujata Iyengar, in *Shades of Difference: Mythologies of Skin Color in Early Modern England* (Philadelphia: University of Pennsylvania Press, 2005), uses the term "mythologies of color" to describe "the complex of early modern beliefs surrounding the significance of skin of all perceived shades—white, black, red, green, brown, yellow, and transparent" (14). For an influential account of early modern race, see Kim F. Hall, *Things of Darkness: Economies of Race and Gender in Early Modern England* (Ithaca, NY: Cornell University Press, 1995). Hall argues that the descriptions of race in early modern literature, long dismissed as idiomatic or nonracialized, in fact evince a clear connection to slavery and imperialism.

18. Ian Smith, "Othello's Black Handkerchief," *Shakespeare Quarterly* 64, no. 1 (Spring 2013): 9.

19. Stephen Greenblatt, *Renaissance Self-Fashioning* (Chicago: University of Chicago Press, 1980), 233–34.

20. All citations from *Othello* are from the Arden Third Series edition, ed. E. A. J. Honigman (New York: Bloomsbury, 1996).

21. Urvashi Chakravarty, "Race, Natality, and the Biopolitics of Early Modern Political Theology," *Journal for Early Modern Cultural Studies* 18, no. 2 (Spring 2018): 144, emphasis in the original.

22. Jonathan Gil Harris, "Shakespeare and Race," in *The New Cambridge Companion to Shakespeare* (Cambridge: Cambridge University Press, 2010), 206.

23. Emily Weissbourd, "'I have done the state some service': Reading Slavery in *Othello* through *Juan Latino*," *Comparative Drama* 47, no. 4 (2013): 533.

24. Camille Wells Slights, "Slaves and Subjects in Othello," *Shakespeare Quarterly* 48, no. 1 (Winter 1997): 383.

25. One other possible counter to the claim that Othello was "Black" in some sense close to our contemporary one is that, as he was conceived of being performed by a white actor, he is overdetermined as a material representation as white; for this account—far more complicated and historically enmeshed than my brief précis indicates—see Dympna Callaghan, "'Othello was a white man': Properties of Race on Shakespeare's Stage," *Shakespeare Without Women* (Abingdon, UK: Taylor & Francis, 1999), 75–96.

26. Peter Garnsey, *Ideas of Slavery from Aristotle to Augustine* (Cambridge: Cambridge University Press, 1996), 12.

27. Garnsey, *Ideas of Slavery from Aristotle to Augustine*, 16.

28. Cicero, *The Booke of Marcus Tullius Cicero entitled Paradoxa Stoicorum*, trans. Thomas Newton (London, 1569), n.p.

29. Seneca, *Workes*, trans. Lodge, 50–51.

30. Seneca, *Workes*, trans. Lodge, 53.

31. Seneca, *Workes*, trans. Lodge, 56.

32. Lipsius, *Two Bookes of Constancie*, trans. Stradling, 122.

33. John Leo (Leo Africanus), *A Geographical Historie of Africa*, trans. John Pory (London, 1600), 40–41.

34. Robert Burton, *The Anatomy of Melancholy*, ed. Holbrook Jackson (New York: New York Review of Books, 2001), 264.

35. Ania Loomba, *Shakespeare, Race, and Colonialism* (Oxford: Oxford University Press, 2002), 107.
36. Eliot, "Shakespeare and the Stoicism of Seneca," 130–31, emphasis in the original.
37. Eliot, "Shakespeare and the Stoicism of Seneca," 131.
38. Eliot, "Seneca in Elizabethan Translation," 72.
39. Eliot, "Seneca in Elizabethan Translation," 73.
40. F. L. Lucas, *Seneca and Elizabethan Tragedy* (Cambridge: Cambridge University Press, 1922), 48.
41. Seneca, *Workes*, trans. Lodge, 208.
42. Seneca, *Workes*, trans. Lodge, 807.
43. Seneca, *Workes*, trans. Lodge, 556.
44. Seneca, *Workes*, trans. Lodge, 204.
45. Seneca, *Workes*, trans. Lodge, 210.
46. Epictetus, *Manuell*, trans. Sanford, 13.
47. Hadot, *Philosophy as a Way of Life*, 139.
48. *The Geneva Bible*, 1 Corinthians 15:10.
49. Daniel Vitkus, "Turning Turk in *Othello*: The Conversion and Damnation of the Moor," *Shakespeare Quarterly* 48, no. 2 (1997): 176.
50. Braden, *Anger's Privilege*, 169.
51. Julia Reinhard Lupton, *Citizen-Saints: Shakespeare and Political Theology* (Chicago: University of Chicago Press, 2005), 120.
52. Lupton, *Citizen-Saints*, 122.
53. Both Chakravarty and Lupton develop their concepts of "natality" in dialogue with Hannah Arendt, who coins the term in *The Human Condition* (Chicago: University of Chicago Press, 2018).
54. Chakravarty, "Race, Natality," 142.
55. Christopher Pye, "'To throw out our eyes for brave Othello': Shakespeare and Aesthetic Ideology," *Shakespeare Quarterly* 60, no. 4 (Winter 2009): 428.
56. Matthew Steggle, "Othello, the Moor of London: Shakespeare's Black Britons," in *Othello: A Critical Reader*, ed. Robert C. Evans (New York: Bloomsbury, 2015), 124.
57. Graham, "Consciousness, Self-Spectatorship," 268.
58. Ian Smith, "We Are Othello: Speaking of Race in Early Modern Studies," *Shakespeare Quarterly* 67, no. 1 (2016): 109.
59. Miles Grier, "Inkface: The Slave Stigma in England's Early Imperial Imagination," in *Scripturalizing the Human: The Written as Political*, ed. Vincent L. Wimbush (New York: Routledge, 2015), 211.
60. Grier, "Inkface," 211.

Conclusion

1. Rhodri Lewis, *Hamlet and the Vision of Darkness* (Princeton, NJ: Princeton University Press, 2017), 14.
2. Lewis, *Hamlet and the Vision of Darkness*, 31.
3. Lewis, *Hamlet and the Vision of Darkness*, 34.
4. Lewis, *Hamlet and the Vision of Darkness*, 299, emphasis added.

5. Michael Dobson, "Elsinore's Star Bullshitter," *London Review of Books* 40, no. 17 (September 2018), https://www.lrb.co.uk/the-paper/v40/n17/michael-dobson/elsinore-s-star-bullshitter.

6. Seneca, *Letters on Ethics*, 88.35.

7. Seneca, *Letters on Ethics*, 88.28.

8. Seneca, *Letters on Ethics*, 88.18–19.

9. Seneca, *Letters on Ethics*, 88.39.

10. Nussbaum, *The Therapy of Desire*, 330.

11. John Schafer, "Seneca's *Epistulae Morales* as Dramatized Education," *Classical Philology* 106 (2011): 35.

12. There are exceptions, of course; for one salient case, see the collection *Sensuous Curriculum: Politics and the Senses in Education*, ed. William H. Schubert and Ming Fang He (Charlotte, NC: Information Age Publishing, 2019). The powerful work of the teacher and activist Paolo Freire looms large in pedagogy theory that seeks to dismantle the neoliberal focus on information accumulation and capitalist advancement; see his totemic work *Pedagogy of the Oppressed* (New York: Bloomsbury, 2018). For theatrical implications of Freire's work, see Augusto Boal, *Theatre of the Oppressed*, trans. Charles McBride (New York: Theatre Communications Group, 1993). Nancy Kindelan, in *Artistic Literacy: Theatre Studies for a Contemporary Liberal Education* (New York: Palgrave, 2012), makes the less revolutionary but still bracing argument for theater's incorporation in a range of professional activities.

13. Scott Newstok, "How to Think Like Shakespeare," *Chronicle of Higher Education*, 63, no. 3 (September 2016): B12.

14. The Stoics in the early modern imagination could at times be indistinguishable from Aristotelians, even in their defining qualities, as Joshua Scodel explains in *Excess and the Mean in Early Modern English Literature* (Princeton, NJ: Princeton University Press, 2002). Early modern Stoicism, Scodel writes, "often minimized its differences from Aristotelianism by characterizing them as merely terminological in order to claim that Stoics, like Aristotelians, called for regulating rather than eliminating emotions" (2).

15. Aristotle, *Nicomachean Ethics*, trans. Robert C. Bartlett and Susan D. Collins (Chicago: University of Chicago Press, 2011), 12–13.

16. Martha Nussbaum, *Creating Capabilities: The Human Development Approach* (Cambridge, MA: Harvard University Press, 2011), 123.

17. Nussbaum, *Creating Capabilities*, 131.

18. Martha Nussbaum, *Poetic Justice: The Literary Imagination and Public Life* (Boston: Beacon Press, 1995), 3.

19. Nussbaum, *Poetic Justice*, 4.

20. Julia Annas, *Intelligent Virtue* (New York: Oxford University Press, 2011), 84.

INDEX